"Wonderful! A spellbinding story that tugs at the emotions. This breathtaking, powerful tale, woven by a superb talent, is impossible to put down."
—SARA ORWIG
author of *Warrior Moon*

Praise for Dinah McCall's
DREAMCATCHER

"Moving, poignant, gripping. This book will stir your heart and warm your dreams."

—Janis Reams Hudson,
author of *Remember My Heart*

"A great talent destined for stardom. . . . I highly recommend it!"

—Georgina Gentry,
author of *Cheyenne Splendor*

"Wonderfully provocative, complemented by a fascinating story, characters you can't forget, and pacing that has you panting for breath. This book has it all!"

—Carol Finch,
author of *Canyon Moon*

DREAMCATCHER

Dinah McCall

HarperPaperbacks
A Division of HarperCollinsPublishers

HarperPaperbacks   *A Division of* HarperCollins*Publishers*
                    10 East 53rd Street, New York, N.Y. 10022

Copyright © 1996 by Sharon Sala
All rights reserved. No part of this book may be used or
reproduced in any manner whatsoever without written
permission of the publisher, except in the case of brief
quotations embodied in critical articles and reviews. For
information address HarperCollins*Publishers*,
10 East 53rd Street, New York, N.Y. 10022.

Cover and stepback illustration by John Ennis

First printing: January 1996

Printed in the United States of America

HarperPaperbacks and colophon are trademarks of
HarperCollins*Publishers*

❖ 10 9 8 7 6 5 4 3 2 1

Throughout history, dreamers have been portrayed as people who are unable to accomplish anything of worth. As an inveterate daydreamer, I beg to differ. This book of my heart is dedicated to dreamers— everyone, everywhere, who sees a better place within themselves than that place in which they live.

ACKNOWLEDGMENTS

I must thank some very special people for sharing the richness and beauty of their heritage with me, and enabling me to have a better understanding of the power that exists within the minds and hearts of the American Indian.

My thanks to Weaver (Sonny) Cheek, and his daughter, who is also my daughter-in-law, Kristie Ann Cheek Sala, for helping me with the research concerning the Muskogee Indians, the tribe to which they belong—which later in history became commonly known as Creek Indians.

When I began this book, it was just a story. When I was finished, it had become a part of me, just as my daughter-in-law has become a part of our family.

The American Indian's unswerving belief in things that cannot be seen, but must be taken on trust, is not unlike that of anyone who believes in a higher power. During my research, I have truly come to believe that just because you cannot see it, does not mean it is not there.

Any license taken with the actual Muskogee Indian beliefs has been purely for fictional reasons, and any errors are mine. The truth of the Muskogee people and their beliefs is still there waiting, for any who wish to see.

PROLOGUE

Sweat ran in rivulets like molten copper down the burnished band of his chest muscles, and yet he did not feel the heat of the fire before him.

Wind roared past his ears, lifting his long, dark hair away from his shoulders until it became part of the night around him. Spirits that rode with the sound invaded his body, entrapping him even more deeply into the vision, and yet he could only stand with legs braced, feet apart, unable to move as he was pulled into the dream.

Wide-eyed, he stared blankly into the space just beyond the precipice upon which he stood and watched her coming toward him . . . on the air . . . through the air . . . as part of the air.

Though she was dressed in what looked to be a strange fashion of the white man's clothing, her sex was still unmistakable. And although no one told him, and there was no sound to confirm what was in his heart, he knew her name to be Amanda.

Panic was in every movement of her body as she ran with arms outstretched, her thick auburn hair flowing out behind her like a fiery veil. Tears ran unheeded down her cheeks, streaking her face with a war paint of despair. The terror in her eyes burned into his soul. His body trembled beneath its impact. He tried to move . . . to reach out . . .

or call out. But he was here, and she was there, and it was just a dream.

Blood raced wildly from nerve point to nerve point as his heart thundered and his fingers twitched loosely at his sides. The vision had moved him beyond words, emotionally, but his body remained immobile as he stared across the fire and into the space beyond the darkness of night.

He knew her. She'd been with him forever—hiding somewhere within his heart, waiting for him to find her. And now that she was here, he was helpless. He was unable to reach out and touch the pure alabaster beauty of her skin, unable to thrust his hands into the mane of hair flying out behind her, unable to pull her to him . . . beneath him.

She beckoned with one hand, her mouth opened wide in an ear-piercing scream he could not hear, and then she was gone.

He shuddered and fell forward upon his hands and knees and felt, for the first time, the heat of his fire. Staggered by the emotions still roiling within, he found it difficult even to move. But as quickly as he could manage, he was compelled to begin the creation of their link. His reluctance to turn away from the mountain precipice was great. In doing so, he would be severing any lingering emotion of the woman in his vision . . . his woman.

But he knew what must be done. Whispering a quick prayer to the spirits to guide him, he retrieved the knife that he'd dropped beside the fire, then headed for the surrounding trees.

It didn't take long to choose the tree. Even in the dark, his knowledge of the forest in which he lived was vast. With a swift slash of the knife, the thin, green branch came away in his hands. Calmer now that his mission was clear, he hurried back to the dying embers of his fire and tossed another stick into it, squinting his eyes against the sparks and smoke that popped and then rose into the air above it. Satisfied that he had sufficient light by which to work, he squatted on his heels as he began to dig through his gear.

Twice as he sought the things that he needed, he stopped to toss back the long cloak of black hair that fell across his face and eyes.

They were amber, whiskey-colored eyes, like those of a white man. They did not belong to the rest of him. His heart and his soul were Indian. He was Nokose, which meant Bear in the language of his people, the Muskogee. But whether he liked it or not, thanks to his French trapper father and his Indian mother, he was a man of two worlds.

Impervious to the sweat that ran across his bare upper body, he sat down, using his soft deerskin leggings as a lap table upon which to work.

Within moments he'd fashioned the thin, supple branchling that he'd cut from the tree into a circle, fastening it tightly with a strip of green rawhide. As it dried, it would shrink and hold the ends of the green willow firmly in place.

Then he took a long, continuous strand of string-thin leather and began the weave, forming a web-like design inside the circle as a spider would a web. He was ever careful to leave a small opening in the center of the web itself.

Off and on as time passed, he would toss another small stick onto the fire, for light with which to see. The heat from its blaze kept a steady stream of sweat running down the middle of his chest, staining his deerskins as well as the breechcloth and leather pieces covering his manhood. But his discomfort did not come from the heat or lack of light. It came from the urgency of knowing that without his help, Amanda would perish.

Hours passed, and when he was finished, he held it up to the firelight, turning it carefully, first one way then the other to check for flaws. Finally, nodding with satisfaction at his handiwork, he set it down upon his knees.

With slow, measured movement, he removed a single eagle feather from his pouch and tied it onto the webbing, at once giving the talisman he had just completed the swiftness and keen eyesight of the eagle to whom the feather had belonged. Then he lifted his arms and removed the bear claw hanging from a thong around his neck and tied it to the webbing as well. He grunted with satisfaction as it dangled against the wood. She would need all the power and magic the claw possessed.

His fingers ran the length of the claw, then paused at the tip, felt the talon-like curve, and shuddered. This, and others like it, had ripped him from his mother's belly, and flung him into the bushes to die. Had it not been for his father, Jacques LeClerc, he would have done so.

But his father's grief and a wet nurse's persistence had saved him, a tiny baby, from certain death, and he had grown to be a man both feared and revered within his people. Few among the Muskogee had the nerve to scoff at the great magic of his birth. There were none who did it to his face.

He blinked once, returning his thoughts to the task at hand, and set aside the memories for another day. A day when there would be time to remember the laughing, full-of-life trapper who'd been his father, and the wild fight for survival that they'd endured without complaint. It was, after all, the only way they knew.

His medicine bag dangled from a leather thong around his neck, and he fingered it carefully, considering the seriousness of what he was about to do. But he knew that to make this talisman work its magic, he must give it a bit of himself.

Without further hesitation, he opened it.

A tilt of the pouch sent a tiny medallion fashioned of beads and porcupine quills tumbling into the palm of his hand. And as it did, he thought of the mother he'd never known. Of the hours that she must have worked, and the joy with which it must have been made.

He wondered if she'd laughed with pleasure as she'd tied it to the cradleboard his father had made for him, an unborn child, and then wondered again if the tie that had bound his mother and father was as strong and as tight as the tie that bound him to the woman in his dreams.

The thought of his Amanda reminded him of the task

at hand. He laid the small beaded medallion onto the web and tied it firmly into place, imbuing the piece with something of his spirit, as well.

It is done!

He sat back on his heels, staring at the thing that he had made. His muscles quivered and then relaxed. Breathing came easily now that it was over.

His eyes glittered, and then narrowed. His lips, full and shaped as if with a sculptor's knife, firmed as he stood and then walked away.

The smoke from his dying fire drifted past his face as he paused at the precipice overlooking the valley below. The prayer he whispered as he held the talisman up to the vast expanse of night sky was older than his People, older than Mother Earth herself.

The Dreamcatcher was complete.

From this moment on, all of Amanda's dreams would filter through the webbing, and only the good dreams would be allowed out through the tiny hole in the center of the web.

There was but one thing left for him to do, and he struggled with it, trying to remember the unpracticed words of his father's second tongue. He closed his eyes, recalling her face and her form, and finally spoke, and when he did, it was a cry from the heart.

"Amanda! Do not be afraid. I will come for you!" he shouted.

The words fell from the edge of the precipice and drifted out into the waiting silence in sure, but halting English. And then he turned and walked back to his camp, swiftly put out what was left of the fire, and gathered his things about him. Without a backward glance, he walked down off the mountain with the magic in his hands.

ONE

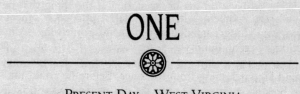

"Catch her! She's going to fall!"

Detective Jefferson Dupree turned at the shout just in time to see the young woman teetering at the edge of the makeshift stage set up in the center of the park.

He lunged, arms outstretched, and took the weight of her body against his as they both tumbled to the ground. There was little time for him to register her softness and the subtle scent of her perfume. Or how perfectly she seemed to fit within his embrace. There was only time to brace himself as he cushioned her body with his own.

Amanda had known she was going to fall. There was no time for shock or fear. Just the thought that it was going to be embarrassing as hell if she didn't die. Because only then would the fall have been forgivable. Congressmen's wives did not fall from stages in front of crowds of voters.

But the expected pain of landing on the ground didn't come. Instead she found herself cradled against a broad, thundering chest, and held so gently that for a heartbeat she wished never to move.

"Oh my God," she whispered.

Forgetting to feel embarrassed, she found herself lost in gentle, brown eyes that were shot through with just enough gold to remind her of warm whiskey. His nostrils were flared slightly from the strength he'd exerted in breaking her fall. His upper lip was sharply chiseled, the lower, full and sensual, but at the moment, twisted slightly in a grimace of pain.

Everything about him that she saw came and went within a millisecond, and then she thought, *David is going to kill me.*

In the moment when they stared into each other's eyes, something passed between them. Something swift. Sudden. Urgent. But it was never voiced.

From the corner of his eye, Jefferson Dupree saw David Potter dashing from the stage. Before he could find the breath or impetus to speak, the woman was yanked from his arms. He would have sworn that for an instant Amanda Potter had clung to him as if dodging her husband's hands. The moment he thought it he told himself he was a fool. She was married to one of West Virginia's brightest and most charming congressmen. Her world had to be just about perfect.

"Oh, my! I'm sorry," she whispered, and looked up into her husband's face, searching the handsome perfection for approval.

Dupree wasn't certain whom she'd just apologized to, but he assumed it would have been to him.

"No need to apologize," he said, brushing off his jacket and slacks. "I'm just glad I was here. Are you all right? That was quite a fall." Out of habit, he started to check her for injuries.

But Amanda Potter wasn't allowed to answer. She was busy being engulfed within her husband's embrace. Jefferson Dupree was shocked at the odd shaft of resentment he felt when he saw it happen. Moments ago it had been *his* arms that had sheltered her. It had been *his* chest she'd laid her head upon.

What the hell is wrong with you, Dupree? he asked himself.

He hardly knew this woman. The last thing he should be thinking was what was on his mind. The gathering crowd of concerned onlookers gave him time to regroup.

"I can't thank you enough," David Potter said, and shook the detective's hand, ever conscious of the flashbulbs going off around them. "You saved Amanda from a terrible fall, I'm sure."

"I was just in the right place at the right time," Dupree said, and smiled at Amanda, wishing he had the right to tuck the stray lock of chestnut hair away from her wide, frightened eyes and kiss the small red spot on her cheek that had collided with his chin.

Amanda smiled nervously and brushed at her clothing, unable to look either man in the face. All she had left of the moment was a lingering feeling of the way their bodies had collided and then joined, and the security of being held. Her face was suffused with a wild blush. Here they were in the middle of a public celebration, and she'd made a fool of herself, as well as ruined David's speech. He was going to be furious.

She shrugged. What else was new.

"Darling . . . tell me you're all right?" David's hand cupped her cheek as he tilted her face toward him.

She smiled at her husband, nodding without speaking as he carefully brushed at the dirt and grass stains on the sleeve of her pink suit.

His concern was appropriate, and his clean-cut, handsome face reflected his distress. Quickly he assured the members of the committee who'd staged the rally that it was certainly not their fault the end of the stage had collapsed. Accidents happened.

Dupree's hawk-like eyes narrowed as he watched David Potter cup his wife's elbow and usher her carefully toward a waiting car. Ever the politician, he was constantly assuring everyone they passed that Amanda was perfectly fine. With the skill of one to the manor born, he seated her inside, tucked the tail of her skirt in the car, and then slammed the door.

Amanda shuddered as the force reverberated within the confines of the car.

Waving to his constituents while mouthing platitudes, he motioned to the chauffeur behind the steering wheel, then smiled as they drove away.

Amanda felt the heat of David's occasional glance as Marcus Havasute, their chauffeur, wove through traffic. David's sigh of relief was evident as the massive iron gates of the family estate came into view.

"Thank God," he muttered. "We're home."

Amanda shuddered. Home didn't have the same connotation to her that it obviously did to him. Before she was ready to move, the car had pulled up to the door and stopped. By the time she'd unbuckled her seat belt, Marcus was at her door and was gently helping her out and to her feet while David exited on his own. Without waiting for her, David entered his house with Amanda at his heels.

"Mrs. Potter! What happened?" Mabel cried, as she hurried into the hallway. The state of Amanda's clothing was impossible to miss and the housekeeper flitted about her in concern.

But David waved her away with a sweep of his hand as he pulled Amanda up the stairs behind him. All of his solicitation for Amanda's welfare was gone. They continued up the stairs and down the hall to their room. The door shut behind her with a cool, metallic click.

"You stupid bitch! Can't you do anything right?"

His hand hit the middle of her back, dead center, propelling her forward, face down upon the bed. His anger was instant and alive, thickening the air in the room until it was hard for her to breathe. He yanked at her arm, turning her onto her back, and although she thought about protesting, she knew from experience that it would only make things worse.

"You've ruined your suit. And it's a Givenchy original. No one will remember my speech. The only Potter who'll make the news tonight is you falling off that goddamned stage!"

"David, don't."

She hated the whine in her voice. But it was there before she had time to stop it. Her arms flew up to ward off the second blow, but were too late as his hand connected with the side of her face. Her head popped backward on her neck. Light exploded behind her eyelids. She moaned, and tried to roll away.

"Shut up," he snarled, and thrust himself against her crotch, using his knee as a pry bar to separate her legs.

"David . . . please . . . for God's sake don't," she begged, and then flinched when he pinned her to the bed.

The sharp, staccato rap upon the bedroom door made him freeze in mid-action. David's face was a caricature of its former beauty. The perfectly shaped lips were thinned and pulled back in a snarl. Wide blue eyes had gone narrow and colorless with fury. His blond hair, usually so well groomed, hung down across his eyes and forehead like a pale shroud.

"What is it?" he shouted to whomever was there. When Amanda would have moved, he wrapped his hand around her throat and held her down on the bed like a pinned butterfly. "You know better than to disturb us in our room!"

Amanda closed her eyes, and tried to swallow, unwilling to watch his nostrils flare. But it was impossible for saliva to get past the grip he had on her throat. Instead, it trickled out the side of her mouth with the blood.

The housekeeper's voice was loud and shrill. "The mayor's on the phone. And I thought you would want to know that a television crew has pulled up in the yard."

David shuddered. The fist he'd made of his hand went slack and the one he'd wrapped around her throat slid off her body. He dropped onto all fours over Amanda's body as his erection, along with his muscles, went lax.

Long seconds passed as he hung there, suspended above her body on all fours, willing his breathing back to normal and that black emotion back into the cellar in his mind. Finally he spoke.

"I'll be right there."

He stared down at the raw, spreading bruise on the side of Amanda's face and the trickle of blood at the corner of her lips.

"Darling . . . you hurt yourself when you fell. I'll have Mabel get you some ice for that."

He leaned forward. Perspiration from his forehead dripped onto her cheek. He pressed a soft, sensual kiss at the corner of her eye and then across her lips, using the tip of his tongue to remove the last traces of the blood that he'd drawn. His hand slid up her skirt and cupped her rudely as his hot whisper raked her face.

"You're so beautiful, Amanda. If you would only learn not to disobey me, then I wouldn't be forced to reprimand you. Try to remember that, darling. It's so important that a politician's wife be above reproach."

Then, as if nothing untoward had just happened, he pulled himself off her shaking body and left the room, combing his fingers through his perfectly cut blond hair and readjusting his clothes as he went to meet his public.

As he was on his way out, the housekeeper hovered just out of reach.

"Mabel . . . Mrs. Potter had a fall in the park. See to her."

"Yes, sir. Right away, sir," she mumbled, and ducked her head.

Mabel waited until he was out of sight and then made a beeline for Amanda. She knew what had happened. All the servants on the Potter estate knew what their employer was like. And they all knew that to intervene on Amanda's behalf was impossible. It had been done at times, but it was dangerous, and it had even been fatal.

"Are you all right?" Mabel asked, as she darted into the room and quickly shut the door behind her.

Amanda's eyes teared. The elderly housekeeper's presence was all that kept her sane. She shrugged and started to crawl from the bed, then groaned as her sore and aching muscles protested.

"Here, Missy, let me help," Mabel said, and offered a hand.

Amanda took it.

"What happened?" Mabel asked.

"Does it matter?" Amanda said. "No matter what precipitates it, the end results are still the same."

Her quiet despair pierced the old housekeeper's heart. But there was little either could do. Mabel's spirit was willing, but her aged body wasn't able. And Amanda flatly refused to allow another soul to interfere on her behalf . . . ever.

She'd done it once, three years ago, and still had nightmares about opening the morning paper and reading the headlines.

BEDSIDE SUICIDE!

And the smaller lines added below: *Local lawyer ends own life as illegalities in practice are revealed.*

The only wrong Larry Feingold had committed was helping plan Amanda Potter's escape and she knew it.

"Here, dear, let me help," Mabel said, and quietly began unbuttoning the ruined blouse that Amanda had worn beneath the suit. She clucked in distress as the blouse came off of Amanda's shoulders, and tried not to look at the new bruises or the old scars.

With Mabel's aid, Amanda solemnly removed the rest of her clothing, then staggered to the bath and climbed into the warm, soothing waters that Mabel had drawn.

"Sit, girl," she ordered, and helped Amanda slide into a reclining position.

Amanda closed her eyes and leaned her head against the white tiles while Mabel moved a cold compress across the wounds on her face in a slow, gentle motion.

"'Tisn't right," Mabel muttered. "'Tisn't right at all! No man should be striking his woman, I don't care what excuse he gives."

Painful tears spurted from beneath Amanda's lashes as Mabel pressed the cloth against the swelling bruise at her temple. She was caught in hell, between her husband and fate, with no obvious way out except death.

"Just stay out of it, Mabel. I can't bear to have any more *consequences* on my conscience. Do you hear me?"

Amanda's voice was strong, and her grip sure as she grabbed her housekeeper's wrist and shook it to make her point.

"I hear you. I hear you," Mabel replied as she hustled around the outer room, gathering the ruined and soiled clothing. "But it still don't make it right. Someone should do something about that man. If you ask me, he's not right in the head."

"No one asked you," Amanda reminded her.

Mabel huffed. She picked up an earring from the floor and then searched the bed as well as beneath it for its mate.

"Missy," Mabel called. "I can't seem to find your other earring."

Amanda slid lower into the water and closed her eyes. "It'll show up," she said. "It's probably lost in the bedcovers somewhere."

Mabel laid the orphan diamond stud on the dresser and made a quick and quiet exit.

Amanda shuddered and rubbed her hands up and down her bare arms as she listened to Mabel's footsteps disappearing down the hall. Her fingertips brushed across the upper portion of her left arm. When she connected with more bruised flesh she winced, and then oddly enough, smiled when she remembered how she'd come by those. David hadn't put those there. She remembered the man in the park, and his firm grip. He'd kept her from falling on her face in the dirt.

"At least I came by some of these bruises honestly," she muttered.

The water enveloped her like a jealous lover, and no sooner came the feeling than she bolted out of the bath, grabbing for a towel. The idea of getting caught wet and naked by David made her sick. She didn't need any more reminders of lovers and their jealousies. She was living a double life as it was. Pretending all was perfect when it was a living hell.

As she dried, she thought again of the man in the park, of how safe she'd felt in his arms, and how close she'd come to whispering in his ear a plea for help. But she'd caught herself in time. Remembering, instead, the last man she'd asked for help. She couldn't have another Larry Feingold on her conscience. The next time, she wouldn't survive the guilt.

Amanda knew now that asking David for a divorce was futile. He would never let her go. It wouldn't be good politics. All she could do was bide her time. Somewhere . . . somehow . . . the opportunity would present itself. And when it did, she was going to run like hell and never look back. That thought was all that kept her going. That hope was all that kept her sane.

"Say, Dupree, you made a fine flying catch out there this afternoon."

Jefferson Dupree looked up to see his superior, Orvis Morrell, standing by his desk. "Thanks, Chief." He grinned and shrugged. "Someone yelled catch. It was reflex that made me do it." For some reason, he felt the need to minimize his part in the incident.

"Spoken like a true running back," Morrell said. "But you still made the department look good, boy. No one can say that we weren't on the job. Not today, at least."

Dupree shuffled some papers on his desk as Morrell ambled into his office.

Yeah, I was on the job all right, he said to himself. But his gut told him that he had missed something.

He couldn't shake his instincts. They'd been on alert ever since David Potter had yanked Amanda from his arms. It was something about his smile. Then he told himself that there was nothing about David Potter that was different from any other politician. They all smiled in public . . . too much and too often.

Thirty-six years old, Jefferson Dupree had been a detective on the Morgantown, West Virginia, force for the last six years, and before that, a military policeman in the Marines. In those six years, he'd probably seen David Potter and his wife at least once a week, either driving by in their chauffeured limousine, or written up in the society section of the local newspaper. Today was the first time he'd had any personal contact with them, though, and he felt as if he'd been sideswiped.

He shuddered and closed his eyes as he swallowed a lump in his throat. Some contact. He could still remember the way it felt to hold her. It felt comfortable. It felt right. And the most puzzling thing of all . . . it felt downright familiar.

His wayward thoughts were shattered by a disgruntled complainant. One, unfortunately, whom he knew all too well:

"Where's Detective Dupree? I wanna talk to Detective Dupree. I know my rights. I may live on the streets, but I've still got rights. I wanna talk to Dupree."

Dupree looked up and stifled a sigh.

"Hey, Beaner. Don't raise such a fuss, man. I'm right here," he said.

He stood and waved the old man over, wondering as he did how long he would be able to hold his breath. Unlike a lot of homeless people who took every opportunity they got to bathe and change, Beaner wasn't fond of changing clothes *or* bathing. In fact, if Dupree wasn't mistaken, Beaner wore everything he owned . . . and had for some years now. And the only time the clothes . . . or Beaner, got wet . . . was when they got rained on.

"What seems to be the fuss?" he asked, and hoped that Beaner's story wasn't going to be a long one.

Beaner wistfully eyed a doughnut beside Dupree's phone, settled himself in the chair beside his desk, and sighed.

Dupree winced. Beaner's breath was as bad as his body odor. And the fact that he sat down, intending to stay a while, didn't bode well for the atmosphere inside the office.

"Help yourself, Beaner," he said.

"Oh no," Beaner muttered, and looked away. "I couldn't eat another bite."

"Suit yourself, man," Dupree said. But he knew the

routine. And it had to be done just right or Beaner would be insulted beyond belief. "I'm gonna fill up my coffee cup. Be right back, and then we'll talk."

Beaner nodded importantly. And the moment Dupree walked away, he stuffed the entire doughnut into his mouth, chewed twice, and swallowed the chunks in a single gulp.

"Have some on me," Dupree said, setting a styrofoam cup of coffee at Beaner's elbow. He knew Beaner was going to need it, or whatever he had to tell him was going to be peppered with doughnut and powdered sugar.

Beaner took one sip and then settled the cup between his knees, cradling it in his hands as if it were a sack of gold.

"I'll just save the rest for later," he said.

Dupree hid a grin and nodded. "Now then," he said. "What is it you needed to tell me?"

Beaner shifted in the chair, and his mouth pursed over his last three teeth.

"I found something in the park," he said. "It ain't mine. I don't keep what ain't mine." He set the coffee on the desk as he dug in his pocket.

Jefferson Dupree took a long gulp of his own coffee, ignoring the fact that it was way too hot to swallow. At this point, anything was better than breathing too deeply. And then he looked down at the sparkle in Beaner's hand and nearly choked.

Sitting in the midst of the filth, its perfect beauty was nearly obscene. But its worth was obvious.

"Where did you get that?" he asked, lifting it from Beaner's palm.

"I told you it ain't mine," Beaner repeated. He recognized the detective's interest. "I told you . . . I found it in the park . . . remember?"

Dupree nodded, and turned it over in his hand, trying to remember where he'd seen the earring that matched this one.

"I found it down by the stage . . . after the speeches,"

Beaner went on. "I always do my duty and listen to the politicians. Might wanna vote again one of these days," he added, and snickered once to make his point.

Jefferson Dupree's hand clenched over the diamond as sweat broke out across his upper lip. Now he remembered where he'd seen this. One just like it had been on Amanda Potter's ear. She must have lost it in the fall.

"Beaner . . . you did the right thing," he said, and started to dig in his pocket for his wallet.

Beaner frowned and jumped up. "Don't pay me!" he shouted. "I don't take money for doing the right thing. I ain't a beggar. I just ain't got a home."

Dupree winced. He'd known that Beaner was sensitive . . . as were many of the homeless people on the streets that he'd come to know.

"Hey man, I didn't mean it like that," Dupree said softly. "This is really valuable. The owner will be real happy to get it back. I was just going to give you a reward. People can accept rewards, can't they?"

Beaner's frown turned upside down. The smile that split his face framed his three remaining teeth to perfection.

"Well now. I guess they can," he said. He palmed the twenty dollars Dupree handed him, and disappeared from the office much quicker and quieter than he'd come.

"Good Lord," Morrell said, as he walked out of the office with a can of air freshener aimed before him. "It doesn't seem possible, but I swear he smelled worse than last time."

Dupree blinked and coughed as Piney Forest Fresh mingled with the remnants of Beaner.

"My God, Chief. You made it worse."

They both laughed. Such things were part of their everyday life.

"Look at this," Dupree said, and opened his hand.

Orvis Morrell gawked. "Is that thing real?"

Dupree nodded. "It belongs to Amanda Potter. Guess she lost it when she fell."

"Here," Morrell said, and held out his hand. "I'll give

the Potter house a call. Someone can come down and claim it."

"No! I'll take it myself," Dupree said, and then flushed at his insistence. It was obvious, even to himself, that he was too eager to go to a place where he didn't belong.

Morrell's eyebrows arched. "You better watch what you're doing out there, Dupree. It doesn't pay to mess with Potter."

"What the hell does that mean?"

"Nothing," Morrell said, and turned away. "Just remember what I said. Get rid of the earring . . . and whatever else you're carrying around inside that damned hard head of yours." The door slammed behind him as he disappeared into his office.

Jefferson Dupree blinked at the sound, and then looked down at the earring in his hand.

Then, without further ado, he set out to return what wasn't his.

TWO

❋

The sound of footsteps on the stairs sent Amanda into a panic as she finished drying from her bath. David was coming back and she wasn't dressed. The last thing she wanted was the sight of her nudity to instigate a revival of what he considered lovemaking.

There was no time for underwear. Her only hope was the jade brocade jumpsuit he'd given her for her birthday. It would be easy to get into, and the rich fabric and dark color would hide her lack of lingerie. What David didn't know wouldn't hurt her.

She bolted to the closet and quickly found what she'd been searching for. She yanked at the hanger and then cursed helplessly when the jumpsuit caught at the neck.

"Oh God, no," she muttered, then willed herself to a calmness she didn't feel.

With sure fingers, she quickly unwound the single thread that had entangled itself. Then, using the wall to steady herself, she jammed first one foot and then the other into the legs of the garment. In seven steps David would be inside the room and she knew it. She'd spent too many nights lying awake, counting the distance between herself and hell, to lose track now.

Six. Five.

She stuffed one arm into the sleeve and then shrugged

the other up and over her shoulder, ignoring her aching muscles and her new, tender bruises from her latest bout with David and the platform.

Four. Three.

The zipper tab did its part to make her crazy by twice slipping from her shaky fingers. But then her fingers caught a firm, sure hold.

"Please let this work the first time," she said, and pulled.

Two. One.

"Darling! You're already out of your bath!" David pursed his lips. "I had envisioned joining you."

Amanda slid a small, practiced smile in place and pretended to be as disappointed as he, when in fact the thought made her sick. She didn't know how much longer her sanity and her strength would hold out against his.

"The water got chilly. It was making me stiffen up," she explained, hoping it served to remind him that her suffering was not only from the accident, but at his hands as well.

If his conscience tugged, maybe he'd leave her alone for tonight. Maybe . . . if she was lucky . . . he'd actually leave and search out one of his *women*. He had them. He'd always had them. But it had taken Amanda years to realize that she didn't care.

"Your hair got damp," David said. "Mabel should have put it up for you." He frowned at the thick tangle of curls hanging down the back of her jumpsuit, as well as the moisture that was turning it to a darker shade of jade.

Amanda's heart jerked. Whenever anyone failed him, in whatever manner, invariably she was the one who suffered.

"I asked her not to," Amanda said quickly. "I was so sore I wanted to get right into the tub. It was my fault. Really!"

She sat down in front of the dresser and picked up her brush. In spite of her determination not to let him know he'd hurt her earlier, she winced.

He saw it. Instantly he was at her side.

"Darling. Let me," David coaxed, and took the brush from her hand.

The scent of his cologne, as well as the not-so-subtle shift of his manhood against her back, made her nauseous. She bit the inside of her lip to keep from screaming. This scenario had been played out so many times in the past that she could almost pinpoint the minute he'd drag her to her feet and remove her clothes.

David's fingers dug through her hair and into her scalp. Slowly, steadily, he massaged her head from neck to crown, and then back again, all the while working out the muscle knots he'd created.

Amanda closed her eyes. She couldn't bear to watch his face grow slack with desire. When it did, she knew that his eyes would lighten until the blue was little more than a white glitter, and that his body would grow hard and hot and she would be the one to suffer his quixotic tenderness.

She knew he was an abuser, but she would never understand the mindset of a man who could beat the hell out of a woman one minute, and then stick himself inside of her, exalt in his climax while blood ran down her face, and then cry like a baby for what he'd done.

Because of him, Amanda's opinion of men ran from fear to hatred to indifference. But it didn't matter. While David Potter had ruined her forever, she knew in her heart that she would survive him. She also knew that someday she would get away. But never . . . not ever in this lifetime . . . would she allow another man to touch her or hold her. The pain was too great.

David's fingers dug into her scalp and then suddenly fisted, balling up the hair that was within his grasp. Unbidden tears sprang to her eyes as he yanked her head back against his belly.

"Amanda . . . where is your other earring?"

The low, threatening tone of his voice made her knees feel weak. If she hadn't been sitting, she would have fallen on the spot. Hiding the fear that his question evoked, she shrugged out of his grasp and stood, maintaining a cool, calm demeanor as she looked down at the single piece of jewelry on the dresser, then back at him.

"I don't know," she said. "Mabel asked the same thing when I was in the bath. I assume it got lost on the bed during the . . . *scuffle*." She stared him fully in the face and had the pleasure of watching a swift, but sure, flash of guilt come and go.

"They were Mother's," he said.

"I know that," Amanda said. "I was about to search for it when you came in."

"Then I suggest you do so," David said softly. "It must be found. They're a family heirloom, you know."

"I don't lose my jewelry, David."

"People have to be taught to take care of possessions," he muttered, completely ignoring her comment, as well as the fact that he was probably responsible for the earring being missing to begin with.

Amanda's stomach fluttered. She'd heard that censorious tone before, and it had always culminated in what David liked to call "behavior modification." She called it torture.

She leaned over the bed and began running her hand across the patterned coverlet, certain that within moments she would find the earring. But when her search had covered the entire bed, as well as beneath the pillow shams, and it was nowhere to be seen, she began to panic.

Dear God, please let me find it!

Beads of sweat ran down the middle of her back. Amanda felt the silk brocade sticking to her body as she dropped to her hands and knees and began crawling around the floor, splaying her fingers desperately.

"Amanda . . . "

The warning was thick in his voice.

"You *could* help me look," she muttered beneath her breath.

The kick caught her mid-stomach, instantly moving her from a crawling to a sitting position as she struggled for breath. Her rib cage, along with the inside of her lip, began to throb, and when she tasted blood, she realized that she'd inadvertently bitten the inside of her mouth.

Damn you to a bloody hell, she thought. But the wish did nothing for the immediate lack of air in her lungs.

"You've lost Mother's earring!" His accusation was high-pitched and shrill, almost childish.

Amanda held up her hand to ward off the oncoming blow as she shook her head. Had she a breath of air left in her lungs she would have screamed at him in fury.

The angry glow in her eyes surprised him. That and the sound of the doorbell echoing throughout the house stopped the second kick in mid-swing.

"Oh, who the hell could that be?" he muttered, glaring at her. "Probably more journalists inquiring after your health." Once again, he straightened his clothing and smoothed down his hair. "When I come back, that earring better be lying beside the other one on the dresser . . . or you'll be sorry."

I already am, she thought, as she watched him leave.

As soon as she could stand up, she did. The woman staring back at her from the mirror was unrecognizable. A large bruise was darkening by the moment. Her lower lip was puffed and bloody. She looked defeated and afraid, and the pain on her face was impossible to hide.

"Damn you, David," she whispered, and hated herself for the tremble of her chin. "And damn you," she told herself, "for letting this happen . . . over . . . and over . . . again. If you weren't such a bloody coward, you'd end it now."

An impassible expression replaced the one of pain. Contemplating suicide was an old, almost comfortable, enemy.

But as quickly as the thought came, it went. If she killed herself, then David would still come out the winner. And the thought of him using her death to garner more votes in the next election made her furious. If she died, she was taking him with her.

"I've got to get out of here," she said, and began pulling herself together.

If she could make it downstairs into public company before David had a chance to come back to their room and resume his mind and body games, she knew that she'd be safe. It would be temporary. But in Amanda Potter's world, any kind of safety was acceptable.

As she jerked the brush through her hair, she remembered her lack of underwear and started to undress. But the thought of David coming back and catching her nude killed the thought before it became deed. Instead she slipped her feet into matching slippers, splashed some cold water on her battered face, and left her bedroom as quickly as her aching body would allow her.

She made it all the way down the stairs and was going toward the kitchen area and the safety of Mabel's company when she heard the sound of David's voice and the argument that ensued.

"Look, Detective. I greatly appreciate what you did for me . . . and for Amanda. But I must insist that whatever you have to say, you say to me. Amanda is, at the moment, indisposed. Her fall was a serious one, you know."

Jefferson Dupree wasn't having any of it. Amanda Potter's fall would have hurt him a hell of a lot more than her. He'd been on the receiving end of her flying leap off the platform.

"I'm not trying to be difficult, Congressman. It's just that I need her to identify something," Dupree said.

"And what might that be, Detective?" Amanda asked.

Both men turned at the sound of her voice. David was furious that she'd come downstairs and entered into a conversation he had every intention of keeping to himself. He glared as she entered the library.

Jefferson Dupree was in shock. He couldn't find the words to even answer her question. He couldn't do anything but watch the way she spread her hand across her belly as she walked, as if she were making certain nothing slipped out of place. He wondered how she'd gone from grass stains to bloodstains in less than two hours.

Her mouth was swollen. There was a bruise spreading across the upper side of her face. And he hated himself for realizing, through all the horror, that she had to be naked beneath the jade silk. Her body was too fluid to be otherwise.

"Dear God," he whispered. "I'm sorry. I had no idea that you'd been hurt this badly. What did the doctor say?"

"She hasn't been," David replied for her. "They're only bruises. We're tending to them here. No need making bad press of such a little incident. It would only make the city fathers look incompetent, you know. It would seem as if they couldn't provide a safe environment for public affairs."

Only bruises? Dupree could not believe Potter's assessment of his wife's suffering.

Amanda grimaced. Yes, she had bruises, along with what felt like a cracked rib or two. But they would heal. She knew what a real broken rib felt like, and this wasn't nearly painful enough to worry about.

"What was it you wanted to ask me, Detective?"

Amanda's soft voice yanked Dupree back into focus. He dug his handkerchief out of his pocket and unfolded it, revealing what lay inside.

"My earring!"

Amanda's gasp was inadvertent. It killed the relief of seeing the lost earring as her lungs inflated and sent a shaft of pain spiraling against bruised ribs. She staggered, and then felt herself being lowered into the seat cushion of the chair behind her.

"Are you *sure* you're all right?"

Dupree's voice was soft, the touch of his hands upon her arms, solicitous. The seduction of his sympathy was overwhelming. But the memory of David's fury, and the scope of his power, was enough to stop her fleeting idea of asking for help.

"I'm fine," she said quickly, and looked away, unwilling to give David any grounds for further anger.

"Amanda . . . darling. Isn't this wonderful news? It's been found!"

David's voice, as well as the way he inserted himself between her and the detective, told her more than she wanted to know. He was already suspicious.

"You see, Detective, we'd already missed the earring," David said. "And had launched our own search on the premises, unaware that it had been lost elsewhere. Where, may I ask, was it found?"

Dupree knew when to argue, and when to shut up. And even though he sensed a high degree of tension between the Potters, as well as the antagonism that Potter exhibited toward him, he knew that this was one of those times when interfering between a man and his wife was out of line. Way out of line.

"It was found at the park. Somewhere near the platform. I suspect she lost it in the fall."

"Of course, of course," David said, and lifted the earring from Dupree's handkerchief as if he were lifting it from something foul.

"I suggest you have it cleaned before Mrs. Potter wears them again," Dupree added, thinking of Beaner's filthy palm, and wherever else he might have had it before he'd turned it in to the authorities.

David's eyebrow raised, just enough to let Dupree know he was amused. "But of course," he drawled, and glanced back at the handkerchief the detective was putting in his pocket. "I had already intended to."

Jefferson Dupree flushed. The insult was flagrant. The urge to put his fist between Potter's nose and chin was fierce. He knew his limits, and they'd just about been reached. It was time to leave while he still had a job and a reputation.

"I've finished what I came to do," Dupree said, and then, although he knew his opinion was not welcome here, felt compelled to add, "Mrs. Potter, I highly recommend a trip to the doctor."

Without waiting for an answer, he started out of the library. "Don't bother to move," he said without looking back. "I'll let myself out."

Moments later, the sound of a slamming door told David Potter that he'd done just that. And, before he could think to act, the housekeeper bustled into the library.

"Mabel, will you help me dress?" Amanda asked. "David is going to call the doctor and make an appointment for me. I think I may have hurt myself, after all, when I fell."

Mabel hurried to her mistress's aid. With her help, Amanda managed to get back upstairs, leaving David alone in the room.

David was in shock. A moment ago when Amanda had begun issuing orders, she'd reminded him of his mother. It made him feel small and helpless, and he didn't like that feeling. He didn't like it at all. Amanda had just issued a directive without his authority, and yet he'd stood there and let her do it. *It's no big deal,* he told himself. *I'll let her have her trip to the doctor. It will probably make good press.*

And then he remembered the detective's expression of disbelief, and the way Amanda had all but fallen into his arms, and felt the anger returning.

I have Mother's earring, he reminded himself. *That's good! Everything is back in place.*

And although he tried to convince himself that all was well, a darkness began to envelop him from the inside out. He walked to the desk to pick up the phone and then couldn't remember the doctor's number. With shaking hands, he began to sift through the Rolodex, but it was hopeless. The rage was upon him so swiftly he could not see.

The contents of his desk went flying as a roar filled his ears. Without thought, he slapped the glass surface of the desk with the flat of his hand. The force of the blow echoed loudly into the silence of the room, and then there was nothing to be heard but a soft, almost nonexistent whimper.

It was that sound and a blinding pain that brought him slowly back to his senses. When he could think, and when he could see, the reason for the fiery throb shafting through his hand and running up his arm became obvious.

The earring . . . his mother's earring . . . was imbedded in the center of his palm as if it had been set in flesh instead of gold. He stared down at the sight and started to smile. The smile turned into a chuckle, and then the chuckle to an outright laugh.

"I say! I believe I've found Mother's earring."

The absurdity of the remark sent him into further fits of laughter that evolved into something dark and ugly. It sent the nearby servants scurrying to other parts of the house.

David opened a drawer and selected a letter opener from the scattered contents. The dagger-like design, as well as the narrow, rapier-sharp blade, would serve his purpose.

Without taking a breath or considering the pain, he plunged the blade into his palm just to the side of the two-carat stone, and then gave it an upward twist. The diamond stud popped out and then rolled to a stop on the desktop as slickly as if it had just been birthed.

Nerve impulses began registering pain, and David shuddered and stared blankly at the blood that was dripping onto the desk pad. But then he smiled. It was a thin expression of the real thing.

Casually, as if he were about to brush lint from his clothes, he popped the handkerchief from his jacket pocket and then wrapped it in place around his hand. Moments later, a thin line of blood began to seep through, coloring first one thread, and then another, until a bright patch of red centered in the makeshift bandage.

He picked up the earring and swiveled the chair in which he was sitting until he was facing the mullioned glass of the massive French doors behind him. Angling for the best light, he held the earring up, and turned it first one way and then the other, noting how many of the facets were covered in blood. He frowned.

Without waste of motion, he slipped the precious jewel into his mouth as one would eat a grape, rolling it around inside as if tasting for flavor, mentally marking the somewhat salty taste of himself for future reference.

Then, ever so carefully, he pushed it out between his lips with his tongue, caught it between thumb and forefinger, and once again, held it up to the light for observation.

"There now," he said softly. "There now. It's all shiny and clean. Won't Mother be proud?"

It might have been true, had *Mother* not been dead these last ten years. But in David Potter's twisted mind, that bit of information did not, at the moment, compute.

Jefferson Dupree drove all the way down to the station, parked, and locked his car. He was halfway across the parking lot before he realized that the bruise on Amanda Potter's face was on the wrong side to have happened in the fall.

The thought caught him in mid-step. He froze in place and considered the ramifications of what he was thinking.

"I'm just imagining it," he muttered, then closed his eyes and did a mental playback of the incident, from the moment someone yelled "catch her" until she was yanked from his arms.

It still came out the same. There was no way her face, or the rest of her body, could have been injured so severely by that fall. But . . . what occurred after she'd gone home was another story altogether.

"Hey, Dupree, are you asleep on your feet?"

He jerked and then opened his eyes. His chief, Orvis Morrell, was grinning at him.

"Chief . . . I think I may have just stumbled on a case of physical abuse."

Morrell's smile died a slow death. "Now just what the hell do you mean?" he asked. "I thought you'd gone out to the Potter estate to take back that earring?"

"I did. And when Mrs. Potter came down to identify it, she looked like she'd been through a hammermill."

Morrell frowned and looked away. "Hell, boy, she fell off a platform, remember? I know you're a smooth operator, but you're not exactly satin-covered and down-filled. It had to hurt her."

"No, dammit. I know what I saw. And the woman who picked herself up from the ground in the park was walking upright and steady. The one I saw just now couldn't stand up straight. She also had a busted lip and the whole side of her face was a solid bruise. That didn't happen in the goddamned fall."

"Stay out of it."

Dupree couldn't have been more surprised had Morrell just offered him a bribe, because the man was as honest and above reproach as the day was long.

"What the hell do you mean, stay out of it?" he demanded, unaware that his voice was shaking from shock and anger.

"Just what I said. There are some things around here that you don't go poking your nose into, Dupree."

Jefferson frowned. "But I can't just ignore what I saw."

"Oh, but you can . . . and you will. I said stay out of it. That's an order."

But Morrell knew his man well enough to know that an explosion was bound to come. It did.

"Sonofabitch!"

Morrell took a step back in reflex.

Dupree leaned forward until their noses were nearly touching. "I'll go to hell first," he warned Morrell.

"That's just about where you'll be if you don't heed my warning," Morrell said softly.

Dupree pivoted and started walking away. The length of his stride and the set of his posture were evidence of his unbridled fury. He was a man on the run from himself.

He was inside his car, had started the engine and slammed it into gear, before he realized he'd even moved. As he left a quarter-inch of rubber behind him on the pavement, the realization of what he'd just done sank in. Countermanding direct orders and then breaking city traffic ordinances in plain view of the law were not swift career moves.

"Oh hell," he muttered, as he drove into traffic. "I was looking for a job when I took this one, anyway."

* * *

"Mabel, please tell David that I'm downstairs and waiting," Amanda said, as she sat down in a chair in the hall.

Mabel nodded and hurried away, a little surprised by her mistress's quiet, purposeful attitude. She couldn't remember a time when Mrs. Potter had taken the initiative in such a manner, and she feared the outcome of the stunt.

She peered into the library, but he was nowhere to be seen. Frowning, she turned and then gasped, clutching her throat in shock as he stood less than a foot away with a hard, intent look on his face.

"Oh my, Mr. Potter, but you gave me a fright! I didn't hear you come up."

"I had a little accident myself," he said, and held up his hand, indicating a neat gauze and adhesive patch in the palm. "Is Amanda ready?"

"Yes, sir, she's waiting for you in the hall."

Once again, Mabel was surprised by this odd turn of events. In the past, David Potter would have been furious by now. She wondered what on earth had taken possession of these two, then sighed. The less she knew about the goings-on in this household, the better off she probably was.

"I've called Marcus. He'll be driving us," David said as he walked away. "If I have any calls, take a message. I'll get back to them as soon as possible."

"Yes, sir," Mabel said, and watched him walk away.

David entered the long hallway, eyeing the polished marble and gleaming crystal with pride. He loved beautiful things. It was one of the reasons he took such pride in his wife. She was a beautiful woman.

And then he saw her sitting upright and silent, awaiting his arrival. He frowned at her appearance. Right now, Amanda was not at her best and he didn't like that. He didn't like that at all.

"Amanda, darling, are you ready?" he asked.

Lost in thought, she hadn't been aware of his arrival, and jumped at the sound of his voice.

"Yes," she said, willing herself not to look down, and looking instead at a point just over his shoulder. "Are you driving me?"

He held up his hand once more. "I had a little accident." He smiled, and the beauty of it illuminated his face. "It seems to be the day for Potter incidents, so I called Marcus around with the car. He should be here soon."

At that moment, both of them heard the sounds of tires crunching on the gravel driveway.

Amanda started to get up and then moaned softly as a new spear of pain dug another path through her belly.

"Darling . . . I'm so sorry," David whispered. "Let me help you."

Amanda flinched, but didn't speak as his hand slid beneath her elbow and gently helped her to her feet. By the time they were on their way, Amanda already envisioned the upcoming scene at the hospital. She was going to be the beloved but injured wife, and he was playing the part of the devoted and concerned husband.

Bile rose at the back of her throat, and tears burned behind her eyelids. She clenched her teeth and stared out the window at the passing scenery. Somewhere out there was a man—or possibly a woman—who was going to be brave enough, and willing enough, to help her. And when she found him, or her, she was going to run and never look back. Until then, she had to bide her time. The blueblood lineage of David Potter, his status as congressman extraordinaire, and the long arms of his multimillions of dollars were more than she could fight alone.

The hospital came into view, and minutes later, Amanda found herself being ushered into a private examination room with David still playing the part of dutiful husband.

The door closed and for a moment they were left alone.

"Be careful what you say, Amanda," David said softly.

She looked up. And this time, she met his gaze full force. "I'm *always* careful what I say."

The door opened and Doctor Ihnike entered. He was small and dark, and his almond-shaped eyes, the most expressive feature on his face, registered the shock he was feeling.

"Mrs. Potter! They didn't tell me it was you."

After the last time, he'd warned David Potter that there must be no more "incidents" such as these and had strongly suggested therapy. Obviously, his warning hadn't been severe enough. He glared at the congressman, willing him to look back, but he didn't. David Potter was too busy watching his wife's reaction.

"As I suppose you've heard by now, I suffered a fall off the stage in the park," Amanda said quietly.

Dr. Ihnike frowned. "I also heard that one of our illustrious detectives, Jefferson Dupree, caught you in a flying leap that would have shamed the best running back in the NFL. Was I wrong?"

Amanda shook her head. "No. He caught me. But it seems that I've suffered some delayed reactions to the incident."

"So it seems," he said softly.

This time David Potter met his gaze without flinching. "I'm most concerned about her ribs," he said. "They must have been bruised or cracked in the fall . . . don't you agree?"

The cool warning was in place. Dr. Ihnike frowned. He hated being put in this position. But after his last report, the hospital board had come down on him like an avalanche. He could practice medicine, or he could pack. They'd given him little alternative.

"I really can't say what's wrong with her . . . this time . . . until I see her X rays."

David swallowed angrily. The threat was subtle, but it was still there. *Damn the man. Doesn't he know what's good for him?* David thought. *He's got a wife and three children to consider . . . just as I've got my image to protect. He needs to get his priorities in order.*

"I'll call for a wheelchair," Dr. Inhike added, and

patted Amanda gently on the shoulder. "You need to take a ride to X-ray."

"I walked in, I can walk down there," she said. "Besides . . . I know the way in my sleep."

"Humor me," he said. "I'll call a nurse and see you after your X rays have been developed."

He left the office, muttering beneath his breath. The wry twist to her mouth made him sick. Inhike wondered why a woman would stay with a man like that, and then knew that it wasn't for him to get involved.

Unlike child abuse cases, which he was obligated to report, this woman was an adult and perfectly capable of making her own complaints. Oddly enough, she didn't.

Maybe Potter's status and money were enough to make the punishment worthwhile. But the moment he thought it, he knew that he didn't really believe it. Not about Amanda Potter. There had to be another reason. And he hoped to hell that whatever it was, she got it resolved before it killed her.

A few minutes later, an orderly wheeled Amanda from the office and down the hall toward X-ray. The long hall was chilly, and reminiscent of a meat locker: sterile walls and a constant blast of cold air, coupled with the constant motion of people dressed in white, moving about like so many slabs of beef on constantly moving racks.

Amanda shuddered and closed her eyes, aware that her husband was hard on the heels of the orderly who was pushing her chair.

His angry curse startled her. She looked up . . . and straight into the whiskey-brown eyes of the tall, angry man who was leaning against the doorway at the end of the hall.

"Detective Dupree!" She was surprised to see him here.

"What the hell are you doing here?" David asked, and then caught himself, aware that by his profession alone, the man had a right to be almost anywhere.

Dupree crossed his arms across his chest, letting his finger slide along the bulge of his shoulder holster for assurance, and looked down at the toe of his boot, considering his answer carefully before making it.

"I guess you could say I'm following up on the loose ends of a situation I didn't like . . . unofficially, of course."

David stared, shocked by the taunt in the detective's voice. The trio stood frozen while the orderly fidgeted, uncertain as to how to handle this delay.

Amanda's heart skipped a beat. It was a sobering thought that here was a man who'd made a suggestion that he expected to be carried out. In fact, he'd been so certain that it would be done, he'd come to the hospital himself to make sure.

David was livid. When he got home, he'd make a call to this man's superiors. That would put a stop to this meddling before it had a chance to escalate.

Shock and some unexpected tears made Amanda momentarily mute. She couldn't remember the last time someone had guts enough to thwart her husband, or cared enough for her well-being to take the second step.

"Excuse me, Mrs. Potter, but I need to get you down to X-ray. They're waiting," the orderly said.

"Go ahead," David said, and felt the detective's stare as they passed.

Dupree was unable to take his gaze away from her battered face and the lost, hopeless expression in her eyes. Something dark and hateful expanded within him. A territorial, possessive emotion almost overwhelmed him. He had the strongest urge to grab David Potter as he walked past and beat him senseless, just as he knew he'd done his wife.

"I don't expect I'll see you here again, Mrs. Potter," Dupree said.

It was nothing more than a thinly disguised warning. Amanda wasn't the only one to get the message. She sensed David's displeasure and ignored it.

"I certainly hope not, Detective," she said softly.

The elevator door opened, and they got on. The

orderly turned Amanda's chair so that she was facing out when the doors began to close. Her last impression of Dupree was that of a predator, just waiting for his prey to make a mistake. Somehow, it gave her comfort.

THREE

Two months had come and gone. It was the downhill side of spring, and the season fading fast was once again taking Amanda's chances of escape with it.

Ever since the incident in the park and the detective's short intrusion into their lives, David had been overzealous in his efforts to have her watched. She wasn't allowed to drive herself anywhere. It wasn't safe, he said. The wife of a prominent man such as himself was a prime target for terrorists. He took pride in the fact that she was too precious to him to risk her safety. Amanda knew that he was scared to death that she'd tell. Or she'd run. Or both.

She sighed, remembering the other time when she'd tried, and Larry Feingold's "suicide" as a result. She had to live the rest of her life with the knowledge that, inadvertently, she may have caused the death of another human being. And, because of that one time, she knew that David would never trust her again.

Thus, he had posted round-the-clock bodyguards for her and kept her life as cloistered as possible so that his reputation would never be marred. That couldn't happen. Not to a Potter.

She and their chauffeur, Marcus Havasute, became the odd couple of Morgantown. She went nowhere without him, not even to the beauty parlor. His hulking six-foot-seven-inch frame was more than out of place in the feminine salon, but he stoically ignored the giggles and comments that came his way. And because Marcus was of Samoan descent and quite handsome in his own exotic fashion, he also got more than his share of offers, which he did *not* always ignore.

And so they existed: Amanda Potter, the fashionably correct wife of Congressman David Potter, and her jailer named Marcus.

Time passed as she dwelled on the outside of hell, waiting to fall in and be consumed by its fires.

The morning sun broke through a thin layer of cloud cover, illuminating the crystal figurines on the shelf over the breakfast nook. Amanda glanced up, and then out the window, wishing with all her heart that she had a good excuse for spending the day outdoors. Not in the yard, but away somewhere, enjoying the early summer and the clear, fresh air.

The morning paper rustled beneath David's hands as he casually turned the page from the financial section to the local news. In the same moment, he cursed beneath his breath. "Well, damn. Wouldn't you know it?" he muttered.

"What's wrong?" Amanda asked, and silently shook her head at the maid who stood just outside the door, awaiting a sign to come in and clear the table. If David was disturbed, adding a fresh face to the situation wasn't wise.

"The Leder auction is this weekend. I've been waiting for weeks for them to announce the date and now I won't be able to make it after all."

Amanda felt a swift surge of hope. Maybe . . . just maybe . . . if she worked this right, she'd get her chance to get out of this palatial mausoleum.

"That's too bad," she said. "I don't suppose canceling your flight to D.C. is in order, is it? After all, aren't you chairman of this particular committee?"

"Yes, indeed," David said, refolding the pages of the newspaper into virgin order. "I'm in charge. It's impossible for me to miss it."

Amanda looked away, unwilling for him to see how desperately she wanted to hear the words. To actually volunteer her for the trip to the auction, instead.

"Maybe it's all for the best," she said. "The pipe rack may be in poor condition. Ruben Leder had let everything else go to ruin. Remember how poor everything looked when we were by there last fall?"

David nodded, caught off guard by Amanda's quiet concern for the fact that he might miss adding a precious new piece to his collection of antique pipe racks. Greed for the things that he coveted overrode his normal caution.

"I'd like for you to consider going to the auction in my stead," he said, and waved for the maid to come clear the table of their breakfast dishes.

His statement required no answer on Amanda's part. If he'd uttered the wish, then it was to be considered a command.

"I don't know," she said, unwilling to let him see how badly she wanted this chance to get away from the cloying walls of the Potter estate, if only for a day. "I don't think I remember the way." She looked up, judging the impact her hesitation would have upon him.

David caught the fire in her eyes and noted how the green had turned to a darker shade of jade. Just for a moment, he wondered if he'd been had, and then discarded the thought as quickly as it had come. It must be the sunlight reflecting from the crystal behind him and into her eyes. David Potter couldn't be *had*.

And, as she'd expected, her hesitation was just the right note. If she didn't want to do it, then of course he would insist that she did. Control was David Potter's nemesis, as well as his constant companion.

"Of course I would insist that Marcus drive you," he said.

"Of course," Amanda echoed, relishing the thrill that skittered throughout her system. "But you must give me all the details. What, for instance, would be your highest bid? The condition of the piece before I consider bidding? That sort of information."

David nodded, suddenly excited about the prospect of acquiring a new piece for his collection.

"I've got a book on the pieces of that period," he said. "I'll get it for you before I leave today. That way, you can read up on the subject before the sale. And of course, as always, money is no object."

Amanda smiled once. But it was a small, cold smile, and was nowhere near her heart. *Of course,* she thought. *Money is never an object.*

Two days later she waved David off at the airport, crawled back into the black limousine, and nodded to the driver.

"Do you know the way to the auction, Marcus?"

"Yes, ma'am," he said, keeping a careful eye on the traffic as he turned the big car toward the highway leading south out of town, toward the small, nearby hamlet where the estate auction was to be held.

Amanda shivered with excitement and smoothed the palms of her hands against the fabric of her slacks. Thankful for their comfort, she tried to ignore the neat, beige color. Rusty orange or a royal blue would have been her choice of color. But Amanda had few choices in life, and choosing her style of clothes was not one of them.

"Marcus . . . I'd like some air," she said. When he turned on the air conditioner, she added, "I mean fresh air. Would you please roll down the window an inch or two?"

"Yes, ma'am," Marcus replied, and proceeded to oblige.

The breeze was brisk and fresh, and Amanda untied the white bow at the nape of her neck, freeing her chestnut hair and letting it tangle around her head with abandon. She laughed aloud at the carefree feeling it gave her, and missed Marcus's look of surprise and then sympathy.

He was secretly appalled at her situation, but a job was a job, and his was to do what David Potter ordered. If he valued the job . . . as well as his life, he knew not to let Amanda Potter out of his sight.

She unbuttoned the top two buttons on her white, oxford shirt, and dumped the sweater she'd brought along on the seat beside her. The day was too beautiful to be buried beneath anything, especially clothing.

All too soon the signs began to appear on the side of the road that gave directions to the sale. Marcus began slowing down, and before she knew it, had pulled into a driveway and parked inside a roped-off area beyond the old, crumbling walls of the three-story brick mansion. Seconds later, he was at the back door, extending a hand to help her out.

People were milling everywhere. The soft rumble of their voices was music to Amanda's ears, and she loved the fact that no one seemed to notice that she'd pulled into the drive in a limousine, when everyone else in sight seemed to have come in sedans or pickup trucks.

Enticing scents of homemade pies and steamy coffee filled the air. Amanda suspected that, as was normally the case at sales such as these, some neighborhood ladies' organization had volunteered to furnish food for the sight-seers in order to make a little extra money for their club.

"I'm suddenly starving," Amanda said. "Marcus, please be my guest. David gave me enough cash for food." A childlike smile softened the severity of her expression as she waited for him to answer.

It was not lost on Marcus that she'd all but admitted that she had no money of her own. He forgot to answer as he looked deeply into the shadows in her eyes and saw her waiting for his answer. And in that moment, he almost hated his employer for what he did to his wife.

"No, ma'am. You will please let me pay for the food," he said quietly. His words more of an order than a request. "You can keep your money . . . this time."

Amanda's shock was evident. Her small smile slid a little bit off center. It wasn't in her to refuse his offer. If Marcus paid, then she could add this small amount of money to her secret stash. Someday she would need every penny she could get her hands on. Someday . . .

She quickly stuffed the thought to the back of her mind and headed for the lunch wagon, aware that Marcus was never far behind.

Hours had come and gone since their arrival. It hadn't taken Amanda long to sign up as a prospective bidder, or to receive her number, which would be used as a means of identification should she bid or buy. And it had taken even less time to discern that the pipe rack David coveted was in prime condition, and in one of the smaller lots that wouldn't be auctioned until late afternoon. She was pleased about the delay. The longer it took to buy what she came for, the longer she got to stay away.

The sun had intensified. Mid-afternoon had given way to a near-stifling heat and many bidders had taken what was theirs and gone about their business, unwilling to out-wait the auctioneers' delays for the promise of a cool home and an even cooler drink.

Amanda wandered around, perusing the odds and ends scattered around the premises, wondering why a man such as Ruben Leder would collect such an odd assortment of things in his ninety-two years.

Marcus was deep in discussion with one of the pretty young things who'd helped serve the food. Amanda smiled to herself as she heard his occasional boom of laughter. At least she wasn't the only one enjoying the day.

Casting a glance over her shoulder, just to make certain that the auctioneers were still where she'd left them, she headed for an abandoned folding chair beneath the wide branches of an ancient oak tree.

"I never thought anything this hard would feel this good," she muttered as she sank wearily into the chair and lifted her aching feet from the dusty earth.

"Worn out, are you?"

Amanda jumped. The old woman's voice startled her so, she almost fell off of the chair.

"Sorry, honey. Didn't mean to scare you," the old lady

said, and chuckled to herself as she continued to dig through the contents of a rusty trunk.

Amanda turned. "It's okay," she said, glancing up to see if Marcus was watching.

The last thing she needed was for him to report back to David that she'd actually carried on a conversation with someone. David would instantly assume the worst. She sighed in relief. Marcus was shirking his duty, at least toward her, because he'd completely disappeared from sight.

"My name is Dorothy," the old lady said, as she swiped a handkerchief across her sweaty face then stuffed it back in the pocket of her blue gingham dress. The motion plastered damp wisps of graying hair that had escaped from her topknot down against her forehead.

Amanda held her breath. She knew what manners bade her do next. It took all her nerve to say it, and then when she did, she found that it hadn't been as difficult as she'd imagined.

"I'm Amanda."

Two words said quickly. But they were all the more sweet for the relief that came with them.

"Bought anything yet?" Dorothy asked.

Amanda shook her head. "I'm still waiting. They haven't gotten to the lot I'm interested in."

Dorothy nodded as she continued to poke through the trunk. "Smart buyer," she said. "Some folks come to these affairs, get caught up in the competition of bidding, and then buy all sorts of junk. Go home later, wondering what on earth they'll do with it." She laughed, and pointed at the pile of rotting linens and yellowed clothing that she'd pulled from her trunk. "See what I mean?"

Amanda nodded. Dorothy was so open and genuine, and so deeply engrossed in digging through the contents of the trunk, that Amanda became intrigued in spite of a small voice warning her to mind her own business.

"This trunk yours?" she asked.

"Yep. And everything that's in it. Unfortunately, the

everything needs to be burned. Just look at this thing, will you? I can't imagine what on earth anyone would want with something like this." She held up a tattered dress, then pointed to a stack of old magazines and an even smaller stack of picture frames. It was then that she noted Amanda's interest.

"Here, honey," she said, motioning toward the pile of things. "I only bought the trunk. I refinish and sell them at my shop. If there's anything there that you want, feel free. I planned to ask to have it hauled away with the rest of the day's trash. Someone besides me can deal with disposing of it."

Amanda shook her head. "No. I'd better not," she said, and stood up, looking toward the auctioneers.

They were no closer to the lot she had come for than they'd been fifteen minutes earlier. She shoved her hands in her pockets and looked around for Marcus. He was still missing.

Her fingers fairly itched to dig through the ancient stacks . . . just to look . . . she wouldn't dare take anything home that David hadn't approved of first. Everything in the Potter estate coordinated with something else. She couldn't imagine what she'd find that he would like.

The next thing she knew, she was down in the dust on her knees, the fine fabric of her slacks forgotten in her haste to look before the old woman changed her mind.

Dorothy laughed as she finished sorting through the last of the contents from the trunk. "There's nothing here I want. If something takes your fancy, it's yours. Have a nice day, dear," she said, and hefted the trunk sideways onto a red wagon and hauled it away.

It didn't take long for Amanda to see that Dorothy had been right about the linens. They were ready for the dump heap and that was a fact. The old magazines held no interest for her, and she sifted through them quickly, seeing nothing that even a collector would want. That left the old frames and the pictures.

She stood, quickly checking the auctioneers and their

progress toward David's prize that she had yet to buy. From the looks of the crowd, she'd better hurry. It seemed as though they'd shifted slightly toward the last lot.

Most of the frames were old, and the pictures all but faded to a near-white. It was obvious that there were no hidden masterpieces in these. And then she lifted the last, intent on searching behind the frame, just to see if something was hidden beneath, when she saw it lying on the ground, half covered by a heap of rags.

It was small, no larger than a dinner plate, and it had been mounted and framed in a manner similar to that of the shadow-box era. The glass covering the top had long ago been broken and removed. Only the small narrow trench remained around the frame where it once had rested.

Amanda squinted, and held the piece up to the light, trying to read the engraving on the small brass nameplate beneath. It was unlike anything she'd ever seen.

DREAMCATCHER – circa 1800

She caught her breath. What a fanciful name. If only there was such a thing, she thought wistfully.

It was so old! She looked down at the pile of musty cloth and rotting paper in which it had been hidden, and frowned. To have existed so long only to come to this? It didn't seem fair.

The piece inside the frame was obviously American Indian in origin. The leather thongs and ancient feathers, as well as the small, tattered remnants of beadwork were vaguely familiar only because their style was similar to other hand-worked pieces that she'd seen.

But that was where her expertise stopped, because this piece was so different. It looked as if someone had tried to fashion a spiderweb and hadn't quite succeeded. The circle of wood in which the web had been woven was obviously quite crude, and looked like a piece of limb had been fastened together by bits of leather wound about it. The webbing inside it was also of leather, but much thinner, and much more fragile in appearance. She tested it with her fingertip and found that it was stiff and hard. But then, remembering the date on the brass plate, she was amazed that it was still in one piece.

Several objects had been fastened upon the webbing in no special order. With the lightest of touches, she traced them, one to the other, marveling at their endurance through time.

An obsidian-colored claw was caught in the webbing. When she traced its shape, she shuddered. In spite of the heat of the day, it felt cold to the touch.

Quickly, Amanda turned her attention to the next object on the webbing. For some reason, she felt uncomfortable dwelling on the creature to which the claw must once have belonged.

A bit of feather was tied near the edge closest to her heart. And then out of nowhere, an outlaw breeze sprang up and lifted the ancient feather, sending it fluttering.

A screech, high up and far away, caught her attention. She looked up to see a large bird circling way above her in the clear blue sky. She could only watch with mouth agape as it circled higher and higher until it was no longer in sight, and then couldn't believe what she had seen. The massive wingspan was unmistakable. It had been an eagle, of that she was certain.

Eagles were an endangered bird and rarely seen, especially in these parts. And to have spotted one now, just at the moment that the bit of feather had fluttered in the breeze, seemed something of an omen.

The breeze quickened, suddenly lifting the hair from her shoulders, as if a hand had just slid along her neck. She shivered, imagining she heard a voice whispering in her ear, then told herself she'd probably gotten too hot, and swiftly focused on the next object hanging on the web.

"How dear," she whispered, as she traced the tiny beaded medallion hanging near the center, and thought of someone long dead who must have fashioned it from love.

David would hate this. It was old. It looked dirty. And Amanda had never wanted anything as badly in her life as she wanted this oddity.

Carefully, she turned it over, searching for more clues to its purpose. There was a small, handwritten note that had been glued onto the backing. Some of the words were blurry. And the spidery writing was difficult to decipher.

It read: *The owner of a Dreamcatcher is a blessed man indeed. For all of his life, his dreams will be filtered through the webbing, and only the good dreams will be allowed through the hole in the center.*

A loud burst of laughter and the wild, staccato cry of the auctioneer as he instigated a flurry of anxious bets caught her ears.

"Oh my!"

Amanda jumped to her feet, clutching the Dreamcatcher as she hurried toward the shouts inside the tent. If she missed buying that pipe rack, David would, quite literally, kill her.

Unaware of the picture she made as she dashed into the tent waving her number with the small brown frame pressed against her breast, she was intent only on the fact that David's pipe rack was in bid, and that bidding had been going on for some time.

"Going once, twice . . . "

"Fifty dollars above the last bid . . . whatever it was," she shouted, and then blushed beet-red when laughter skittered across the crowd.

"Sold . . . to the little lady with the smudge on her cheek."

The auctioneer's teasing remark went right over Amanda's head. She would have willingly stripped naked and danced on a table to get that rack. Going home without it just wasn't an option.

Amanda grinned slightly, her embarrassment giving way to relief as she took the pipe rack . . . and her number . . . and went toward the travel trailer that doubled as an office to pay for her prize. And then she remembered the Dreamcatcher.

"Oh Lord," she muttered, looking down at the prize clutched against her breast. "What am I going to do with this? David will have a . . . "

"Mrs. Potter. Would you like me to put your things in the car while you pay?"

Marcus's unexpected arrival ended the joy of the day. She'd been caught with the goods. And then she did something impulsive. She looked up . . . and then up some more, until she found herself staring straight into his warm, brown eyes.

"I, uh . . ." She clutched the Dreamcatcher even tighter to her chest, unwilling to relinquish what had been . . . for a very short time . . . hers alone.

"Mr. Potter sent a case for the pipe rack, ma'am."

"I know," she said, and sighed in defeat, expecting her found treasure to be taken away, also.

Marcus took the pipe rack from her hands and started toward the car.

"But Marcus, aren't you going to take the . . . ?"

He turned. A long, silent moment passed between them as he looked into her face and then down at the old, dusty piece she held clutched to her chest.

"Take what, ma'am? I have what we came after. I don't see anything else that requires my attention . . . do you?"

Tears welled up in her eyes. She bit her lower lip and looked quickly down at the ground, unable to face his sympathy.

"Thank you," she finally managed to whisper.

"I did nothing," he said softly, and walked away.

"Right . . . nothing," she echoed, and looked down at the Dreamcatcher, remembering the promise on the back. *Only the good dreams.* Dear God, if it would only deliver.

The hotel room was in darkness. Sounds of traffic on the street far below were almost nonexistent. Washington D.C.

penthouses were known for their comfort, as well as their privacy.

David sat on the edge of the bed and dialed the phone, wearily rotating his head and neck as he waited for the rings to begin. And when they did, he counted them, one, two, three . . .

"Hello."

The voice was deep and lacked expression. David smiled to himself. Marcus was where he should be, and therefore Amanda would be, also.

"So, Marcus, how did the day go? Did Amanda get my pipe rack?"

Marcus frowned and wondered why his boss was asking him something he should have been asking his wife. "Yes, sir. She purchased the rack, just as you wished."

"Were there many bidders?" He fidgeted as he kicked off his shoes, mentally picturing the thrill of the competition, as well as savoring the joy of winning the prize.

"I wouldn't know, Mr. Potter. I can't ever tell who's bidding and who's scratching."

David sucked in his breath. For a moment, he would have sworn that he detected sarcasm, but he told himself he was imagining it. He laughed at the mental image Marcus's words painted instead.

"I know what you mean. It took me years to catch on to the game."

Marcus waited. Carrying on a friendly conversation with this man was somehow wrong. This man could never be his friend.

"So . . ." David loosened his tie and then fell back on the bed, glancing up at the mirrors above it and smiling to himself. "Is Amanda home?"

"I would assume so, sir. She was dining . . . alone . . . when I last saw her."

David frowned. "Who's watching her now?" he asked.

"I don't know, sir. I think I heard her say she was going to retire to her room after her meal."

"Please tell Mabel to put her on the phone," David said. "I want to tell my wife goodnight."

"Yes, sir. Just a moment, sir," Marcus said, and put the call on hold while he went to do his master's bidding.

David fiddled with the buckle to his belt and then finished removing his tie while he waited for Amanda to come to the phone.

The sound of water running in the adjoining bathroom made him smile in anticipation. He turned his head and stared intently at the thin, yellow line of light beneath the closed door and felt his pulse beginning to accelerate.

And then the water went off. The door opened. She stood naked in the doorway, with the light behind her, and the darkness before her, waiting for his command.

"Come here to me," David said, his voice deepening with each breath that he took.

The woman tossed her head, and he imagined that she smiled as she began a slow, sexual saunter toward him. His breath began to quicken, as did his body. She slid onto the bed beside him, wrapping her nudity around him like a snake to a tree, then began a seductive striptease of his clothing until David was as naked as she.

"Hello?" Amanda said.

The voice in his ear never registered as David closed his eyes and bit his lip, groaning softly to himself as the woman's hands and mouth slid over his manhood and began a dance of their own that was making him mad.

"Hello?" she repeated.

David shuddered. "Amanda?"

He arched to the woman's touch and tried to concentrate on Amanda's voice, enjoying the vicarious thrill of sexual satisfaction at the prostitute's hands while carrying on a conversation with his wife.

"Yes, David. It's me. Sorry I took so long to get to the phone. I was about to take a bath."

He pictured his wife's slender body as it would look with the water refracting her image, then shuddered as the woman let go of his manhood and mounted him like a horse. She leaned forward, her breasts close to his lips as she began to move upon his body. He closed his eyes and gritted his teeth as he concentrated once again on continuing his conversation.

"How did the auction go?" he asked, when he knew full well the results. But it was his nature to see if what Amanda told him jibed with what her bodyguard had claimed.

"It went fine," Amanda said. "I got your pipe rack. I think for a good price. It was a hundred and fifty dollars less than the last one you bought."

"Oh my God," David gasped, as the woman above him took his hard, aching manhood and suddenly squeezed it between her knees.

Amanda frowned. She'd known David would be happy, but not like that. "David . . . ?"

"Listen . . . darling . . ." his breath was coming faster and faster as the madness came upon him. "I've got to go. Room service is at the door. I can't tell you . . ." he gasped and then wrapped his hand in the woman's hair, forcing her down upon him, forcing her to take him inside her mouth, forcing her compliance. She didn't demur. She was being paid well for this performance. In her business, the customer was always right. "I'm very happy with your behavior, Amanda. I'll call you tomorrow," David said quickly, and then flung the phone across the room, oblivious to the fact that it unplugged itself from the wall as it flew through the air.

The line went dead in her ear. Amanda shrugged and hung up. She didn't care. Chit-chatting with her husband was the last thing on her mind.

David's heart was thundering, a thin film of sweat had covered his body as the woman took him where he wanted . . . where he needed to go.

The pressure became unbearable. Waiting was no longer an option. He wrapped both of his hands tightly into her hair and thrust, unaware of the pain that she suffered, uncaring that he was more than she could accommodate. He came, over and over in harsh, shuddering gasps.

Finally he let go of the woman, and she fell limply onto the floor beside the bed, choking on tears and the remnants of David Potter's pleasure, while gasping for air.

Long moments passed while both of them tried to collect themselves. The woman was the first to move. She crawled to her feet and began staggering toward the bathroom. David rolled from the bed and followed her.

His hand snaked around her from behind. He palmed one of her voluptuous breasts, and then the other, and thrust his rejuvenating lust roughly against her buttocks.

"Not so fast, honey," he growled in her ear. "I paid for the night . . . and it's just begun."

He didn't see her blanch. Nor did he feel her pulse rate accelerate from fear. If he had, he wouldn't have cared. She was just a prostitute. He was Congressman David Potter, of the West Virginia Potters. He was above reproach . . . and above the law.

FOUR

The room was so quiet. There was nothing left but the echo of her own voice telling David goodbye. Amanda stood in place and stared at the comfort and the opulence before her, and knew that she'd trade it all in a heartbeat for her freedom.

The only difference between her life and that of a death-row inmate was that the walls of her cell were pristine white and decorated with original works of art. The end result was still the same; she was most likely interred for life as well.

She walked to a window overlooking the grounds of the estate, blinking back tears as she watched David's Dobermans running a silent watch through the yellow circles of light the floodlights made on the manicured lawns, then disappearing into the darkness beneath the ring of trees surrounding the estate. Even though she could no longer see them, she knew that they, like David, hovered too close for escape.

Memories of her life before David Potter were few and far between. There was little left of the naive, wide-eyed college freshman who'd been swept away by a handsome senior. David had been, among other things, captain of the debate team as well as president of his fraternity and all-around BMOC.

Amanda laughed through her tears. Big Man On

Campus. Nabbing one of those had been the ultimate goal of nearly every girl at school, and she'd landed one of the biggest. The only problem was, she no longer wanted him, and she didn't know how to throw him back.

She leaned against the windowpanes, relishing the coolness of the glass upon her brow, and wished that her parents had lived longer. If they had, maybe they'd have seen past David's outer beauty into the black heart that he possessed. Then she sighed. Even if they had, she probably wouldn't have believed them. She'd been infatuated with what she thought to be a real-life prince, when in fact, she'd actually married the toad.

The clock in the hall chimed once, announcing the half-hour, and Amanda turned to check the time. It was already half-past ten, but she wasn't sleepy. Remembering college days had brought back other memories that made her wish for another kind of freedom, as well. Here she was, a grown woman as well as a wife, and she didn't even have free rein in her own house. Her stomach growled. Cook had certainly retired, but dammit, she was hungry.

A spurt of defiance surfaced as she turned from the window and stomped toward her closet. It didn't take long to slip out of her nightgown and into some sweats. Her flat-soled mules made a slap-slap sound against the floor as she walked, and without thinking, she slipped out of them and started toward the door in her bare feet.

Thoughts of a roast beef sandwich and some cold iced tea were uppermost in her mind as she turned the knob and opened the door. The hallway was in shadow, and she unseeingly collided with Marcus, who'd been outside her door, on guard.

Her squeal of shock coincided with his grunt of dismay when he felt himself stepping on her bare feet in his haste to stop her flight.

"For Pete's sake," Amanda groaned, as she bent down and massaged the two smallest toes on her left foot. "I didn't know you were here. You scared me half to death."

"Is there something I can do for you?" he asked as he

continued to maintain a gentle, but firm, hold on her upper arm.

"I'm fine," she muttered. "You can let go of me now."

It was only when he didn't answer and she looked up into his glacial stare that she realized what he'd thought.

Her laughter was hard and almost shrill. It startled him enough that his grip loosened and then he dropped his hands to his sides.

"When I run," she hissed softly, "it won't be in the middle of the night, or through those damned cannibals in the yard. And," she added, wincing as she tried to wiggle her injured toes, "I won't be barefoot."

Marcus flushed and looked down.

"I'm sorry, ma'am," he said quietly. "I was only doing what I was . . ."

"Save it," Amanda said. "I *was* going to get a sandwich. But I've suddenly lost my appetite."

She turned and walked back into her bedroom, quietly closing the door in his face.

For a moment, neither moved as they stood on opposite sides of the door, listening. Amanda was the first to do so, and when she did, it was to lock her door from the inside.

Marcus heard the click and knew it for what it was; a rejection of the slight camaraderie they'd experienced today. Now they were back on firm and recognizable ground. While he worked for her husband, he would be her jailer, not her friend.

Amanda heard his footsteps as he walked down the hallway. But she knew he wouldn't go far. He had a job to do. It was only after she could no longer hear sounds of his presence, that she realized what she'd admitted to him out in the hall.

She'd said . . . when I run, not *if*, but *when*.

"Oh my God," she moaned, and dropped to her knees. "Dear Lord, don't let him tell David what I said. Please . . . don't let him tell." Her hands shook as she buried her face in her hands. "I don't know how much longer I can hold on to my faith."

Nausea overwhelmed her. It took everything she had to drag herself up and into bed before turning out the lights. Although it was very warm outside, and the central air-conditioning was running full blast within the house, every inch of her body felt numb. She knew it was shock. And . . . like everything else in her life, she knew it would pass.

Something poked into the crown of her scalp, and she reached over her head, feeling in the darkness for the source of her pain. Her fingers touched, and then traced the Dreamcatcher's frame, and she remembered then secreting her gift from the auction into the house and into her bedroom by hiding it beneath her sweater.

A Dreamcatcher. What a joke! The last thing she wanted to do was close her eyes and dream. If she did, they were bound to be nightmares. She could not escape the hell in her life . . . not even in her sleep.

Tears began to fall in earnest as she pulled the Dreamcatcher from beneath her sweater and laid it on the pillow close to her cheek. The last thing she remembered was the scent of old leather and moonlight reflecting off of the claw hanging from the web, giving it an eerie, luminescent glow.

And then she slept.

He came through the light. A dark silhouette within a white so bright that it was impossible to look away. Compelled by the power with which he moved, she gazed upon the breadth of his shoulders, the length of his legs, and waited to see his face.

She sighed restlessly, curling into an even tighter ball upon the bed and fought the urge to scream. He was close. So close. She imagined that she could feel his breath, hear the rush of his blood as it thundered through his body, feel the silken brush of his hair as it cloaked her shoulders and her arms.

She feared the pain of his touch. In Amanda's world,

with men, there was always pain. David had never shown her anything else, and he'd been her first. But as the man came closer, she waited for a pain that never came.

Instead, she imagined that she felt the bed give beneath her. Then she felt the weight of his body as it slid along the length of her back, coaxing her body from its coiled shell into relaxing against the warmth and the strength of his own. The chill of fear slid away, along with her worries, as he enfolded her within his arms.

The last thing she remembered was the scent of leather and wood smoke, the touch of his lips upon her brow, and the thought that she'd been held like this before.

Inner peace flowed throughout her body, and Amanda slept.

"Mrs. Potter! Mrs. Potter! Please . . . open your door!"

Amanda sat up with a start, looking around in fright for the man with whom she thought she'd spent the night. He . . . like the darkness . . . was gone.

She blinked in sudden confusion. Bright sunlight was pouring through the gap in the curtains, and she thought she heard woodpeckers hammering against the eaves of the three-story colonial. If David were here, she knew he'd already be on the phone ordering exterminators to prevent further damage to his beloved eighteenth-century home.

A sharp series of knocks sounded at the door again, and this time, Amanda realized that it was Mabel, not woodpeckers, that had called her from her sleep.

"I'm coming. I'm coming," she muttered, as she swung her legs over the side of the bed. She moved with reluctance, because when she let Mabel in, she would be shutting out the last remnants of her dream. For some reason, letting go of the memory was almost painful.

"And what a dream," she mumbled to herself, remembering the power, as well as the gentleness, of her dream lover.

And then she stopped short, shocked by the way she'd mentally tagged him. Why on earth had she thought of him as a lover? Nothing seductive had happened in the dream. Only a gentleness and a strength that she was unwilling to forget.

"Oh no! My Dreamcatcher," she said, and looked wildly back toward the bed.

She had to hide it. If someone saw it, even her dear and trusted friend Mabel, there was always the chance that something might be said to give her away. And while the thing was of little value, its presence in her life had become vastly important. It stood for a defiance that she thought she had lost.

Mabel rapped on the door again, this time, adding a verbal warning of her own. "You open that door right now, Missy, or I'm calling Marcus," she said.

Amanda swiftly hid the small frame behind the great bedstead. For the time being, it would have to do. She opened the door, and then grinned at Mabel's frazzled appearance.

"What? Did you think you were going to find me lying in a pool of blood?" Then she shrugged. "I wouldn't give him the satisfaction. And . . . I wouldn't do that to you. You'd be the one to have to clean it up."

Mabel made a face at the thought, and then sighed with relief. "You scared me half to death. I can't remember the last time this door was locked from the inside. Usually it's the . . ." She had the grace to flush.

"Right. Usually it's the other way around."

"Will you be coming down for breakfast?" Mabel asked, eyeing the sweats that Amanda must have slept in.

Amanda stretched. "Yes. I'm starved. And I don't want any of that low-fat, high-fiber stuff either. There's nothing wrong with my health . . . or my weight. Tell Cook I want Belgian waffles with strawberries . . . and whipped cream. Real whipped cream. Give me ten minutes, and I'll be right down."

Mabel could only stare in shock at the odd change in Amanda's behavior. Where had the subdued, meek-

mannered woman who was married to David Potter gone?
Better yet, where had this bright-eyed, almost happy,
young thing come from?

"Oh . . . and Mabel . . . "

"Yes, ma'am," she said.

"Tell Marcus to bring the car around. I've decided a
change is in order in my life. I think I'll go down to the
Delia Potter Shelter for the Homeless. There's a crate of
clothing that David said must be disposed of. I intend to
see that it gets to where it's needed."

"But Missy, Mister will have a fit if he sees your old
clothing on the backs of some of those street people,"
Mabel argued.

"He can't be angry. His mother started the project
years ago, long before it was fashionable to be concerned
with such issues."

Mabel frowned and shook her head, convinced that
she was asking for trouble.

Amanda hugged the elderly housekeeper and then
grinned. "Just think of the great press it will make. Last year
Congressman Potter's suit was at the White House. This
year . . . who knows? It might be on its way to a flophouse."

"The Mister will be mad at you," Mabel warned.

"What else is new?" Amanda asked, and turned away,
unwilling to watch the growing concern on her housekeeper's face. No matter what she did, David didn't like it.
Why shouldn't she do something to try and please herself
for a change?

Amanda tore through the clothes in her closet, searching for something to wear that expressed her state of mind.

She went to breakfast in blue jeans and sneakers and
ignored the staff's whispers and stares at her unusual attire.
She kept telling herself that she had just as much right to
be in charge of something as David did.

Her own warning system was going off in spades. Yet
for some reason, somewhere between David's departure to
D.C. and the aftermath of the auction, she'd found a new
sense of self.

An hour later, she stuffed the last bite of strawberry and waffle into her mouth, sighed with satisfaction, and pushed back her chair. It was time to get moving. Amanda had a purpose, if only for today.

She refused to feel silly that her defiance consisted of the distribution of some unwanted clothes. There had to be a starting place for a new direction in her life. The homeless shelter was going to be it.

"I know who you are!"

Amanda turned from her task of sorting through the huge box of clothes that she'd brought, to see an elderly and extremely bedraggled man, poking at her shoulder. She tried not to smile at his comical appearance. He must be wearing everything he owned. His clothing hung in layers . . . tattered, filthy layers.

"Then you have me at a disadvantage, sir," she said softly, and extended her hand. "I don't believe I've had the pleasure."

Marcus was halfway across the room when he saw Potter's wife start to shake hands with the beggar. Short of shouting "No!", which he desperately wanted to do, he could do nothing but push his way past the lines of people who were inside waiting for their free daily meal, in hopes that he reached her before any harm was done.

For Beaner, it had been years since anything had gotten through the miasma of simply existing within poverty. But when Amanda Potter offered to shake his hand, he felt a lump come up into his throat, and the need to renew identification with himself, as well as this sweet, pretty woman.

"My name is Dewey Miller," he mumbled, and glanced away as he said his name aloud. It hurt to hear it spoken, because it had been years since Beaner had admitted to himself that he'd ever had another sort of life. "But you can call me Beaner. Everyone does." Then he looked back up and grinned.

Amanda didn't flinch as his grubby fingers curled around her hand. And when he smiled, it was easy to see that "Beaner" had exactly three viable teeth left in his head. She wondered how on earth he chewed his food, and then her heart tugged when she remembered. There were probably many days when he had nothing at all to eat. Teeth would be the least of Beaner's worries.

"I'm pleased to meet you, Dewey. I suppose you're an old hand at how all of this is run." She waved her hand around the shelter, encompassing the food lines as well as a room off the front where boxes of donated clothing were being sorted.

He nodded importantly. "Yessiree bob. I know all there is to know in here."

He squinted his eyes and pursed his mouth, sucking his teeth as he considered revealing anything else about his personal life. But the pretty lady's eyes were green, and clear, and sparkled when she smiled. He decided that maybe . . . just maybe . . . she could be trusted. But only to a point, he reminded himself. It didn't pay to trust anyone too far. In his experience, somewhere along the way, they always let you down.

"This is my first day here," Amanda said. And then she remembered his opening line. "How do you know who I am?"

"You're the lady I saw fall off of the stage in the park a few months back. You're that congressman's wife." Beaner grinned and then whistled. The air rushed through the vacancies in his mouth like wind whistling through the trees. "That wasn't exactly your best giant leap for mankind," he added, grinning at his own wit.

Amanda gawked in suprise at the comparison, and then her lips parted and the laugh that came up and out of her throat was more unexpected and genuine than anything she'd experienced in years.

"Ma'am . . . are you all right?" Marcus asked as he bolted through the last couple separating him from his charge, and took a quick step between Amanda and the beggar.

But she was laughing. And he didn't think he'd ever, not in the five years that he'd worked for David Potter, ever heard her laugh. Not like this.

"I'm perfectly fine," she said, between giggles, as Beaner jumped several steps backward at Marcus's arrival and pulled nervously at the layers of his clothing. "I was just having a wonderful conversation with Dewey."

"Who's Dewey?" Marcus growled, then watched as Amanda waved toward the beggar.

"Dewey, this is my chauffeur, Marcus Havasute."

Marcus didn't offer his hand, and Beaner wouldn't have taken it had he done so. Neither man even considered the possibility of doing anything but ignoring the other.

"I'm the one who found your earring," Beaner announced importantly, and glared up at the huge, dark man, trying to reestablish some of his credibility.

Amanda's face lit up again. "Oh my," she said, and for the first time since the strange conversation began, really looked at the raggedy man.

A wave of shame swept over her. Had she seen this man on a street, the last thing she would have expected him to have was a shred of honesty. She stared at his gnarled and filth-encrusted hands and wondered what there was inside of a man like Beaner to have been able to give back a two-carat diamond without a qualm.

"Dewey."

The solemnity in her voice startled him, reminding him of times gone by when he'd been called on the carpet for one thing or another. He looked toward the front door, and then the back, gauging the distance between himself and freedom, and wished he'd never started this conversation.

"You'll never know how much that meant to me," Amanda said softly. "I would have . . . "

Her pause on the word made Marcus look away in shame. This woman endured much because of everyone else's silence.

". . . I would have suffered greatly had you not found it and returned it in such a timely fashion."

Beaner was amazed to see that there were tears in her eyes. On the streets where he came from, crying was a private thing. And the only privacy a homeless person had was anonymity. Beaner didn't know whether to look at her or not.

Amanda caught her breath as she realized she'd just terribly embarrassed both men, and quickly changed the subject.

"You know, Dewey, I think you and my husband are about the same height. There's a really nice coat in here that got too tight under the arms for him. Would you . . . I'd like for you to . . . "

Amanda didn't know how to offer charity. In the past, it had all been done so impersonally. Seeing a recipient face-to-face was an entirely different story.

Beaner drew himself up to his full height and combed his fingers through the wispy white remnants of his hair.

"I'd be most honored to accept your gift, Mrs. Potter," he said formally, and then he felt obligated to add, "although I already spent the reward money Detective Dupree gave me."

Amanda nodded and turned. She began digging through the stacks of clothing that Marcus had unloaded for her and tried not to let her shock show.

So, that nice detective, the one who'd saved her from the fall, had also given a reward to this man in their name. Shame overwhelmed her. It was a gesture that neither she, nor David, had even considered.

Minutes later, Beaner/Dewey was gone with the long, gray topcoat now his newest addition to the layers that he was wearing.

"Please . . . Mrs. Potter . . . we must go home now," Marcus said.

Amanda nodded. She felt suddenly weary all the way to her bones, and wondered where her spurt of joy and defiance had gone.

As Marcus settled her inside the limousine and waited for her to buckle up, she felt an old, familiar tension beginning to coil inside of her. Tonight, David would be home. And when he came, she would have to tell him what she'd done. It was imperative that he hear the words from her lips before someone else told him.

Maybe he would be glad. Maybe he wouldn't care that she'd taken the initiative and gone out into the public eye alone.

A bitter smile twisted her lips as Marcus pulled into traffic.

Right, Amanda. And birds don't fly.

The minute they entered the house, she had an overwhelming urge to sleep. And although it was barely noon, Amanda had read enough about severe depression to know that a constant need to sleep was one of the early warning symptoms. But knowing the reason, and being able to fix it, were two entirely different matters.

Mabel dawdled in the hall as Marcus locked the front door behind them.

"I won't be having lunch," Amanda told her. "I'm too tired. I think I'll just take a nap before David comes home. I need to be alert and fresh."

Amanda walked up the stairs and headed toward the master quarters.

Mabel frowned at Marcus, as if to say, "What have you done?"

He shrugged angrily, and then muttered beneath his breath as he walked away toward his own quarters. He had enough to worry about on his own front without worrying whether that woman made it to her room or not. She should have known better, he kept telling himself. She should have known not to go.

Amanda slipped into the bedroom and closed the door behind her. The vacant, king-size bed against the wall beckoned. Without thinking, she reached behind her and turned the deadbolt, then began stripping off her clothes as she headed for the bath. By the time she got to the tub, she was nude. Without even waiting to turn on the water first, she crawled inside, curled into a ball, and then turned on the taps.

As the tub filled, the water lapped at her belly, and then her breasts, rocking against her body like a gentle lover. And in the same moment she had that thought, she remembered her dream and shuddered.

"You're losing it, Amanda," she told herself. "Yearning for a man who doesn't exist will get you locked up faster than David can say 'vote for me.'"

With little wasted motion, she soaped, rinsed, and climbed out of the tub to dry as the water emptied down the drain. The friction of the terrycloth against her body brought her breasts to a swift, aching peak. She hated herself for the arousal. But shame kept her from acknowledging what her body already knew. She needed to be loved. And it wasn't going to happen.

The comforter was soft and cool against her nakedness as Amanda stretched out face down upon it. It yielded to her weight by letting her settle and then conforming to her shape.

Amanda turned her head sideways, using her hands for pillows, and closed her eyes. Just before sleep claimed her, she remembered thinking that she needed to check and see if her Dreamcatcher was still safely hidden from prying eyes. Discovery was the last thing she wanted.

Amanda dreamed. Black thoughts filled with terror. Pain-filled memories that surfaced from her subconscious to remind her that when she'd made the choice, it had been wrong. Very, very wrong. Weight and guilt settled around her heart. Even in her sleep, she knew that it came from the dread of her husband's imminent return.

Her muscles jerked, and her eyelids twitched as the dream rolled on through her mind like a rerun locked into perpetual motion. Tears began to burn her eyes, and she thought she heard herself sob.

And then she felt it. The white-hot heat from a light so bright and so strong that it had to come from either heaven or hell. Sweat beaded across her body as she struggled with the need to run.

Just when she might have screamed out in fright, she saw him, just as before, coming through the light. He moved swiftly, yet seemingly in slow-motion. A long swath of dark hair flowed out from his neck and shoulders as he ran, giving her the impression that he was flying.

She almost called out to him and then realized that she did not know his name. And so she waited, as before. And as before, he kept coming closer and closer.

His breathing was heavy, as if he'd been running a long distance. She tried to see his face, but once again, could not fathom a single feature.

But when she felt his weight upon her back and the slight give to the mattress as he crawled upon her bed, she knew a sensation of relief, the likes of which she'd never felt. It was the certainty of safety, and the peace of coming home.

She thought she heard him sigh as his arms slid beneath her body and turned her in his arms. And although she knew it was impossible, she felt herself being held, face to face, body to body, against muscle and warmth. His strength flowed through her and she knew a surprising absence of fear.

Amanda slept.

"Where is she?"

David's angry shout echoed throughout the downstairs of his palatial home as he slammed the front door behind him to punctuate his question.

Mabel scurried from the kitchen with her hands clasped. When she entered the foyer and saw his face, fear for Amanda overwhelmed her. What had he learned? What had she done that had angered him to this degree? She wondered if this was the day he was finally going to go too far.

"She's in her room, sir," Mabel said. "She wasn't feeling well earlier and decided to skip her lunch."

David frowned. He was still fuming. His feet had no

more than touched the tarmac of the airport before some meddling reporter had set a round of flashbulbs off in his face and then bombarded him with questions concerning his wife's unscheduled appearance at the Delia Potter Shelter for the Homeless.

What on earth had possessed her? He was still in a state of disbelief. Had she thought to insinuate herself into other people's lives and try to escape from him in this manner? Did she think so little of herself that she would willingly lower herself to the status of a street person just to elude pursuit?

David let his coat and bag lie where they fell. He took the stairs up two at a time, certain that when he confronted her, she would be on her knees, begging for his forgivness. The thought of her on her knees made him hard. But his sudden anticipation quickly disappeared when he hit the door, turned the knob, and it refused to give.

Shock suffused his face. A dull red came up from beneath his collar and flashed past his hairline in the space of seconds.

"Amanda!"

His angry roar came as an unwelcome intrusion into Amanda's deep, dreamless sleep. She turned over on her side, befuddled by the noise, and watched in sleepy confusion as the door flew open. A faint imprint of his shoe near the knob was her only indication that she must have unthinkingly locked it behind her.

It was hard to say who was the more shocked. David for the fact that Amanda was stark naked, and had obviously just awakened, or Amanda for the fact that he'd just caught her in the state he so desired. Nude.

Oh no! she thought. But covering herself now was a little like closing the floodgates after the water had already escaped.

"What on earth?" David asked. The defensiveness was still in his voice, but the sight of Amanda's lush body and unclothed limbs was making him forget everything but the growing hard-on behind his fly.

"The morning was so hot that when I came in, I took a cool bath and then fell asleep," Amanda said, and gauged the distance from her closet, wondering if she could slip on a robe before he got to the bed. "I locked the door so no one would walk in on me. Had you waited a moment, I could have saved us the price of a new door and lock."

Her quiet rebuke slid past his consciousness like a whisper in the wind as he shrugged out of his suit coat.

Amanda swallowed harshly. She didn't know if she could face this. Not now. Not after the gentleness of the other man.

And then she stifled a quiet sob. What was wrong with her? There was no other man. Only a figment of her imagination. Unfortunately, her reality was coming toward her with a look on his face she knew all too well.

"David . . . the door," Amanda said, reminding him that it stood ajar. Anyone who came up the stairs would see directly into the room.

He pivoted swiftly and slammed it shut, but it didn't fasten. It was broken.

Amanda closed her eyes and imagined the servants overseeing the coupling. She imagined their sly whispers and disgusted laughter downstairs and wanted to die. But . . . if she didn't see them watching her . . . she could tell herself it hadn't happened.

And then all she felt were David's hands pulling her to a sitting position, and then the feel of his shirt against her breasts, and the sound of his zipper opening. She wanted to scream. He hadn't even waited to undress.

"Amanda . . . darling. Put your arms around me. This is going to be so good."

Only for you, David. Only for you.

And then there were no more sounds other than the grunt that he made when he jammed himself into her body, and her soft sigh that sounded more like a sob.

Amanda kept her eyes closed and let her mind drift into another place where David Potter did not exist. And when his hands squeezed a little too brutally upon her breasts, and his teeth took too deep a bite into the tender skin at the base of her throat, she was hardly aware. She was remembering another man with arms too strong to let her fall, and a heart so gentle that pain was not a word he knew.

FIVE

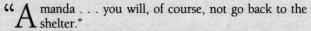

"Amanda . . . you will, of course, not go back to the shelter."

David's quiet demand followed the bite of broiled salmon she had started to swallow. Her throat swelled instantly as a combination of anger and defeat overwhelmed her.

And then something unexpected happened. Something she hadn't experienced before. Her throat muscles loosened and the food slid down as smoothly as melted butter. The fork that had started to shake in her fingers stilled. And the look that she turned upon David startled him as much as it did the servant hovering just outside the door.

"I don't see why," she said coolly, and forked another bite of fish, inserting it into her mouth and chewing calmly. She frowned. "Do you think Cook over-seasoned this? It tastes a bit too strongly of tarragon for me."

David was shocked. Amanda had just done something unheard of. She'd contradicted him, and then ignored him.

"Now look here," he growled, as he wadded the napkin in his lap into a ball. "You don't . . . "

"I believe your mother started that shelter, didn't she, David?" She didn't even wait for him to acknowledge her statement. They both knew it was a well-known fact. "Why on earth would you care if I simply continued something that your mother thought so highly of? You surely don't think your mother was at fault . . . do you?"

He was shaking with fury. "What Mother did has nothing to do with us!"

Amanda arched an eyebrow. "It's a good thing she's no longer around to hear you talk like that, David. She would be devastated. Your mother loved me, remember?"

David's face fell. His eyes narrowed. He cast swift, furtive glances about the room, as if checking to make certain his remarks were not overheard.

"She loved me more," David said, and then hated the childish whine in his voice. "And she raised me to be the man in the family. Remember? Father died when I was ten. I've always made the decisions in this house, and I have no intention of stopping now."

Amanda simply stared. Something inside of her had snapped. She no longer had the need to grovel or cower in the hopes that it would allay one of his fits. In fact, she wasn't so sure she wouldn't welcome it. Maybe the battle would be their last. At least then her suffering would be over.

"Would you excuse me?" she said, and pushed back her chair without waiting for his approval. "I believe that I'm finished. Quite finished."

As she rose, she dropped her napkin beside her plate and gave him a placid smile, then smoothed the skirt of her rose-colored chiffon dress as she walked from the room.

David stared, mouth open, eyes glazing with fury, and watched his wife disappear from the dining room like a pink shadow.

"Sir . . . will you be wanting dessert?"

"Hell, no!" David shouted, and jumped from his chair, uncaring of the fact that it fell backwards against the wall and scraped the paint. "Clear the table . . . and then get out of my sight! Do you hear me?"

"Yes, sir," the servant said. "Right away, sir."

David followed in Amanda's path, blinded to everything but the need to regain control of his world.

Inside their room, Amanda heard him coming up the stairs. But the need to run was gone. She inhaled deeply, girding herself for battle, and pivoted to face the door just as it flew back against the wall.

"You will never . . . ever . . . walk out of a room like that again. Do you hear me?"

His near-perfect features were mottled red as fury enveloped him. He shook with rage at the woman standing before him and the defiance on her face. Then he lifted his arm and swung.

His fist caught the side of her jaw with a glancing blow. Amanda staggered and then fell backward onto the bed, catching herself on her elbows and then rolling up and away before he could follow. She retrieved a flashlight from the bedside table and now held it out, weapon-like, within her grasp.

"David!"

When he would have followed the first blow with a second, her shout caught him unawares. The flashlight in her hand, as well as the stance that she had taken, shocked him. Surprise mellowed his anger. It spilled from his system, leaving him weak and shaken.

"Put that down," he ordered. Then he tried to regain his control by giving her a reprieve. "I don't think you have need of further discipline . . . at least not tonight."

Her immaculate hairdo had come undone from its clasp. Ignoring the faint bruise already apparent on the side of her cheek, David stared at the loose, auburn curls dangling across her forehead and imagined that they gave her a sex-tousled appearance. Her defiance was startling, intriguing . . . and oddly, it only made him want her more. He started toward her.

Amanda recognized the look on his face. A wave of nausea almost overwhelmed her as she drew the flashlight back, brandishing it like a club. She would not suffer him again.

"That's the last time you touch me," she whispered. "If there's ever a next time, when you start, you better finish the job. If I'm alive when it's over, I'll kill you."

David paused in mid-step. His mouth dropped open. He couldn't have been more shocked if she'd just kicked him in the stomach.

Mabel hovered just outside the door of the master bedroom, her fingers pressed against her lips, her fierce glare warning Marcus, who'd come upstairs with her when the shouting started, to stay silent. At the moment, the play was in Amanda's hands. It was to her benefit that they remained out of sight.

"You don't know what you're saying," David said. And then his self-righteousness reappeared as he added, "And . . . you don't mean that. You can't threaten . . . "

"I'm warning you, David," Amanda said, interrupting him before he could finish another threat. "You will not touch me again. Not in hate. Not in anger. Not in love."

The room felt off center. He tried to focus on his anger, concentrating on the way she'd defied him, but it was no use. He was lost in the middle of an unfamiliar war. All he could think to do was argue.

"You can't tell me what to do. And you can't refuse me my conjugal rights. You're my wife."

"I want a divorce, but I'll settle for being left alone."

The calmness with which she spoke made him furious. He threw a pillow across the room in frustration, and then hated her for the fact that she didn't even duck.

"A Potter does not divorce," he said, and took a step forward. "And you'll never make me believe you've thought this up on your own. You're seeing someone behind my back, aren't you?"

She laughed. It was a cold, bitter sound. "There isn't a man on this earth that I want. You've taught me to fear and distrust your entire gender, David. You've ruined every chance of happiness I might have had. But I won't let you ruin what's left of my life. I said it before, and I'll say it again. Either kill me now, or get the hell out of the room. I will never sleep with you again."

He laughed. "You can't keep me out. The lock is broken."

"There are other rooms, with other doors and other locks."

"They can go the same way this one did." David was reluctant to give up, even though she had him over a barrel.

"Touch me again and I'll tell. Kill me and everyone who works in this house will tell. They won't jeopardize their futures to protect yours."

He paled. It was the threat of exposure that did it.

"You'll be sorry," he whispered, pointing an accusing finger in her face.

"I've been sorry since the day I said 'I do.'"

From the silence that followed her remark, Mabel knew it would only be a matter of seconds before David either followed through on Amanda's taunt, or left the house altogether. Whichever it was, she had no intention of letting him know that she and Marcus had overheard every word of the argument. Frantically, she waved Marcus away, then hid in an adjoining room.

Marcus took the back stairs down to the lower level and tried to forget that the woman he'd been hired to protect had just been in mortal danger, and he'd stood in silence without making a move to help her. Guilt overwhelmed him. Not for the first time, he wished he'd never left his beautiful island of Samoa.

But Samoa was a lifetime ago. The NFL had taught him to love the finer things in life. And when he'd blown his knee, losing those luxuries had seemed impossible to bear. David Potter's offer had seemed like a gift from heaven. In reality, it had been an invitation to hell.

David's curses filled the air as he made his departure from the room. Amanda held the flashlight until she heard his footsteps down the stairs, heard the door slam, and then, moments later, the sound of his car as he drove away.

"Oh my God," she whispered, and fell to her knees. She didn't know where the strength to defy him had come from. But she had no illusions that her reprieve was permanent. To save herself, first she had to get out of this room. Later, when she could think, she would find a way to get out of his life . . . permanently.

"Missy . . . are you all right?"

Mabel's voice was weak and shaky. Amanda looked up to see the housekeeper coming into the room.

"I'm fine," Amanda said.

"I was so worried about you," Mabel said. "I can't believe that you actually defied him. I wanted to help . . . but I didn't know what to do."

Amanda nodded, and would have smiled, but the pain in her jaw was too great. She grasped Mabel by the shoulders.

"You want to help? Then we haven't got much time. I need to move all of my things to the small bedroom down the hall." Then she winced again. It hurt even to talk. "And I need an ice bag for my face."

Mabel nodded and hurried to the house phone to order up the ice. Then she hung up the phone and began wringing her hands in panic as she spoke. "But Missy, what if he . . . "

"Please. Move my clothes now!" Amanda said. "I've spent my last night in the same bed with that man."

Mabel sighed, then nodded and rang for extra help. Less than an hour later, every garment, every personal item, every bit of makeup and toiletries belonging to Amanda had been transferred to the single guest room three doors down.

While they were busy moving her things, Amanda knew that she had something of her own to move. She pulled the Dreamcatcher from behind the bed frame, slid it inside her pillowcase, and then left the room with it clutched to her chest.

"I'm taking my pillow," she said, as she entered her new bedroom and flopped down on the lounge chair while they continued to move her belongings. "You can replace it with one from that bed."

The maid did as she was told, and neither she, nor Mabel, was the wiser for the fact that Amanda had moved more than herself and her personal possessions this night.

When she left the bedroom of her husband, she'd taken hope with her.

Somewhere in town a siren sounded, screaming a warning for all in its path to move aside as a police car took pursuit. And then the clock in the hall struck three times.

Three A.M. Am I ever going to be able to sleep?

Amanda rolled over in bed and stared at the ceiling, holding her breath as she listened for the dreaded sounds she'd been waiting for. And when they came, they brought terror with them.

David was home! The front door went shut with a sharp click. For a moment, she heard nothing, and suspected that he was doing some listening of his own.

And then he started up the staircase. Amanda stuffed her hand in her mouth to keep from screaming.

God give me strength.

Far down the hall, the footsteps paused, and Amanda knew that David had taken in the fact that much in their bedroom, including his wife, was missing.

And then he started down the hallway, walking from door to door, testing each one as he went. Each time a door opened, it closed moments later with a snap, accompanied by her husband's frustrated curse.

And then he came to the end of the hall. To her bedroom. She sat up in bed and curled her knees beneath her. If need be, readying herself for battle. The doorknob turned. She heard his weight push against the door, and then the familiar curse when it refused to budge.

"Amanda . . . sweetheart . . . let me in. I promise it will be different. We can go to a counselor. Things can be worked out. You'll see."

She held her breath.

"Please, darling. This is silly." The tone of his voice lowered as the timbre raised. "You can't spend the rest of our married life behind a locked door."

Oh but I could, Amanda thought.

She bit her lip and stared at the knob as it twisted one way then another, expecting at any moment to see the door go flying inward and then have to face her husband's deadly wrath.

David listened, expecting a response. When none was forthcoming, his anger grew. How dare she do this? Humiliate him in front of his employees, and in his own home? What on earth would the papers print if word of this got out?

Amanda crawled quietly from the bed and got to her feet. If she had to fight, it wasn't going to be flat on her back.

"Amanda! Open this door now!" he ordered, and began pounding on it with his fist.

"Sir! Would you be needing any assistance?"

David jerked back in shock, his hand still doubled in anger. The chauffeur's bulk was nothing more than an enormous shadow at the end of the hall, yet he knew instantly who it was.

"No," David muttered, and took a step back from Amanda's door. "We were just having a marital disagreement. You know how it is. Go back to your quarters. If I need you, I'll ring."

"Yes, sir," Marcus said, but he didn't move.

David fidgeted. It had become a waiting game, and finally, Marcus won.

David stalked back up the hall, walked into his bedroom, and tried to slam the door. But it bounced back on the broken lock and then swung until it came to rest, half open.

"I want this door fixed tomorrow!" David shouted.

"Yes, sir," Marcus said, and then he was gone.

Amanda stepped backward. When the bed connected with the back of her legs, she slid down onto the side of the mattress in shaky relief. Only after the room stopped spinning did she realize that she'd been holding the Dreamcatcher against her chest like a shield.

"Oh my God," she whispered, and leaned her forehead against the back of the frame, relishing the roughness of the wood as a tangible reminder that she was still alive.

She rolled over into the middle of the bed, taking the Dreamcatcher with her. The wisp of feather tickled the side of her cheek as she laid it beside her. She reached out in the darkness, letting her fingertips trace the shape of the claw, as well as the tiny beaded medallion, before she groaned helplessly.

Tears tracked her cheeks as she swallowed over and over, refusing to acknowledge the terror that she felt.

"I'm so tired of being afraid. I'm so damned tired of being afraid."

But there was no one to hear her whispered plea, and soon, she closed her eyes, praying for sleep to claim her.

It did.

Amanda held her breath, watching in dreamsleep as he walked toward her through the light. This time she'd been waiting.

You came, she thought, and felt the bed give behind her as he took his place at her side.

She sighed in her sleep and shifted on the mattress, making room for his body as he reclaimed his place and cradled her head upon his chest. The weight of him was welcome. It meant she was no longer alone. She felt his breath upon her cheeks, the sweep of his hair against her neck, and then his hands as they pulled her firmly against the pounding of his heart.

My Amanda.

Even in sleep, her heart leaped. It was the first time she'd heard his voice. She sighed again, and shifted restlessly.

Rest, my Amanda, rest. Do not be afraid. I am with you always.

As before, peace enveloped her, and she slept.

*   *   *

The sound of loud hammering awoke her. Sunlight was in her eyes, and this time there was no mistaking the sounds for those of woodpeckers. Obviously, Marcus was following his orders. Carpenters had arrived, and the bedroom door was in the process of being fixed.

Amanda yawned and then stretched. Her elbow bumped the Dreamcatcher. She smiled at a private memory and rolled over, to secrete it behind the wicker headboard of her bed. Then she got up and sauntered to the bathroom. It wasn't as opulent as the one in the master bedroom, and there was only a shower stall, not a tub. But to Amanda, it meant peace and privacy. Heaven.

Half an hour later, dressed casually in blue slacks and matching cotton sweater, she made her way downstairs, only to meet David on the way up. A flicker of muscles along the side of her jaw was the only indication of her concern. She met his startled gaze full force and gave him an impersonal smile.

"Good morning, David. Did you save me any coffee?"

He stared, unable to answer. He was still too furious, and too busy planning his retaliation.

"Never mind," Amanda said, taking the stairs down two at a time. "I can always have tea. See you later."

The sounds of her footsteps were lost in the echoes of the hammering coming from above.

"Dammit all to hell," David mumbled, as he headed for his room. "She will pay. She will pay dearly for this."

Amanda purposely dawdled through breakfast, hoping that David would take it upon himself to leave, and she could make her way back upstairs to some semblance of safety while she made her plans.

Last night, while waiting for David's return, she'd counted her secret stash of money, and to her delight, realized that she had nearly five hundred dollars. A pitiful sum, considering the Potter millions and how long it had taken her to acquire it. But it was still enough to get her away.

Twice during breakfast, she'd almost given up on her

plan before she'd even started. In the back of her mind, *The Plan* had always been there. But implementing it a second time scared the hell out of her. She still had nightmares about what he'd done to her when she'd run before, as well as the threat he'd made if she ever tried it again. If she ran and he found her, her next home would not be the Potter mansion, it would be an asylum.

Despite all of her earlier bravado and daring behavior, therein lay most of Amanda's problems. Her husband had enough bureaucrats on his payroll to do whatever he wished. He might not be able to kill her and get away with it, but he could damn sure have her locked away for the rest of her life. She didn't know which would be worse; living with just one maniac, or spending the rest of her life with an entire asylum full.

A maid entered the breakfast room to clear the table. Amanda smiled at her.

"When you've finished, would you mind telling Marcus that I'd like to go out for a few hours this morning?"

The girl nodded, and then looked away. She hurried from the room with plates stacked in her hands. Amanda frowned at her odd behavior and then shrugged. She couldn't blame any of them for being nervous. From the way he behaved, it was a wonder David could keep any kind of help.

She walked into the hallway to wait for Marcus to bring around the car, thinking that the morning was going better than she'd expected. It was when she went back upstairs to get a jacket that she made her first mistake.

The carpenters were nowhere in sight. The mess was gone and from the appearance of the new door on the master bedroom, everything was back in working order. Amanda scurried past the open doorway, telling herself that it was simply a case of nerves that was making her wary.

One of the maids had cleaned her room. The bed was made. Fresh towels hung on the bar in the bath. Amanda opened the closet door and began to search for the jacket she wanted when she heard a sound.

She stepped back from the closet, gazing quickly around the room for a sign of intrusion. There was none. She was still alone. It was only when she looked toward the door to her room that she noticed it was shut.

That was strange. She knew she had left it open. The windows were open in the house, so there was no way a draft could have blown it shut. But the mystery was solved when Amanda tried to open the door. It wouldn't budge.

She gasped.

"Amanda. I'm sorry it's come to this."

David's voice was low. She imagined him leaning close to speak so that he would not be overheard.

"I have to be gone for the next five days, and I had to assure myself that you'd be here when I return. We can work out our problems. I'm sure of that. But you've got to give me a chance, and you can't do that if you're gone . . . can you?"

Her eyes narrowed. Hatred for the man on the other side of the door nearly overwhelmed her. But as much as she'd like to vent her anger, she knew that there was something else that would serve her better.

She looked closer at the door. Granted, the carpenters had installed a new lock in the master bedroom. Her own lock, the one she'd locked David out with last night, was still in place on her side of the door. It was then she realized the carpenters had *fixed* more than one door.

"Don't worry, darling," David said. "You'll be checked on hourly. You'll want for nothing, I assure you." He waited for her reaction.

Amanda reached up and turned the dead bolt on her side of the door. It slid into place with a loud, metallic click.

At that moment, had she been able to witness his shocked reaction, she would have laughed aloud. As it was, she had to settle for the fact that she'd had the last word.

David hit the side of the wall with the flat of his hand

and turned aside in fury. And then he saw his housekeeper and his chauffeur coming down the hallway.

"Just in time," he said.

"You sent for me, sir?" Marcus asked.

David nodded, and then pointed to the door. "Mrs. Potter is going to be . . . indisposed . . . for the next five days. Until my return, no one, and I mean no one, is to let her out, or to go inside, other than you or Mabel. Do I make myself clear?"

Marcus didn't answer. David glared at him in warning.

Mabel gasped. This was beyond anything he'd ever done before. She couldn't stop herself from speaking. "Oh, sir. What if there's a fire? What if she takes sick? You can't just lock her up like a dog. Please . . ."

"How is that sick grandson of yours doing, Mabel? I heard he's about to make his third trip to the Shriner's Hospital in Louisiana. Is that right?"

Mabel wrung her hands and looked down at the floor. She'd never hated or feared a man as much as she did her employer right now.

"Yes, sir. That he is," she mumbled.

"Well now," David said, and slid his hand along her shoulder. "I certainly hope nothing untoward delays his scheduled surgery, don't you?"

David's fingers squeezed the nape of her neck. Just enough to make his point. Just enough to send tears spurting.

Mabel dug in her pocket for a tissue and blew loudly. She didn't know whom she was angrier at: David Potter for the threat, or herself for once again bending to his will.

"Run along now," he said. "You can check on my wife later, after I'm gone."

Mabel ducked her head and hurried away.

Satisfied that he'd successfully dealt with one, he turned his full attention to the other. Marcus Havasute was too big for neck squeezes, and David wasn't all that certain that the money he was paying him was enough to buy total loyalty. In fact, in David's estimation, Havasute was the perfect bodyguard, but for one flaw. He had too much character for his own good.

"You will check on her every hour, on the hour, to see if she needs anything."

Marcus's dark eyes seemed fathomless. David stared intently, trying to decipher his chauffeur's state of mind. It was no use. The stoic Samoan had taken a silent stance and was merely listening, with arms folded across his massive chest, waiting for David to continue.

"When I come back at the end of the week, I expect her to be waiting for me. Do I make myself clear?"

Marcus nodded slowly.

David sighed in relief. "Good. I hate to think of anyone disobeying my orders." He gave Marcus a pointed look. "Someone might get hurt."

"No, sir. Not while I'm here," Marcus said. His quiet voice rumbled across David's nerves. "You hired me to protect your wife. I intend to do exactly that. While I'm in this house, no one hurts Mrs. Potter . . . again."

David nodded and smiled, then started down the hall toward the bedroom to pack when something Marcus said made him pause. He turned. Marcus was standing guard at the door, just as David had instructed.

He shrugged and entered his bedroom. It wasn't until he'd closed the door to begin his packing that the last of Marcus's words thoroughly soaked in. Marcus hadn't just been echoing David's orders. He'd been warning him off.

"Damn him," David muttered, as he began stuffing freshly laundered shirts into a bag and then throwing everything else in on top.

He glared at the mess he was making and remembered that Amanda always did his packing. It would be the first, but not the last, time that David had second thoughts about what he had done. Yet he was too stubborn and too single-minded to ever admit a mistake. Potters were too rich to be wrong.

Back in her bedroom, Amanda leaned her forehead against the door and listened to David giving them orders.

Tears rolled silently down her cheeks as she faced the fact that her plan was going to have to be put on hold again. Figuratively speaking, she was, once more, under David Potter's fist.

The silence of the room beckoned.

There's got to be a bright spot in all of this.

And then she realized, with David gone for five days, she'd have plenty of time to rest . . . and to sleep.

The thought of the man who came to her through her dreams made her ache with emptiness. And then the fact that she'd even given credence to his existence told her more than she was ready to face.

"If I'm not careful, David will make me as crazy as he is," she whispered. "I can't pin my hopes on a man who isn't real. I have to find a way out of this by myself."

But her situation was too depressing to consider. Once again, Amanda found herself undressing and crawling into bed. Maybe that was her answer after all. Maybe when she was as crazy as David she would find a way out of this hell.

She pulled a pillow out from beneath the bedspread and bunched it beneath her cheek. Remembering the Dreamcatcher that was safely hidden behind the headboard, she closed her eyes.

By God, if I can't beat David . . . I'll join him.

It was her last conscious thought before she drifted asleep.

SIX

─────────── ❁ ───────────

I can't do this anymore.

Yes, Amanda. You can. I will help you.

Amanda moaned, then tossed and turned, fighting her subconscious; willing away the man from her dreams. But it was no use: His will was stronger than her own.

As before, the light enveloped her. And as before, he came with it, through it, unto her.

The mattress sank beneath his weight. Amanda sighed and rolled toward him, hating herself for the weakness, and at the same time yearning to feel his arms around her once more. She was alone, but in her sleep, no longer lonely.

My Amanda.

The words drifted through her senses. She smiled and tilted her head, trying to see into his face. But the light was too bright, and his hold upon her body was too strong. She gave up the fight, and for the first time, let herself be fully drawn into his power.

Something felt different. He was still aligned behind her, holding . . . protecting . . . not only with his power, but his body as well. His arms cradled her. His heart thundered beneath her ear. She felt his sigh as he exhaled softly against her cheek.

And then he whispered in her ear. She couldn't remember what he asked. All she remembered was turning over and waiting for him to come in.

He did.

Reason splintered. Every need, every wish she'd ever known died and was reborn a thousand times. Her body became fluid, her bones nonexistent. She was light . . . and energy . . . and then they were one.

Her climax was instantaneous. She sat straight up in bed, gasping for air and trying to tell herself it had come because of unfulfilled, subconscious wishes.

But her body was still shaking, her pulse racing, and she would have sworn that she could still feel the imprint of his mouth upon her lips. So great was her experience that had she been forced at that moment to walk, she would have been unable to take a step.

"Oh . . . my . . . God."

She buried her face in her hands and wept. She wept because it was over. She wept because he was gone . . . and it had only been a dream.

"Amanda."

Her eyes burned. Her tears ceased. She imagined that she'd heard his voice . . . again. Only this time, closer than before.

"Amanda . . . Mrs. Potter . . . are you all right? Please open the door. I have your food."

She groaned and fell back onto the bed, covering her face with her hands. Dejection filled her. It wasn't his voice she'd heard, it was Marcus's. She truly was losing her mind.

"Just leave it," she said. "I'm not hungry now."

"Please, Mrs. Potter. At least take it inside your room. I'm only allowed to open your door on the hour. It will be cold if you wait that long."

Muttering to herself, she crawled from the bed and unlocked her side of the door. Without giving Marcus time to begin a conversation, she took the tray from his hands and slammed the door shut in his face before he could argue.

She set it on the table beside the door and locked herself back in. Ignoring the enticing scents of smothered chicken and new peas and potatoes, she was on her way back to bed before Marcus had time to turn his own lock.

She crawled in between the covers, fluffed her pillow, and then closed her eyes. But it was lonely in her room, and too quiet. All she could hear was the sound of her own heartbeat and the clock ticking on the bedside table. She slid her hand down between the mattress and the head-board, felt the familiar wooden frame and the Dreamcatcher inside it, and sighed. But only once. It wouldn't do to think that lightning could strike twice.

Marcus stood in the hallway and tried not to let his imagination run away with him. He knew women. He'd had many. And he knew what a woman who'd been in the throes of passion looked like.

In spite of the fact that Amanda Potter was alone in that room, she'd come to the door with her clothes awry, her hair in tangles, her lips swollen, and her neck and face slightly pink. She looked suspiciously like a woman who'd just been made love to.

He paced the hall in front of the door, considering the wisdom of breaking down the door and checking the premises for himself or ignoring the situation altogether.

A few minutes later, when he could hear nothing on the other side of the door but an occasional squeak of the bed frame and a soft, dejected sigh, he decided he was imagining things. She'd been asleep for God's sake. All he'd done was wake up an angry woman.

He remembered something his father had once told him: There was a very fine line between love and hate. Obviously Amanda hated him for following David's orders. That explained her appearance and her behavior.

Satisfied with his own interpretation of the situation, he folded his arms across his chest and leaned against her door—not in an attempt to eavesdrop, he told himself. He was only making sure that if she called out for help, some-one would be there to answer.

And so the days passed. Each time she opened the door to give back a tray with the food scarcely touched, or to receive a fresh one, Marcus watched. But the woman he expected to see was never there. She was no longer angry and dejected. Nor was she wasting away before his eyes.

She would come to the door wearing nothing but a nightgown, with her hair falling down around her shoulders in a cascade of colors that reminded Marcus of autumn leaves spilling from a basket.

Mabel would stare at her and then beg, "Please, Missy . . . you need to eat."

Amanda would simply hand back the tray and close the door between them.

"But, Missy, don't you want to see the mail? You always do the mail." Her pleas always went unanswered.

Amanda's silence invariably sent Mabel away in a fit of tears, claiming that the "missus" was wasting away and going to be sick.

But Marcus pondered all that was happening and decided Mabel was wrong. In fact, in his opinion, Amanda Potter wasn't wasting anything, including herself. The glow in her eyes seemed to be spreading throughout her body, giving her something she'd previously been lacking: the look of a well-loved woman.

Amanda stood naked before the window, secure in the knowledge that the darkness of the room kept her from any prying eyes outside.

She relished the freedom of standing unclothed as well as the feel of air touching her body in a way *he* could not, and then shuddered and frowned as she realized that the credence she'd given to *his* existence might be all it took to destroy her.

"If only you were real," she said, and turned away, casting a sad eye toward the empty bed she'd left only moments earlier.

Tomorrow David would be home. Tomorrow reality would intrude into her dream world, and in the moment she acknowledged the fact that it *was* a dream world, and not her real world, she began to cry. Soft, nearly unde-tectable sobs born of great despair.

"If I thought you'd follow me into death, I'd be there tomorrow," Amanda whispered, unable to look at the bed.

The instant the words were uttered, her throat tight-ened and she felt as if someone had just put a hand in the center of her chest in a motion of denial. She dropped to her knees on the carpet and buried her face in her hands.

"I close my eyes and find myself happier than I've ever been in my life. But when I wake, I find more misery than I knew possible to exist. What do you expect me to feel?"

Her whispers held a hint of accusation as well as despair. But there was no one to hear her, and no one to blame except herself. She'd walked willingly into her mar-riage with David Potter. And she'd stayed, in spite of the abuse that he'd dealt her.

Yes, somewhere through the years she might have been able to escape him, but at what expense? she asked herself. How many lives would have to be sacrificed so that hers could be happy? If there were sacrifices to be made, Amanda knew they had to come from herself, not the lives and blood of others.

The clock in the hall chimed four times. Morning was too near. Amanda crawled from the floor into bed. The time in which she would be delivered from her room and back into David's life was swiftly returning.

"All I need is one more fix. Just one more dream. Maybe the memories will be enough to keep me sane. Maybe . . . "

The floorboard creaked just outside her door. She closed her eyes and gritted her teeth, aware that Marcus, her jailer, was still outside. Guarding. Listening.

Tears squeezed out from beneath her eyelids as she rolled over onto her side and swallowed a sob. She wouldn't give any of them the satisfaction of knowing that she hurt.

And finally she slept . . . and as before . . . he came.

*   *   *

I don't want to lose you.

It cannot happen. I will be with you always . . . in your heart, and in your mind.

Then take me with you. If you're from heaven, I want to go. If you're not, I don't want to know. Just don't leave me.

I am here. Let me in.

Amanda sighed and rolled over onto her back, even in sleep obeying his commands.

Her pulse accelerated as the light filled her. The silhouette of his body was now as familiar to her as her own. The breadth of his shoulders was such that when he covered her, she knew to the millimeter how deeply into the covers she would be pressed.

She could measure his height by memory, knowing that just before they were one, she imagined she could feel the imprint of his knees along her thighs, sliding her open for him to come in.

Her only regrets were that he had not revealed his name, nor had she ever seen his face.

Amanda.

His breath was upon her cheeks, then her breasts, and then her belly.

"Oh . . . my . . . God."

She felt as if she had screamed the words. But in fact, they had been little more than a whisper as he entered.

Where life flowed within her, now it had doubled. Two hearts pounded, beating as one. Pulses raced with each other to reach a finish line that lay less than a gasp away. Her body was at once too heavy to move and lighter than air.

Now he was inside of her. His spirit was right where it belonged. The warmth began at her toes, traveling up and up until the hair at the back of her head felt hot, as if she'd lain out in the sun too long. Her pulse hummed, her skin tingled.

She struggled with consciousness, feeling the need to

open her eyes and see the face of her beloved, then gasped as he replaced that thought with another and sent her to a different level of glory.

Everything within her began to darken and tighten. Muscles began to draw while breath grew short. The pulse pounding in her ears was deafening as lifeblood spiraled throughout her body. Just when she would have thrown her arms upward to draw him deeper into her embrace, her body exploded.

Heat shattered and left her weak and shaking as she gripped the bed to keep from falling. Light began to emerge from within her consciousness.

Amanda drew a long, shaking breath, imagining that he was coming back, and then cried aloud when her eyelids fluttered open instead.

It was not *his* light that she was seeing. It was the morning sun streaming through the curtain sheers at the window and into her eyes.

"No." Her voice shook as reality intruded. "It's over. He's gone."

She rolled over onto her stomach and buried her face in the covers, unable to face the knowledge.

No, Amanda . . . it will never be over. I will be with you always.

Her tears ceased. The hopelessness with which she'd awakened slid away as easily as his words slid into her mind. For no reason, she leaned over, pulled the Dreamcatcher from behind the bed, gently lifted it from the frame, and then held it up to the light.

The rays from the new morning sun were warm and strong. A promise and a beginning of the dawning day. They radiated through the glass, highlighting the tiny particles of dust dancing in the air.

The ancient leather thongs dangled downward from the Dreamcatcher like dry grass rocking in a breeze. The ivory claw swung back and forth against the webbing, a pendulum on a timeless clock. Absently, Amanda started to trace the small beaded medallion when something happened.

At first she thought she was imagining it. Light did not rearrange itself without something first coming into it to make a shadow. Or so she thought.

Her room began to fade from her sight. Everything around her seemed to darken except for the sunlight that continued to pour into the room through the glass. It seemed to Amanda that the vast array of sunlight began to gather, spiraling around and around, waving energy and light into a rope-like beam that suddenly caught and then burst through the opening in the web like an arrow fired straight at her heart.

Startled, she fell back onto the bed, blinking in confusion as her room came back into focus, and sunlight resettled itself into its rightful position.

"It had to happen," she told herself, shaking her head as she rolled over and slid the Dreamcatcher back into its hiding place. "I knew it would only be a matter of time before I lost my mind. I hope I'm happy. It's finally here."

She ran shaky fingers through the tangles in her hair as she scooted from the bed and headed for the bathroom. If she had guessed correctly, David's plane would be in before noon today. She had no intention of being caught unprepared. Not again.

As she passed the dresser, she gave herself a half-hearted glance and then froze in mid-step. Turning, naked as the day she was born, she came face to face with herself in the mirror.

Her pulse skipped several beats, and then increased as she walked nearer, peering intently at her reflection. Her gaze was caught not on her delicate but full-breasted figure, but on the small red mark just above her heart. It looked as if it should be painful.

Entranced by the oddity of the spot, Amanda reached out her hand and actually touched the surface of the mirror in an attempt to examine herself before she realized what she'd done. Yanking her hand back in embarrassment, and thankful that no one had been present to see her stupidity, she looked down at herself instead, and gently stroked the surface of her skin.

As she'd expected, it did not hurt. But the mark was as vivid and fiery a red as if it she'd just been newly branded.

"What on earth . . . ?"

It was no larger than a silver dollar. It made her think of a cherry Lifesaver, complete with hole in the center.

Amanda looked back at the bed, trying to ascertain if she'd accidentally slept on an object that might have caused the mark. There was nothing there. She looked back in the mirror. The shape of it was so unusual, and yet familiar. It reminded her of . . .

The Dreamcatcher!

It was the exact shape of a miniature Dreamcatcher. And then she remembered holding her own up to the light and imagining that the sun had turned into a fiery bullet.

"Oh God."

She staggered backward upon impact of the knowledge, made her way back to the bed and crawled into it, unable . . . unwilling to face her image again. What was happening to her? Before this, she'd believed that the events of the past days had been her imagination.

"But if this is real, then what's been happening inside my head?" she whispered, and buried her face in her hands.

Footsteps coming down the hall warned her that she didn't have long to tarry. She bolted out of bed and into the bathroom, unable to look in the mirror at herself again.

By the time that she'd dressed, she was better able to face herself and the day. It was time to check her appearance, but facing herself in that mirror again was difficult.

She paused before it and then turned, half-expecting the mark to shine through the lightweight fabric of her dress. It didn't. The navy-blue stripes on a white background were crisp and cool. The square-cut neckline, as well as the form-fitting bodice and flared hemline were extremely flattering to her figure. But Amanda hadn't dressed for David's approval; she had dressed for war. She took a seat in the chair by the door and waited.

Downstairs, David's arrival was imminent. Marcus had already left for the airport to pick him up. It was only a matter of time before he returned, and then it was anyone's guess as to what would happen.

"You swear she never left her room?"

Mabel nodded furiously and wrung her hands as David's voice pounded into her conscience. "I swear," she repeated, and tried not to cry. "In fact, I'm afraid what we'll find when you go inside. She hardly ate a thing the entire time."

David's nerves did a little two-step along his spine. What if the dumb bitch had gone and done something fatal to herself? How on earth could he explain that to the media?

He turned his attention to Marcus. "And you . . . "

Marcus silently accepted the finger his employer was pointing in his face.

". . . you also swear she never left her room?"

"I already told you she has not," Marcus replied.

It was obvious by the way he spoke, as well as the way he was standing, that he was furious at being questioned in such a manner. It was only then that Marcus realized this was nothing more than the way Amanda Potter was treated, day in and day out. He didn't like the thought that he'd contributed to her misery.

"Good," David said. "Now, let's proceed to her room. I want her out of there. It's not healthy."

Neither Marcus nor the housekeeper had the nerve to object to David's diagnosis of the situation. Neither reminded him that it had been his fault she'd been incarcerated in the first place. Instead, they followed him up to the second floor of the Potter mansion and to the room at the end of the hall.

David started to knock, then thought better of it, and motioned for Marcus to come forward, thinking that she'd sooner come out for anyone but himself.

Obeying his orders, Marcus turned the lock. "Amanda
. . . Mrs. Potter. Would you open the door please?"

"Are you alone?" Amanda asked.

David rolled his eyes. He should have known. "Don't
tell her," he hissed.

"I don't lie," Marcus said. "No, ma'am, I'm not."

"Is David there?" she asked.

"Yes, ma'am, he is."

"Good," she said, and the door opened inward,
startling them all into taking a collective step backward in
shock.

Her hair was loose and hanging freely about her face
in thick, wavy curls. Her skin seemed to glow, and the
glance she gave them was alive with vitality and daring.
Her neat, navy-and-white dress flirted graciously about her
knees as she marched out the door. It was hard to say who
was more surprised, David or his servants.

"Amanda . . ." he began.

"When I come back, I want that lock off my door," she
said, her mouth pursed as she absently clicked a fingernail
against one of the buttons on her dress. Then she
shrugged. "For now . . . that's all."

She breezed down the hall, her navy sling-back pumps
making sharp staccato echoes on the polished hardwood
flooring.

"Oh . . . if you need me, I'll be in the library downstairs. I want to use the phone. I have to make my apolo-
gies to Mrs. Tuttle down at the shelter. She expected me a
week ago."

Mabel and Marcus stared at each other. A red flush
swept up David's neck and face as he gawked at
Amanda's disappearing figure. What in hell had happened to the body he'd expected to be dragged from
the room? In fury, he spun around and all but shouted
in their faces.

"I thought you said she wasn't eating!" He pointed a
finger in Mabel's face. Before she could answer, he turned
on Marcus. "And as for you . . . maybe I should have asked

you a different sort of question. You said she didn't come out . . . but I didn't ask who went in. Now I want to know. Who in hell's been sleeping with my wife?"

In spite of his darker color, it was obvious that Marcus paled. But it wasn't from fear. It was anger.

"No one exited, or entered that room. I gave you my word," he said. "And I don't respond to threats."

David couldn't believe his ears. "It was you, wasn't it? You're the one who's been sleeping with my wife. All the while I trusted you and you were . . . "

Marcus's anger reached boiling point. He grabbed David by the shirt collar and lifted him off the floor. "Your wife is a lady. I respect her. And I would never do anything to dishonor her . . . or myself."

"Put me down!" David shouted. Just as his feet touched floor, he added, "You're fired!"

"No, sir," Marcus said. "I quit five days ago. I made up my mind that I can no longer work for a man who has no honor. I only waited until you came back to tell you this."

Mabel thought about running away but was afraid that if either man realized she was still present, they would do her in, right then and there. She pressed her fingers against her mouth and leaned back against the wall, hoping they would not notice her.

"Just so you know," Marcus went on, "If anything . . . *suspicious* . . . ever happens to your wife, I will be the first one to come forward and testify against you. Do you understand?"

David was in shock. A sudden and intense fear overwhelmed him as he looked deeply into the darkness of the big man's face. Millennia of island warriors stared back at him through those dark brown eyes. All he could do was nod. And then he remembered Amanda's flighty departure and bolted toward the stairs.

"God have mercy on our souls," Mabel said, and quickly crossed herself before scurrying down the back stairs.

Marcus felt that a load had lifted from his shoulders and knew that it wouldn't take him long to pack. He had a sudden need to see his beautiful green islands and be re-baptized in the Pacific.

To walk into the clear blue waters surrounding Tutuila, the island on which he was born, and swim until his shoulders ached and the muscles in his legs felt like rubber bands. Only then would he cease to feel dirty for what he'd done.

SEVEN

"Amanda!"

The anger in David's voice made her wince. She looked wildly around the library and then grabbed at a stack of mail, unwilling to let him know that she'd purposely headed for this room to await his arrival. Here she felt somewhat safe, knowing that all of the hired help would be within hearing distance.

The floor seemed to thunder beneath his approach. Suddenly, his hand was upon her arm. She whispered a prayer, and then held her breath as he spun her around to face him.

"Answer me," he demanded. "What were you . . ."

The letter opener she was holding poked into the flesh of his belly. He inhaled sharply as his eyes followed the length of the blade. What had been an ordinary object had suddenly become a weapon. At any moment, David fully expected to see it ripping through his shirt and feel it sinking into his stomach.

Amanda's eyes widened. She looked down, watching in absent fascination the way her fingers curled and recurled around the pearl handle, noting the fact that a mere fraction of an inch separated the tip of the opener from the softest part of her husband's stomach. She looked up, unaware that her eyes were narrowing by the minute. They glittered as she gauged the depth of his fury before answering.

"What was I doing? I'm opening the mail." She shrugged out of his grasp and turned away. "It's piled up beyond belief."

Realizing how close she might have come to ending it all, he began to shake, unable to transfer his fear into anger as quickly as he once might have done.

"Mabel said you didn't eat," he accused, suspicious, and a bit jealous of the vitality in her behavior, as well as the glow beneath her skin.

Amanda slipped the letter opener beneath a second sealed flap. It made a soft ripping sound as it ran through the envelope. She considered the feasibility of truth versus varnish and settled on the latter.

"She exaggerated. I couldn't exercise, so I had no appetite."

"I fired Marcus." A muscle jerked at the side of his mouth as he waited for her reaction.

She glanced up at him. "What on earth for? I thought you hated to drive."

Aha, David thought. *Now comes the truth. She's sorry he's gone! That means they'd become close . . . maybe too close.*

"I don't trust him anymore," he said.

Amanda shrugged. "So hire another."

It wasn't what he'd expected. No gnashing of teeth. No cries of dismay. In fact, little reaction at all other than surprise. *Damn you, woman. You've been up to something. I've never seen you so . . .*

Words failed him. If he could have finished his thought, the word might have been *alive.* He'd never seen her in this light, with an inordinate amount of inner strength, and the casual grace of someone who knows that they are important . . . and loved.

"I'm hiring no one," David muttered. "From now on, when we go anywhere, we go together or not at all."

"That's fine with me," Amanda said. "I've always wanted to accompany you to D.C. Next time you have to go, I'll be ready."

She opened the rest of the mail and then sat down in a

chair to read it, missing the shock and then ruddy flash of color that swept across her husband's face as he realized he'd just damned himself along with her.

If she came along, then his bedroom bouts with his *play pretties,* as he liked to think of them, would have to come to an end. That meant no more games . . . no more . . .

"Here." She handed him a card from the stack she'd been reading. "This concerns you, as well as me. Unfortunately, we've been unforgivably rude by not responding sooner."

David flushed as he yanked the card from her fingers.

"We have to attend, you know," Amanda went on. "The shelter is honoring their founder. And since that happens to be your mother . . ." Her sentence came to an uncertain end, but Amanda's persistence did not. She felt a small surge of power, knowing that for the time being, she had him on the spot. It was a heady feeling.

"I know, I know. Hell, this is tomorrow. There's no possible way I can . . . "

"I guess that means I go alone to represent the Potter family," Amanda said.

David flung the card in her face and stomped toward the phone.

Moments later, Amanda heard his public persona kick into gear as his call was answered. She held her breath as she listened to him mouth some excuse regarding the late response and then assure them that both he and his wife would be honored to attend.

So, David Potter. You knuckled under easier than I'd imagined, she thought, and wondered how she might have fared if she'd had the nerve to try a similar revolt years ago.

"I think I'll wear my pink dress," Amanda said.

David glared. His fingers curled. The palms of his hands itched to connect with the side of her face.

Amanda looked up. A surge of nausea boiled low in her stomach. She read his emotions, as well as his body language, perfectly. He wanted to hit her. He wanted to hurt her, badly. It was all she could do not to give in to the urge to duck her head and scream. But she'd set the play in motion days ago with her earlier threats. Now was not the time to back down or change the rules.

"Don't even think it," she said. "Not unless you intend to kiss your career . . . and your good name goodbye."

"You can't do a thing," David said, and leaned so close he could see himself reflected in her pupils.

"I can bleed . . . and I can talk."

The simple answer made him shudder. Visions of her holding a press conference wavered with those of her lying cool and composed inside a casket. He almost followed through on his impulse, and then his last vision returned with an ending he hadn't considered before. Yes, she was lying in a casket, but when he turned from it to walk away, uniformed officers were standing at the end of the aisle awaiting him with handcuffs. The vision was all too real to ignore.

He shoved himself away from her chair and left the library before he made a mistake he couldn't fix. And all the way up the stairs he kept trying to figure out why she'd changed, and who had caused it.

"She never used to argue with me," he mumbled, and began peeling his traveling clothes from his weary body. "She used to be so nice . . . and compliant. When she misbehaved, she took her punishment like a good girl." Angrily, he ripped the shirt from his body, ignoring the buttons that went flying about the room. "Someone has taught her to be naughty . . . very naughty. It's up to me to find out who and make them pay."

He dropped onto the side of the bed and suddenly smiled. It transformed the look of anger on his face to one of classic handsomeness. "That's what I'll do," he muttered. "I'll make *them* pay."

Downstairs in the library, Amanda sat motionless in the chair. The mail slid slowly from her lap as she watched the open doorway through which David had disappeared. Her knuckles whitened as she gripped the arms of the chair with deathly force. She listened, half expecting David to come ricocheting back.

When she should have been sighing with relief, instead, she felt herself coming unglued. She bolted from the chair and dashed down the hall, beating her rising nausea by a hair's breadth. Moments later, she let it have its way, then collapsed in a weak heap upon the seat of the commode, shaking and gasping for breath.

"Oh God, oh God!" She leaned her forehead against the porcelain sink, while letting the cool, refreshing water trickle between her fingers. "How did I do that?"

But no answers flowed forth with the cleansing water, and finally she stood and began dabbing at her face and neck with a wet cloth, calming her racing pulse, as well as the lingering remnants of nausea.

The woman in the mirror was pale, but the color was familiar. A combination of shock and adrenaline overflow. But the fire in her eyes and the determined twist of her lips was foreign. Somewhere during her five-day incarceration, Amanda had regained a sense of her self and her independence.

"But why? And how?"

She asked, but no one answered. A trickle of water ran down her cheek toward the neckline of her dress. Before she could stop it, it disappeared beneath the fabric.

Amanda grabbed a hand towel from the rack and absently moved her collar as she blotted beneath the neckline of her dress. And as she did, once again she saw the mark of the Dreamcatcher, and remembered.

She closed her eyes, longing to feel his body against hers, longing to hear his thoughts mingling with her own inside her head. And as she thought of him, she remembered his last words to her.

I will be with you always.

Watching herself in the mirror, she lightly touched the mark, and then traced the edges with her fingertips, coming to a reluctant halt at the center. It could be from anything. An odd shape, but explainable as a reaction to an insect bite. Even an allergic reaction to a food. Instinct told her differently as she rejected the explanations, one by one.

"Are you real?" Amanda whispered, and stared deeply into her own eyes. "Or are you just a wish inside my head?"

Unwilling to wait for an answer she might not like, Amanda swiftly exited the bathroom.

Mabel hovered at the end of the marble entryway, wearing an expression as gray as her dress.

"Missy . . . are you all right?"

Amanda turned. She tried a smile. But it didn't work. It only made it as far as a grimace before her mouth turned down at the edges and her chin quivered.

"I don't know, Mabel. But I'm trying to be. I'm trying so very, very hard."

She walked away, leaving the housekeeper with the constant feeling of impending doom.

"Congressman! Congressman Potter! Please, could we have one more picture, this time with the current board of directors?"

The reporter's question was one of David's favorites, and not the first since their arrival at the shelter's reception honoring his mother. He smiled engagingly, turned a perfect profile to the camera while extending one hand in a gesture of camaraderie, and slid another across the shoulder of the dowager beside him.

"Perfect! Now . . . hold that pose . . . "

Cameras clicked and the noise level of the assembly rose as those who were "someone" in Morgantown mingled.

Remembering that during her dive from the platform in the park she'd been wearing pink, Amanda had rejected wearing another pink dress after all and chosen a blue one instead.

The collar was big, loose, and the fabric rippled softly against her body as she moved from group to group, always smiling, sometimes stopping to visit. But never long enough to let David think she was swapping confidences with anyone.

She alternated between consummate joy that she was no longer incarcerated within the four walls of that single room, and dread that when it got dark, she would once again be alone in that house with him.

Amanda tried to scoff at her own fears, telling herself that one couldn't be alone with any man when there were six live-in servants, as well as a host of others who came and went on a daily basis. But, she reminded herself, if those same six servants were virtually blind and deaf to all that went on in the house, she might as well be alone. There was no one, save herself, to whom she could turn. Before, that had never seemed enough. Now . . . she wasn't so sure.

She glanced toward the end of the room, saw that David was still preoccupied, and wished for a bit of silence to soothe her weary nerves. At that same moment, a faint breeze wafted across her face, instantly cooling her cheeks and ruffling the wisps of her hair that had escaped from their clasp.

Turning toward the source, she glanced through the open doorway toward the patio and the flower garden beyond. The evening sun hung halfway between horizon and zenith, a blazing ball of early summer heat. Inadvertently, she stared straight into it. It was a hot, white light of such brightness that she got lost in the glare and swayed dizzily upon her feet.

And then a tall, dark silhouette of a man stepped into the doorway. It seemed as if he just walked out of the light and into the room. The similarity between his action and her dream made her gasp. Her eyes widened and she forgot to breathe. She blinked rapidly, trying to see past the shadow of him into the face of the man beyond, but it was impossible. She'd looked too long into the light.

His size was that of her dream lover. His shoulders were of a width that made her want to reach out and test them for firmness as well as strength. She watched as he came closer. Without thinking, she extended her hand.

Detective Jefferson Dupree was in shock.

He'd cursed roundly for being assigned to this shindig, expecting nothing more than an afternoon of pure boredom. But when the chief said "jump" the appropriate response was always "how high?", and so he was here.

It wasn't until he arrived that he discovered what, and whom, the function was for. He'd watched from afar as Congressman Potter and his wife, Amanda, exited from their cab. It was then he felt the first stirring of an emotion he hadn't experienced since high school. He was jealous. Green-eyed, sick with envy, jealous.

Dupree spent the rest of the afternoon muttering to himself about the money being wasted on this party when it could have been spent on the homeless for which it had been intended. He also tried like the devil not to watch the guests of honor work the crowd, because he wanted nothing more than to rework David Potter's face.

He had such a vivid image of the last time he'd seen them, and the condition Amanda Potter had been in when he'd walked away. He'd already come to the conclusion that, regardless of her reasons for staying with David Potter, the man did not deserve a woman like her.

That was just before he walked from the garden into the room and found himself falling into a pair of eyes so bright and so green that they might have come from the garden he'd just vacated. She stood motionless in the midst of the party-goers, with an expression of shock and wonderment upon her face, gazing at him as if he was a long-lost lover.

He had a notion to turn and look over his shoulder, certain that she must be staring at someone other than himself. But she wasn't, and he didn't. And when she extended her hand, he was drawn across the room by a force stronger than his will.

Her hand was warm within his grasp . . . and yet so fragile.

"Mrs. Potter . . . Amanda? Is there something you need?"

She came within inches of his face before she spoke.

You.

The thought was here and gone so fast that Amanda wasn't certain she hadn't imagined it. Because the moment he'd opened his mouth, she'd known the man . . . and known that he wasn't *hers*.

"I'm sorry," she said, and quickly snatched her hand away before anyone noticed she'd come too close. "I was just on my way out to get a breath of fresh air. I looked into the sun and . . . lost my way."

Dupree noticed that when she talked, there was the beginning of a dimple near the left side of her mouth that teased her listener into forgetting what she was saying.

He stepped aside and motioned toward the patio beyond. "It would be my honor to escort you, ma'am."

"Please, I think we can dispense with formalities. After all, we've been a little too . . . up close and personal . . . for the mister and missus stuff, don't you think?" She grinned, causing her dimple to indent.

Dupree felt something like a teenager in his awkwardness and almost forgot to answer. "Oh . . . you mean the flying catch," he finally said.

"I'm heading for a shady place to sit and have something cool to drink," she said, leaving the detective stunned and mute as he watched her progress out the door.

Livid with jealousy and anger, David watched his wife from the podium. He recognized the detective to whom she was talking, and hated the fact that the man had a legitimate right to strike up a conversation.

His eyes narrowed at the way Amanda was responding. He couldn't remember her ever having the audacity to chit-chat with anyone like that man . . . especially beyond his hearing.

Then he frowned as Amanda began to move through the crowd. He watched her disappear out into the gardens and wondered. *Surely . . . surely this is not the one.* But the seeds of doubt were sown and anger was in place. He stepped down away the podium and began to make his way through the crowd.

Across the room, Dupree's feet refused to move as the woman of his dreams walked away, beyond his reach. His heart pounded so wildly within his chest that he feared it might explode, and the want that had surfaced as they talked was making itself known. What a mess! He was locked in place in the middle of a party, about to experience a heart attack and a hard-on, all at the same time.

And then the situation righted itself. He took a deep breath and then laughed at himself. Without further thought, he took two glasses of something iced from the tray of a passing waiter and followed Amanda Potter outside.

She'd taken a seat in the garden beneath a spreading oak tree. The air was faintly reminiscent of gas and diesel fumes from the intermittent flow of traffic beyond the walls of the garden, but it was still fresher than the heavy atmosphere of party-goers and smokers who lingered inside the lobby of the shelter.

At the same time she looked around, she wondered where the street people who were normally present had gone. She suspected they'd been neatly tucked away out of sight until the party was over. It didn't seem right. Being ashamed of the people they professed to help, while raising money to continue to help them, was something of a contradiction.

She looked past the gate to an old man who was shuffling along on the street beyond. Something about him seemed familiar. And then she focused on the coat he was wearing and began to grin as she hurried to the gate and began to shout.

"Dewey! Dewey! It's me, Amanda."

Beaner almost didn't look up. He hadn't heard his true name called in so long, he'd almost forgotten that it was his. And then he remembered the pretty woman from the shelter. He saw her waving at him through the gate and grinned before making his way toward her, fingering the lapels of his new coat.

"Oh my God!"

David Potter's gasp of horror came at the same time Jefferson Dupree discovered Amanda's whereabouts and frowned at the beggar who seemed to be panhandling at the gate. Unaware that each of them had the same thought, both men began to move toward her.

"Amanda!"

Her name echoed almost simultaneously from separate sides of the garden. She turned at the shouts, surprised to see her husband, as well as Detective Dupree, running toward her. David reached her first.

"Get away from him, Amanda! What on earth do you mean by . . . "

"David, this is the man who found my earring. Say thank you for me, please." A cool smile was in place as she waited for him to do as she'd asked.

David found himself extending his hand through the wrought iron gate, mouthing the words before he thought. As their hands connected, he looked down at the filth on the old man's fingers, gasped, and jerked the hand back just as Dupree arrived on the scene.

"Beaner . . . what the hell are you . . . "

"Detective Dupree . . . I believe you know my friend, Dewey," Amanda said. She remembered the old man's revelation about Dupree rewarding him on their behalf. And the detective had never said a word to reclaim what he'd paid out.

Dupree's mouth dropped. *Dewey? Where had that come from?* "Hey, Beaner . . . uh, I mean Dewey . . . what's up, buddy?"

Watching the expressions on both the detective's and her husband's faces, Amanda suddenly realized that they thought they'd been coming to her rescue. Refusing to make any explanations or excuses, she held her ground.

"Hey, there, Detective. Long time, no see," Beaner said.

Dupree grinned. He knew when he'd been had.

Beaner's near-toothless grin made David shudder and absently run his tongue across his own teeth.

"So, Congressman Potter, do you think that NAFTA will ultimately hurt, or help, the economy?" Beaner asked, knowing that the newly signed North American Free Trade Agreement had been a point of argument on Capitol Hill, as well as in every coffee shop in the nation.

"Uh . . . I uh . . . " David blinked in shock at the informed question.

"I read the paper in bed," Beaner added, and then cackled with delight at his own joke of the fact that often, newspapers served as both mattress and blanket.

Dupree grinned, understanding the connection instantly. David, on the other hand, was still at a loss. He wasn't the kind of politician who communicated with anyone who didn't wear clothes from Brooks Brothers. And then he looked closer at the coat the beggar was wearing and gasped. It was his!

Amanda looked at Dupree and noticed he was grinning, obviously at ease with the situation, as well as with Dewey. She then glanced at David's shocked expression and smiled to herself. *I choose better friends than husbands.*

"Amanda, it's time to go," David said, using his professional expertise to do to Beaner what he did with constituents he couldn't satisfy: ignore them.

She sighed. "Dewey, it was good to see you, again."

He nodded and started to shuffle away when her soft voice stopped him.

"Dewey?"

He turned.

"Do you need anything?" she asked.

Jefferson Dupree's conscience tugged. Here was a woman who could stand having the same question asked of her, and instead, she was thinking of someone else. Hopelessly, uselessly, he fell a little deeper in love.

"No, ma'am, I don't believe I do," Beaner replied after some thought, and then walked away.

David grabbed her by the arm and squeezed until his fingertips almost disappeared within the soft flesh. "Amanda, what do you mean by consorting with . . . ?"

She pulled her arm away and gave him a cool, warning glare as she rubbed the place that he'd hurt. "David, I believe we owe Detective Dupree some money."

Dupree was startled. He was unaware that she'd learned of his generosity toward Beaner. "No, ma'am, you don't," he said abruptly.

David felt weightless. Somewhere between here and the reception he'd lost his way. None of this made sense.

"Why on earth should I give this man money?" he asked her, refusing to ask Dupree directly.

"Because that old man you so casually blew off was the one who found your mother's two-carat diamond earring. He turned it in to Detective Dupree here, who, in turn, gave him a monetary reward. I'm going to tell the hostess goodbye. I'm sure you'll find a way to make this right."

She gave David a pointed look he couldn't ignore. *Just wait,* he thought. *Just wait until we're alone. You won't be so smart then.*

David glared at the detective, who'd suddenly taken an interest in the underside of the tree beneath which they stood.

"I will be waiting in the cab," Amanda said. And then she gave Dupree a thoughtful glance, remembering how elated she'd felt when she thought he'd been her dream lover. She shrugged away her dejection and smiled. "Detective, it was good to see you again, too."

She walked away, leaving the two men standing before each other like two randy tomcats with their tails tied together.

"How much?" David asked.

"Twenty bucks," Dupree answered.

David's eyebrows rose to the edge of his hairline. "For a two-carat diamond?"

Dupree grinned.

Anxious to be free of any indebtedness to this man, David dug through his wallet and grabbed a handful of bills without counting them, then thrust them into the detective's hand.

Dupree looked down and frowned. He counted out two tens, and handed the rest back.

"Gave me too much," he said. "You need to be more careful with your money. I wouldn't want anyone to think you were trying to bribe me . . . now would I?"

David shook with rage as the big man stuffed the bills in his pocket and sauntered away.

He almost hoped this was the man Amanda was cheating on him with. He would enjoy watching him die.

On the ride home, the absence of conversation was glaring. The only one talking was the cabby, who'd quickly figured out he was hauling bigwigs. But his expected tip was not what he'd hoped for, and he roared away, leaving them in a flurry of dust and gravel.

Now they were alone. David was so close Amanda could feel his breath on the side of her face, and yet she refused to let him see her anxiety.

"Is he the one?" David asked in a low voice.

Amanda turned a blank stare toward her husband's maniacal glare. "He?"

David grabbed her by the elbow and squeezed it hard enough to remind her that he overpowered her by several inches, as well as a hundred pounds.

"The man you've been screwing, you bitch."

Amanda didn't have to feign shock. It was there, in every pore of her body. David read it as guilt.

"It's true. He was the one, wasn't he?"

"You're accusing me of sleeping with a cab driver? You're crazy."

The door swung open. Mabel stood on the threshold wearing a smile. "Welcome home, Mr. and Mrs. Potter. Will you two be wanting the evening meal at the usual time?"

It didn't take her long to see the argument in progress and promptly wipe the smile off her face.

"I'm not hungry," Amanda said quickly. "I won't be wanting a meal, but I might have something in my room later."

She quickly made her way upstairs, out of David's sight.

David was left standing on the doorstep, full of righteous indignation and fury that she'd deliberately misunderstood what he had meant. He ran into the house and then paused at the foot of the stairs, yelling up the staircase like some drunk calling for a drink. "You know what I meant!" he shouted. "And you know who I mean. Don't think I'm going to forget this. Not any of it!"

There was no response to his jeers. He turned, fury evident in every gesture, and saw Mabel still standing in the hall, awaiting his decision.

"What?" he yelled.

Her lips thinned, and in spite of the jolt of fear that hit her square in the belly, she stood firm as she repeated her question.

"Dinner at the usual time, sir?"

"No! Hell, no! I'm going where I'm more appreciated," he said.

The front door slammed behind him.

Mabel waited. Minutes later, there was the sound of a car being driven from the garage. She heard the gravel crunching on the driveway, and then the familiar squeal of tires on pavement. When she was certain that he was so far out of earshot that he could not hear her response, she muttered, "I'd like to know where that might be. I hear hell is full up these days."

A smile cracked her face and she hurried away, satisfied that her small defiance had done the most good for what it had been intended . . . her own peace of mind.

EIGHT

———————— ❁ ————————

A cease-fire entered their lives. The war of fists and words between David and Amanda smoldered on the sidelines while a new phase began.

Amanda was using it to her fullest advantage. Day by day her departure drew closer to reality. But the timing would be of utmost importance. She'd waited nearly ten years; she could wait a little longer. While her plans to leave hovered in the background, other plans had already been set into motion. These belonged to David.

Independence Day was imminent. Since early days, the Potters of Morgantown had played host to an all-city Fourth of July picnic. This year was no exception. Anticipating a rousing crowd and always on the lookout for another way to mingle with voters, David's politician persona was in full swing. Orders went out on a daily basis to local caterers, party planners, media, etc. It would be the local bash of the season.

And so, while the world outside went on about its business, the Potters lived within the same walls, at opposite ends of the hallway, and waited for an explosion they knew was bound to come.

It was the day before the picnic. Perfectly manicured lawns surrounding the gracious home had given way to half-erected tents, stacks upon stacks of folding chairs, and an assortment of cocktail napkins that had yet to be put in order.

Dressed in crisp summer whites, David could have posed for an ad in *Gentleman's Quarterly* as he exited the house with a man in tow. He paused at the doorway until he spied his wife among the people working outside and raised his hand in a kingly gesture.

"Amanda! Please come here! There's someone I want you to meet."

It was more of a command than a request. Nevertheless, Amanda obliged, and then tried not to stare at the blond pony-tailed giant standing beside her husband.

"This is Serge." He waited to see her reaction. When there was none, he continued, certain that his next announcement would get under her skin. "Our new chauffeur."

The big man's clothes were subdued, and his features composed. But his professional, businesslike demeanor did not fool Amanda. She knew a hired gun when she saw one. This man fit the Hollywood version of hit man to a T.

Amanda smiled slightly, and then nodded. Minute motions of manners that never reached sincerity. David's expression made her sick to her stomach. She could tell by the look on his face that he thought he'd one-upped her again. Refusing to lower her voice or disguise her disdain, she nailed David with a ruthless question.

"So where did you get this one, *GUNS ARE US?*"

David flushed and cast a wary eye toward Serge, angered that she'd allowed their antagonism to be so evident. And then she staggered both men with a remark that left them speechless.

"Welcome to our home, Serge. And I just love your hair," she said. "You must let me have the name of your stylist." It came out of nowhere. Unable to believe she'd just said that, she shifted the load she was carrying and disappeared into the house.

Serge's response consisted of a slight twitch of his eyebrows and a readjustment of his jacket.

"Come with me," David muttered. "I want to show you the parameters of the estate."

The new "gun" stepped off the patio and followed his employer's hasty trot across the manicured lawn as they dodged the people in charge of setting up the fete.

Amanda dumped her load onto a table in the kitchen and then wiped a hand across her face. What with one thing and then another, it had been a trying morning. Adding Serge to the situation had only made it worse. At this moment, she hated David Potter with a passion. By hiring a bigger, better stooge, he'd rubbed her nose in her own defiance. The newcomer's appearance at their home could do nothing but make her departure more difficult.

The housekeeper came into the kitchen and then dodged an angry Cook, who was in the process of loudly demeaning the skills of the caterer his employer had hired.

"Mabel, tell the caterer that we'll use these," Amanda said, pointing to the samples of party paraphernalia she'd been looking at.

Mabel nodded and hurried off to make the call. The house was in an uproar, and there was no time to waste. Tomorrow was the Fourth of July.

The anticipation of a cool bath and a quick nap was uppermost in Amanda's mind. She had no intention of trading any more remarks with David, or his latest new hire, at least not today. Just as she was about to leave the kitchen, the phone rang. She picked it up on the third ring.

"Hello."

"Hi! Is Davie there?"

The female voice was high-pitched and almost giggly. Amanda pinched the bridge of her nose with her thumb and finger and tried not to laugh. *Davie?* That one was rich!

"Davie who?" Amanda asked.

"Oh! I guess I shoulda asked for Mr. Potter, right? So . . . is he there, Hon? I need to talk to him."

"He's here," Amanda said. "But he's unavailable at the moment. Would you care to leave your name and phone number? He can call you back."

"Oh, I don't know. What if he don't get my message? I really need to talk to him."

"Look," Amanda said, tired of dealing with an airhead who was obviously one of her husband's playthings. "You can leave a message, or you can come to the picnic tomorrow and talk to him in person. It makes no difference to me, okay?"

The woman practically squealed in delight. "Gee, thanks, Hon, you're a doll. What did you say your name was?"

"I didn't," Amanda said. "But just for the record, I'm Davie's wife. See you tomorrow . . . Hon."

Amanda disconnected and grinned, imagining David's reaction if one of his "women" showed up at the fete. As far as she was concerned, the whole damned lot of them could come. Maybe they'd give David something to worry about besides where she was and what she was doing.

"Oh my, Missy, look! Isn't that Senator——?"

Mabel's breathless gasp vaporized as she dashed forward to stop a plate of goodies from sliding off a table in front of some arriving dignitaries.

Amanda rolled her eyes. From the look of it, most of David's congressional peers had arrived, along with most of Morgantown. She'd been dreading this day for weeks. And now that it was here, she knew that the only way to get through it was to wear a smile.

Her fingers absently traced the waist of her red-and-white sailor slacks and sleeveless top, then flew to her hair as she remembered she'd forgotten the matching red-and-white bow for her hair.

She turned to look for Mabel, who was nowhere in sight.

"Pooh," she muttered. "I'll get it myself. David can play host on his own for a minute."

She hurried back inside and started up the stairs.

"Madam . . . may I be of assistance?" Serge's deep voice thundered up the stairwell.

It startled her so much that she stumbled. When she

might have fallen, instead she felt his huge hands steadying her on the stairs.

"Are you all right?" he asked.

"I would have been if you hadn't yelled at me and scared me half to death."

She took several long, deep breaths to calm her frazzled nerves. Putting up with this blond monolith was not on her agenda, not today. She shrugged out of his grasp and headed up the stairs.

Shocked by the sound of his footsteps so close behind her, she pivoted sharply.

"What is it with you? Do you have orders to keep me in full view today? Is that it?"

No emotion registered on his face. "I am following orders, ma'am. I'm to make certain that you have all that you need."

Amanda gritted her teeth. "Well . . . I *need* to go to the bathroom and then I *need* the bow I forgot for my hair."

He didn't even have the grace to flush.

"And . . ." she continued, ". . . I don't *need* any help with either."

Shaking with anger, she slammed the door in his face and then leaned against it and closed her eyes, willing away the spurt of tears that threatened. She hated David. She hated her life. For two cents . . .

I am with you always.

The thought came out of nowhere. And with it, came peace. Amanda's hand flew to her breast; her fingers sliding along her skin searching for the tiny mark that had disappeared days ago. Once, its appearance had shocked and frightened her. Now that it was gone, she felt abandoned.

Reluctantly, she pushed herself away from the door and did what she'd come to do. Minutes later, with bow in place, and defiant flags of color sweeping across her cheeks, she made for the stairs. She exited the house and came to an abrupt halt at the top of the patio steps just as David was coming up.

"Call off the moose," she hissed, indicating Serge, who

hovered just behind her. She smiled benignly and waved at a couple who called out to them from across the lawn, and continued her threat without missing a breath. "If you don't, I swear I'll make such a scene, you'll wish you'd never been born."

With the warning hanging in the air between them, she walked toward the crowd and began doing what was expected of her . . . playing lady of the manor.

David Potter was caught between a rock and a hard place. If he did what he wanted and Amanda made a scene, it would be all over the papers before morning. If he did as she asked and she ran, it would *still* be all over the papers before morning.

"Damn, damn, damn," he muttered, and then turned around and shoved a practiced smile in place as he waved Serge away. "She'll be fine on her own today. See to the security at the gate. Just make sure no troublemakers get inside." *I'll deal with my wife . . . in my own way,* he added to himself.

Serge nodded. It made no difference to him. It all paid the same. He headed for the front gate of the estate. Unfortunately, no one warned him that trouble would come in a size six mini-dress, complete with a head of *Dynamite Red* curls, chewing a wad of three-day-old gum. If they had, he might have stopped her entrance upon the scene and saved his employer from ruin.

Destiny Dawn, aka Sylvia Myers, exited her cab and followed the crowd pouring through the gates of the Potter estate. That she was a bit overdressed for a picnic would have come as no surprise to those who knew her. Destiny believed in flaunting her God-given talents, which consisted of a Barbie-doll face, unaugmented 44D breasts, a minuscule waist, and a shapely butt that made men itch to touch it.

And while she was exceedingly proud of her face and figure, she knew that it would only last as long as her youth. Working on the theory her mother had drummed into her from an early age, to use what she had, she'd used herself. Now she was about to reap the profits.

Three-inch heels sank into the gravel as she made her way up the drive. More than one man noticed her hips as they moved like pistons alternating fire. Up. Down. Up. Down. Molded, melted, and poured. An explosive situation encased in red latex.

As she reached the edge of the grass, she took the gum from her mouth and sighed reluctantly before tossing it into a shrub. It was just getting good.

Then as if girding herself for war, she patted her mop of red curls, hitched the neckline of her dress up, and then pulled the skirt down. Unfortunately for Destiny, each action served to negate the one before. A skittering of anxiety came and went as she considered what she was about to do.

"It's sure to be no big deal. After all, I got a personal invitation from the lady herself. So . . . here goes nothin'."

She giggled once, and then made her way toward the buffets, certain that before the day was out, she'd find David Potter. And when she was through with him, she would never have to work again.

Jefferson Dupree felt like three kinds of a fool as he tried a casual saunter into his boss's office and leaned against the door facing.

"Look, Chief. Don't you think we should drop in on the festivities? Sort of check out the situation and make sure that everything's okay? You know from experience that half of Washington D.C. will be here before the day's out."

Chief Morrell eyed his maverick detective and tried not to let his imagination give life to any more worries than he already had. No matter how much he denied it, Morrell knew that Jefferson Dupree had a fixation on the congressman's wife. It wasn't smart. It wasn't healthy. But it was also none of his business.

"No, Dupree, I don't think we have to worry about their damned picnic. It's on private property. And knowing Potter, he's bound to have hired all sorts of security for the bash. He always does. Besides, you're no longer on patrol.

When you made detective, you were supposed to give all that up, remember?"

Dupree frowned. He'd known before he asked what the chief would say, but he'd been unable to stop himself from trying, just the same.

"Fine," Dupree muttered. "And if something bad happens out there, don't say I didn't warn you."

He was almost out the door when Orvis Morrell's grumble slowed his exit.

"So, go look," Morrell muttered. "Check out the food, the guests, even the walls around the damned place for all I care. But if you know what's good for you, you won't look too long at someone else's wife."

Dupree slammed the door behind him, relishing the sharp crack that it made as it flew shut. The chief was way out of line. He had no claim, either real or imagined, on Amanda Potter. He was just concerned, that's all. *Dammit, there must be several hundred people going over there,* he thought. *I'm only doing my job.*

But the spurt of excitement that kicked his pulse into a higher gear had nothing to do with monitoring a crowd at a party. In a few minutes he knew that he'd see her. He kept telling himself that all he was going to do was look.

He couldn't find her. In distress, he'd sampled three kinds of meat, had two quart-size cups of lemonade, and was strolling around the grounds on the pretense of working, when he heard a laugh. It was so carefree and joyful that he turned without thinking, intent only on seeing what was so funny.

And when he turned, he realized why he hadn't been able to find her earlier. She was not where he'd expected. She was in the midst of a group of children who were flying kites. Her laugh had come and gone, but the joy on her face was still there as she gazed upward in delight, watching, along with the others, as the kites fought for dominance in the air far above their heads.

She laughed again, only softer, and the cookie he was

holding fell from his hand, forgotten in the act of watching her play. Then she turned in his direction and began to run with the string of a kite held fast in her hand. Leaving her shoes on the hill behind her, she ran barefoot with long legs stretched in a full-out run, lightly giving bounce to her breasts and tumbling her curls loose from the clasp at the back of her neck. He watched as a red-and-white bow came undone on her hair, and floated to the ground behind her like a dying bird.

Out of nowhere came the knowledge that she had a small brown freckle on her right breast and that he could span her waist with both of his hands, with the last knuckle of his little finger left over for room.

And with that knowledge came another certainty. Amanda belonged to him. To hell with her husband. Something had to be very, very wrong with this picture. Fate had screwed them up somewhere . . . some way. Of that he was certain.

And then reality surfaced and he shuddered. That kind of thinking could get a man fired . . . even killed. It was impossible. He had no way of knowing anything of the kind about this woman. Granted, the first time they'd met, she'd literally fallen into his arms, but that had lasted only seconds, and . . . she'd been fully clothed. So how could he know this about her? Better yet, whatever made him think he did?

A low groan came up from deep in his belly. A swell of tears gathered in his throat, burning his nose and the backs of his eyes without permission. All sound around him ceased to exist as he became lost in the image of her running toward him.

Then, before his eyes, the image began to change. The light around her seemed to disappear, and suddenly it was dark. Unable to move, he stared into the vision and watched as she continued to run. But the laughter was gone from her face. Her eyes were wide and filled with terror, her mouth opening for a scream that never came.

He blinked, and as quickly as it had come, the image was gone. Dupree shuddered and combed his fingers through his hair, disrupting the short, black strands and making them stick out in all directions. He was losing his mind and that was a fact.

He staggered backwards, stumbling over folding chairs and squashing dropped styrofoam cups beneath his boots. And when the rock wall surrounding the estate stopped his fall, he stood in place and waited for the world to come to an end. It was definitely doomsday, or he was going crazy.

But neither happened. And finally, without ever speaking to either of his hosts, he shoved his hands into his pockets and stalked away as if the hounds of hell were at his heels.

No one noticed the tall detective hastening from the picnic, with the tails of his sport coat flying out behind him, his long, jean-clad legs making short work of the distance back to his car. And if they had, they would have thought little of it. After all, he was an officer of the law. They were always on the run.

Meanwhile, another uninvited guest had made her way through the food lines, nibbling and giggling while constantly searching the crowd for a sign of a familiar head of blond hair and a face like a movie star.

Destiny Dawn was on the prowl. She wasn't leaving until she saw her Davie, and that was a fact. She took a deep breath and then winced when her stomach gurgled in protest. Maybe from its bondage beneath red latex, maybe from the barbecue she'd eaten earlier. At any rate, she was in need of something cool to drink and a place to sit down. Her feet were killing her.

It was because of sore feet and a parched throat that she found him. Beneath a shade tree nearest the drink table, in deep discussion with three other men dressed similarly in summer blazers.

He laughed at something one of his companions had said and then turned to take a drink from his cup when he saw her. It would be hard to say who was the more surprised, Destiny for having found her man . . . or David for having been found.

She giggled and waved, and he turned three shades of

red and motioned her away. She made a playful pout of bee-stung lips and shook her head and her hips in a no, no manner, as if to remind him that he wouldn't be able to call all the shots today. Not here.

David's intestines rumbled threateningly. He mentally cursed women and the ground they walked on, then made polite excuses to his friends before pretending to stroll casually through the guests.

"What the hell are you doing here?" he growled, as he slid past her in the crowd.

She gave another pout and tried to slide her hand beneath his arm. He spun around. The look he gave her made the hair rise on the back of her neck. Had she used the sense she'd been born with, instead of her greed, she might have left then and spared them all.

"Don't be mad at your little Destiny," she whispered playfully, and then pretended to stumble, pushing her breasts against his arm. The flash of fire in his eyes was exactly what she'd hoped to see. It gave her the impetus to continue. "Davie . . . we've got to talk."

"Not here." He turned his back on her and pretended to observe the celebration in progress.

"Yes, here," she persisted.

David winced. He heard determination in her voice. And he knew from experience that this one wouldn't stop until she got her way. He almost got hard just thinking about her. She was one of the few that gave as good as she got. She liked it . . . and him . . . as rough as it came.

"See that line of trees beyond the lawns . . . ?"

"Yes," she said breathlessly, and giggled softly.

David closed his eyes and swallowed a curse as she pressed herself too intimately against the back of his buttocks.

"Work your way through the crowd and then when no one is watching, disappear into the trees. I'll be along soon."

"Okeedokie," she said. Accidentally on purpose, her hand slid between the back of his legs and squeezed just enough to tease him into an erection.

"Oh my God," David muttered, and dropped instantly to his knees, pretending an urgent need to tie his shoes, when in fact, he would have embarrassed himself had he faced the crowd.

It took several minutes to rein in his rising libido. But when he had, he got to his feet, dusting off his knees and checking the crease in his slacks to make certain that he hadn't gotten grass stains.

Mother would be furious if I stained my clothes, he thought, and in the instant he thought it, stumbled. *Dammit, woman, you're dead! Why won't you stay that way?*

Minutes later, he paused at the edge of the immense grassy lawn and turned, taking the time to survey all that was his. With a surge of manly pride, he disappeared into the depths of the trees without looking back.

"There you are," Destiny said with a sigh. She plastered herself against him, like raspberry jelly melting on hot, white bread. "You didn't call little ole me when you were in town."

Her accusation, as well as her seeking hands, was making his ears ring. He glanced around the location. With the dense band of trees at their backs, and a thicket of vines covering the ditch between him and the high rock wall of the estate, he was certain that they were hidden from prying eyes.

"What did you want to talk about?" he asked, and then arched and groaned beneath her touch as she slid a hand through his opened zipper and encircled him with her fingers.

"You like that, don't you, Davie? You like everything little Destiny does for you."

He grabbed her by the shoulders and started to force her to her knees.

Destiny's eyes narrowed. "Oh no, you don't," she said, playfully, and withstood his demands as she staggered slightly and stepped away.

David was swollen to bursting, the heat of passion hard upon him, and she'd stopped? What the hell was the bitch playing at? He grabbed her by the hair and pulled her forward, roughly yanking her and causing her to lose her shoes.

She'd seen that look in his eyes often enough to know that he'd slipped over the edge.

"Don't, Davie. I didn't mean anything," she whined, and began trying to reconnect her groping palm with his engorged manhood.

But David wasn't having any of it. If he wanted to jerk off, he could do it by himself. He didn't need a whore like her calling the shots. No way.

"I want you off this estate . . . now," he whispered, and encircled her neck with one hand, while he continued to hold a fistful of her hair in the other.

She realized that coming here had been a mistake, and then she remembered her reason and got mad all over again. It was her second mistake.

"I'm not going until I tell you something." She struggled to free herself from his fury. "And don't be so rough with me," she added. "I'm pregnant."

She became vile before his eyes. A nausea rose within him as he dropped his hold upon her body and staggered backward in shock.

"You're not!" It was nearly a scream.

"I am." She pouted, and feathered her hands across her abdomen to make her point. "I need some money. I need to get rid of it, Davie. Besides." Her smile turned feral. "You won't want this getting out now, will you? A little thing like this," she pointed to her belly, "could ruin your chances for re-election."

He paled.

"I want a million dollars."

There. She'd said it. Surely he could figure the rest out for himself. She didn't just want an abortion paid for. She was blackmailing him and they both knew it.

"You bitch."

He began to shake. The erection he'd had only moments ago went limp inside his slacks. Spit ran from the corner of his mouth as he rubbed his hands up and down the sides of his slacks in short, jerky motions, trying desperately to cleanse himself of her touch.

"Now, Davie . . . I didn't get this way all by my—"

His hands encircled her neck, squeezing the last of her sentence off in mid-word.

"Shut up! Shut up, you filthy, filthy bitch. Mother will be furious." He was still shaking. His stomach jerked over and over as bile rose and hung at the back of his throat, threatening to boil up and over. "A Potter will not be born of a whore," he moaned, and began to squeeze.

Destiny knew she'd made a mistake. She wanted to tell him she'd changed her mind. But she couldn't speak. In fact, the longer he squeezed, the harder it was for her to remember why she'd even come.

I'm going to die, she thought. *This is not the way I'd planned to retire.*

The world around him ceased to be. David held her for what seemed hours. He wasn't even aware of the sharp little pop that her neck made when it broke. He didn't see her eyes roll back in her head, or see it loll against his fingers. All he could see was his mother's accusing, disapproving glare. He continued to squeeze, desperate to stop the images . . . and his mother . . . from coming.

It was the sound of crying that finally made him stop. And when he turned her loose, he watched in horror as she fell lifelessly, as if in slow motion, to the ground at his feet. Only then did he realize that the sobs were his.

David Henry Potter . . . what have you done?

The shrill voice startled him. Unaware that the sound was coming from inside his own head, he staggered once and stumbled over one of her high-heeled shoes. Just the sight of it made him gag.

"I didn't do anything," he whined, in a childish, singsong voice. "She made me do it. It was all her fault."

He pointed toward the ground, and once again began to rub his hands up and down the sides of his slacks.

"I'll get rid of her," he whispered, and looked wildly around at the area in which he stood. The steep slope of the ditch and the heavy vine covering would be perfect. "Don't be mad, Mother . . . please don't be mad. I'll fix it. I'm your little man, remember? I'll make it go away. You wait and see."

The voice inside his head continued to rant and rail at him for his stupidity. And all the while, he proceeded to finish what he had begun.

He couldn't bring himself to touch her with his hands. Instead, he kicked the body with his shoes until she teetered on the edge of the slope.

"Just one more push," David whispered. And then it was done.

It rolled down . . . down . . . down. Tumbling over and over in the thicket like a broken doll. And the farther it rolled the higher up her dress rode on her body until when it came to rest, it was up above her waist. But there was no one to see her shame. And then one after the other, her red spike heels followed her descent, and became lost in the undergrowth.

The heat of late afternoon beamed down upon the heavy growth as the vines slowly but surely resumed their normal positions, and turned their faces back up to the sun.

David stared so long and hard into the ravine that he lost sight of the place in which she fell. Only then did he regain his equilibrium enough to realize what he'd done.

"Oh my God," he muttered, and began reassembling his hair and clothing in order to return to the picnic.

His eyes were wide and blank, his lips sagging, his movements slow and lethargic. He pivoted slowly about the clearing one more time, just to make sure that he'd been unobserved.

It was okay. He'd done it. He had fixed what he'd broken. Just like his mother taught him. A weight lifted from his shoulders.

As he started to move; he glanced down to check his watch, and something made him pause. Without missing a beat, he reached down and zipped up his fly. He'd have to hurry. It was time for his speech.

NINE

❀

Chuckie Rigola's reputation had preceded him.

He shifted his position in the tree overlooking the palatial Potter estate, angled his camcorder toward the ongoing party just beyond the trees, and cursed the fates—and Madonna—for his ever having been arrested. It was a hazard of his profession. But suffering the arrest without a single picture to sell had been what really needled him.

Today, when he'd tried to get inside the Potter estate along with the other journalists and photographers who were recording the bash, he'd been recognized and turned away. He could just hear his mother now. If he'd gone to college like she'd wanted, he'd have a real job, not this uncertain bullshit a freelance photojournalist had to deal with.

He snorted in disgust, and then winced when a small twig on the limb he was straddling poked his behind. His short legs and stocky body did not lend themselves to furtiveness . . . or to climbing trees.

Photojournalist. Who was he kidding besides himself, he thought. It was a sleaze job and one he would love to kiss goodbye. But until his proverbial ship came in, Chuckie wasn't brave enough to change his way of life.

If only I hadn't tried to do Madonna.

But hiding in that elevator shaft had seemed like such a good idea at the time. He'd been so certain that he'd catch her in the act of something outrageous, and net big bucks. Instead, it had netted him two days in jail and cost him a thousand dollars he'd had to borrow from a local D.C. loan shark. Figuratively, as well as literally, he was up a tree.

He shifted slightly upon the limb and fiddled with his camera lens, using it like a telescope in hopes of spying something he could sell.

Maybe . . . just maybe someone will show up. There are all kinds of bigwigs at this bash. Surely I'll get a shot of something, or someone.

He had to. As it was, he couldn't even go home to D.C. until he came up with some dough. Rent, alimony, and the balance of what he owed the loan shark were all past due.

And then she walked into the clearing.

"Oh man," he whispered, and leaned forward, shifting the camcorder to a firmer position upon the limb he was straddling.

He didn't know who she was, or why she'd slipped so furtively from the trees, but he'd bet any amount of money—if only he had any—that she'd crashed the party.

Chuckie focused the camera, using the lens as a vicarious eye, and let it linger on the cleavage above her red dress.

Then a man in white walked into the picture and Chuckie nearly fell out of the tree.

"Oh man, oh man, oh man."

He inhaled slowly to keep from jiggling the camera, and adjusted the zoom lens so he could get a closer look. Unexpectedly the man turned, facing Chuckie as perfectly as if someone had yelled "cheese."

"Hell-lo, Congressman Potter," Chuckie muttered as the camera continued to roll.

This was his day. He'd just never imagined that when his "ship" actually docked, he'd be up a tree watching it happen.

The woman in red was all over Potter. Chuckie grinned. This shot was going to net him a fortune. And when he saw Potter push her to her knees, Chuckie wrapped his legs a little tighter around his perch and leaned lower, intent on getting every bit of this on tape. He was mentally counting the money and considering retirement locations when it happened. And because he was watching it through the eye of a camera, he almost forgot that what he was watching was real.

Her right shoe fell off, and when she kicked out against the congressman, the other went flying out of sight of the camera. Suddenly she was helpless and dangling in the grip of Potter's hands, like a rag doll dancing in the wind.

Chuckie watched through the camera as her eyes began to bulge. He saw the color of her face go from fair to dark and ruddy, flushed with the blood that was trapped above her neckline. Potter's hands continued to squeeze . . . tighter . . . and tighter. Her head suddenly lolled, and although he was too far away, Chuckie imagined he heard the bones in her neck snap.

When she fell at Potter's feet, Chuckie exhaled slowly and found himself blinking through a watery veil. It might have been sweat. It could have been tears. But he wiped neither away as he continued to stare through the lens. Unmoving. Disbelieving. He'd witnessed a murder!

His first instinct was to notify the police. But the deed had come and gone so quickly, it might never have happened. He needed money. This would be an endless supply from a bottomless source. As the word blackmail skittered across his mind, he fumbled with the camera and his conscience, and nearly fell out of the tree.

In that moment, he lost focus and panicked, fearing that he would miss taping something else. Then he realized that little else could possibly outdo what he'd already filmed.

Out of the corner of his eye, he saw Potter kicking the body over into the bushy ravine. He aimed. The camera whirred one more time, a mechanical accompaniment to the awkward ballet of Destiny Dawn's final roll.

Chuckie suspected the woman was one who'd made her living on her back. As he climbed down from the tree, he realized that she'd died as she lived . . . with a man's hands on her body and her feet off the ground.

But conscience had no place in Chuckie Rigola's plans. He had copies to make, and letters to write. If all went according to plan, at this time next week he could be in Jamaica, strolling on the beach with a girl beneath each arm.

Amanda's feet ached as she kicked off her shoes. But it was a good sort of ache. She couldn't remember the last time she'd run barefoot on grass. She smiled to herself, remembering the children's laughter and delight when she'd joined them.

Hours later, she stood at the window in her bedroom overlooking the tableau of remaining guests. These were the ones who had a special invitation to the fireworks display now in progress.

David was probably furious with her for leaving the picnic early, but she didn't care. Today, while flying the kite, she'd had a glimpse of what it would like to be free again. She needed to be alone now to consider her chances of regaining that freedom.

She grasped the edge of the windowsill as she leaned forward, watching as a red, white, and blue crescendo of gunpowder exploded upon the night sky. With a little imagination, she pretended she could still feel the tug of the kite string within her fingers as the paper sail caught air currents, remembering how it had been able to fly away with little effort. She would have given a year of her life to be able to do the same.

One after the other, the rockets went up, streaking toward the heavens like fiery arrows, bursting open in colorful display, while tears streamed silently down her face. She'd never been so alone . . . or so lonely.

Then one rocket went up, up, up. It seemed to hang

forever, suspended in time and space before its climax came. And when it did, the display it sent forth hung against the darkness of the velvet sky; a frantic glitter of fleeting beauty. A circle of gold within a circle of gold, like the Dreamcatcher behind her bed. And as it broke apart, it fell to the earth in streamers of light, similar to the leather thongs that dangled from the web.

The world around her disappeared. She felt a presence of peace and knew that it came from *him*.

An overwhelming need to crawl into bed and into *his* arms claimed her. She walked away from the window and fell face down across her bed. The pain inside her was too fierce to ignore. Her eyes burned from the need to cry. An ache spiraled through her, and she rolled over on her back and stared up through a veil of tears, fixing her sight upon the gravity-defiant shadows that danced above her on the ceiling.

"Where are you, dammit! Why is it that I can only know you in my sleep? Don't you understand? I can't do this on my own."

I am with you always.

The thought came with overflowing tears, spilling down the sides of her face and onto the bed.

"Then come to me," Amanda demanded, and sobbed as she dug angry fists into the comforter on either side of her body. "I can't exist on dreams . . . not anymore."

The gauntlet had been thrown. And when no man materialized from within the shadows, she flung a pillow across the room and jumped up from the bed. She staggered to a chair by the window, making a nest for herself within the cushions. She would not sleep there again. Not if all she got were dreams. A woman couldn't live forever on dreams.

Much later that night, David Potter finally retired. Assured that his wife was in her usual place, he calmly entered his room and shut the door. Before he reached the bed, he divested himself of every stitch of his clothing and walked blindly into the bathroom and stepped beneath the shower.

The cold water hit him full force, but he didn't flinch. And when it began to run warm, he started to wash. The soap ran in a slick film over all his body and sluiced onto his feet. Bubbles escaped from between his toes, only to flee haphazardly down the drain. He repeated the process over and over until his skin began to burn. Finally he turned off the faucets and stepped out of the shower.

"Now," he murmured. "Now I am clean. See, Mother!"

He held out an arm and stared into the steamy mirror over the sink and into the eyes of the woman in his mind.

Her mouth began to move. Up and down, back and forth, she scissored and chewed the complaints that he imagined were falling from her lips, and when she was through, he sighed. He hated it when she did that.

Moments later, he crawled between the covers and was soon fast asleep in the arms of hell, cradled by memories that wouldn't let go.

Breakfast had come and gone and taken David with it. Amanda glanced at the clock on the library mantel, gauging time as well as distance. He should be landing in D.C. about now. She sighed. While he would return by nightfall, at least she had the day to herself. And, she reminded herself, she definitely had things to do.

Last night had been hell. She'd felt abandoned, her last hope gone with the arrival of morning. Even her dream lover had not been able to come to her aid. She knew it was time to quit playing mind games.

Her fingers absently traced the book spines on the shelves behind David's desk as she considered the possibility of using the shelter as an excuse to get out of the house. If she could get out, then the next step would be to get away. As she toyed with the idea, Serge slipped into the library, unseen.

"Would there be anything you need?"

She jumped. Her "jailer" was obviously doing rounds. He was resplendent in powder blue shirt, ecru slacks so tight that his thigh muscles . . . and everything else . . . bulged when he walked. His ever-present ponytail hung down over his massive back like Rapunzel's locks. Amanda stared at the long, curly length of it and wished that she could escape from this marriage as easily as Rapunzel's lover had climbed up the tower.

At the thought, she shuddered, remembering Rapunzel and her prince's fate. They'd both been found out.

"Rapunzel, Rapunzel, let down your hair," Amanda muttered beneath her breath.

"Pardon me?" Serge said.

She shrugged. "Nothing. Now you have me talking to myself. I was looking for a book when you came in. Please go hover somewhere else. You get on my nerves."

She'd been rude, but couldn't bring herself to care. Moments later, he left as quietly as he'd come, barely missing bumping into Mabel, who bustled in with an armload of mail.

"Would you look at this," she said with a huff, setting it down in the middle of David's desk. "It'll take the better part of your day to go through that."

Amanda sighed. "It'll give me something to do," she said. She had to maintain some normalcy in her routine. It wouldn't do to let on, even to Mabel, that the first chance she got to elude Serge, she was going to run.

An hour passed, and then two, then three. Amanda sorted and read, making stacks of the pieces of mail that were DEO—David's Eyes Only. The rest she did with as she chose, stuffing some into a wastebasket, the rest into piles, some to go to the accountant, others that needed an RSVP.

"Missy . . . ?"

Amanda looked up.

"Won't you have a snack?" Mabel asked, frowning at the pallor of Amanda's face. "You skipped your lunch entirely."

Amanda nodded. "Maybe a cold drink and one of Cook's applesauce muffins. It's too near the evening meal to eat more."

Mabel hurried away, anxious to do what she could for Amanda, always aware that what her mistress needed most, she was unable to provide. A way out.

"Thank goodness this is the last of it," Amanda muttered, as she picked up a padded envelope. This had to be the tape of yesterday's festivities. She remembered hearing David ask for a copy.

Mabel came back with a tray full of goodies.

Amanda smiled. "I thought I only asked for a muffin and a cold drink."

"So, you might want seconds," Mabel said. "Eat! Eat!" she urged, and then closed the library door behind her to give Amanda some privacy.

There was no note inside the envelope, but it didn't matter. The tape would speak for itself. She inserted the video into the VCR and realized that she was a little excited about reliving some of yesterday's events. Maybe the camera had caught the children flying kites. It would be nice to see that again.

She picked up the remote along with a soft drink and a cookie, and flopped down into an easy chair in front of the television screen.

Expecting pictures, she was surprised to hear a voice superimposed over the blank tape instead.

"Congressman. A lofty title for an important man, right? This is the voice of your conscience."

Amanda sat up, her cookie forgotten as she stared at the screen. What on earth? This must be one of his buddies' ideas of a joke. She continued to watch and listen.

"What you are about to see will amaze you. Even shock you. But not because of the subject matter. Oh no, Congressman Potter. You won't be surprised, will you? Because you've already seen it . . . up close and VERY personal. What WILL surprise you is that someone else did, too."

"Watch. Listen. I will contact your office tomorrow. I

expect you to take my call, or you'll be sorry. I think you can figure out the rest."

Amanda leaned forward. The image of a woman came onto the screen. She stared, trying to figure out why what she was seeing seemed so familiar, when it dawned on her. The woman was on their property. That was the view from the back of their estate. Amanda watched intently. She could tell that the tape had been taken yesterday, because from time to time, bits and pieces of the celebration were visible beyond the treetops.

Then David walked into the clearing and the camera zoomed in, focusing perfectly upon his figure, and then upon his face. He turned, and seemed to stare straight into the lens. The look on his face made her shudder. Amanda knew that David would kill whoever had done this.

And then they began to move, and Amanda realized why the tape had been sent. David's liaisons were about to catch up with him. What she was seeing was a tawdry romp of sexual degradation that made her gag. Sickened by what she was watching, she jumped up, intent on yanking it from the machine. But before she could, the scene had escalated from sordid to sinister, and she froze in place, terrified by the sight now before her eyes.

When David's hands closed around the woman's throat, Amanda felt as if she was choking. And the harder the woman seemed to struggle, the tighter the band became across Amanda's chest. Finally, when the woman's head snapped and she fell limp and lifeless to the ground, Amanda fell to her knees upon the carpet and buried her face in her hands, knowing that time and time again, that had been her fate. But for the grace of God, only the ending had been different.

With that realization came another. There was no time left for dawdling. She had to get away.

"Dear God! Dear God!" she cried.

But her legs refused to move and she sat weak and helpless as the scene played and replayed within her mind.

Long minutes passed. The tape had long since played

through. Amanda came to herself slowly as one thing at a time assaulted her numbed senses.

The scent of peanut butter.

She looked down to see that she'd crumbled the cookie beneath her knees.

The hum of the VCR.

She picked up the remote and stopped the machine, oblivious to the fact that all the color had disappeared from her face, or that her eyes were wide and filled with horror. She found herself dialing the phone, unaware of what she was doing until she heard someone answer. . . .

"Morgantown Police Department."

Amanda had to swallow twice before she could speak. And later she would wonder what had made her ask for him when she did speak.

"Detective Dupree, please."

Seconds later he was on the line. His voice resonated inside her head, bouncing reason against fear until she almost forgot why she'd called. Finally she managed to whisper, "Is this . . . you're Detective Dupree?"

"Yes, ma'am," he repeated.

"I need help." She shuddered and swallowed an errant sob. "Dear God . . . please. I don't know where to . . . "

The sound of David's voice echoed outside the door. Before she could think, she'd slammed down the phone and cut off her only source of help. He was already home! From the sound of his voice, he had to be nearby.

Oh God! Oh God! There was no time for her to rewind the tape. She knew that even if she stuffed it back into the envelope and managed to reseal it in time, when he watched it himself, he would know that she had seen it. Then she would be as dead as that girl on the tape.

She glanced around the room. Trapped by the situation, she made an instant decision. She yanked the film from the VCR and at the same time, quickly unbuttoned a button on the front of her shirt. Her hands were shaking as she slipped the film inside her shirt, thankful for its loose, blousey fit. Carefully, she tucked it back into her slacks, then rebuttoned her clothing, and smoothed down her hair. Nothing must be out of place.

The envelope the tape had come in went into the trash underneath the junk mail, and she began gathering up her uneaten snack as if it was something she did every day.

She was standing at the door with the fully laden tray in her hands, waiting with an emotionless expression on her face when the door opened. David entered the room and then took a startled step backward.

"Amanda? I didn't know you were in here."

"Just in time," she said, and slipped through the doorway with the tray held before her like a shield. "My hands were too full to open the door. I was about to have a snack when I heard you arrive. Your mail is on the desk. I'll have the snack in my room instead, so you won't be disturbed."

His eyes narrowed as he watched her slip up the stairs, balancing the tray carefully in front of her as if she were carrying crown jewels instead of a damned soda and a plate of cookies. Since when had she become so considerate of him?

The thought came and went quickly. He realized that he couldn't care less. He had too much on his mind to try and play mind games with her, especially today. All during his flight home, he'd been trying to figure out a way to get that body off his property. But try as he might, he couldn't think of a solution that didn't require enlisting the aid of hired help, which he refused to do.

He dropped into his chair and then suddenly sniffed the air in disbelief. He leaned over, following the scent to the cookie crumbs on the floor beside his desk.

He hit the intercom with the flat of his hand. "Mabel . . . get a broom and a pan in here now! There are crumbs in my Aubusson!"

Jefferson Dupree frowned. His adrenaline had surged, then subsided, leaving him oddly weak and shaky as he hung up the phone. That was an odd one. Usually the crank callers went a bit further before ending their drama.

He picked up his pen and tried to refocus on the paperwork in front of him. But it was no use. The woman's voice had sounded so desperate. And the worst thing of all was, it had sounded too damned familiar.

"Ah, hell, Dupree, you're just working too hard," he told himself.

"Talking to yourself, boy?"

Dupree looked up. Chief Morrell was standing in front of his desk. Before he could answer him, the big man dropped a half-dozen bulging files on top of the others, and winked.

"Knock yourself out, kiddo," then ambled back into his office.

Dupree tossed his pen up in the air and rolled his eyes. Did this never end? He got up and stretched, then picked up his coffee cup. If he had to ride a desk all day, he was going to have to be wired full of caffeine. Paperwork made him sleepy as hell.

Using the water cooler for a sink, he rinsed out his coffee cup. As he did, he realized that one of these days he was going to have to wash it instead. The mug was starting to look as green on the inside as it was on the outside.

Green! The color made him think of Amanda Potter's eyes. The cup fell to the floor with a crash, breaking, unnoticed, into several pieces. The woman on the phone! She'd sounded like Amanda!

He was all the way back to his desk and ripping through the phone book in search of her number when he realized what he was doing. He'd already given himself a pep talk about this. Obviously it had done little good.

He sank down into his chair and buried his face in his hands. *I am losing my mind. I cannot let this happen.*

With his dark hair spiking in unruly bunches from the knuckles that he'd dug into his scalp, he closed his eyes and willed it not to happen again.

"She doesn't belong to me. She doesn't."

But she does.
He had the last word with himself.

Crumbs were the last thing on Amanda's mind as she all but ran down the hallway toward her lonely room. She made it inside and then set down her tray with a clank, ignoring the soda that sloshed and the cookies that broke.

"Thank you, Lord," she muttered.

She dashed back to the door and tried to turn the lock, but her fingers were shaking too hard to get a grip. All she could see was the image of that poor girl's head going slack on her neck. When the tumblers slid into place with a loud click, she jumped, thinking that it was the sound of bones snapping that she'd heard.

"My God," she whispered, and leaned her forehead against the door as she realized she was safe, for the moment. Only then did she remove the cassette from inside her blouse.

It was a Pandora's Box of black plastic and magnetic tape that would prove to be someone's undoing. Amanda was determined it wouldn't be hers.

She closed her eyes and concentrated, trying to remember the voice at the beginning, before the images had overtaken her senses and driven her to the brink of madness. And then she remembered! He would call David at his office. That's what he'd said. But David wasn't at his office. Good! That meant she had at least until tomorrow.

She had until tomorrow to do what?

Amanda crawled into the middle of her bed with the videocassette held firmly in her grasp and realized that her first move should be to get the tape to the authorities. And . . . if David hadn't come home when he had, they'd already be on their way.

Suddenly, she began to shake. The moment she thought of the law, she realized how close she'd come to revealing herself to a man she hardly knew. She remembered the other times when David's deeds had been outside of the law and he'd gotten away with them. The times when she'd been beaten to near death, and his money had been enough to make a doctor ignore the oath he'd taken in exchange for a new wing on a hospital.

Her fear grew. Who could she trust? Where could she go? Again, her thoughts went back to Detective Dupree. Oddly enough, he'd seemed willing to buck David on her behalf on several issues. But the moment she thought of him, she recalled the young lawyer whom David had ruined. Could she take the chance on being responsible for ruining another man's life? Or what if David owned Dupree, as well as all the other officers on the force? Then where would she be?

"But he's a sworn officer of the law," she muttered. "He's supposed to protect people like me from people like David. Maybe I can trust him. Oh God . . . and maybe I can't."

She jumped off of the bed and began to race around the room, searching out things she should take, refusing to consider what she would leave. As she packed, she made the decision. For her, it was the only one she could make.

She'd get the tape to Detective Dupree, but not in person. By the time it arrived on his desk, she'd be long gone. If he was trustworthy, her husband's arrest would be all over the news. Then, and only then, would she come home. And if Dupree could be bought off like all the others, then she would have already disappeared.

She began sorting through her closet. When it was time to go down to the evening meal, she did so with butterflies committing suicide in her stomach. But she had to maintain the order of the day. Routine would be her best accomplice.

"The Mister is gone, Missy," Mabel said, as she put a warm plate at Amanda's place.

"Too bad," Amanda said, and smiled when Mabel winked.

"Said something came up. Said he'd be back day after tomorrow," Mabel continued, and nodded for the maid to bring in the first course.

Just as Amanda lifted her soup spoon to her lips, she saw a large shadow move across the wall in front of her and knew that Serge was in the hallway behind her. On duty.

"Anyone ever tell you that you're too big to lurk?" she asked softly, knowing full well he would hear everything she said. She smiled in her soup when she saw his shadow stop suddenly, then move away as quickly as it had come.

Hours later, relieved to be free of David's observation, she was back in her room, working on her escape plan.

A rather worn-out, navy-blue duffle bag was all she could find without arousing suspicion, and it was almost too large for what she had in mind.

Two changes of clothes. Handfuls of underwear. An extra pair of shoes. A fanny pack that held her life savings of seven hundred plus dollars. And the Dreamcatcher. She'd been about to zip the bag when she'd remembered it and pulled it out from behind the bed.

Even inside the wooden frame, it was still so fragile, but impossible to leave behind. She laid it on the bed and studied it for several minutes before she came up with an idea she thought might work. Rummaging through the small desk in the corner of the room, she found some tape. With a couple of magazines to give stability, she was ready to proceed.

Amanda sandwiched the Dreamcatcher between the two magazines. With tape as a binder, she began winding it from top to bottom and then side to side, until the wooden frame had all but disappeared beneath the paper folds.

She pushed once or twice upon the surfaces, pleased to see that they did not give way to the pressure of her hand. She knew that it was as safely packaged as she could manage.

She'd chosen her clothing wisely. With only hours until dawn, Amanda began to dress. First the jeans. She needed durability, and anonymity. Everyone wore jeans.

Then a shirt of no particular style. Just a nondescript blue and white stripe.

Tennis shoes came next. For running . . . for running away.

And when she was dressed, she turned and stared at herself in the mirror. Expecting to see fear reflected, she was shocked to see excitement, instead.

"This is it," she warned her image.

She looked at herself again. Something was yet to be done. But what? Her hair! She had to disguise it in some way.

She went back to the closet again, only to come up empty-handed. There was no time to worry about details. She made for the bathroom and minutes later came back with it woven into one long braid and hanging down the center of her back. If worst came to worst, she could always stick it inside her shirt and hope that no one looked too closely.

Now for the incriminating evidence—the videotape. Amanda went back to the desk and pulled out a padded mailer. With her heart thumping near the back of her throat, she started to address it and then realized that she didn't even know the detective's first name.

"Fine," she muttered, scrawling the words, *Detective Dupree, Morgantown Police Department, Morgantown, West Virginia.*

There was only one department, only one Morgantown. Surely there was only one Dupree.

She dug deeper into the desk and came out with a fistful of stamps. It would be hard to guess how much it would cost to mail, but it would be deathly ironic if it was refused for lack of postage.

Soon a line of stamps went from end to end across the top. Nearly four dollars worth. It was more than enough.

And suddenly it was done. There was nothing left to do but take her best shot. Escaping on foot was going to be difficult enough. Getting past those damned dogs was going to be nearly impossible.

She paced the room for nearly half an hour before she remembered the fire they'd had in a gardener's shack a few years back. When the fire department had been called, the dogs had immediately been put up to allow the firemen free access to the grounds without danger of being attacked. That might work!

But she couldn't do this alone. This was where trust came in. And in this house, there was only one person she could ask.

She picked up the house phone and dialed the house-keeper's room, knowing full well that Mabel would be sound asleep. She answered on the second ring.

"Mabel . . . don't say my name. Are you alone?"

On the other end of the line, Mabel's eyes grew round. Out of habit, she grabbed for her eyeglasses on the bedside table, although she didn't need them to hear. She knew that voice. She'd just never expected to hear that request.

"Yes," she answered, and hugged her pillow to her breasts.

"If I ask you to do something for me . . . will you?"

Mabel's chin quivered and her heart thumped loudly. She took a deep breath. "Yes. Anything."

Oh God, Amanda thought. *This is actually going to happen.* And although she knew their conversation could not be overheard, she still began to whisper.

"I need a fire. A really big fire . . . but outside, where no one is hurt. Remember when the gardener's shack burned? Someone had to put up the dogs, didn't they?"

Mabel grinned. "Yes they did. They did, at that!"

"I'm going to bed, now," Amanda said quietly.

"Sweet dreams," Mabel said softly. *And Godspeed.* She realized she was crying.

TEN

———— ❁ ————

Beaner heard the sirens and shifted in his sleep, uncon-
sciously pulling his sock cap further over his ears to
block out the sounds. But they got louder . . . and closer.
Finally in disgust he stumbled to his feet and staggered
back through the storm drain in which he'd been sleeping.

"A man can't get a decent night's sleep, no matter
where it is," he muttered.

He heard wind rustling through the leaves, saw a faint
glow of light in front of him, and realized he must be close
to the other end of the drain.

The sirens seemed fainter now. Then they suddenly
ceased altogether. Satisfied that he'd gone far enough to
finish out the night relatively undisturbed, he kicked at the
sticks and leaves in the floor of the pipe, feebly feeling his
way in the dark until he'd cleaned away a comfortable spot
on which to lie.

No sooner did his head touch the cold, metallic floor
than he relaxed, turned over on his right side facing the
faint glow of light, and began to snore.

Amanda stood in the dark, on a street corner two blocks
over, and watched as the fire trucks sped past on their way
to the estate. Her heart was pounding, her legs shaking
from the sprint that she'd made through the gates, thankful

that the moment the fire department had been called, someone inside the house had not only put up the dogs, but had made sure the gates were open for the trucks' access.

A soft breeze lifted a loose curl that had escaped from her braid and tickled the side of her face. Intermittent streetlights along the sidewalks gave her a path in which to walk, but she chose the shadows instead. Another woman might have been afraid, either of the dark, or of men lurking in it. But those unknowns held no fear for Amanda. It was what she'd left behind that gave her reason to hurry. Her very life depended upon escape.

Some time later she stepped out onto Main Street and for the first time, realized just how far she'd come, and how late it was getting to be. From the faint pink glow above the horizon, the sun must be poised just below, awaiting liftoff into the day.

Anxiety lent speed to her movements as she ran through the near-empty streets, searching for a mailbox in which to drop the video. She turned a corner on the run and almost stumbled into one in her haste to disappear before daylight caught her. Without hesitation, she dug into the duffle bag hanging from her shoulder, yanked out the padded mailer, and dropped it in the box.

It was done!

The evidence that could ruin David Potter was in the mail. By this time tomorrow, the next day at the latest, Detective Dupree would get it. What he did with it after that remained to be seen. She intended to be as far away as possible if and when the world came tumbling down.

She headed for the bus station, and an hour later, was on the first bus south out of Morgantown. Only when she saw the city limits sign did she relax. And then only enough to take her first deep breath of the day.

Hours later, Amanda got off the bus on its third stop, and entered the sparse pedestrian traffic on a thoroughfare that led downtown.

No one paid any attention to the nondescript young

woman with a braid hanging down her back. Her jeans weren't new and while her shirt was clean, it was also loose and wrinkled. With a duffle bag on her shoulder and tennis shoes on her feet, Amanda looked no different from any other person on the move.

One would have to look closely to see the small, telltale signs of wealth—the perfectly manicured nails, the obvious softness of her skin and hands. And if someone chose to look deeper, into her eyes, the horror and fear would have been evident.

But no one looked. Amanda didn't stop to see if they had. She was on her way to the store across the street where a sign was swinging lazily in the breeze.

THRIFTY RENT – CARS FOR HIRE.

The second step of her exodus.

In this town, her face would be less familiar, but she still felt slightly uneasy in laying down her first paper trail. Using a false name was impossible, because to rent the car, she had to produce a valid driver's license. And, because she had no credit cards, she also had to put up a large cash deposit. Her money was shrinking fast. Yet, except for hitchhiking, which she refused to consider, she had no other choice. She needed to put a lot of distance between herself and David, and a bus was not the best way to do it. With not enough money for a plane, this was her only option.

Her plan was to be on the next leg of her journey when the car and the paper trail came to light. The southern half of the United States was an immense place in which to disappear . . . and David's status as congressman held less weight there than it did in his home state.

The girl behind the rental desk didn't look old enough to vote. Amanda hoped she'd never heard of Congressman David Potter. And because Potter was a fairly common name, Amanda felt reasonably safe when she drove out of the car lot behind the wheel of their cheapest model.

The beige compact was full of gas. A loaner map lay on the seat beside her. Amanda's hands shook as she gripped the steering wheel and watched for the highway sign that would take her south, out of town.

She stopped once at a small gas station to buy a soft drink and some snacks. She ate while she drove, constantly choosing the smaller side roads to reduce the chance of being spotted, in case someone was looking for her.

As she drove, a strange thing began to happen. Her pulse rate steadied. The knot in her stomach loosened two hitches. And the weight she'd been carrying upon her conscience for the last few years began to disappear. Amanda began to smile. And the farther she drove, the wider the smile became.

Heat from the morning sun beamed down on Beaner's face, warming his cheeks and highlighting the bits of dust and fuzz caught in the scraggly growth of a week-old beard. He scrunched his eyes a little tighter, trying to ignore the fact that morning had come, but finally gave it up as a lost cause.

He yawned, then opened his eyes, a little curious as to where he'd spent the night, since he'd more or less done his "bed shopping" in the dark.

The first surprise came when he realized he'd just spent the night with a woman. But not in the manner one might expect. And not with the kind of woman he'd have chosen for himself. This one was dead.

Beaner jumped to his feet and ran. His footsteps echoed within the empty drain, ricocheting from the walls and into his ears. His pulse pounded erratically, his stomach churned. Finally he gained the outer entrance, only to see that he was virtually alone at the edge of the wash.

"Oh man, oh man," Beaner muttered, and wiped a shaky hand across his bushy face.

But while a lesser man might have chosen to simply lose himself within the multitudes on the streets and ignore what he had seen, the same conscience that had driven Beaner to return the diamond earring that he had found, now set his feet in the direction of the police department. He would tell Dupree. Dupree would know what to do.

At about the same time Beaner came to this conclusion, Serge was at the Potter estate making a choice of his own. He could either stand his ground and try to explain why Amanda Potter was no longer in her room . . . or on the estate. Or he could simply pack his bags and leave Congressman Potter to deal with the situation.

He was leaning fast toward the latter option when the phone rang. And because he answered it without thinking, the decision was taken out of his hands. David Potter had phoned home.

"Potter's residence."

"Serge! Potter here. How is everything?"

Serge inhaled. His chest swelled like an inflated balloon. The normal rumble in his voice gravitated toward thunderous as he answered. "There was a fire last night."

He held the phone away from his ear, letting Potter's shrieks of dismay subside before he continued.

"No, sir. It was not inside the main dwelling. It was an outbuilding. The fire trucks arrived almost instantly and soon had it under control. There was no damage to any other structure."

"Was anyone injured? Has Amanda called the insurance adjustor yet? Let me speak to her," David said.

"No one was hurt. And . . . I wouldn't know if Mrs. Potter has called anyone . . . because she's not at home."

Potter was quiet. All the panic and confusion of the last few moments might never have been. "What do you mean . . . she's not at home?"

The ominous lack of emotion in Potter's voice startled Serge. "I mean . . . sir . . . that when she did not come down for breakfast, I went up to check. She was not in her room."

"Did you check the grounds?"

"Yes. Thoroughly."

David's mind blanked. For a moment, he could see nothing and hear nothing but a deafening roar thundering in his ears. His first conscious thought was that Mother was going to be furious!

"I don't like to hear this," David said softly. "This is exactly what I told you to expect when I hired you, wasn't it, Serge? You came highly recommended. I was assured that you knew how to do a job well. I'm not pleased. I want you to know that."

Serge didn't answer. He wasn't too pleased with the situation either. He listened as David continued.

"I will be home this afternoon," David said. "When I get there, I expect my wife to be in residence. If she's not, I expect to know why not, and where she can be found. Do I make myself clear?"

"Yes, sir," Serge answered. That was an order he knew how to follow. Search and destroy were his specialties.

The line went dead in his ear. Moments later he was on his way out.

Jefferson Dupree walked into his office and plunked a new coffee cup onto his desk before he even sat down.

The headache he'd brought with him to work was a remnant of a long night with little sleep. Every time he'd closed his eyes he'd gotten a mental replay of the woman who'd called for help and then disconnected before he could get her name. Experience told him it had been a prank. Instinct told him it had not.

Steam from the hot coffee wafted up into his face as he filled, then lifted the cup. Heat radiated close to his lips. Years of practice warned him it was too hot to drink. Out of habit, he blew twice before taking the first sip.

"Dupree! I gotta talk to you now!"

Startled by the sudden shout in what had been a quiet moment, he choked. The coffee scalded his throat all the way down.

Blinking back sudden tears of pain, he turned to see Beaner coming across the room in a dead run. The old man's coattail flew out behind him as he waved his arms up and down like a landlocked bird trying to take flight.

"What's up, Beaner?" He set his cup down, far enough away from the agitated old man so that the rest of his coffee wouldn't wind up on the front of his shirt.

"Bad stuff's afoot," Beaner said between gasps, then cast a furtive glance around the room before sidling a little closer to the detective.

Dupree held his breath and hoped that this would be over with fast. He hadn't had breakfast, and old Beaner didn't smell any better than he had the last time he'd seen him. Then his conscience pricked. He doubted if Beaner had eaten either.

"Want some coffee, Beaner? If you're hungry, I bet I can round us up a couple of doughnuts, too."

Beaner shook his head. "No time . . . no time to waste on eating."

That caught Dupree's attention. He'd never known Beaner to turn down free food. "So what is it that's bothering you?" he asked.

Beaner folded his arms across his belly, leaned forward until his mouth was only inches away from Dupree's ear, and whispered, "I saw a dead body."

Dupree jerked back as if he'd been shot. His eyes narrowed. The old man wasn't in the habit of lying . . . not about anything. If he said he saw a body, Jefferson knew the odds were that someone was dead.

"Who was it?" Dupree asked.

Beaner shrugged. "I don't know. It's a woman. A young woman. Real pretty from what I could see of her." And then he frowned and glanced around the room, as if expecting someone to accuse him of the deed. "But I didn't get too close," he said. "I know about not messing up crime scenes and the like."

Dupree frowned. "Let me tell the chief where we're going," he said. "Then I want you to take me to the place."

Beaner nodded importantly. "I'll do it. I'll do it because it's my duty as a citizen."

Dupree felt another jolt of guilt at Beaner's words. Homeless people had a tendency to get lost in the cracks of bureaucracy. It was amazing to Dupree that Beaner/Dewey had managed to maintain his integrity when all else had abandoned him.

"Where is the body located?" Dupree asked, just before he entered the chief's office.

"Behind that congressman's place," Beaner said, as he slid a finger beneath his sock cap and absently scratched.

Dupree froze. His fingers gripped the doorknob, but he couldn't make them turn it. "Are you referring to Potter? Congressman Potter?"

Beaner nodded. "Yeah. And we better hurry. It's gonna be a hot one today and that little lady needs to get out of this heat."

Jefferson Dupree felt that single swallow of coffee threatening to come up. He turned cold all over. All at once. A flashback of the woman who'd called yesterday pleading for help came over him. Along with that, an image of Amanda as he'd last seen her.

Somehow he got into the squad car. His first rational thought came when he stopped at the street above the storm drain that emptied into the wash below.

"You say she's inside . . . in there?" he asked, as Beaner paused at the entrance to the drain.

Beaner nodded. "But you have to go all the way through. She's at the edge on the other side. If you want I can show you where to . . . "

"No! Stay here!" Dupree ordered. And then softened his warning by patting Beaner's shoulder. "Please?"

Beaner sat down. "I didn't really *want* to go back. I just thought I *should*."

Dupree squeezed Beaner's shoulder again in sympathy and stood at the opening to the drain, trying to get up the guts to walk inside.

The morning sun gleamed down upon his head.

Nervously he combed his fingers through his hair, making inky furrows in its length. He shifted his shoulder holster beneath his jacket, ran his finger absently over the belt buckle above his button-fly jeans, and kicked at a stick beneath the toe of his boots as he started inside.

To go from bright sunlight to the dim reality of Beaner's bedroom was startling and depressing. He began to walk. And when the odor first appeared, it stopped him in mid-stride like a fist.

"Holy Jesus."

It was meant as a prayer. Dupree came face to face with a thought that up until now he'd been unwilling to consider. If this was Amanda's body he was about to find, he didn't want to face what might have happened to her. He didn't want to think that the call he'd had yesterday could have been from her and he'd ignored it like so much spilled salt.

He staggered, and then reached out, skinning his knuckles on the side of the drain as he tried to steady himself.

"Oh God," he whispered, and took a step forward. "Please don't let this be her. Not Amanda. Not my Amanda."

He began to walk toward the light at the end of the pipe.

She was lying on her back staring up at the sun. Dupree waved at a swarm of flies and cursed, needing to look, but trying not to see how this once beautiful body had been despoiled. This was the part of his job that he hated with a vengeance. It constantly appalled him that one human being could mangle another to the point that the victim was often unrecognizable.

Little was left of her panty hose save a webbing of snags and runs. Beneath them, her long legs were covered with dark bruises and deep, black scratches. The blood was old and dried, along with the mud on her cheeks. The necklace of bruises around her throat told Dupree as much about her death as the angle of her head to her neck.

A faint breeze made its way down into the steep

ravine, blowing wisps of red curls that had escaped being plastered by mud to the side of her face. Although every bit of her lingerie was still in place, the dress she was wearing was up around her waist.

Dupree fought tears as he stared down into the vacancy of the young woman's face and could feel no shame for his joy. It wasn't Amanda!

"Thank you, God."

It was all he could say. He turned from the sight, his legs shaking as he started out the way he'd come in. Before he reached the exit, he found himself running. And when he burst into the sunlight and took a long deep breath, Beaner looked up and nodded.

"I did the same thing this morning," he remarked.

Together they walked back to the squad car. Dupree called for the crime lab and then settled down to wait. As he did, he began to take down Beaner's story. His fingers shook from lingering remnants of the earlier shock as he started to write.

"Let's see, now," Dupree said. "Your name is . . . Dewey?"

It took Beaner a moment to consider the implications of revealing his true identity again. It was so much safer on the streets if no one knew your name. And while he wasn't wanted by the law, and had no living relatives, it was still the only thing of his past that he had left. Saying the name aloud was a hard reminder of what he'd been and what he'd lost. Finally he answered.

"That's right, Detective. My name is Dewey. Dewey Miller, from Godebo, Oklahoma. Before FHA foreclosed on my place . . . I was a farmer."

Dupree began to write.

Mabel jumped as the front door swung open. *He* was home. There was no getting around the fact that he would have to be faced. She smoothed down the front of her apron, patted her fluff of gray curls, and said a prayer.

"Good afternoon, sir," she said.

David dropped his bag in the hallway. He looked as if he'd just walked off the page of a fashion magazine. His pale green blazer, oatmeal-colored slacks and open-collared shirt complemented his blond hair and dark tan to perfection. He nudged his bag with the toe of a shoe, careful not to scuff the soft Italian leather, and then turned on Mabel with deadly calm.

"Where did she go?"

Four words. Spoken with as much viciousness as she'd ever heard come out of a man's mouth. Mabel folded her hands in front of her and stood her ground, willing to lie, up to a point. She knew that most of what she said had to be the truth or he'd know it.

"I don't know, sir. The last time I spoke with her was last night." A frown furrowed her forehead as she thought. "I was having popcorn in my room. She called down to ask about a book she'd been reading . . . before going to sleep, you know."

Mabel watched a vein corrugate at his temple and knew he was hanging on the edge of her every word. She had to be careful.

"And . . ." David prodded.

Mabel nodded. "And when I told her I'd put it back on the library shelf, thinking she was finished with it, she told me to never mind. Her last words to me were 'I'm going to bed.' And that's the truth, so help me God."

The ring of truth was too obvious to be denied. David wanted to hit. He wanted to scream. He wanted to kill. He did none of the above.

"Is Serge here?"

"No, sir," she answered.

"Have someone take my bags to my room," he said. "When he comes back, I want to know."

"Yes, sir," Mabel said, and hurried away, thankful to have the initial confrontation over with.

David took the stairs two at a time, then ran down the hallway. The door to her room was standing ajar. He walked inside and went straight to her closet. What he saw made him furious. She hadn't taken a thing. It would be impossible to guess at what she was wearing. Probably something nondescript.

He went through every drawer and every shelf, certain that he'd find letters, notes, suspicious phone numbers. Anything to convince himself that she'd had help. An accomplice . . . maybe even a lover. A rage came upon him, and then everything went dark.

Glass shattered. David blinked and slowly focused as light re-emerged and centered on the mirror across the room. Pie-shaped wedges of glass clung to the frame. A small bronze paperweight lay on the floor beneath.

He stared at it. The last thing he remembered was holding it in his hands.

It's all your fault, you know.

"Moth-err."

If you hadn't been a bad boy, none of this would have happened.

"Dammit, Mother, don't start."

You can't do anything right. I'm sick and tired of paying for your mistakes.

"I fix my own mistakes. I always have."

Not always. Remember?

"Nooooo."

The scream resonated beyond the bedroom, out into the hallway and down the stairwell. A maid crossed herself and shuddered at the eerie shriek before scurrying toward the servants' wing.

The last thing she wanted was to be alone and caught by the boss. Everyone knew what he was like. Everyone knew what he'd do to a young girl . . . if she was willing. And sometimes . . . even if she was not.

"Okay, boys. That's a wrap." The coroner swept the area carefully with his gaze, giving the crime scene one last look. "It's all yours, Dupree."

The coroner wiped sweat with a forearm as he absently peeled the paper-thin latex gloves from his hands and stuffed them into his pockets.

Almost instantly, they began to vacate the area, leaving the vine-covered ravine as quiet and isolated as it had been before the arrival of the police. The only difference was the frame of yellow crime-scene tape marking the boundaries of the incident.

Destiny Dawn's travel dress was nothing like that in which she'd arrived. She'd traded shiny red latex for a black plastic body bag. She would not have been happy. It did nothing for her figure.

Orvis Morrell mopped his forehead with a handkerchief and swiped at a swarm of gnats and flies that had refused to leave the premises along with Destiny Dawn.

"I'm going to question the nearest residents," Dupree said. He tried not to let it, but what he'd said sounded like a warning, and he knew it.

Morrell stared. "Don't let personal feelings get in the way of good police work, boy. You hear me?"

Dupree frowned. "You can't be trying to tell me not to question the Potters. The damned murder took place on their property, for God's sake."

"I know that," Morrell said. "And you heard the coroner. Jane Doe's been dead about two days. That puts it the day of the Fourth of July picnic. Hell, boy. Half the state was here, remember?"

Dupree frowned. Oh yes. He remembered. He remembered walking onto the place and coming unglued at the sight of Amanda running toward him. He remembered seeing stuff that wasn't even there. How in blazes could he forget?

"I know that. I won't overstep any bounds. But I've got to have a starting point." He turned and pointed toward the house. The top floor of the elegant three-story colonial gleamed white above the treetops like frosting on a cake. "That happens to be it."

Morrell nodded. "Let me know if you need extra help. The sooner this one is solved, the better off we'll all be."

Then he shoved his hands in his pants and ambled back through the storm drain, mentally girding himself for the messages he knew would be on his desk. The mayor, the senator, hell, for all he knew, the president would be calling. On that, he'd bet his pension.

Dupree glanced at his watch. It was half-past three. This had taken the better part of a day. His stomach growled. Only then did he remember he hadn't eaten all day. He looked down at the dirt on his hands and back at the place where the woman had been lying and knew he wouldn't be able to eat a bite. Not today. But he could wash. And his throat was so dry, he felt like he could drink forever.

When he exited the drain, he stopped and stared at the view before him. It was as if he'd walked from one dimension into another. Mentally, he knew that to be true. He'd been so focused on the investigation, he hadn't even noticed when Beaner had wandered away. But it was all right. If he needed him, Dupree knew where to look.

Moments later he was in his car and out on the thoroughfare, searching for a gas station. After that, he was going to call on the Potters, and something told him he wouldn't be welcome.

Chuckie Rigola was seething. He'd made calls all day to David Potter's office in D.C. and the piss-ant secretary had refused to put them through. That's when he'd changed his tactics and decided that he'd call his home. He couldn't let this opportunity slide by. Not when he'd already gone this far.

He'd done his research before he sent the tape. He had all the phone numbers he needed to stay in touch with the congressman. He even knew the name of the woman who'd been murdered and where she'd worked.

He dialed and waited, counting the rings. A woman answered, and when he asked to be put through to Potter, she started to refuse.

"Look, lady," he snarled. "It's urgent business. Get Potter on the phone now."

Moments later David Potter answered.

"Hello, buddy. Did you like the movie?" Rigola asked.

David frowned. "If this is a joke, I'm not in the mood," he said. "Is there something I can do for you?"

Rigola frowned. "This is no joke, you jerk. I'm talking about the little video I caught of you and Miss Destiny Dawn, late of Talk of the Town, as well as the ravine behind your little home-on-the-range."

The man chuckled in his ear and David almost dropped the phone. How could he know? The body hadn't even been found . . . had it?

"I didn't get any video," David said. "I don't know what you're talking about. Now, if you'll excuse me, I've got better . . . "

Rigola cursed. "You got it, you asshole! Yesterday! It was signed for by someone named Mabel."

David felt the room sway beneath his feet. Where could it be? He'd come home yesterday and gone through everything on his . . .

Oh shit. He had a flashback of Amanda standing at the doorway when he entered, holding that damned tray in front of her like a shield. The last thing she'd told him when she left was *the mail was on his desk!*

She'd seen it! That was the only explanation! It also explained why she was gone now. What shocked him was the fact that he hadn't already been arrested. If Amanda had the video, what on earth was she planning to do? And then it hit him. She, too, had her own little plans to get some money out of him. That had to be it. He made a decision.

"Look, I believe you," David said quickly, anxious to placate the man until he could formulate a plan. "The problem is . . . I didn't get it."

"Well I did," Rigola said. "I got plenty. Right down to the part where you rolled Destiny Dawn down that ravine and then zipped up your pants."

Oh my God. He did see it. There was no other way he could know a detail like that.

David was sick. Cold sweat broke out on his forehead as he dropped into a chair. He could just hear his mother now. She'd never let him hear the end of this one.

"What do you want?" David asked.

Rigola grinned. "Now we're talking," he said. "I want a million dollars. In mixed, unmarked bills. None of them larger than a fifty. I want it by tomorrow morning. And this is where you drop it."

David made quick notes, realizing as he did that his blackmailer was obviously calling from D.C. since the drop was to take place there. The man ended with a warning.

"I won't call back. I won't renegotiate. This is your only deal. Your final deal. Pay up or read about it in the papers."

"I'll pay. I'll pay," David said. "But I get all the copies. You make sure, or I'll find you. Don't try to screw me. You won't win. I'm the master at that."

Rigola frowned, thinking that he just might be in over his head, and then shook it off. A million dollars. It was worth the risk. He hung up.

David stared at the phone in his hand and tried not to come unglued. But he could hear her voice . . . whining . . . carping . . . just like always. He could never do anything right.

He shook off the mood, picked up the phone, and dialed his banker in Washington D.C. It was after hours, but he knew him well. They had a lot of the same tastes. In fact, if memory served him, his banker had tasted Destiny Dawn, too.

"Marley? This is David. Listen to me. Here's what I need."

He began to talk. When he finished, he poured himself a Scotch and strolled out onto his patio to enjoy the evening sun. That was when he saw the men crawling on their hands and knees at the far edge of the estate.

"Dammit!" He flung the whiskey in the bushes as he dashed back into the house. "Mabel. Get in here!" He looked over his shoulder, unable to believe his own eyes, and then muttered, "And where the hell is that damned bulkhead I hired? These days, it's impossible to get good help."

Mabel scurried into the alcove like a gray mouse. Her radar was on high. The urge to run was uppermost in her mind. He must have discovered her duplicity. Someone must have seen her in the vicinity of the shed that had burned. It was all she could think of.

"What the hell is going on out there?" he asked, pointing to the men in the distance.

Relief swamped her. "Oh that. It's the police, sir. I thought you knew. They're investigating."

His gut kicked, and he frowned. Almost afraid to ask. "Investigating what? The fire? I thought fire marshals did that sort of thing."

"No, sir. They're investigating a murder. Someone found a body down by that storm drain." She folded her hands. "Will that be all, sir?"

All? Hell yes. Isn't that enough?

"Do they know who she is?" he asked.

"I don't know, sir. All I know is . . . someone came to the door and told us they'd be on the premises for a while."

"Fine. Let me know when dinner's ready. I'm starved."

"Yes, sir," Mabel muttered, and left the room before he could think of something else to fuss about.

It was only after she'd returned to the kitchen that she realized what he'd said. How did he know it was a woman's body they'd found? She stopped in mid-step and started to shake. How had he known that?

ELEVEN

The martini was perfect. David popped the olive in his mouth and then winced when the doorbell rang in the middle of the crunch. Moments later Mabel came into the library and finished ruining his aperitif.

"Detective Dupree to see you, sir. He says it's about the murder."

David choked as he tried to swallow. Embarrassed, he pointed toward the martini. "The olive had a pit." Then, more to himself than to Mabel, he began to mutter. "Doesn't the man have any social graces at all? It's the dinner hour. Couldn't it have waited until later?"

"Death waits for no man," Jefferson Dupree said, stepping aside as Mabel hurried out of the room.

David's eyebrows arched. Literary quotes from a homicide detective? He was vaguely surprised. He forced a smile he didn't feel and motioned for Dupree to take a seat.

"Thanks," Dupree said. "Been on my feet all day out in that ravine. Feels good to sit down." He straightened his denim-clad legs as he sat. When he looked down, he noticed dust on the tops of both boots and absently rubbed them, one at a time, on the back of his pants legs.

He grinned when he saw he'd been caught at the motion, then shrugged. He and David Potter were cut from two separate bolts of cloth. It was something Potter would never have thought to do, but Dupree did without thought.

David ignored the man's ingenuous approach, and turned away to refresh his drink, certain that his face showed the turmoil he was feeling.

"May I offer you a martini?" he asked.

"No thanks," Dupree said. "On duty." He settled deeper into his chair.

David's stomach lurched. *Has he come to arrest me?* The detective seemed quite at ease in his clothes, as well as his skin. It crossed David's mind that this big man was probably very attractive to women. He wondered if Amanda thought so. He remembered the man's undue interest in her at the hospital, as well as the day of the shelter's celebration honoring his mother, and wondered if Dupree had helped her get away.

"I suppose you know by now a body was found on your property," Dupree began.

David's pulse skipped. He sipped at his drink and managed a nod. "My housekeeper told me. Such a tragedy for one so young."

Dupree's pen stilled above his paper. He forced his facial expression to be blank, and the tone of his voice lowered a good two octaves. "How did you know her age?"

David flushed and started to stammer. "Well . . . my housekeeper said that a woman had been found. I just assumed that she was young. Am I wrong?"

"No."

It was the way he said it that told David he'd just made a blunder. It was his first. It had to be his last. He decided to take the initiative and get this over with fast. "Look, Detective. I appreciate your job. Really I do. But there's little I can tell you."

"She died the day of the picnic."

The martini sloshed on his hand. David cursed and set the glass down upon the credenza. "There were over five hundred people here that day. I knew less than a quarter of them by face, even less by name. You understand how it is. A politician meets so many."

Dupree grinned. It wasn't a friendly smile. "Right. And after the election, remembers so few."

The flush on the congressman's face told Dupree that he'd scored a point he shouldn't have been making. He forced himself back to the facts. "Just a joke, man," Dupree said. "Okay, you say you don't know this woman. Let me show you her picture, then tell me that again."

David felt bile rising. His left eye twitched as that whine resurrected itself inside his head. *I told you this wasn't going to work!*

"Get it over with," David growled.

Dupree pulled the picture from his pocket. It was a Polaroid, obviously taken when Destiny Dawn was not at her best. He laid it on the desk beside Potter and then watched for a reaction.

Most of the ants had been brushed off her face before the snapshot had been taken. But they'd missed one. It was right in the center of the picture . . . crawling out of Destiny's nose and onto her upper lip. David had a vivid memory of other times . . . and that mouth . . . on his body.

"Oh my God!"

The picture fluttered to the floor at his feet. David leaned over his desk and took several long deep breaths, willing himself not to throw up on the Aubusson. When he could talk, he went on the attack.

"How dare you come in here and show me something so offensive?" He pushed the picture toward the detective with the toe of his shoe and then glared. "No. I don't know that poor unfortunate woman. Now, if you'll excuse me, I have things to attend to."

Dupree bent down and picked up the snapshot. He slipped it into his pocket and gave Potter a cool stare, careful to frame his request so that it was nothing but proper. "I'd like for your wife to look at this, too. It's possible that she might know her."

David flushed. "She can't look. She's not here. And she wouldn't know someone like that. I'm afraid I'll have to ask you to leave."

Dupree's instincts jumped on the description . . . *someone like that.* What was it about Potter that made him keep categorizing a woman he claimed he didn't know?

"I hate to insist," Dupree said softly, though he really didn't, "but I need her to look, as well as the other members of your staff. When will she be back?"

"I don't have any idea," David said, and then took a deep breath. That last answer had sounded too close to a shout. "But you may feel free to speak to all of my staff at any time."

Dupree nodded, but he couldn't get past the fact that Congressman Potter was making a claim that he didn't believe. He'd seen them together. He knew how closely David Potter watched his wife. Something didn't feel right. Out of nowhere, a thought surfaced that made him ask, "By the way, exactly where is your wife?"

Potter fidgeted. He seemed to be considering his choices. Finally, he answered. "Look, Detective . . . I don't know, and that's the truth. If you must know, we've been having some . . . spats. Being in the public eye is a constant strain. She decided to take a trip to clear her head. I'll be hearing from her any day now. When I do . . . I'll pass on your request. Are you satisfied?"

She was gone?

Dupree broke out in a sweat as his world went awry. It took several seconds for him to get himself back in gear. And when he did, he was anything but satisfied.

Having been a fairly successful running back in college, Jefferson Dupree knew when someone was on the defensive. The congressman was running behind a mile-high wall of unwarranted indignation. He had a body on his property he claimed not to know. He had a wife who was missing, who probably had left him. And all he could say was "I don't know."

Dupree had been in the business a long time. He knew liars when he heard them, knew fear when he smelled it, and knew when to make an exit.

"Sorry to intrude," Dupree said. "Have a good evening . . . and enjoy your meal."

He heard Potter gagging as he walked from the room.

Amanda was exhausted. Lack of sleep the night before while she'd been planning and packing was catching up with her. Running away from home was a tiring business.

She glanced at her watch. Almost four in the evening. The afternoon sun was still a persistent presence. Should she take a chance and try to sleep, or should she continue to drive?

While she was considering her answer, the yellow line wavered in front of her car. Before she knew it, she found herself on the wrong side of the road and she skidded to a stop just inches away from a steep embankment.

She was so exhausted, the near-miss didn't even faze her. And no one argued her decision to find somewhere to stop and sleep. It was a heady thing, having the freedom to make a choice as simple as that. Carefully, she pulled back into the correct lane and started searching the small, two-lane highway for signs of civilization.

Steep hills peppered with very tall trees and a variety of underbrush rose on either side of the roadway, leaving little to no shoulder on which to park. Had she found even a rest area, she would have considered pulling off the highway and sleeping in the car. But nothing appeared, and she was forced to drive on.

And then her much-needed oasis appeared as she topped a hill. The small group of buildings was, virtually, in the middle of nowhere. As she drove closer, she realized that it was a kind of truck stop/campground with all the amenities that a weary traveler might desire: a large parking lot complete with trailer hookups, a small diner with a sign that said *EAT HERE,* and a building labeled *LAUNDRY.* This was the first time she'd ever considered that truckers might need such services. She suddenly realized what a skewed and sheltered world she had lived in.

ROOMS FOR RENT. That was the sign she'd been looking for. A closer check revealed that it resembled a "no-tell motel" but at this point, Amanda couldn't afford to be choosy.

She crawled out of her car and stretched. Her legs were stiff, and her feet felt two sizes too big for her shoes. She'd been sitting too long. As she staggered toward the sign marked *OFFICE*, her stomach rumbled.

First she would get her room. Eat, then sleep. After that, back on the run.

With the duffle bag slung over her shoulder, Amanda entered the diner. The smells of cigarette smoke and grease, along with a plethora of other odors she chose not to identify, assailed her. Ignoring the stares of interested customers, she slipped into an empty booth and picked up a menu from behind the napkin holder. The words blurred before her eyes.

"What'll it be?" the waitress asked.

Amanda looked up. Staggered by the amount of hair that had been whipped and sprayed into place upon the waitress's head, she tried not to stare.

"What's already cooked?" she asked, knowing full well she wouldn't be able to stay awake much longer.

"The blue plate special."

"I'll have that," Amanda said, and stuck the menu back behind the napkins. "And lots of tea. Iced tea."

"You got it," the waitress said. "Be right back."

The waitress had seen plenty of road-weary travelers in her day and this little girl fit the bill. She knew when it was prudent not to dawdle.

Moments later, a cold glass of iced tea made a wet trail across the scarred tabletop as the waitress slid it toward Amanda. She caught it on the slide and lifted it to her lips in one smooth motion. When she set it down, it was empty. Silently, the waitress filled it, then smiled and went away. A couple of minutes later she was back with a steaming plate in one hand and a basket of hot rolls in the other.

"One blue plate special," she said. "Dig in, honey. Knock yourself out."

Amanda stared in amazement. If she ate all of this, that just might happen. The plate was piled high with slabs of roast beef, the juice of which oozed enticingly into a volcano of mashed potatoes erupting with brown gravy. Hot rolls, a mound of steaming corn, and the salad of the day accompanied the feast. *What was it that waitress said? Oh yes . . . dig in.*

She picked up her fork and dug.

An hour later, she was standing beneath the showerhead of the musty stall in her bathroom. Blissfully, she ignored the mold and grime that had taken root in the grout between the black and white ceramic tiles, focusing instead on the warm, steady stream of water sluicing across her face and body.

When the water ran cold, she barely managed to dry herself off. The last thing she remembered doing before falling naked onto the bed was to push a chair beneath the doorknob. The single lock and tiny chain stretching from door to facing did little to assure her she would be safe or undisturbed.

In minutes she was asleep, the problem no longer worth worrying about.

The sound of David's voice shrieked in her ear. Amanda jerked in her sleep as she tried to escape from the nightmare. But it was hopeless. Memories of the murder were too fresh and her fear was too deep.

His fingers dug into her shoulder as he yanked her around to face him. She tried to scream, and then found she couldn't even breathe. His hands locked tight around her throat in a repeat performance of what was on the tape. Unable to watch the face of her killer as she died, she closed her eyes and said a prayer for her immortal soul, preparing for her life to end in the same manner as the woman's on the tape.

Fight, Amanda! Do not quit.

She shuddered and jerked, kicking off the hateful images for another much more desired. The familiar voice of her dream lover was back . . . and so welcome. Peace centered within her, dissipating fear. She turned to face the light.

He came toward her. A dark silhouette in the center of brilliance. Running. Arms outstretched.

So great was her relief, that tears slid from the corners of her eyes as she slept.

Amanda. I am coming.

And then he was there. Just as before, she struggled within herself, desperate to touch the intangible, grasp the impossible. And then as she slept, she imagined falling sobbing into his arms.

I am here. I am here. You have no need to be afraid.

That's where you're wrong. Without you, I am always afraid, she thought.

He sighed. His breath was on her cheek, his hands on her body. She opened herself for him to come in. At the moment of joining, her breath actually stopped. And when it began again, it seemed to come from a source other than her own.

Tremors began, from the ends of her toes to the crown of her head. It was as if every molecule in her body moved aside for another set to enter. Two separate hearts began to intermingle, then beat as one. Her limbs became heavy.

Stroke, upon stroke, upon stroke. There wasn't a space on her skin that didn't burn, but from a fire that did no harm. Everything within her needed to hold, to touch, to praise. But sleep's hold kept her mute, and his presence was too strong for her to control.

All around her the air hummed like a tuning fork. Just when she would have gone up in flames, the climax was upon her. Spilling warmth and love, like a dam bursting from overflow.

And then she was one . . . but not alone. Replete from the knowledge that she was loved and beloved, Amanda turned in his arms and fell deeper asleep, secure that David could no longer hurt her. Not even in her dreams.

And the night passed without incident.

The drapery across her window was hanging awry. Three hooks were missing at the place where the two panels met. Sunlight spilled in through the crack and onto Amanda's face as she slept into morning. But it wasn't the sun's warmth that awakened her. It was an urgent voice in her ear.

Get up, Amanda! You must run!

She flew off the bed and yanked on her clothes before she realized she'd been dreaming. But, she told herself as she pulled on her jeans, her instincts hadn't led her wrong yet. Her hands were shaking as she sat down on the bed to tie her tennis shoes. Maybe something more than instinct was at work here. Maybe David *was* close on her trail. Her heart skipped a beat. Maybe he was just outside her door, waiting with a perfect smile in place, and a mind gone crazy.

She didn't take long to pack. It was a simple matter of brushing her hair and shoving toilet articles back in her bag. Holding her breath, she peeked through the curtain, half-expecting to see Serge's face looking back. No one was there.

Laughing nervously at her own imagination, she tossed the room key on the unmade bed and headed for her car. Within the space of fifteen minutes, she'd refueled the car, bought breakfast to go, and was on the road, unaware that her fears were a little too close to the truth.

At the moment she took the first bite of her sausage and biscuit sandwich, Serge was in a phone booth across from the place where she'd rented her car, making a report to his boss, who had just landed in D.C.

"She took a bus out of town and rode all the way to Crawley before renting a car," Serge said.

"Sonofabitch!" That was more than a hundred miles south of Morgantown. There was no telling where she'd gone from there.

Suddenly realizing that he'd shouted, David flushed and looked around, praying that no one had noticed. At this point, being paged in an airport was risky. Receiving news like this only added to his frustration.

"So follow her," he ordered.

Serge rolled his eyes, allowing himself that little freedom, simply because he was alone. "Follow her where, sir? I don't know which direction she went from here. There are seven roads leading out of this town that fork off into a variety of directions."

"Dammit to hell . . . hire help!"

"Yes, sir."

This time someone did hear him. A woman frowned at David as she passed, dragging a small child by the hand. David shrugged, giving her his best charming smile, and turned his back to the throng of people circulating inside the airport. He took a deep breath.

"Get them on the trail, and then I need you to go home and keep an eye on things there," he went on. "Wait for my call."

"Yes, sir."

"And Serge . . . "

"Yes, sir?"

"If anything . . . shall we say . . . unusual happens at home, I want to be notified immediately. Do you understand?"

Serge got the message. It was the only kind he ever heard.

"I understand."

After hanging up, David left the airport for his meeting with Marley. The money had to be ready. He didn't have time for delays.

He gave his cabby the address, then leaned back and smiled. Oh, he'd pay the money. He had no choice. It would be all over the papers if he didn't. Of that he had no doubt. He grinned again. So much for newsmen and their deadlines. His blackmailer had a deadline of his own. He just didn't know it.

*   *   *

"Mail, Dupree. You got some mail."

A female officer waved the package beneath Jefferson Dupree's nose.

"It's about time," he said, looking at his watch to emphasize his statement. "It's past noon. What have you been doing with it, steaming it open before you pass it out?"

Officer Travillo grinned and fluffed at her hair. It was a wasted motion. Her hair was slick and tight, pulled back into a neat, professional bun at the back of her head. She fingered the package like a child testing presents, even shaking it once to make her point.

"This feels like a video. Hey, Dupree. Are you into watching porno now?" She leaned forward teasingly. "You good-lookin' hunk, if you were into that, you shoulda' called. I get the wants myself now and then."

Dupree snatched the package from the officer's hands and grinned. "I'll tell Barney you said so."

She grinned. Barney was the sergeant on duty. He was also her husband. And she was the office clown.

Dupree leaned back in his chair as he opened the envelope. Just as she'd predicted. A video. He shook the envelope and then dug inside, expecting a written explanation, but nothing came out. There was only one way to solve this problem.

"Hey, Chief," he called. "Does that VCR in your office still work?"

Morrell grinned as he poured himself a fresh cup of coffee. "If we're watching movies, I want some popcorn. Anyone got any popcorn?"

Dupree ignored the catcalls as he walked into the chief's office and turned on the TV and VCR. Whistling absently beneath his breath, he started to slide the video-cassette into the slot when he noticed that it needed to be rewound. He picked up the remote and punched the proper button before pulling up a chair.

"Cheap seats," he said as he straddled a chair, then leaned forward, using the back of the chair for a chin rest.

"Let 'er roll," Morrell said, and took a sip of coffee.

The rewind sequence had ended. Dupree pressed *Play*.

When the voice came on instead of a picture, Dupree began to make notes. By the time the scene began to unfold, he had a knot in his stomach. When it ended, he felt as if he needed to throw up. With his eyes closed against the ugliness of what he'd seen, he leaned his forehead against the back of the chair and began to curse.

"Where the hell did this come from?" Morrell asked when he could talk.

"The mail," Dupree said, and bolted for his desk to take another look at the envelope it had come in. He slipped it into a plastic bag. It was now a piece of evidence that would indict David Potter for murder.

There were no other clues except the video itself. As his mind raced, he kept trying to breathe. But terror had set in . . . in a big way. The woman on the phone. Her voice had seemed familiar. After the arrival of this video, his instincts were screaming *Amanda Potter*.

When she'd seen this tape, she must have been terrified . . . as terrified as the woman on the phone had sounded. And then he thought of something else and started to sweat as the date on the postmark also became a factor.

"Oh, Jesus. It came in the mail."

Morrell couldn't figure out what was going on. All he could see was that his detective was losing it.

"What the hell's wrong with you?" Morrell asked.

Dupree started to pace the floor, mentally counting backward from today to the postmark, taking into consideration the length of time it would take to go through the local postal system. At the earliest, it would have been mailed the same day he got that frantic phone call from an unidentified woman. But where was she now? What had happened to her while this was en route?

"Okay, let's look at the facts," he muttered.

"That's always good," Morrell said, and got a glare for his comment.

"The fact that the video hadn't been rewound when we got it tells me several things," Dupree said.

"Such as?" Morrell asked.

"One. Someone viewed this. And . . . even if they'd been scared out of their wits by it, they probably would still have rewound it." His eyes glittered with frustration and fear. "Unless . . . they were interrupted. This would explain why we got it in the mail in this condition. If Amanda Potter saw it and was the one who panicked and mailed it in, this would also explain why she was gone. She would be running away from her husband before she was next."

"Look," Morrell began. "Get a warrant for Potter's arrest. Do it now. And when you find Amanda Potter, I want to talk to her. I need to know if she's guilty in any way."

Dupree went still. The look on his face was feral as he remembered something else. "Potter said they'd had a fight."

"Shit," Morrell said, and set his cup on the desk. "This puts a whole new light on things. If she saw this . . . and Potter knows it . . . then it's just possible she'll turn up dead, too."

"Like hell," Dupree said, and stalked from the room.

"Where are you going?" Morrell shouted.

"To get that goddamned warrant like you ordered. And after the sonofabitch is picked up . . . I'm going to find my Amanda."

Morrell went pale, and then flushed. "You fool! She's not yours. And there's no guarantee that she's not involved in some way."

"She's involved all right," Dupree said. "How the hell else do you think that got here?" He pointed toward the VCR and the video they'd watched.

"How can you be so certain that *she* sent it?"

Because my heart tells me so. "Instinct."

"Why didn't she just bring it down here herself?" Morrell argued.

By this time, their argument had reached shouting proportions. Some of the detectives tried to ignore it. Others stopped to watch.

"Why? I don't know why," Dupree yelled. "Maybe it was for the same reason she kept getting treated at the hospital for falling down a flight of stairs, when we both know she got the hell beat out of her and no one helped her, including me. Or maybe it was because when someone actually tried to intervene on her behalf, others told them to mind their own business," he added, referring to the day the chief had told him to butt out. "Hell. Maybe she doesn't know who to trust. I don't know! But when I find her . . . I'll tell her you asked."

Guilt overwhelmed Morrell. He got the message loud and clear, along with everyone else in the department. What Dupree accused him of hurt. What was worse, it was true. More than once, he'd suspected Amanda Potter was being abused. And like everyone else, he'd done nothing, said nothing.

He took the video out of the machine and bagged it as evidence. If she was dead, he wouldn't be able to live with himself.

Chuckie Rigola was as jumpy as an addict watching someone else get a much-needed fix. With one eye on the traffic at the busy D.C. newsstand, and the other on the constant ebb and flow of cars pulling up to it, he was about to lose his cool. The more he thought about what he was doing, the worse he got.

All of his life, he'd tried to do the right thing, and look where it had gotten him. He was nothing but a down-and-out stringer for a trade rag that had a reputation as sorry as that woman who'd been murdered.

But all of that would change when he got his money. He'd go straight. He'd give to charity. He'd visit his mother more. He'd be able to set up his own printing business and not be looked down upon by every journalist he knew.

He was so busy justifying his actions to himself, he almost missed the congressman's arrival. And when he noticed the tall blond man and the casual yet elegant cut of his clothes, he knew that the moment was at hand.

Chuck hitched up his pants, readjusted his slouch hat, grabbed his suitcase, and headed for the newsstand.

"Afternoon, Emory," David said. He set his suitcase down at his side and handed the newsboy a ten dollar bill. "*Playboy*, please . . . and keep the change."

David tore off the plastic and began to browse, waiting anxiously for the blackmailer to show. A minute passed. And in that time, he became so engrossed in his magazine that he almost forgot why he was there.

"*Wall Street Journal*, please." Chuck set down his suitcase and dug around in his pocket for the money to pay.

David went still. It was the prearranged code he'd been waiting to hear. Realizing that the man had come when he wasn't watching, he instantly thought of his money and glanced down. Now there were two identical suitcases, sitting side by side. He knew what was in his. What he wanted had to be in the blackmailer's bag. He started to turn.

"Hunh uh," the man warned softly. "Don't turn around."

David froze, his gaze pinned on the centerfold and the dark delta between the woman's legs.

"Just keep reading," Chuck added. "We're gonna do a little trade . . . and then you can be on your way."

"You asshole," David hissed.

"No . . . you're the asshole," Chuck said, and picked up the other suitcase. "I didn't kill. I didn't lie."

He ducked behind the newsstand and darted through traffic. When he realized that he'd made it across the street and inside his car without being shot in the back, he began to laugh.

"I did it! I did it!" he shouted.

Gleefully, he started the car and pulled into traffic,

accidentally taking a street that led toward the White House, instead of the one that led out of the area.

Before David could think of a suitable reply, he found himself alone. He grabbed the remaining suitcase and all but ran to a nearby bench. His hands were shaking as the latch popped. Holding his breath, he opened the lid and then looked inside. He laid his *Playboy* inside on top of the cassettes and began to grin.

Only then did he venture a glance in the direction he thought the blackmailer had gone. And while nothing and no one obvious caught his eye, he knew locating the little scumbag was not a problem.

Glancing down at his watch, he began to count. When the second hand had counted out thirty seconds, David stuck his hand in his pocket. The remote was small and cool in his hand as he stood. With the suitcase in one hand, his other hand in his pocket, he began to walk toward the curb.

"Taxi!" he called. When a yellow cab streaked toward him, he rubbed the button on the remote, fantasizing that it was something else, and pressed.

The climax came as an explosion rocked the ground on which they stood. Everyone in the area, including David, instinctively ducked. There was instant hysteria and a few moments later, the wailing of sirens as they began to close on the column of smoke now visible above the trees.

"My word," David muttered, and helped a woman to her feet. "What on earth do you suppose happened?"

The woman crossed herself and then glanced across the greens toward the smoke.

"Oh God. Right in the middle of rush hour!" She clasped a hand to her throat. "Just like the New York Trade Center bombing. We're very close to the White House, you know."

David didn't answer. There was no need. The rumors had already started. He got into his taxi. Destination: penthouse.

*   *   *

Dupree knocked on the door to the Potter mansion. He, along with a squad of officers, was ready to place David Potter under arrest. The warrant in his pocket was a crisp reminder that when they had to, the wheels of justice could turn swiftly.

Mabel answered.

"I need to speak with David Potter," Dupree said.

Mabel's eyes grew round. She could tell by the assortment of men behind him that this wasn't a social call.

Her voice rose two octaves and began to quiver. "He isn't here," she said.

"Is something wrong?" Serge stepped forward and braced himself against the doorway with one arm, confident that his bulk alone would make entry impossible.

Dupree frowned at the appearance of the bruiser who had all but pushed the housekeeper aside. *Aha! Hired muscle. Now we're getting somewhere,* he thought.

"I'm Detective Dupree, of the Morgantown Police. I need to speak with Mr. Potter."

"Identification, please," Serge said, and waited patiently while Dupree dug out his shield and showed it to him. "As Mabel says . . . Mr. Potter isn't here," he added.

"We have reason to believe that he is," Dupree said. "All his cars are in the garage."

"He doesn't care to drive himself. I believe he's in D.C. at this moment."

"Would you mind if we came in and looked around . . . just in case you've been mistaken?" Dupree asked. It wasn't much of a request, it was more of an order, and both men knew it.

"Do you have a warrant?" Serge asked.

Dupree grinned. Somehow it didn't surprise him that this man knew all the right questions to ask.

"Actually, I do." He presented it for inspection as well.

"This isn't a search warrant. This is a . . . "

"Right," Dupree said. "It's a warrant for his arrest. Now please, step aside."

Serge did as he was told. "If you do not need me further . . . I will be at the garage, washing the cars," he added, and strolled out the front door as if he owned the place while the officers swarmed the premises.

One by one, the officers slipped inside the mansion and began to make their way throughout, doing a room-by-room sweep in order to ascertain that the man in question was actually gone.

Dupree headed for the library with Mabel at his heels.

Once inside the garage, Serge headed for the phone. In his estimation this would qualify as the "something unusual" that his employer had wanted to be notified of.

In a state of sexual arousal, David answered. Moments later the woman on his lap slid to the floor as the smile on his face fell.

"Get out," he said.

She didn't have to hear it twice. Within three minutes she was dressed and on her way down the hotel elevator.

David closed his eyes and tried to concentrate. He couldn't hear what Serge was saying for his mother's shouts and screams inside his head. If she would only shut up . . . he could fix this. He could fix anything. He was a Potter.

And then a light dawned, and his smile slid back into place. He began to speak.

"I will be out of here within five minutes. Wear your beeper at all times. I will call you when I've relocated. When you return my calls, either go to a pay phone, or use one of the car phones. They might put a trace on the phones at the house."

Serge listened and did as he was told. But all the while he kept thinking, wouldn't it be a wiser move on Potter's part to just get out of the country while he could, instead of trying to get even with his wife?

Meanwhile, unaware that David Potter had been warned of the pending arrest warrant, Dupree, along with the squad of officers, continued to search, room by room, floor by floor. And every step they took, a matching set of tears rolled down the elderly housekeeper's face. By the time they started a search of the second floor down the bedroom wing, she was in full flow.

Dupree stopped and took her gently by the arm. "Ma'am, if this is too painful for you, you don't have to accompany me," he said. He felt sorry for her. The few times he'd been here, she'd been genuinely friendly to him.

"It's not that," Mabel said, and began to sob. "I'm just so upset. This is all quite distressing. Could you tell me why Mr. Potter is being arrested? If it's not a secret . . . that is?"

"It's no secret, ma'am. He's being arrested for the murder of the woman who was killed on these premises."

She sobbed even louder. "Oh Lord. It could as easily have been my Missy."

Dupree went cold. He knew that she meant Amanda.

"Is there something you're not telling me?" he asked.

She mopped at her tears and shook her head as she stepped aside for him to continue.

Dupree frowned, for the moment willing to let her comment slide. He started inside the next room and then stopped and stood in the doorway, staring mutely at the king-size bed while his belly did a flip-flop and his conscience reminded him that what he was thinking was still none of his personal concern.

"This is the master bedroom," Mabel said and blew her nose loudly.

Dupree nodded, and made for the closets. He opened the doors and then stared. Something wasn't right.

"There are no women's clothes in here," he said. "Did Amanda take everything with her when she left?"

"Oh no!" Mabel gasped, and fluttered toward the doorway, mopping her eyes and blowing her nose with every step. "She didn't sleep in here. Not anymore. One day she just up and announced she wanted her stuff moved. Guess she'd had enough," she added beneath her breath.

But Dupree heard her last comment. His heart skittered.

He wasn't sure how he felt about what he'd learned, but he thought the emotion was elation.

"Show me her room," he ordered.

Moments later, they were at the end of the hall. Just as they started inside, Dupree noticed something above the doorknob and frowned. He ran his finger along the wood, testing the holes that had yet to be filled, and the scratches along the facing on the other side.

"Something's been removed," he said.

"It was a lock," Mabel said without thinking. The moment it came out, she realized what conclusion he would draw. She'd been right. The look on his face made her tears start all over again.

"She was locked in her room?" Horror filled him. He remembered thinking she'd been one of the beautiful people, with a beautiful life. He couldn't have been more wrong.

Mabel sobbed harder. "You just don't understand. There wasn't anything *we* could do. Every time someone tried to help her, something bad happened to them. Something bad, I say."

"Jesus Christ!" he growled. "Was she even fed? Did you people care for her at all?" His voice raised two octaves as shock began to set in.

He didn't wait to hear the housekeeper's answer. If he had, he wouldn't have believed it. He walked inside the room, expecting to see a chamber of horrors. Instead, he saw a small, nondescript room with a single bed. And at the same instant, the room began to spin. A darkness settled within him. If he dared, he could have closed his eyes and felt the hopelessness with which she'd lived.

"She didn't take anything with her," Mabel said. "She left almost everything behind."

Even her despair, Dupree thought. He could feel it.

"Oh my," Mabel gasped. "The mirror is broken. I didn't know. I'll get someone up to fix it."

"A hell of a lot more than a mirror is broken around here," Dupree said, and stomped from the room.

Moments later, the police were gone, satisfied that David Potter was not on the premises. An APB was put out for his arrest, as well as one for Amanda, as a possible material witness.

Dupree went back to the office to digest what he had learned. Most of it boiled down to the fact that the woman he'd somehow come to love, even without knowing her, probably hated men with an undying passion. She'd suffered horror at the hands of a man who'd sworn to honor and love her. She'd been let down by those around her. He felt sick. Even if he found her, what he'd dreamed of would never be. How could he possibly make such a woman love him?

TWELVE

❁

Amanda adjusted the radio as she drove, frowning, then shaking her head in disbelief as a bulletin came on the air. A bombing had just occurred in the nation's capital near the White House, giving rise to the supposition that it was the latest in a rash of terrorist attacks throughout the country.

"There's too much death in this world," she muttered, and then would have laughed at her ridiculous remark, had it not been so painful. She was on the run because of death. And her horror was more complete due to it having been committed by her own husband's hands.

As she drove, she prayed, checking every station on the hour, hoping that the next time she tuned in, she would hear that a prominent member of Congress had been arrested for murder. Then she would be safe. Only then could she return home.

But there was no news of an arrest. Her hopes sank. Had she been that wrong about Dupree? She didn't want to believe it. If he didn't come through for her, David was going to get away with murder.

The midday sun was on the wane when she entered a particularly steep patch of roadway. Halfway up the second hill, the car sputtered, hacked, and died.

The suddenness with which her escape stalled was unexpected. She guided the rental car onto a narrow shoulder of the road and then tried to restart it. Over and over. Nothing happened. The little engine didn't even make an effort.

"Oh no." Her voice was tinged with despair. She doubled her fists and hit the steering wheel in helpless fury. And as she did, panic surfaced.

This just figured. Here she was, in the middle of nowhere with a murderer at her heels. She stared down at the gauges in defeat. Little lights blinked back at her from the dashboard. Red lights. Yellow lights. The colors were symbolic of the way she'd gone through life. Red light. Stop! Yellow light. Warning! She felt as if the car itself was trying to predict her future.

She checked her map, then checked again, hoping to find that she'd miscalculated distance. She hadn't. The best she could figure, there was help twenty miles back, or fifteen miles ahead.

And then she remembered the way in which she'd awakened this morning, hearing the voice that made her jump out of bed.

He'd told her to run, so she had. But now it would seem she was down to a walk. Without further hesitation, Amanda began to gather her belongings.

After stuffing all of the food she had left in her bag, she got out of the car and locked it. Step by step, she went up the hill without looking back. There was no need. She'd looked over her shoulder for the last time. Either she got away, or she didn't. The decision seemed to be out of her hands.

For over thirty minutes no vehicle approached her or passed her by. Her frustration at being alone and stranded changed to relief as she suddenly heard the sound of an engine some distance behind her, and coming at a high rate of speed.

"Finally," she muttered, and stepped to the side of the road, absently wondering which thumb one used when hitching a ride.

She never knew what made her do it. Later, she would

remember thinking that it felt as if she'd been pushed. But when she raised her nose from the dirt to see the car streaking past, she was looking out at the highway from within the forest at the edge. She'd jumped!

"For Pete's sake," Amanda said, and pounded her fists angrily in the dirt, and then started to crawl out from beneath the undergrowth. Why on earth had she done that? Now she was still stranded, and it would be dark soon.

Her stomach growled. Well, she told herself, since she was sitting down, now seemed as good a time as any to take advantage of the snacks that she'd bought.

Unable to consider anything except the moment at hand, she dug in her pack and pulled out an apple. Two bites later, she nervously eyed the dense Appalachian woods behind her, wondering what unknown beast might lurk within.

And then another sort of beast resurfaced, and Amanda found herself back beneath the underbrush, watching with her heart in her mouth as a car came by, but from the opposite direction in which she'd been walking, and at a much slower rate of speed.

"Oh my God," she muttered, and dropped her apple in the dirt as she peered through the leaves beneath which she lay. It was the same car!

The two men inside seemed to be searching the roadside as well as the forest. *For what?* And then it hit her. *For me! Oh God! David found my car. He knows I'm on foot.*

There were other explanations for what just happened. But instinct for survival, and her knowledge of the extent of David's power, told her she was right. The second the car went over the hill and out of sight, Amanda jumped up and began to run. Away from the road. Deeper into the forest. More lost than she'd been before.

The mechanic pulled into the storage and rental units. He idled his truck slowly down the alley until his passenger pointed to a particular unit. Brake lights went on. The engine died. His passenger exited the truck with a mincing step. The handbag at her elbow rocked with every motion of her body. Her mouth made a mauve moue as she looked down. The street was wet.

"It just can't be helped," she said, readjusting her coiffure, and hurried toward the unit, trying to ignore the puddles she was forced to cross.

As she walked, her sturdy, sensible shoes made little splat, splat sounds and scattered pin-dots of water along the edge of her no-nonsense slacks and matching button-down shirt.

She reached the door with a satisfied smile, swung her handbag across her belly, and began digging within its depths until she found what she'd been searching for. Seconds later the key to the rental unit was in the lock. It turned with little fuss.

The overhead door slid up in a series of jerks and squeaks, and when the contents were revealed, she smiled in perfect satisfaction and dusted off her hands.

"There. Just as I told you. It's as good as new. Now . . . if this nice man will just make it go, we'll be on our way."

The mechanic eyed his passenger and fought the urge to spit. It was a free country. He supposed it took all kinds to populate it. But he'd be damned if he could see the reason for one like this. Besides the fact that the man—he was sure it was a man in women's clothing—was a little light in the britches, he was wearing one of the lamest wigs he'd ever seen. It was his personal opinion that the sucker was crazy, because he'd been talking to himself nonstop since the ride had begun.

"Got the battery right here," the mechanic said, and went about the business for which he'd been hired.

"And the gasoline. We'll need gasoline. My little go-mobile won't run without fuel, will it, darling?"

The mechanic froze. For a moment he thought the guy had been talking to him. Battery or not, he wasn't going anywhere near that building with a man who called him darling. But the more he thought about it, the more he decided that the nut was still talking to himself. Careful to give himself plenty of running room should it be necessary, the mechanic got out his tools and set to work.

A short time later, he was two hundred dollars to the good as the go-mobile/motor home pulled out of the rental unit and onto the highway with the bewigged man behind the wheel, still talking to no one but himelf. The mechanic shuddered. Self-preservation told him that might have been a very close call.

The motor home was like a dinosaur on the freeway. Its lumbering maneuvers caused a trucker to lay on his horn as he quickly changed lanes to avert a collision.

The sound of the horn caused David to swerve. Careful of the traffic both in front and behind, he slowly inched his way back into the slow lane and then glanced up in the rearview mirror and frowned.

"What are you doing here?" he asked, and yanked the wig off of his head and tossed it onto the floor without considering the oddity of his reaction to his own reflection.

Someone had to get you out of the city safely. Who else but your mother?

"Well, I'm out," he said. "And I wish to hell you'd stay where you belong."

I am where I belong, my darling. With you. Forever.

David took some tissues from the glove box and began to wipe his mouth. Lipstick came away in his hands, leaving thick, mauve swaths across the delicate paper. When he could no longer taste his mother upon his person, he tossed the tissues behind him. They fell unheeded upon the wig he'd already abandoned. Unfortunately for David Potter, he could not get rid of his mother so easily.

He drove south toward the town where Amanda had rented the car. But it was only a starting point. She could be anywhere by now. He remembered Serge and wondered how far the search for Amanda had developed. With one eye on the traffic, he carefully dug into the handbag on the seat beside him until he found his portable phone, then dialed the pager number, left a message, and waited.

A few minutes later, the phone rang. After a short conversation, David began to smile.

"Perfect," he said. "You've done well, Serge. Now get the men that I asked for . . . and dogs as well. I want her found before nightfall. Do you hear me? Before I leave the country, she will pay for what she's done."

He disconnected the call and made an adjustment in his direction of travel. He no longer needed a starting point. Instead he was already mentally planning his reunion with his wife. He should have her in his hands before morning. And when he did, she would pay. After all, this was all her fault.

A hound bayed and then moments later another joined in. An eerie, bugled warning to their prey that trail had been struck.

Amanda rolled over and then sat straight up, staring around the darkened woods in sleepy confusion. For a second she couldn't place where she was or how she'd gotten there. And then she remembered and shuddered. But not from the moonless night or the chill. It was the dogs that made her bolt to her feet.

Once, right after she and David had been married, they'd visited some shirt-tail royalty in England and been invited to ride to hounds. She could still remember the sound of the dog pack as they struck the fox's trail. And the sound they'd made when he'd been found. It was this same sound she was hearing now.

While she knew full well that running hounds was a popular pastime in parts of West Virginia, instinct told her that tonight they were after bigger game.

Her!

And while it was instinct that warned her, it was self-preservation that made her run. Up the mountain. Away from the dogs and the men who would be following them.

She ran. Onward. Upward. And fear became a constant companion, because no matter how fast she moved through the trees, it was evident that the people behind her were closing the gap.

The hounds' mournful howls were louder. And she could now hear the sounds of men's voices. Urging on the hounds. Shouting her name.

Her legs shook. The duffle bag she was carrying bounced against her rib cage, alternating its impact with those of her feet hitting earth. Breath came in harsh gasps that burned up her throat and out through her mouth and nose. Moisture ran from her hairline down into the collar of her shirt. Part of it sweat. Part of it blood. The low-hanging tree limbs and dense undergrowth had done their part in hindering her escape.

"AAA . . . MAN . . . DA."

David's voice, and the sound of her name on his lips startled her. Knowing her enemies were close enough that she could discern not only her name, but who was calling it, lent a fresh burst of speed to her flight. And yet as swiftly as she was moving, she knew it wouldn't last long. Her strength was almost gone.

Oh God! Oh God! I need help. I cannot do this alone.

A few hundred yards behind her a hound suddenly bayed. A sure sign that he'd marked prey and was nearing attack. Amanda's breath caught on a sob as a sharp pain beneath her rib cage sent her staggering . . . staggering into the man who stepped out of the trees in front of her.

Before she could adjust her headlong flight or think to scream, his arm snaked out and slid around her neck, pulling her upright and then against his broad bare chest with a sharp, unsettling jolt. Just when she thought it was over, he grabbed her by the wrist and pulled her even closer, pressing his mouth against her ear. It was a rough whisper. A warning and at the same time, a deliverance.

"Do not be afraid, my Amanda. I have come for you. Now run!"

Within the space of a millisecond, she knew the voice,

the touch, even the whisper of his long hair that moved across her face as he gave the urgent warning, and knew that it had finally happened. She was either mad . . . or already dead. Either way, it no longer mattered. Because the man's voice . . . and his touch . . . were as familiar to her as her own face.

Suddenly she found herself flying through the air, her feet barely touching the ground as he led her in a full-out run. Somehow dodging trees she would have run full tilt into. Moving in a certain path when she would have blundered along in wild, panicked flight. Silently but surely. And just when she thought her legs could no longer move, the fleeing couple went from the faint light of the moonless night into a darkness that was so sudden and so dense it felt thick.

Amanda gasped in shock. Although he still held her arm and continued to move along some path, she automatically extended her arm before her as a blind woman might. She was feeling her way through the darkness, unable to completely trust the man's hold . . . or her sanity. Any moment now she expected him to disappear as quickly as he had before. And when he did, she knew she would be face to face with her devil. With David and his hounds from hell.

And then he stopped. Suddenly. Unexpectedly. She walked into his back and grunted from surprise rather than pain. She heard the shuffle of his feet as he turned toward her, then lifted the bag from her neck. It fell to the ground with a soft plop.

"My bag!" she cried. "It has all my things in it."

She felt his hand slide across her shoulder and then cup her cheek. "It has nothing you need," he said softly. "Come. Follow me."

Once more, without question or remark, she did as she was told. The sound of his hand sliding along rock told her that he must be searching for an entrance . . . or an exit to something. Expecting it to be another cave, she was unprepared for the place that they entered.

It was a vacuum where no air, sound, or substance existed. Amanda froze and prepared to die. The pressure upon her body was vast. A loud humming penetrated her skin clear through to her bones. Then she felt his hand tightening around her wrist, heard him grunt, as if from great effort, and felt herself being yanked from here to there.

Where darkness had abounded, there was now only light. Full, broad sunlight. And trees. And birds. And clouds scattering across a sky so blue it made her eyes hurt. Instinctively, her hands flew to her face, because after the darkness, the light was too bright to bear.

There behind the safety of her own hands, she began to calm. Her heart rate went down to just below the level of a full-blown attack. And her breathing, and his, were softening with each drag of air through their lungs.

She remembered thinking that if this was still a dream, she never wanted to awaken. Slowly, slowly, she let her fingers part. Let in light . . . and the sight of his face. A little at a time.

She wasn't prepared for it. Or him. Her hands fell limply to her sides. Her lips went slack as her pupils blossomed, widening in green confusion.

"Who . . . what . . . are you?"

"It is I, Amanda. You called for me, and I came."

Her eyes rolled back in her head. The last thing she saw was the blue sky above her, and his dark visage as he leaned over her. Fate was kind. She fainted.

"Sonofabitch! What the hell's wrong with those dogs?"

David was in rare fury. The hounds had been just ahead of them, running full out, their noses to the ground, their tails a flag of their flight, when they'd stopped. Just like that. Without warning. As if they'd run into a brick wall.

The hounds whined, a high-pitched wail of fear, then rolled on the ground and bared their bellies in an act of subjugation. Before the hunter could stop his dogs, they leaped up and ran back down the mountain the way that they'd come.

"Aw, hell," the hunter said, and started scratching his head and looking nervously around, suddenly aware that maybe they should be the ones on the run. "I ain't never seen them act like that before. It was like they'd done seen a ghost."

"There's no such thing as a ghost. Just dumb dogs," David shouted, and fired his gun in the air two or three times to emphasize his point.

Serge frowned. His boss was out of control. He'd just announced their presence to anyone who happened to be within hearing of gunshots. It was an extremely stupid thing for a man on the run to do. Serge fully understood the desire for revenge. Most of his previous employers had, at one time or another, acted upon it themselves. But this man was wanted for a murder. He should be hiding, or running. Not chasing away in the darkness up the side of a mountain and shooting off his mouth as often as he shot off his gun.

The hunter nervously peered around again, and then made his decision.

"I gotta go get my dogs," he said, and quickly disappeared through the trees.

Serge quickly added his opinion to the pot. "Boss, I think we should leave. It will be morning soon."

"Good," David said. "Light will make it easier to track her."

Serge considered the answer and knew that it was now time for him to make a decision of his own. Did he stay with the man who paid him? Or did he get out before he became implicated in a murder that for once he hadn't committed? He considered the odds.

"Amanda! You can't get away from me. I'll kill you first!" David shouted, and fired his gun into the air until it clicked on empty chambers.

Serge sighed. The odds had just shifted against David Potter. "Are you coming, boss?" he asked.

"No! In fact, hell, no!" David shouted, ejecting the empty clip onto the ground, and fumbling inside his jacket pocket for a fresh one.

David's only warning was a snapping twig. He swung around, pointing his empty gun at the place where Serge had been standing. There was no one there.

"Serge!"

His shout echoed up and down the mountain with no answer.

"You sniveling coward! Come back! Come back, dammit! You can't leave me up here alone on this mountain. I own you."

You're not alone, David. You still have me. You will always have me.

David shut his eyes against the sound of her voice and still she came, persistently, constantly, resurrecting herself.

"Dammit, Mother, I don't need you," David cried, and dropped to his knees on the ground. "I can fix this myself." He moaned beneath his breath, then wrapped his arms around himself and began to rock. "I'm a big boy. I'm a real big boy."

Nokose sighed as he lifted Amanda from the ground and into his arms. Her reaction was to be expected. And yet he'd felt strangely betrayed by her shock. Pained by the fear that he'd seen in her eyes. How could she doubt so when they'd been as one?

He shifted her gently, wincing at the mass of tiny scratches upon her delicate skin, and the faint outline of bruising beneath her eyes. She had suffered so much. And he'd almost been too late.

He lifted his head and looked carefully about the clearing, his gaze clear but sharp, constantly searching the depth of trees through which they must go before he would have her home . . . and safe.

A thunder of guns rumbled, like storm clouds building on the horizon. Nokose frowned, remembering a time in his land when the few strangers who'd come had come without thought of overtaking or changing those who were already here. Who'd come simply to become lost in the greatness of the land he called home.

But now British were here. Their red coats and noisy, metal accoutrements were a constant display of garishness against the spartan lives of those who lived within the land's harshness, as well as its abundance. And on their heels, the French. They waged a war, trying to prove who owned what, when Nokose, like all his Indian brothers, felt it was a dangerous but foolish white man's game. Land belonged to no one . . . and everyone.

He thought of his mother's people, the Muskogee, who were far to the south, and wondered if it had been wise to stay here after his father, Jacques LeClerc, had died. Wondered if he should have gone back to the creek banks of the Chattahoochee, far beyond the sound of guns . . . and strangers in stiff clothing . . . who did not know how to bend with the land. Who tried to make it bend to their will, instead.

And yet he knew that when he'd had his vision of Amanda, leaving had no longer been an option. Creating the Dreamcatcher had been his way to forge their link. With its completion, the waiting for her arrival began.

The rumble came again, from far beyond the mountains. But it was not a natural storm that was approaching. The turmoil within the continent was just past simmer and about to boil over. Within the year, a British officer named Braddock would lead his men to fight against battlefield tactics he did not understand. Fort Duquesne, and the French who manned it, along with their Indian allies, would become his nemesis and ultimately render his defeat.

Nokose's nostrils flared as he sniffed the air. He watched. And he waited. And when he was certain he could move about freely within the forest, he walked away with Amanda in his arms.

By the time he got to the clearing surrounding his

father's house, he knew every nuance of Amanda's face. From the curve of her chin, to the tilt of her nose. The way her generously curved lips tilted up, even in sleep. The shadows her long, thick eyelashes left on her cheeks. The way she molded her body against his as if she'd been carved to fit him.

It was with great regret that he entered his father's cabin and laid her gently down upon the bed of furs in the corner. He would have willingly held her for the rest of his life, so great was his love for this stranger who'd just entered his world.

She stirred, then winced. Even in a semiconscious state, she suffered. Nokose stared intently at her odd garments, wondering how to divest her of them, for they were muddy, and bloody, and he needed to tend to her wounds.

Then before his eyes, she inhaled deeply, and a button that had been straining the fabric across her breast suddenly slipped through its hole. Even in sleep, she'd shown him the way.

With a tender touch and a shaking hand, he leaned over her and went to work. And when he was through, she lay naked upon the skin of the bear that had given him his name. As he gazed upon her beauty, a rage began to burn in him. Everywhere he looked, the mark of another man was upon her body. Yet they were not the marks of love. They were the marks of a beast.

A small scar followed the curve of her left knee, and another the inside of her right thigh. And she was almost too thin. Only the fullness of her breasts gave her substance.

His fingers traced the curve of her rib cage and counted more than four separate places where ribs had been broken and healed. The tiny knots were not visible to the eye, only to the touch . . . and to his soul.

Nokose's eyes narrowed. Amber fire glittered beneath his hooded lids as his mouth thinned and his heart hammered against his chest like a war drum. He stood upright with a jerk, unable to face the extent of his woman's suffering, and made for the shelf in the corner where small bags and pots held an assortment of healing herbs. Minutes later, with the handmade ointment lightly applied to her wounds, he prepared a comfortable place for himself to wait. And wait he did.

Hours later, a small fire continued to burn in the fireplace, while a rabbit that had been killed and dressed just that morning hung from a spit. Bits of its fat dripped into the fire as it cooked, making an occasional hiss and spit. It was the rabbit's last complaint.

Nokose squatted before the fire to check the meat. His hair cloaked his shoulders. His thighs bulged against the soft deerskin of his leggings, and his breechcloth fell loose between his legs and across his buttocks. While he was engrossed in his work, Amanda woke.

Her limbs felt stiff. Her body ached. The only things she could move without pain were her eyes. And they could not see enough to satisfy her shock, or answer her questions.

The room in which she lay was dark and windowless. A single door stood slightly ajar, letting in a crack of bright sunlight, as well as the faintest of breezes from beyond. The roof above her head was log. From what she could see of the walls surrounding her, they were the same. Rough-hewn, with the bark still remaining in spots. A clean but smoky scent filled the air, along with a variety of drying herbs she could not identify hanging from the rafters above her head.

A fireplace dominated one wall of the cabin. A fire burning deep within its depths gave off an intense light at the end of the room, along with shadows that danced at the periphery of her vision. The stones were gray and massive, and looked as if they'd sprouted on the spot. A mantel ran the length of the wall above it. Small objects were scattered along the shelf. The only thing she recognized upon it was a rifle, with a barrel so long she could hardly believe that one person could hold it without assistance, let alone aim it and fire it.

Leather pouches hung from pegs on the wall about the room. A single table sat near the fire with a bench on either side.

Oh God! Either I've lost my mind, or heaven is not what I'd imagined.

Nokose sensed movement on the bed behind him. But instead of rushing to her side, he stared into the fire, searching for the right way to approach this woman of his heart. And the moment he thought, he knew there was but one way. The same way that he'd come to her before. From the light.

He rose from the floor, a dark shadow between Amanda and the fire, and then turned to face her. She gasped and dug herself deeper into the furs. Her skin, sore and sensitive from her dash through the forest, slid along the pelt as easily as silk against satin. The sensation was at once pleasurable as well as foreign. It was then she realized. She was naked!

"Don't hurt me."

The words came without thought. And had Amanda searched her entire vocabulary for a lifetime, she could not have chosen three more powerful words with which to stop Nokose in his tracks.

His powerful limbs shook as the breath slid from his body in one long, slow draught. Arms hanging limply at his side, his shoulders ramrod stiff, prepared to bear the brunt of anything but her fear, he shook his head and turned away.

And as he did, Amanda got her first good look at the man within the silhouette and sighed. It was the man from the forest! He was real! And she thought that she'd been dreaming.

It was all too much! She curled in upon herself, rolling over onto her stomach and burying her face within her hands. Unable to bear another shock, her shoulders shook from the harshness of her sobs as she let grief and despair overwhelm her.

Nokose spun. The sound of her pain tore through his

gut like the swipe of the bear who'd unearthed him from his mother's belly. Within seconds he was at her side and had crawled onto the bed of furs beside her. The only thought in his mind was to give comfort.

His arms slipped beneath her shoulders, reveling in the pure joy of finally being able to touch her. As he'd done every night in spirit, he was now able to do in the flesh. He turned his woman within his arms and held her close against his chest. Absorbing her fear and her grief . . . because she was too fragile to bear it alone.

So great was her breakdown, that at first, Amanda was unaware that she was no longer alone. Then sensation returned, and memory came with it. She knew this man in whose arms she lay. She knew the shape of him. The way her shape conformed to his. Even the scent of him . . . and his tenderness. And when he moved to hold her closer, and the long curtain of his hair brushed her shoulders, she sobbed with newfound relief and lifted her arms around his neck.

Nokose's spirit soared. The burden of her rejection was no more. Her arms slid around him as easily as he'd slid into her body in the past. He closed his eyes and said a prayer of thanksgiving to the Great Spirit for guiding him to her in time.

"Amanda," he whispered. "My Amanda."

He held her so tightly that she could not move. But there was no need. Amanda was right where she belonged.

THIRTEEN

Jefferson Dupree was in hell. The autopsy on the murder victim found on the Potter estate had come back. Destiny Dawn, aka Sylvia Myers, had been pregnant. Memories of that video resurfaced as he stared at the report.

It made a sick sort of sense. But the motive was pathetic. Dupree buried his face in his hands, trying to shut out the image. She'd literally dangled from David Potter's hands, knowing all along that the life was being choked out of her. Added to that panic was knowing she wasn't the only one who was about to die. An unborn child had also suffered and perished at David Potter's hands. And Dupree would bet his retirement that the murderer was also the father-to-be.

The phone rang. Thankful that his morbid thoughts had been interrupted, he answered it on the second ring, and out of habit, picked up a pencil and slid a pad of paper in front of him.

"Homicide, Dupree," he said.

"Detective Dupree, I was told that you're in charge of the investigation on the murder that happened on the Potter Estate."

"That's right," Dupree said, and thought he heard his caller take a long deep breath. "What can I do for you?"

"My name is Marcus Havasute," he said. "I used to

work for David Potter . . . as chauffeur. I heard on the news about Mr. Potter being wanted for a murder, and that Mrs. Potter has not been located for comment. What I want to know is . . . is Amanda Potter believed to be a victim as well?"

Dupree tried to ignore the knot of nerves that twisted his belly in warning, but it was no use. His own voice cracked as he answered.

"We don't think so. Why? Do you have information to the contrary?" He heard another slow intake of breath from the other end of the line and decided to expedite the conversation. "Mr. Havasute, why don't we get to the point of your call. Okay?"

"If Amanda Potter is dead, I will testify against her husband on the grounds that he abused her, both mentally and physically, during the time of my employment."

The pencil in Dupree's hand snapped. Sweat broke out across his upper lip. He took several deep breaths before he could trust himself to speak.

"Mr. Havasute, please give me your address, and a number at which you can be reached." He wrote quickly, and then before he could talk himself out of the notion, added a personal question of his own: "I'd like to know something. If you were aware of her abuse . . . and her suffering . . . why didn't you help her? Why didn't you say something to the authorities sooner? Why the hell did you wait until now, when you think she's dead?"

"I don't know," Marcus replied softly. "And if she is dead . . . if Mr. Potter hurt her . . . I will see her face in my mind, for the rest of my life. So you see, Detective, I will pay for my silence."

"Thank you for calling," Dupree said, unable to trust himself to continue this conversation. "If I need you, I'll be in touch."

The line went dead in his ear. He shuddered and hoped it was not an omen of things to come as the image of Amanda's face slid back into place within his mind.

A file dropped onto the desk in front of him.

"Got another one for you," Chief Morrell said, and started to walk away.

Dupree looked up, his expression blank, his eyes dull and unfocused. *Another what?* Right now, there was only one thing in his life that he could concentrate on, and that was finding Amanda Potter.

"I'm still on the Potter case," Dupree said.

The harshness of Dupree's voice, as well as his haggard expression, were symptoms of his sleepless nights and anxiety-ridden days. Morrell was understandably unhappy with the fact that one of his men had gotten personally involved with a suspect in a murder case—even if the involvement was only in the guy's head.

"No you're not," Morrell said shortly. "Thanks to the arrival of that tape, it's been solved. The murderer just hasn't been picked up. Just because your brain is below your belt right now doesn't mean crime has stopped. Get to work on the next one, boy. That's how we get through it."

Dupree stared at the folder Morrell was pointing at, unable to focus on it, or anything else but the woman who haunted his dreams. "Amanda Potter is still missing," he said.

Morrell sighed. "Then turn it over to Missing Persons. Hell's bells, Dupree. Until they give us a body, we don't show up. This is Homicide . . . remember?"

Dupree hands fisted. "I would like to request a leave of absence."

"You're crossing lines, Dupree. You can't mess with stuff out of your territory."

"I can't sleep. All I hear is that voice. She asked for help. I didn't respond." A clammy sweat seeped from his body onto his clothes, leaving him with an odd lassitude he couldn't seem to shake.

The look on Dupree's face tore at Morrell's conscience.

"It's not your fault," Morrell said. "And you still don't know that call was from her. It could have been any crackpot and we both know it."

"It *was* her." Dupree glared. His whiskey-colored eyes narrowed until nothing was visible except a hard, angry glitter. "Instinct . . . and my heart . . . already know."

Morrell shoved his hands in his pockets and muttered beneath his breath about the obstinacy of certain people.

Dupree rubbed a hand across his face in frustration. The rough whiskers raking across his palm startled him. He hadn't shaved! The last time that he'd come to work in this condition was when he'd lost his partner to a sniper's bullet. He dug his fingers through his hair and relished the pain as his fingernails raked his scalp. He had to find Amanda. He couldn't face losing another partner.

He didn't consider it strange that he thought of her in those terms. In fact, partner was a weak term for the emotion he felt for her. He couldn't explain it. Not even to himself. He only knew he had to find her. She belonged to him. She just didn't know it yet.

Suddenly he realized that he'd just made a decision he hadn't been able to voice. He shoved his chair back from the desk and picked up the folder Morrell had dropped.

"Give it to someone else, Chief. I'm not going to be any good to you . . . or to myself until this is over. I can't work, or rest, or concentrate on anything else until I find her." His voice cracked. "And bring her home."

"And if she's dead when you do?"

Dupree grabbed his jacket from the back of the chair and stalked out of the room without answering. The hubbub of the office continued with hardly a ripple. Only the chief had noticed Dupree's outburst.

"I'll say a prayer for you, boy," he muttered. "But I think you need more than prayers. I think you need your damned head examined." He dumped the file on another detective's desk and ambled back into his office, hoping this would be over soon. Dupree had better find her or he'd never be back. Because Dupree was the kind of man who would look forever.

Morrell sat down, staring blankly across the room at Dupree's empty desk. A shadow from one of the men in the outer office moved across his line of vision. He shuddered. In light of what had just happened, it seemed like an ill-fated omen. He hoped he was wrong.

Dupree's apartment was spare. A bachelor's kind of quarters. All the necessities without any of the trimmings.

His cabinets yielded few groceries, and the refrigerator even less.

An autographed football from his senior year at college sat on the mantel over his faux fireplace next to a black garter, which he'd caught at his brother's wedding. A framed picture of his mother and father at the party celebrating their twenty-fifth wedding anniversary was on a table next to a copy of *The Rubaiyat of Omar Khayyam*. A grocery receipt served as a bookmark.

The hodgepodge of decor was dominated by the massive painting hanging on the wall opposite the door. Upon entry into his apartment, it was impossible to miss. Dupree called it his "watch bear," claiming he was gone too often to keep a dog.

The plants he'd occasionally bought kept dying from his on-again-off-again watering habits. The oil painting, however, required no care, only a strong constitution. Not everyone appreciated a painting of a bear on the attack, with blood dripping from his mighty jaws and paws, and the soulless expression of a predator in his small, black eyes. Not even Jefferson could explain why he had it. But it had been with him through officer's training, plus three moves, and had now earned a permanent place in his life.

He tossed his keys onto a coffee table littered with dirty coffee cups and empty soft drink cans. He gave the bear an absent glance. As always, his eyes went first to the blood, and then his mind seemed to blank out any further examination.

He picked up the remote with one hand and unbuttoned his shirt with the other, absently pulling it out of his jeans when he had finished. His boots marked his anger with solid thumps as he headed for his bedroom. He aimed the remote over his shoulder and hit the power button. The television came to life behind him.

"Good shot, Dupree," he told himself as he adjusted the volume and tossed the remote onto his bed along with his gun and shoulder holster.

Clothes came next. Boots. Jeans. Shirt. He had a sudden need to wash. All over. He couldn't get the ugliness of his job from his mind, but he could wash its remnants from his body.

The shower was cold when he walked in, and slowly warmed as he soaped and scrubbed. But the spiraling ache that had centered itself inside his belly did not respond to soap or scrub. It wouldn't budge. It was a blot on his soul he couldn't wash away.

"Ah, God," he muttered, and leaned forward, letting the water sluice him from head to toe.

Tall enough that he had to bend to get beneath the shower head, he braced himself with arms outstretched against the walls of the stall, his muscles knotting and drawing from tension. His coal-black hair plastered to his head and around his face as water continued to run.

He closed his eyes and instantly his mind shifted back to the first time he'd seen Amanda Potter. In mid-air, falling toward him with a terrified expression on her face. He took a breath and shuddered, remembering the last time that he'd heard her voice. Again, she'd seemed terrified . . . breathless.

His fingers curled and his legs went weak as he opened the door to his pain. He slid to the floor of the shower and buried his face in his hands, unable to deal with the thought of losing a woman he'd never had. Water pelted against his back. Stinging hot, then running cold. Like the bitter tears he continued to swallow.

But when he emerged, resolve had replaced remorse. He hadn't lost her. She was only misplaced. And it was up to him to find her.

The television continued to blare, good company for a

man who didn't want to talk. Wearing nothing but a towel, he went through his closet with a calmness he didn't feel and chose only the kinds of clothes that would weather stake-outs. The kind you could sleep in and still not be thrown out of the diner the next morning.

And when he was packed and dressed, he stared down at his gun and his bag and wondered aloud: "Where do I go from here?"

He got his answer faster than he could have imagined as regular programming on his television was interrupted.

"*This bulletin just in,* the announcer said. "*Yesterday's suspected terrorist bombing in the nation's capital has been re-categorized as a crime in progress. It is now believed that the man who was driving the car was not a terrorist, but possibly the perpetrator of some kind of extortion.*"

Dupree went into the living room and dropped into a chair opposite the set as he continued to listen.

"*When bomb experts began sifting through the remains, remnants of a large amount of money were found in the car, as well as what looked to have been a large suitcase, possibly what the money had been picked up in . . . or was about to be used in a drop.*"

Dupree frowned. Large amounts of money on bodies always made cops suspicious.

"*Charles, aka Chuckie, Rigola, part-time hustler, sometime paparazzo, has been identified as the driver of the car. While speculation is rife, there has been no statement from the D.C.P.D. to indicate that the man was involved in anything illegal.*"

Dupree straightened in his chair. Paparazzo? Someone who sneaks around and takes pictures of important people without their knowledge? Possibly videos of murders? That would take an extremely large amount of money to buy off.

The scenario spun around in his head until he thought he was crazy. He picked up the phone and called his office. Morrell answered on the second ring.

"Chief—" Dupree began.

"I thought you were on leave of absence," Morrell

growled, while secretly glad to hear a sane tone to his detective's voice.

"I was listening to the news," Dupree said.

"It must be nice," Morrell said. "I was working."

Dupree grinned. Even when he was pissed, the chief was an all-right guy. "So am I. Picture this. We receive a video of a murder in the mail. Anonymously. The same day, two states away in the nation's capital, a half-assed photojournalist blows up in his car, with a suitcase full of money beside him. What does that sound like to you?"

"A coincidence," Morrell said. "Put the man at the scene, and it sounds like a good clue."

"I'm calling D.C.," Dupree said. "And then I'm leaving town for a few days."

"I'm not surprised," Morrell answered. "Keep in touch."

Several hours later, Jefferson Dupree hung up the phone and stared across the room in shock.

When he'd made the first call to Washington D.C., the detective in charge of the bombing had been more than interested in the West Virginia detective's theory. With a search warrant to Chuck Rigola's apartment in his hands as they spoke, the detective promised to be on the lookout for incriminating evidence that might link David Potter to the bombing.

Two hours passed before Dupree got a return call. The D.C. detective was jubilant. Dupree's hunch had been on the money. Several copies of the same incriminating tape were found in Rigola's apartment, secreted in out-of-the-way places for obvious safekeeping. At that point, Potter's financial records had been subpoenaed.

And, the D.C. detective continued, less than six hours before the bombing incident, Congressman David Potter had withdrawn a staggering sum of money from an obscure account. The coincidences were too neat not to fit. The bombing was as good as solved, as was the murder of Destiny Dawn. All they needed was Potter himself, to tie up the loose ends of his dirty deeds.

Dupree grinned to himself, picturing the incriminating

video in mass reproduction. Whatever Potter had paid for, he hadn't gotten his money's worth. Guilt, like a bad taste, lasted longer than the thing that had instigated it.

He hung up the phone with a feeling of having successfully completed one mission, but having left the most important still undone.

It was time to get on the move. With Amanda on his mind and in his heart, he slipped his holster over his shoulder and buckled it down, then slid the gun in place, secreting it beneath his denim jacket.

He stood at the door, his gaze sweeping his apartment to make certain he hadn't forgotten anything important. The bear's portrait snarled at him from across the room.

"Same to you, buddy," Dupree said, and shut the door in its face.

David Potter stumbled through the dense forest, constantly moving upward in the direction they'd last heard Amanda moving. And although they'd not actually seen her, he had no doubt that the person the dogs had been trailing was his wife. It was how she'd gotten away that was making him crazy. Once again, she'd been the cause of his plans going awry.

The hunter had left him, chasing those damned stupid dogs, and Serge afterward, abandoning the man who paid him. A wiser man would have followed suit, but no one had ever said David Potter was wise. Only wealthy.

"I'll find you," he mumbled, fighting the branches that slapped at his face and neck as he ran. "And when I do, you'll be sorry. So sorry."

Time passed. Evening on the mountain was short. Before David was ready for it to come, nightfall arrived. His flashlight now became his eyes as he continued to move ever upward without destination.

A cool night wind began to buffet the trees, rustling the leaves and bushes all around him. David cursed away his fears.

"Big boys are not afraid of the dark," he muttered. It became his litany as he continued his search.

It happened by accident. Had the small animal not run into the opening, he would never have noticed it. But there, carefully concealed behind massive boulders and a thick growth of bush, was what looked to be a cave.

"So that's where you disappeared to," he snickered, and bolted forward, pushing aside the limbs as he entered the opening.

Something small and furry flew past him, its wings flapping softly against the air like a child's hands clapping in the dark. He gasped, and windmilled his flashlight like a club. And then he saw it.

A duffle bag, lying against a wall in the dirt. He began to grin, and dropped to his hands and knees. The zipper rasped, revealing Amanda's assortment of foodstuffs, as well as her meager belongings.

"Food. Thank you, my dear, for furnishing this simple repast. It was so thoughtful of you."

David grinned at his own wit and bit into an apple as he leaned against the cave wall and began to count the money she'd left behind. His eyebrows arched with surprise, unable to believe that she'd kept such devious secrets from him.

He took another bite. Juice ran from both corners of his mouth as he continued to eat, gloating all the while about his success in escaping justice. As soon as he'd meted out Amanda's, he'd be out of the country, and no one would be any the wiser. He'd found her bag. It stood to reason she'd be back for it. How else would she get away?

Feeling satisfied for the first time in days, David rolled over on his side and fell asleep.

More than two centuries into the past, his wife had done the same.

A slight shudder and an occasional sleepy sob were all

that was left of Amanda's breakdown. She lay within Nokose's arms, her body pliant to his every contour. The trust of that gesture was not lost on him. And because it was so unexpected, it was all the more treasured.

"I'm dreaming. You can't be real."

Nokose smiled to himself and buried his face in the rich depth of tangles beneath his nose. Her hair smelled of pine, the smoke from his fire, the musk of his body.

"Can you not feel me?" he asked, taking her hands and splaying them across his chest.

Amanda's fingers curled instinctively, an involuntary reaction after everything she'd endured at her husband's hands. Nokose sensed her panic, but was uncertain how to face it. It hurt to know that because of another man's actions, he, too, might be rejected. But he did not force the issue, nor demand her compliance, and slowly her fingers straightened.

Wildly beat his heart. Soft came his breath upon her face. Slowly . . . slowly, the space between their bodies widened as she tilted her head for a closer inspection of him.

So strong.

She could feel the tension of his muscles beneath her hands and yet he neither moved nor spoke, allowing her to investigate at will. Only a slight flare to his nostrils and a brighter glow in his amber-colored eyes let her know he was affected by her.

So big.

She hadn't imagined the breadth of his shoulders, nor the length of his legs as he and Amanda lay face to face upon the bed of furs. His size alone should have been enough to send her into a panic. It didn't. Instead, it was oddly comforting to know that a man this big had stood between her and imminent danger.

So brown.

His skin was somewhere between teak and tanned. Burnished to a warm, coffee glow from the fire across the room, it tantalized . . . beckoned . . . for her to touch. She did, and caught her lower lip between her teeth when she felt a muscle jerk beneath his skin. Would this be what it took for him to lose control? Would this be the time when her dreams changed into nightmares? In a panic, she looked up into his face.

So wild.

The expression in his eyes was a reflection of his inner turmoil. He sensed her fear and knew the reason. And he resented the hell out of it . . . and her . . . for doubting.

Then he moved and she caught her breath. It slid out of her body in a slow, silent sigh as his fingers threaded through her hair and pulled her toward him.

When his lips touched her forehead, and he laid her head upon his chest, tears sprang forth unannounced beneath her eyelids. She hadn't expected the tenderness. It was his salvation and her undoing.

"I don't even care if you're not real," Amanda said, and let herself be held that much closer. "Any minute now I'll wake up. And when I do, I'll lose you, just like before. I don't want that to happen. I'd rather sleep forever."

Nokose sighed. If only that could be true.

"You're not asleep, my Amanda. And I am no longer a spirit. You can never lose me. I am in here."

He splayed his hand across her breast, touching the place above her heartbeat. He felt her flinch.

"I would never . . . could never hurt you," he said softly. "It would be like killing a part of myself."

Amanda began to shake. *No longer a spirit?* What was this man talking about?

This was all becoming so unbelievable. If she was awake, then she needed some other answers. Answers that didn't come from her dreams and imagination.

"If you're real . . . you're not who I thought you were. And you don't understand . . . I can't stay in this cabin forever. David will find me."

Nokose released her. In one smooth motion, he'd moved from her arms to the doorway and swung the door wide, gesturing toward the grand outdoors visible through the opening.

"You are in the mountains. The nearest settlement is Fort Duquesne. My father is . . . was . . . *français*. A trapper." He frowned as he stumbled over the words, and when he resorted to French, Amanda was even more confused.

"A Frenchman?"

"*Oui*," Nokose said, smiling with relief when he realized that she understood his father's native tongue. "And your man will not find you here," he added.

Amanda wasn't as positive about that last statement as he was, but she let it go for the moment. She was too amazed by what he'd said before.

"Was? Then your father is dead?" Despite his struggle with English, Amanda hadn't missed the sadness in the big man's voice. She tried not to stare at his strange mode of dress, or the fact that his hair, raven black and bone straight, was longer than her own.

Nokose nodded. "He is dead . . . two winters."

She stared at him. Again the odd phrasing caught her attention.

"Why are you up here on the mountain alone? Why don't you just come back to the city?"

Nokose frowned. He did not understand the word "city," but knew that there would be a lot of things between them that neither would understand. At this point, it was obvious to him that Amanda had no grasp of what had happened.

"I could not go back to my mother's People. I waited for you."

Amanda frowned. None of this was making sense. His parents must have been some old hippies, or possibly survivalists.

"Where are your mother's people? And how on earth would you even know that I'd come this way? Even I didn't know that myself until it happened."

"I am Nokose . . . an Indian. Son of Little Bird, a daughter of the Muskogee. They are many in number and live on the banks of the Chattahoochee. The great river has many creeks. My people, the Muskogee, live among them."

Amanda pulled a fur up in front of her as if to protect herself. This man was beautiful. And strong. And if she didn't miss her guess, crazy as they came. What did he think he was, a wild Indian? If it hadn't been so sad, she might have laughed. She looked away, unable to face the fact that the man who'd saved her from David was as crazy as he had been.

"Do not turn away from me."

The cry in his voice tore at her heart. It was impossible to ignore his plea.

"You've got to understand," Amanda said softly. "I'm so very grateful that you saved me last night . . . or today . . . or whenever it was. I've lost track of time." She shrugged to make her point. "But . . . there's no way you could have known I'd be coming."

She chose to ignore the fact that when she'd first awakened and seen him, she'd thought him to be the man from her dreams. Now that she was awake she knew that was impossible.

"I knew you would come . . . because I called you. I came for you out of the light."

"Oh my God!" Amanda crawled to her knees, pulling frantically at the furs beneath. "You can't possibly know about that! How did you . . . ?" Then understanding dawned on her. "I know. I must have said all of this in my sleep. That's what happened . . . isn't it?"

Her eyes were wide and green, her mouth trembling as she awaited his answer. And then he pointed to the wall behind her.

Amanda turned on the furs to stare upward at the Dreamcatcher hanging on the wall over the bed.

"That's my . . . how did you . . . ? But it's not . . . "

"I had a vision. You called out to me from far, far away, my Amanda. I had no way to come to you . . . so I made a way for you to come to me."

She started to shake and then stood up and touched

the thing of which he spoke. Shocked at what she saw, she was unaware that the furs fell from her hands, leaving her naked and helpless before him.

It was her Dreamcatcher. Only it wasn't. This one was new. Even the wood felt green; the leather soft and supple. The feather hanging from the web was beautiful. A stroke of white and brown that flew from its leather tether, rather than the bird it had once belonged to. The claw was there, as was the beaded medallion. There was no difference between this one and hers . . . save two centuries and the magic of love.

"I don't understand," Amanda said. "I left this back in the cave. It was in the bag. You told me I didn't need it."

Nokose sighed. This was so difficult. And yet she had to understand. If she didn't, all of this would have been in vain. "In this world, it is mine. In your world, it belongs to you. Only time separates the owners."

She started to shake. *My world? Your world?*

"I don't know what you're trying to pull," she said, and began stalking around the room, looking for something to wear. "And where the hell are my clothes?"

Nokose grinned. She was truly beautiful when she was angry.

"Don't laugh, dammit!" Amanda said. "Just get my clothes."

He crossed the room, then bent down before a trunk in a corner. Moments later, he was back with a soft, deerskin tunic in his hands.

"Your clothes were torn and bloody. This was my mother's. It would please her if you wore it." It took all of his integrity to do so, but he managed to ignore the small, brown freckle on her right breast and focused on her wide green eyes instead.

Amanda gawked. The deerskin was as close to white as leather could get, and felt like the finest of suede beneath her fingers.

"She won't like you giving her clothes away," Amanda said, reluctantly handing it back in spite of an overwhelming need to cover herself. "Just get my own clothes . . . please!"

"She has no need for it," Nokose said, laying the tunic in her hands. She could not be seen outside in her own clothes. Both British and French would instantly assume she was some kind of spy.

She held it, but refused to put it on. Something inside of her said that once she did, she would have taken one step too many into the realm of disbelief.

"She has no need. She is no longer of this earth."

Amanda's eyes teared. Even though he was a little crazy, she knew what it meant to lose parents.

"I'm sorry," she said softly. "I understand your grief. Both of my parents are dead, also."

"I have no grief for her. Only regret that I never knew her. The mighty nokose killed her. His medicine was strong . . . but the medicine of *mon père* was stronger. We survived."

Finally Amanda allowed the deerskin tunic to slide over her head. It came to a point just below her knees, and the soft border of fringe at the hemline tickled the backs of her legs. In an odd sort of way, it felt good . . . even comfortable.

"Who is No-ko-se?" She stumbled over the unfamiliar word, thinking it to be the name of the man who'd committed a deed resulting in his mother's death.

He pointed to the bed of furs. "You sleep on his fur. His claw hangs from the Dreamcatcher. His spirit is now in you . . . just as it is in me. I have his name . . . and his strength. It is great magic."

Amanda stared at the fur on which she'd been lying and faintly recognized the outline of a skinned bear, although the head and claws were missing.

"A bear? No-ko-se is a bear? Are you saying that a bear killed your mother?"

Nokose nodded.

"And you survived? How?" She searched his body for signs of scars.

Nokose shrugged. "I survived because it was my destiny to be here for you. This I believe."

Amanda trembled. The walls of the cabin were closing in. The Dreamcatcher mocked her from across the room. The man's presence between her and the door made her think of David and the way he had kept her subdued.

In a panic, she bolted, expecting him to grab for her as she ran past him. When she burst out into the warmth of the late afternoon sun, she staggered and had to stop until her eyesight adjusted to the difference.

She stood in the clearing beyond the cabin like a frightened child. Her body was lost beneath the looseness of the garment she was wearing, just as her soul was lost in the world into which she'd been thrust. Unable to tell which path led away from David, she turned helplessly back to the cabin. Surprised, she saw that the big man had made no move whatsoever to chase, or stop her.

Silhouetted against the open doorway, he stood immobile, his face impassive. And yet Amanda sensed that there was great turmoil within him.

He caught her gaze. His head went back. His chin up. He said her name once. Softly. From several yards away. She closed her eyes and listened. He repeated it. And when he did, she knew him for who he truly was. It didn't make sense. But his voice. His touch. His shape were the same. This man . . . who called himself a bear . . . was the man from her dreams.

Tears came. Falling from her eyes in quiet defeat. And then she felt his hands upon her cheeks, and his breath upon her brow.

"Trust me, Amanda. You came with me once. Come with me now."

"No-ko-se?"

He smiled and touched the side of her face. "If you cannot say my name, I have another."

She waited.

"I am Nokose, but *mon père* would also call me Seth."

"Seth?" she repeated.

He held out his hand and waited for her to take it. She did.

FOURTEEN

As they walked through the forest, Amanda was amazed at the height, as well as the variety and abundance, of trees and bushes. Some of the small plants beneath their feet were completely unfamiliar to her, and often as they crossed a creek bank or started up a hill, they would come upon wildlife that took little heed of their presence. She imagined that the Garden of Eden must have once been so.

The big Indian moved through the woods like a shadow, rarely disturbing leaf or bush. She'd tried not to notice how tantalizingly sexual he was as he walked. It took some time before Amanda could put her finger on why she perceived him as thus. She finally decided it was because Nokose was so at home within his own skin. He was a man and knew it.

Her musing was interrupted when they suddenly paused. She glanced up at his face and saw excitement dancing in his eyes.

"What?" she asked.

He tugged at her hand and put his finger to his lips to indicate silence. Amanda followed the direction of his gaze, then smiled in delight when she finally spied the furry little bandit washing his food in the gently flowing water of the creek.

"*Wotko*," Nokose said, and then his eyes grew sad with remembrance. "*Mon père* called him *raton*."

"Raccoon," Amanda added, and tried to ignore the kick of longing she felt when a smile broke across his face.

"Rac-coon," he repeated, and drew a line from her eye to the corner of her mouth with his fingertip, teasing it to tilt just for him.

Amanda couldn't resist. She smiled, and then caught her breath at the fire of desire that transformed his features. Just when she expected him to make a move towards her, he quietly turned away. Retaining possession of her hand, he led her deeper into the woods, higher up the mountain.

There were warning signs everywhere that told her she was a lot farther than lost, but Amanda chose to ignore them. Her rational mind told her that something would click in soon, and she would be able to make sense of what she'd seen and what she'd been told.

I would be crazy to accept this man's claim. There is no way that he actually came to me through my dreams.

No sooner had the doubt arisen than Nokose stopped her motion with a gentle tug. "You frown," he said softly, and traced the furrow between her eyebrows.

His touch evoked memories she'd just told herself didn't exist. Of a time when he'd done more than stroke her forehead. When he'd entered her . . . body and soul . . . like a thunderbolt from heaven. The thought made her blush.

Nokose smiled to himself. Her face was so expressive. Without asking, he knew what had just crossed her mind. He felt her eyes raking his body, lingering longer than was probably necessary on his chest and the breechcloth covering his manhood.

"I was just thinking. I'm sorry," she said quickly. She hated herself for the conditioned response that she'd made. David had wreaked such havoc on her spirit that she automatically apologized, no matter if it was her fault or not.

Now it was his turn to frown. "I do not find fault with you, Amanda. I am only concerned. Come a bit farther. There is a place that I would like you to see."

And so he led her, up the mountain, through the trees.

The clearing was small. Remnants of old campfires were scattered around the area. But their presence was of no concern. At one time or another, they'd all been made by him.

Through the years, when he had endured all that he could of the confines of his father's cabin, he would come up here to sleep beneath the sky and the stars.

Nokose, like all of his Indian brothers, felt a kinship to the land that few white men understood. And although he had been greatly influenced by his French father, at heart he belonged to his mother's way of life. He was Indian. Nokose, a son of the Muskogee, who lived along the banks of the waters.

Amanda was staggered by the view. It went on for miles. The outcrop on which they stood was so high, she could actually look down and see birds flying below.

"Oh look! Down there! That looks like an eagle. There! Is that another . . . and yet another? They're so rare I wouldn't have . . . "

She gasped and then swayed at the edge of the cliff. The revelation was overwhelming.

"No! No!" Disbelief slowly moved to acceptance, because it was no longer possible to ignore what was right before her eyes. "Oh . . . my . . . God!"

Nokose grabbed her before she moved too close the edge, and Amanda dropped to her knees, suddenly unable to stand. "What? I see no enemy. What has given you fear, *ma chérie?*"

It took several seconds for her to realize that the thunder she heard was her pulse racing in her ears. Twice she tried to speak, but the words wouldn't come. All she could do was stare blindly out from the precipice, down onto the tops of the forest, far out across the valleys, beyond the next and the next hilltops.

The abundant carpet of green trees went on forever, as far as the eye could see and then some. And no matter where she looked, or in which direction, the total absence of civilization told her something she could no longer deny.

Everything that should have been, was not. All that Amanda accepted as normal in her world was vividly missing. The trees were lush. The sky was clear. Far below, an occasional glimpse of a river was evident as it wound its way through the valleys. But that was all.

Missing were the metal towers of the twentieth century that straddled hill and dale, stretching heavenward, stringing their webbing of lines that carried electrical power, linking city to state to world. There were no gouges in the sides of mountains through which highways had been laid. No clearings along roadsides that led to towns or cities. No advertisements. No smokestacks far in the distance marking the presence of a mighty metropolis. No jet trails mapping the heaven above their heads. No horns. No smog. Not a sign whatsoever that man even existed . . . except for the one beside her. No sounds save the wind rustling the leaves in the trees around them, and an occasional bird's chirp from the joy of being alive.

"What happened to my world?"

Her cry pierced his heart. Nokose grasped her shoulders and gently turned her away from the view. Forced by his determination, she had nowhere to look but into his face and those eyes . . . his father's eyes. Brilliant amber . . . so out of place in a warrior's face.

"It isn't there, my Amanda. This is my world that you see. Yours is yet to be."

"Oh God, I'm crazy. And if I'm not . . . how . . . why am I here?"

Heat sparked within his eyes. Amanda saw it spiral into a blaze, and felt herself spinning toward it. She reached out to steady herself, and found that she'd been caught in a whirlwind instead.

"You are not crazy, Amanda. You are a whole woman. In here." He touched her head. "And here." He touched her heart. "And you are here because I brought you."

"But why?" she whispered.

"Because you had no one and were afraid. You are here because you need to be healed by me. To be loved by me. It is my *destin*, as well as yours, that we are to be together."

Destiny. Amanda sighed, noticing that he often reverted to French when his English abandoned him. He must have already decided she had no adeptness in speaking Muskogee, his mother tongue, since she'd stumbled over the simple pronunciation of his name. She lifted her face, her eyes glistening with tears, her chin trembling from the impact of her own emotions.

"Then heal me. Love me as you did before."

Joy pierced his heart as she walked into his arms.

"Amanda."

Her name was a whisper on his lips as he cradled her shoulders, then gently lowered her onto the grass. Restraint was in every motion that he made as he slowly straddled her legs and then rested his hands upon bent knees, awaiting her pleasure. This would be their first time, other than in spirit. Because of that, Amanda must instigate whatever happened between them.

She neither moved, nor spoke. But her resistance melted, along with her fears, as the familiarity of his actions began to surface. As in her dreams, she looked up at his dark silhouette framed by the bright light behind him and recognized his presence. Fenced by his knees, she felt them tremble and saw that he patiently, but anxiously, awaited her decision. She held up her arms and made room for him to come in.

The wind lifted her hair from her forehead, cooling the heat of her brow, tangling the chestnut curls he loved to touch. He looked down into her eyes and smiled. Green as the forest he knew and loved, the same color that surrounded them, welcomed him home.

"I would see you, *ma chérie*." His hands shook as he lifted the tunic from her body, and then gently laid her back upon the carpet of grass. "I have great need to touch you." His hands began by cupping her cheeks, then using his thumbs to map the contours of her face and body as he began a delicate sweep of her person.

Amanda moaned and caught his hands. This touching of bodies seemed familiar, yet so much more than their joining of souls. She felt frightened, yet exhilarated.

Nokose paused, giving her time to adjust to his presence. And when he felt the panic, once again, sliding away from her body, he began to stroke her. Along the bottoms of her feet. Up the sides of her legs. Across the plane of her belly. And down to her womanhood. His hands touched, then tested that most secret place hidden beneath his fingers. She sighed, and then moaned when, once again, his thumbs delved deep, centering on the nub hidden beneath the curls.

"During your dreams, it was my joy to join with you. But it was a torment as well, that I could not feel your body against mine. Our hearts have connected over and over, but never our flesh. It is time."

"No-ko . . ."

He lowered his head and blew across the peaks of her breasts. His manhood grew, larger and tighter, angling toward her in response. As he pushed aside his breechcloth, it quickly sprang forward. Hard. Aching. Unrestrained.

A curtain of his hair sheltered her face from the burning sun, as did the breadth of his shoulders. Then his breath whispered across her face as he laid his cheek against her own and reminded her that she had no need to struggle with his Indian name.

"When you call my name . . . remember the name that my father used."

"Seth?"

"*Oui, ma chérie.* Seth."

His lips touched the peaks of her breasts that reached up to him. His tongue circled, then tasted. He shuddered, and stifled a groan. This pleasure must be hers. It was not his time.

"Oh, Seth."

The whisper of his name was understood. He heard her plea for continuance. To do so was his greatest desire.

His hands slid between the grass and her hips, tilting her body to receive him.

She bit her lower lip in anticipation of pain that never came. The throb between her legs began to match the pulse racing within her system. Just for a moment, when she felt his manhood testing the juncture of her thighs, she stiffened, remembering her husband's brutality. And then just as quickly, she heard the assurance in his voice, felt the gentleness of his touch, and knew that she might die after all at the hands of a man. But not from his abuse. From his love.

Nokose braced himself above her and without pause or pain, slid inside his woman as easily as if he'd done it countless times before. His body burned. His brain fogged. He struggled to maintain control of his emotions as her warmth encompassed him.

The heat of her, and the ache of his unfulfillment were medicines too strong for woman or warrior to deny. He began to thrust. Moving steadily, rhythmically. Like a drum beat through the air.

Amanda lost track of everything. Sanity disappeared along with consciousness. There was no cognizance of time or place. Only this man above her, and his body inside her. Filling what had so long been empty. Filling not only her body, but her heart.

Stroke upon stroke, he gave without care for his own desires. Time after time he resisted the urge to spill into the woman beneath him by concentrating on the changing expressions of her face.

The flash of her fear had long since disappeared. He'd seen shock replaced by desire. Pleasure swept away by a blinding need. When he saw her mouth part, and her eyes fall shut, he sensed that it was time.

Just when he thought he would die from the restraint he'd put upon himself, she arched upward beneath him. Her arms tightened around his body as she wound her hands in the length of his hair, using it as reins to complete their ride.

His mind whirled. Lost to everything but the fire within them, he drove himself deep and then burst, spilling into her . . . over and over and over . . . before his arms gave out and he collapsed upon her shaking body.

And when the *petite morte* had passed, and lassitude permeated every bone, he levered himself up, then rolled, taking her with him until they lay side by side, face to face.

Tears ran down Amanda's face. And when he might have worried, the soft smile parting her lips told him they were not tears of pain or regret. He had given her pleasure. She had given him joy.

"Amanda . . . my Amanda . . . *mon coeur.*"

She traced the shape of his face with her fingertip and smiled through her tears.

"Seth?"

He watched her eyes. The windows of a soul told all. Nokose needed to know all there was to know of his woman.

"*Oui,* Amanda?"

"I suffered long at the hands of my husband."

Pain shafted through him. He cupped her face and then tasted the words upon her lips. Sighing with regret, he answered, "I know. If it had been in my power, I would have changed your life years ago."

She wiggled a little within his touch, a little shy, yet daring to dare.

"Because of my suffering I will have need of more than one of these healing treatments . . . don't you think?"

Understanding dawned in him. She was asking him for more of what she'd just received. Surprised and delighted by her naivete, as well as her request, his laughter rang out within the forest.

A jay rose from a treetop, scolding the noisemakers within its domain. A squirrel that had been busily digging an acorn from its shell scampered swiftly up a tree trunk with the nut clutched firmly in its mouth.

And long before night fell, they had loved again and again. Late at night, and far into morning, Nokose lay upon his bed of furs in the cabin with Amanda cradled safely within his embrace. Caught in a draft from the partially open door, the Dreamcatcher's feather moved to and fro against the webbing like a bird bound to a perch.

Nokose closed his eyes and tried to sleep. Amanda sighed and moved a little closer, and as she did, her soft, bare breasts flattened slightly against his massive chest. A muscle jerked in her leg, a dreamsleep sprint he recognized and quickly quieted with a touch of his hand upon her thigh. His heart swelled within him, and even while he thought he would die from the love he felt for the woman in his arms, he wished for an answer that wouldn't come.

It was useless. He felt like that feather, caught within a trap of his own making. He'd called her to him. But when it was time to let her go, he wasn't sure if he would survive.

The diner on the outskirts of Miller's Crossing was small, noisy, and crowded. Nestled along a two-lane highway with a small green valley below, and an Appalachian peak for a backdrop, it was what was known as unique and picturesque.

Jefferson Dupree didn't care what it looked like. If they had hot coffee and a place to sit down, it was just what he needed.

But when he entered and saw the small dining area at the point of overflow, he grimaced. Two days of an all-out search had netted one plain fact. And that was that Amanda Potter had left Morgantown on a bus and then rented a car a hundred miles south.

This morning, when he'd discovered that the same car had been found abandoned in the mountains several miles from here and towed back to the rental agency, his hopes had plummeted. She could have caught a ride with nearly anyone. Be just about anywhere in the world by now. Or . . . she could be lost in the mountains and no one would ever be the wiser.

David Potter damn sure wouldn't turn her in as missing. He was as absent as his wife. The APB was still active on both of them, and although a nationwide search was still in effect, not a trace of either could be found. It was as if they'd disappeared from the face of the earth. Dupree shuddered. He didn't want to consider what that meant.

The background check he'd done revealed that she had no living relatives. A surge of panic resurfaced in him. What if he never found her? Or worse yet . . . what if he found her, and then had to bury her?

"Goddammit!" he muttered, unable to face the thought.

"Hang on, honey," a waitress said, as she sailed by with a tray of dirty dishes in her hands. "Don't lose your cool yet. I'll clear you off a place just as soon as I can."

Ashamed of himself, and the fact that the woman thought he'd been cursing at her, Dupree tried a smile. He caught a glimpse of himself in a dusty mirror over the cash register and stopped before it got any worse. Obviously, his mouth wasn't in the mood.

While he was waiting for the waitress to come back, a stool at the counter became vacant. Before anyone could beat him to it, he slid into place and shoved aside the dirty dishes that the trucker had left behind.

"Coffee," he said, and then added, "Please," when he saw it was the same little woman who'd caught his earlier anger.

He gave his order, and nursed his second cup while he waited for it to arrive. He began to relax, and he tuned in to the various conversations around him. Some were humorous. Some too personal to be discussed in so public a place. And then he zeroed in on one that made him forget his tired feet and an empty heart.

". . . plumb crazy," the man said.

"The hell you say," his buddy remarked. "But did he pay you up front?"

"Naw. And I counted myself lucky just to git away with my dogs. You never saw the like. Big, money-lookin' man. You know the kind. Had this fancy motor home. Even had himself a hired man with a long blond ponytail that went clear to his butt." He snickered. "Shoot. Them two might have been sweethearts, for all I care. That story about hirin'

me and my dogs to find his lost wife still don't sit right with
me. If I lost my wife . . . and there's been a time or two I
considered tryin' it," he snickered again for effect, "I damn
sure wouldn't be lookin' for her up in the Appalachians. I'd
go to the nearest damn mall. That's where."

Jefferson Dupree's heart jerked, then settled down into
a calmer routine. *Ah, God. Surely I couldn't be this lucky.*

"I hear you," the buddy said. "As for the haints your
dogs run across . . . I heard tell of a time when . . . "

Dupree spun around and stared at the two men in the
booth opposite. Ignoring the food the waitress put before
him, he picked up his coffee cup and walked over to where
they were sitting.

"Gentlemen," he whipped out his badge, "I'm more
than a little sorry to say I was eavesdropping on your conversation." Their eyes widened as they stared at the official
insignia. Then, before they could clam up, or take offense,
he began to explain.

The two men listened eagerly, ready to add to the
adventure the hunter had been on. It was when Dupree
asked the hunter if he'd seen the woman he'd been hired to
find, that the facts began to fall into place.

"Naw . . ." the hunter admitted. "The husband . . . he
yelled off and on all the way up the mountains. But no one
answered. And when my dogs hit that spooky trail and
hightailed it back down the mountain, I followed right
behind. I didn't have no desire to stand there and watch
that crazy sonofabitch shoot off his gun no more."

Ah hell, Dupree thought. He should have known Potter
would be armed.

"Who was he shooting at?" he asked.

The hunter snorted. "Nothin'. Everythin'. I never seen
anyone as spooked, except for my dogs, of course. I was
pretty sure we were trailin' someone, 'cause my dogs had
struck trail early. And I know my dogs. I know their separate
calls when they get on a trail. They were on to someone . . .
but I couldn't say who. If it was that Amanda woman, she
wadn't in no mood to be caught."

Dupree grabbed the hunter's hand. His voice deepened. His pulse rocketed. "What did you say her name was?" he growled.

"Hey! That's right! I didn't say before, did I? Oh, hell. That sucker yelled it so many times goin' up that I can still hear it in my sleep. He called her Amanda. And every time he called and she didn't answer, he'd shoot off his gun."

"Where?" Dupree asked.

"Oh, up in the air," the hunter mumbled. "Kind of careless like."

"No," Dupree said. "I mean . . . where did this happen? How far from here? And could you find the place again?"

The hunter snorted. "I know these mountains like the back of my old lady's butt. Hell yes, I can find it. When do you want to go? But I have to say that I'm only goin' so far. Them dogs sensed somethin' I don't want to mess with. Might be a Bigfoot, or the like."

"Could be them haints I was gonna tell you about," the buddy argued.

Dupree interrupted before any more wild tales began concerning ghosts. Stories about haunts, or "haints" as mountain people called them, abounded. As difficult as it was to face, looking for Amanda was proving to be just as futile as ghost hunting.

David Potter slept, curled in a ball, rocking to a lullaby only he could hear. His jacket had become a pillow, Amanda's duffle bag a teddy bear he hugged tightly against his chest.

The first day he'd spent in the cave in a high degree of anticipation. At any moment, he expected Amanda to reappear to claim her belongings. Plans for her punishment had come and gone, along with the daylight.

When the second day had disappeared, as well as most of the food that she'd left behind, he had begun to panic. If he left now, she would get away with what she'd done. That couldn't happen. She'd done a bad thing.

On the other hand, if his food ran out before she returned, David had to make a decision. Either he waited and starved, or he came down off the mountain and possibly walked into the arms of the law. He hated his options. Distressed over the fact that he hadn't been able to come up with another idea, he'd resorted to sleep while waiting for time to pass. Also, if he slept, his mother couldn't come, and he didn't want her to know that he was in trouble. She would be mad at him, again.

The sun rose and then set on the third and fourth days since Amanda's escape. David did little but wake to relieve himself, snatch a bite or two of the remaining bits of snack food in her bag, and then return to his dusty nest inside the cave.

Had he been able to see himself, he would have been shocked and dismayed. The carefully groomed, perfectly tailored congressman from an ultra-conservative, old-monied family was nowhere to be found. He'd become nothing more than a mirror-image of the filthy vagrant he'd ignored. His flight from justice, as well as his hunt through the woods for Amanda, had turned him into a poor replica of Beaner.

A scraggly beard was even beginning to disguise the perfection of his features. Congressman David Potter was disappearing, but not as he'd planned. Had he walked out of the woods in this condition and onto the streets of some city, mingling with the street people he'd long looked down upon, he might possibly have gotten away with murder.

But the urge in him for revenge was too strong. By mailing that tape to Detective Dupree, as he was certain she had, Amanda had exposed him as Destiny Dawn's murderer and had ruined their perfect world. It was all her fault that this had happened. No matter what it took, she would have to pay.

And so he continued to sleep, waiting for fate to hand

Amanda back to him on a silver platter. He saw no oddity in simply sitting there to get what he wanted. After all, everything else in his life had come exactly the same way.

Halfway up the mountain, Dupree paused near a tree to catch his breath, and then staggered when an image of Amanda's face superimposed itself upon his brain.

Panic came out of nowhere, stifling his breath and blinding him to everything but what he was feeling. While sanity told him it was impossible, instinct told him that he'd just walked through a miasma of lingering fear and he knew that Amanda had walked this way before.

"Get a grip," he muttered, and shook off the feeling. If he didn't, he wouldn't do Amanda, or himself, a damn bit of good.

He looked over at the two men who'd accompanied him up the mountain and wondered exactly who was really leading whom. For the better part of an hour, the two would-be big shots, whose names he'd learned were Stanley and Curtis, were busily trading tall tales while he'd pushed steadily upward, leaving them to follow suit.

"Are we still on the right track?" Dupree asked, and slapped at a gnat. Both men nodded.

He tried to imagine Amanda lost in a wilderness like this, and as soon as he did, wished he'd skipped the thought. Chances were, if she *was* lost in this, she had either fallen into one of the countless canyons and now lay helpless, possibly dying from injuries, or David Potter had found her first and she was already dead.

"I will not accept that thought."

"What's that you said?" Stanley asked, and wiped sweat from his brow with the back of his arm.

"Nothing," Dupree said. "Just thinking out loud."

Stanley shivered. "Hell, Detective, don't be tellin' me none of that. The last man I guided up here was talkin' to hisself too."

Dupree sighed. "I'm not crazy. I'm just pissed. I'm a

cop, for God's sake. A woman is in danger, and I can't seem to do a damned thing about it. Okay?"

Stanley nodded. "I wished I'da knowed before what kinda man he was. I'da never took that job. I can't believe he was aimin' to kill her once she was found. Why . . . if I'd led him to her . . . it would as good as have been my fault."

Dupree shook his head. "If Potter had found his wife, I doubt you'd have come off the mountain to tell it."

Stanley paled. "The hell you say! I never thought about that! Hey, Curtis, did you hear that. I was his next victim."

"That was a maybe, not a for-sure," Dupree said. "Now come on. We're wasting daylight. You said we were close. Show me where the dogs stopped."

Five minutes later Stanley stopped and pointed. "It would be about here," he said, peering up through the trees toward the sky. "I distinctly remember because I could see the top of Rainey Ridge yonder." He pointed. "See? There it is."

The anvil-shaped crest of the neighboring mountain was plainly evident.

"Two or three days ago, there wasn't much moonlight. How can you be sure?" Dupree insisted.

"There was enough to get up here. There's always enough to get back. I know what I saw," Stanley persisted. "It was right about here he started to shoot off that gun again."

Dupree began to walk the site, looking for anything that would tell him he was on the right track.

The light beamed down through the thick umbrella of trees, casting alternating patterns of light and shade along the ground, as well on the heads of the men who were deep in search.

Sunlight crowned Dupree's head with a halo of heat, bringing the rich, black highlights in his hair to a radiant glow. His posture was stiff, his attitude on the alert as he moved quietly through the woods. A stiff breeze sprang up, lifting the collar of his blue denim shirt and whirling the leaves beneath their feet. Had it not, Dupree knew that he would have passed the object by without knowing it was there. He leaned over and picked it up.

It was an empty ammunition clip.

"What kind of gun did the man fire?" Dupree asked.

"Some kind of handgun. I ain't for sure because I didn't even know he had it till we got in the woods. And then it was too dark to tell for certain."

Dupree grinned to himself. Potter was getting careless. He dropped the clip into a plastic bag, which he put in his pocket. Things might be looking up.

"Hey! Lookee here."

Stanley's buddy, Curtis, held up his own prize. "I found a ring of keys . . . with an I.D. tag."

"Let me see," Dupree said.

The keys flew through the intermittent sunlight, jangling against one another on their wayward flight, before Dupree snatched them from the air. He looked down at them lying in his hand, and then grinned again. It kept getting better and better.

"If found, return to Potter Estate, Morgantown, West Virginia," he read. "Oh yes!"

"What are we going to do now?" Stanley asked. "Do we keep looking, or what?"

Dupree shook his head. "No way, buddy. You've done more than your fair share. I'm gonna get you and Curtis back off the mountain, and then we're calling in a search team. There's an APB out for this man. He's killed once. I doubt he'd have qualms about repeating the process."

Both men shuddered and nodded, anxious to return to the safety of small-town life and the familiarity of their diner.

Hours later, Jefferson Dupree dropped the key to his motel room by the phone and himself onto the bed. He picked up the receiver and dialed, taking inventory of his scratched boots and torn blue jeans as he waited for Morrell to answer.

"Chief," he said when Morrell did.

"Dupree? Where the hell have you been? I've been waiting for you to call in for two days."

Dupree's gut knotted. "What's wrong?"

Morrell snorted softly. "Wrong? Nothing's wrong. In fact, I've got some good news."

"Amanda's back!"

Morrell sighed and absently cracked his knuckles. He should have known his news would fall short of Dupree's expectations.

"No, boy. Not quite that good. But a good clue, all the same."

Dupree sighed and wearily closed his eyes as he fell backward onto the mattress with a soft thump.

"I'm waiting," he said.

"Potter's goon, one Serge Markovic, was picked up outside of Richmond driving Delia Potter's motor home."

"Delia Potter is dead," Dupree muttered, and scratched at a bug bite.

"Yeah, I know that. And you know that. Even Serge Markovic knows that. But . . . he claims he's not so sure about David Potter. Look, Dupree, according to Markovic, Potter has gone off the deep end. He talks to himself . . . and his dead mother . . . all the time. Hell, he says they even have arguments."

"Oh, great," Dupree said, imagining Amanda's fate at the hands of such a maniac. "And here I thought we just had a rich bad-ass on our hands." He groaned softly into the phone. "Why didn't someone tell us the bastard had a screw loose?"

"How should I know? Maybe everything that happened pushed him over the edge. Maybe he's smarter than we give him credit for. Maybe this is just an act in case he's caught. He could always plead insanity, right?"

Dupree shivered, and swallowed a knot in his throat. "Did this Markovic say anything else?"

"Only that the last time he saw him, Potter was on some mountain and refused to come down. The muscle swears that he didn't know anything about the murder, or that Potter was trying to harm his wife until Potter started firing off a gun as they trailed her."

"It fits."

Morrell blinked and shifted the phone to his other ear. "What the hell do you mean?"

"Because I found the mountain, Chief. And an empty clip from a gun . . . and a set of keys belonging to Potter. I also found the man who guided him part way up. What I don't have is Potter . . . or Amanda. I think they're somewhere farther up, possibly holed up in some sort of shelter. It's impossible to guess. The place is like a jungle."

"What do you want me to do?"

For a moment, Dupree was silenced by his chief's blanket acceptance of his assessment of the situation. And then Amanda's face flashed into his mind and it didn't take him long to decide.

"I want you to call the local authorities and fill them in. Then I want authorization to be included in the search. When they go up that mountain after Potter and Amanda, I *will* be there. I would just like it to be official."

"You got it, boy," Morrell said softly. And then he added. "Dupree?"

"Yes, Chief."

"Good luck, son. I think you're going to need it."

Dupree couldn't answer. And finally when it registered that his boss had already disconnected, he dropped the phone back on its cradle and buried his face in his hands.

His body ached. His head throbbed. He'd never even come close to considering what it would be like to kiss her, and the woman was so deep in his gut he might never be able to get her out. Not even if she laughed in his face when he found her.

"Amanda. My God, woman, what spell have you woven in me? I've lost my heart to you and I don't even know what makes you laugh."

He rolled from the bed and headed for the bathroom, stripping off his clothes as he walked.

FIFTEEN

———————— ❁ ————————

Water from the creek bed ran cool between Amanda's toes as she waded along the bank, a basket clutched tightly to her stomach containing the berries she was picking from the heavily laden, overhanging blackberry vines.

Two berries into the basket. One into her mouth. And so the ritual continued until her fingertips, as well as her lips, were as red as wine and the basket close to full.

Her single braid of chestnut hair hung over her shoulder to rest upon her breast. Every now and then it caught on a particularly persistent vine and she had to stop her harvest long enough to untangle herself from the briars. It was a small price to pay for the perfection of the moment.

She couldn't be happier. David was not of this world. Here, she felt safe, beloved, and protected. Waking to a day with no clocks was a pleasure, as was knowing the man who came for her with open arms, offering a love she could never have imagined.

The sun heated a path on the water, sending the tiny minnows swimming in the shallows to seek deeper, cooler pools. Bees buzzed among the berries, alighting occasionally on a late-blooming blossom, taking their share of the nectar from the rich abundance.

Amanda's borrowed tunic hung loose from her shoulders, while a faint breeze circulated through the trees, moving the deerskin to and fro upon her body just enough for an observer to get a tantalizing glimpse of the seductive shape beneath.

From the opposite bank, eight pairs of obsidian dark eyes watched her every movement. The observers had partially shaven heads with scalp locks spiking defiantly upward, while colorful feathers and beads dangled against their cheekbones.

Each of their faces was painted one half in ghostly white, the other half in deathly black. When they smiled, as they did silently to one another at the sight of the lone woman in the creek, their teeth gleamed ivory, a sharp, feral contrast to the unnatural colors on their skin.

Sweat glistened upon eight brown bodies, while the breechcloths, leggings, and moccasins they wore blended into the forest like saplings among the trees. They stood motionless, holding war clubs in their hands, waiting.

Amanda sang beneath her breath as she continued to gather her fruit, unaware that her life hung in the balance of a warrior's whim.

Nokose was less than a hundred yards from the creek bank when he sensed the danger. Moments ago the woods had abounded with the sounds of wildlife within it. Now the only thing he could hear was the beating of his heart. As if to emphasize the signs, a cloud moved across the face of the sun.

Amanda!

He slid his knife from its sheath and darted away from the path he'd been walking, into the trees, moving as one with the constantly dancing shadows created by the breeze. The air carried the sound of her song, an absent hum that meant nothing to him . . . except the fact that she was still alive. Whatever or whoever was approaching had not harmed her . . . yet!

Fear lent speed to his movements, and in seconds, he was at the edge of the trees, looking down at the top of her head as she moved beneath the berry branches. Relief shot a new surge of adrenalin into his system as he realized she was unharmed. Ever conscious of life's frailty in his world, he began to scan the opposite side of the banks for danger.

Eyes met simultaneously. Amber to black. One to eight. Ignoring the odds, he walked out of the trees and into the sunlight, standing with the knife in his hands, his chin up, his head back. The challenge in his posture was unmistakable.

"Amanda! Come to me." His voice was low but sharp.

She jumped. The berries she'd been about to drop into the basket fell into the water instead with intermittent plops. She looked up and started to smile, when she saw the knife in his hands and the look on his face.

The water splashed as she ran, making tiny rainbows before her flight. But there was no time to admire nature's little gift of beauty. She had no thought but one: to get to Seth.

Droplets dappled her long, slender legs and wet the edge of her tunic. Berries bounced within the basket as she bolted for the steep creek bank. She didn't look back as she lifted her hand for him to pull her up.

He bent down without taking his attention from the opposite shore and wrapped his fingers around her wrist. In one smooth movement, she cleared the bank, berries and all. Just as she turned to look behind her, the warriors stepped out of the trees.

"Oh my God," she muttered, and felt her legs go weak. But she took a deep breath instead of dropping on the spot, and whispered his name in panic. "Seth?"

He shook his head to signal silence, and then took one step to the right, putting himself between Amanda and the war party.

Then one of the warriors spoke. A loud, challenging string of words she could not understand. Nokose's answer shot back across the bank like a lance. Sharp, guttural intonations were traded, accompanied by swift hand signs that Amanda wished she could read.

The only word Amanda grasped was "Nokose." It was repeated several times, by Seth, as well as the Indian across the creek. Suddenly all was silent. The eight warriors on the opposite bank slid back into the trees as silently as they'd come. When they were no longer in sight, Nokose turned and looked down at her.

"What did they want?" she whispered, trying not to shake. It was embarrassing to show fear when this man had not even raised his voice.

"You."

"Oh my God. Why didn't they attack? There were eight of them. Only one of you."

"I am Nokose. They fear the power of the bear."

And then because he knew she would not understand their ways, or the powers in which certain animals gave spirit to the men who were marked by them, he added with a teasing smile. "And . . . I told them that you were lazy and complained all the time. They have women like that in their own lodges. Adding another would only make matters worse."

She laughed through her tears, knowing he'd lied to allay her fears.

"I didn't scream," she said.

He lifted the basket of berries from her arms, and cupped her face with his hand. "I know, my Amanda."

"I did just what you said without question."

"I know that also. And I thank you for trusting in my command. It probably saved your life."

She turned her lips toward his hand and smiled against his palm. "That's twice you've saved my life. By the time we're old, I should be very good at this, don't you think?"

The berries fell to the ground between them as he clasped her to his chest and buried his face in the warm chestnut curls that had escaped her braid.

His heart ached. He would not have the pleasure of knowing Amanda in that way. Their time together was destined to be brief. From the moment he'd seen her in his vision, he'd known and accepted that fact without reservation. What he hadn't realized was how difficult it was going to be to let her go.

"*Amour . . .* " The rest of his words were lost to her as she lifted her face to his kiss.

The world rocked. Slowly the cloud passed from across the sun's face . . . and sometime later, Amanda knelt to retrieve her berries.

"You spilled our supper," she said, trying to tease away the lingering remnants of danger that had intruded into their world.

"If you'd spilled it into the water, we would not have eaten tonight."

He smiled. "But yes, Amanda. I would feast. Upon you." The flush on her face delighted him so, he chuckled to himself all the way to the cabin.

That night, while darkness held the forest within its embrace, Nokose held Amanda within his. Wisps of smoke from the dying embers of the fire in the fireplace told him that unless he moved to replenish it, it would be out by morning. And while building a new fire was not difficult, it was a chore he didn't enjoy.

Quietly, so as not to disturb Amanda's sleep, he slipped his arm from beneath her neck and crawled out of the furs, to walk naked toward the wood stacked by the hearth.

He leaned over to lay a small log upon the coals, unaware that Amanda watched from across the room.

The lack of warmth against her back had wakened her instantly. Desperate to find him, needing to assure herself she wasn't alone, she searched the cabin's shadows. Only when she saw the outline of his face against the flickering firelight did she relax.

Amanda saw that he moved through the dark like a night owl, seeing all that was before him, choosing that which he needed in order to survive. At this moment, it was a stick of wood. Earlier today it had been his knife—to save her life. She'd seen him hunt and kill so that they might eat. She'd seen him risk life and limb to save her from David.

She'd learned that the man she loved was truly wise,

and a gentle lover beyond belief. But today had been a revelation. He had a wilder side he'd kept hidden from her. Today he would have killed. And it would have been for her. It should have frightened her. Instead she felt a small pride. She meant enough to someone that he was willing to lay down his life for her.

He dropped a log upon the fire, which bounced tiny orange embers onto the earthen floor and sent them shooting up the chimney. And in the moment before he straightened, she saw his face and knew that she could easily fight to the death for him. Between her yesterdays and her todays, she'd learned that anything worth having was worth fighting for. Living without this man was not something she could consider. Living in his world might be difficult, but she was willing to give it a try.

She stood, then called his name and waited in the shadows for him to come to her.

"Seth."

A heartbeat later, he was at her side. "I woke you," he whispered. "I am sorry."

She laid her face against his chest and smoothed her hands around his rib cage before locking them in place beneath his shoulder blades.

"I wasn't afraid. I was alone. Two different needs that only a man . . . my man . . . could change."

Bodies realigned, woman to man, heart to heart. Nokose combed his fingers through her hair and then captured her face within his palms, tilting her chin upward so he could feel her breath upon his face.

"Am I your man, Amanda?"

The question felt awkward upon his lips. His heart already knew the answer. But his pride needed to hear it repeated.

"Yes, and my love," she added.

He pressed her face to his chest and gazed over her head at the Dreamcatcher above his bed. *What do I do now? Tell her the truth and break her heart, or take her to bed and lose my own?*

He urged her back down on the furs. "I want to lie with you, my Amanda."

Her hands urged him on. His body betrayed his need as it swelled and surged against the softness of her skin.

"Forever," she whispered, and made room for him to come in.

Therein lay their problem. He had not told her that their forever would consist of only two more days. After that, she must go back. He would cease to exist, and she would have to live with what he'd taught her. He only prayed that she would know where to look for the answers that awaited her in her world.

"You are already forever in my heart," he whispered, ignoring the remorse that filled his conscience as he entered her and then began to move.

Darkness enveloped them as the ancient ritual began. An arch, and a thrust. A simultaneous meeting of bodies that joined and withdrew in order to prolong the pleasure. For if one arched too high, or one thrust too deep, then neither would survive, and the dance would be over before it had begun.

Amanda's body began to coil inward. The pressure of his presence was making itself known. She raked his back with her fingers, searching for handholds on his sleek, sweaty body, trying not to fall from a bed that was beginning to spin.

But it was futile. Before she could find the breath to say his name, pleasure shattered within her.

The tremors of her body drew him deep and kept him past the point of no return. He buried his face in the valley between her breasts and emptied himself inside her, his forever love.

When it was over, he moved from atop, to beside her, gathered her close, and waited for her breathing to soften in sleep.

As darkness began to wither with the oncoming heat of a new sun, Nokose dreamt. Visions that foretold what was to come. He faced the truth and knew no regrets. If he had it to do all over again tomorrow, he would still do the same. Losing his life was a small price to pay for finding his love.

The hours between their loving had come and gone. At dawn, Nokose whispered her awake, then urged her to return to sleep after claiming necessity for a hunt to give them food.

Amanda sighed and raised her arms to encompass his neck. He laughed against her ear and swiftly ravaged her mouth with his own before dropping her back into the furs with an order to bar the door while he was gone.

A swift vision of yesterday's encounter with the marauding band of Indians surfaced. Amanda bolted naked from the bed. The last image she had of him before she dropped the latch on the door was fleeting. But his buckskin backside was enough fuel for her dreams.

He was tall and brown, like the straight trunks of trees surrounding the cabin. His hair, which was as dark as a raven's wing, began to lift in flight as he moved to a trot. A man of the forest. Nokose. A god among men.

Hours later, dressed and roaming the cabin's shadowy interior with curious hand and eye, Amanda examined the various objects for a more thorough understanding of him . . . and of her. There was little to see that explained the drama of their lives.

Time passed. And her patience slid away into panic. Something must have happened! He'd been gone so long. And then she laughed at herself. He'd gone out to get food, but she had to remember that it wasn't as easy as going to the supermarket. Their food was either on the vine, in the ground, or on the hoof. Satisfied with her explanation, panic diffused. And then the Dreamcatcher caught her eye.

"So," Amanda said, as she came to stand before it, gazing up at the feather dangling lifelessly without benefit of breeze. "You are what brought me here. Seth says all of these things are great magic." She touched the claw, feather, and medallion, each in turn.

And then an idea occurred to her. If personal mementos gave the Dreamcatcher more power, then something was missing. The love she felt for him was overwhelming. The Dreamcatcher needed a bit of herself.

A quick search of the few shelves along one wall netted what she needed to complete her task. Satisfied that she had a project of import, Amanda dropped to the bed of furs and began to comb her fingers through her tangled curls.

Before she could change her mind, she sectioned off a small part along the side of her hair, and began to braid. Three equal lengths of hair. Back and forth. Over and under. When she came to the end, she fastened it tightly with a narrow strip of rawhide, and then took a knife and severed the braid's root from her scalp, quickly fastening it before it became unwound.

"There," she said, holding the tiny loop of hair up for inspection. "Infinity." Thanks to the rawhide, the circle was complete.

On tiptoes, she reached toward the Dreamcatcher upon the wall and tied the braid to the webbing. It lay between the bear's claw and the eagle's feather. A small thing, she thought. Hardly of comparable power, but a bit of herself nonetheless.

Amanda could not have been more wrong. It was the missing link between their worlds. He'd called to her with a part of himself. Unknowingly she'd come, bringing a part of herself she would leave behind.

She stood back, hands on her hips, and gazed at the token she'd added to the web. Then she clapped her hands, hardly able to wait until Seth would return so she could show him what she'd done.

No sooner had she thought his name than she heard the sound that signaled his return. A dove cooed twice from beyond the clearing. Amanda held her breath, waiting for the last of the greeting to come. The dove's coo echoed twice again.

She lifted the bar, and flung the door wide. A quick spurt of tears shot through her eyes. But they weren't tears of remorse. They were only tears of joy.

"You're back," she called, and burst from the door into the clearing.

Surefooted to the point of grace nearly all of his life, Nokose stumbled when he saw her running toward him. A burst of heat, white-hot and enduring, swept through him, accompanied by a love so strong that he choked on the greeting he'd been about to call.

Great Spirit, give me strength, he prayed. The birds that he'd snared dropped into the dirt at their feet as she jumped into his outstretched arms.

"Oh Seth, I thought you were never coming back," Amanda cried, and plastered every spare inch of his body with kisses of thanksgiving.

Nokose's heart tugged. Her smiling face tilted toward his, offering all that she was for his approval and his taking. He whirled her around and around where they stood, laughing when her hair flew out behind her like a chestnut fan.

"So . . . am I to believe that you missed me?"

She laughed and thumped his arm with her fist before begging to be put down. "Only a little," she said. "Only a little."

"Come," he said softly. "Soon we will eat."

"What will we do while they cook?" she asked shyly.

His laughter rang out. "You choose," he said, delighting in the way that she suddenly blushed, and then her expression became solemn.

"I choose you," she said.

The burst of need had come and gone, leaving comforting remnants of their lovemaking that surfaced in silent looks, swift glances, and unnecessary touches. As they finished their meal, their eyes burned bright with remembered promises, whispered in the throes of passion.

The door to the cabin stood ajar. A cool mountain breeze came in and flitted about the room, teasing at the drying herbs above their heads, sweeping across the shelves and mantelpiece, lifting damp curls from Amanda's neck, cooling the lingering heat of Nokose's lust for the woman at his side.

A butterfly darted inside, hovered in the doorway as if testing the vicinity for promising victuals, and then swooped back outside, riding the current of breeze like a leaf on the wind.

Amanda pointed and laughed. Nokose turned to see what had given her joy when he noticed the Dreamcatcher above their bed. The added totem was impossible to miss. Caught in a ray of sun, the burnished reds and browns of the tiny braid hung like a jewel upon the webbing.

He stood without speaking and began to walk toward it with arm outstretched. His heart hammered within his chest. His eyes misted unexpectedly from the gift of her love.

The sunshine had been there long enough for the braid to have captured its heat. Nokose's finger traced the delicate loop of her hair. It was hot to the touch, and so fragile. He turned. His eyes fixed upon the woman at the table. There was an emotion whirling within him that he could not voice.

Amanda held her breath. He'd seen it! Suddenly the impulsive gift seemed silly. Maybe even intrusive. She bit her lower lip and clutched her hands in her lap, uncertain of how to behave. An old fear came back without warning. What would happen if she'd done something she shouldn't have?

"I hope it wasn't wrong," she said, mixing nervous laughter with her breathless inquiry.

He shook his head and opened his arms.

Amanda flew across the room.

"*Mon coeur,* it was exactly right," he whispered, suddenly cold from the inside out at the knowledge that the end had already begun.

Her body aligned itself to his, conforming, warming.

He held her close, unwilling to admit, even to himself, the fear that had come with the gift.

"I wanted to give you something," she said, then shrugged. "It was all I had."

"It was of you. Because of that, it is perfect."

She smiled and nuzzled closer, blessing Seth, as well as her good fortune. Everything had been so wrong before. Now it was so very right.

"I have a gift for you," Nokose said suddenly, and went back to the trunk he'd searched when giving her the tunic that she wore.

He returned with a small necklace of leather and bead dangling from his hand.

"*C'était à ma maman.*"

"It belonged to your mother?" Amanda repeated.

He nodded and placed it over her head, onto her neck. Amanda's hand automatically went to the beads. She rolled them beneath her fingertips, feeling the smoothness, as well as their individual shapes.

"They look like turquoise! I didn't know such stones were found here."

Nokose shrugged. "I do not think that they are. *Mon père*, he traded for them at *rendez-vous,* one year." And then he grinned. "After he convinced the man who owned them to trade."

Amanda's eyes widened, then she grinned. "I think I understand. It was a friendly argument, of course."

Nokose smiled back. "Of course," he repeated.

"Thank you," Amanda said shyly, fingering the beads.

A memory flashed through her mind, of diamonds and pearls set in silver and gold, lying loose and unattended in her jewelry box back home. This gift was so humble, yet much more treasured, than anything David could ever have given her. Like his love, her Seth gave without thought of return. She looked up and smiled.

"I will wear it always."

Nokose frowned. He hadn't thought of that. She couldn't wear it always. But while she remained, it was hers.

His expression moved from satisfied to somber. Amanda noticed it and shuddered unexpectedly. She knew, as well as she knew the shape of his mouth against hers, that there was something he wasn't telling.

"What is it?" she asked. "Did something happen while you were hunting? Did you see more Indians?"

He turned away and busied himself with replacing the items inside the trunk that he'd removed during his search for the beads.

"I saw nothing, Amanda. You imagine things."

She knelt at his side and when he would have lingered, closed the lid to the trunk to end his tactical delay.

"Talk to me, Seth. I love and trust you with all my heart. Whatever you need to tell me . . . I will understand."

How could he tell her? *It must be done.* Their time together was nearly over. He couldn't just wake her day after tomorrow and take her back without preparing her for the shock.

But the moment was snatched away by a rumble of faraway thunder. Nokose bolted to his feet. He knew its origin. Fear lent speed to his movements as he ran out of the cabin and into the trees beyond the clearing, unaware that Amanda was right at his heels.

By the time he realized that she was with him, it was too late to take her back. And although he might have wished to spare her this anxiety, it could also serve to illustrate the importance of what she had to learn.

"What was that?" she whispered, then shivered as the sudden silence of the forest in which they stood invaded her senses. She looked up through the trees to the sky above. Even the birds had taken flight.

"*Les Anglais,*" Nokose said. "Redcoats. They come."

Far below, Amanda could see a moving thread of red; men on foot marching through the mountains in single file. Sunlight ricocheted off of their swords and accoutrements; a dazzling, but misleading clue as to what was about to occur.

Redcoats? English? As in British subjects of the Crown?

Something Amanda had never considered occurred to her now. "Seth. Exactly what year is this?"

He shrugged. "My people do not keep time as do yours. I am not sure."

"Do you remember what year it was when your father died?"

His amber eyes darkened with memory. "Come," he said suddenly, and took her by the hand, leading her through the trees to a destination several meters away.

The mound was nearly obliterated by underbrush and fallen leaves. The handmade cross was wooden, and set at a listing angle to the tree behind it.

"*Mon père.*"

It was his father's grave. Amanda knelt and began moving aside the debris to get to the cross beneath. Nokose was puzzled as to her purpose, but he aided her by lifting all but the smallest of twigs hindering her sight.

She rocked on her heels at the words burned into the wood.

"Who wrote this?" she whispered as she reverently traced the letters carved into the wood.

Nokose shrugged. "*Mon père,* as he waited to die."

His father had made his own tombstone? It was beyond belief. The date of birth, as well as the date of death were both in place. Amazement colored her question.

"How could he? How did he know when he was going to die?"

"A man often knows these things, Amanda. Is this not so in your world, also?"

She shuddered, and buried her face in her hands, remembering when she'd thought her own death was imminent.

"Sometimes," she answered, touching the numbers beside the name.

Jacques LeClerc. 1690–1747

Her voice shook as she asked. "Your father's been dead how long?"

"Two winters . . . nearly three."

"Then this would be about . . . 1750. Oh dear Lord! If I remember my history, we're about to experience the French and Indian Wars firsthand."

Nokose heard, but did not heed. It mattered not what her time had labeled his. He already knew what lay ahead for them.

"We've got to get away," Amanda said suddenly, and jumped to her feet. "It isn't safe here. Soon fighting will be everywhere! British and French will fight for your . . . "

The expression on his face made her forget what she'd been about to say. She read it in his posture, as well as the determination in his eyes.

"A man does not run from what is his, Amanda. *Les Anglais et les Français* have no rights to this land. It was here long before I came . . . and will be here long after I am gone. The land belongs to no one. We belong to the land."

"Some things never change," Amanda muttered.

"What?"

"Never mind," she said. "I think I understand. But I don't know if you do. There will be danger."

Nokose smiled gently. "Amanda, no world is without danger. Whether it is mine or yours. But there is always a way to find joy . . . and to find happiness. You have to know where to look."

"Then we aren't leaving, are we?" she asked.

"I am not."

She nodded her head, satisfied with his answer. She'd already learned about fighting for what was right. Standing beside this man to hold what was theirs didn't seem so out of reach.

He took her hand and started to lead her away, when something he'd said suddenly sank in. She stopped and jerked her hand from his.

"What do you mean . . . I? Shouldn't that have been . . . we?"

His eyes mirrored his pain. Amanda bit her lip and cried out. "I don't know what you're thinking, but I won't go!" she shouted, and glared mutinously into his face. "Where you go, I go. We're a team, remember?"

His silence frightened her.

"You said you loved me."

He took her in his arms. Pain made them both shake.

"You said we were forever," she accused, and began to sob.

An answering jerk tugged at his lungs, but he could show no emotion. A man of the People knew to give nothing of himself away. It would only make him weak. But Nokose was also half French. A race of people swept through history by emotional outbursts of equal passion and pain. That half of him surfaced.

Tears burned at the back of his eyelids. Unwilling to admit, even to himself, that they were there, he settled for the weight of her body against his chest as a point on which to focus. Maybe then he wouldn't lose face. Maybe then he would be strong enough so that when it was time, he could let her go.

"You know it would kill me to leave you," Amanda sobbed, and held on to him with all her might.

No, my Amanda. It will kill me.

SIXTEEN

"I don't understand. You brought me back here to teach me to trust a man again . . . and then you expect me to walk away without you? What kind of trust is that?" Terror at losing him intensified her pain.

Nokose paced the cabin floor, trapped by walls, as well as fate. "You must understand," he said. "Otherwise it will be of no avail."

"Oh great! There you go again, speaking in riddles."

Her shout rang in his ears as her fury erupted and she threw an iron pot across the room. It clanked against the logs and tumbled to the floor behind him. He looked up in time to see her reaching for another and darted to her side before it, too, went flying.

"Stop!" He grabbed her hand. "You cannot throw away your pain."

She collapsed in his arms and sobbed against his chest. "Then show me how to accept what I know will surely kill me."

He wrapped his hands in her hair and tugged sharply, making her yield to the demand of his gaze. Forced to face him, she blinked back angry tears as she stared into a blaze of amber.

"Oh God," she whispered, and felt the room tilt at her feet. Whatever emotions he'd held in check were loose. She watched a muscle jerk near his eye, heard the hiss of his indrawn breath, and then winced as his hold tightened upon her hair.

"*Mon Dieu,*" Nokose whispered, his hands shaking as he divested himself of the curls entwined around his fingers. "I would not hurt you . . . even by mistake. I live to give you joy."

Before she could think, he'd lifted the tunic from her body, and her into his arms. He pivoted toward the corner of the cabin. Within two strides, she was lying on the furs, wearing nothing but the simple necklace of leather and beads that he'd given her earlier. No motion was wasted as his own clothing fell away. He stood before her, as God made man. Proud, strong, awaiting his mate.

For both of them, anxiety made speech impossible. From the look on Nokose's face, talk was unnecessary. A desire stronger than the one to be understood overwhelmed her. Finally, there was only a resurrecting throb between her legs and blood thundering through her veins.

"You will accept because you must," he said fiercely, standing tall above her. "You will do what you must . . . as I do. But you will not forget me. I promise, Amanda. I will be with you . . . always."

And then he was beside her. Moving against and then upon her with solemn intent. There was no time for play, or to ready for his coming. Before her next breath was drawn, he'd taken her by storm. Pinned beneath his body, she looked up into the face of her love.

"See me, Amanda," he whispered, and took her face in his hand, piercing her with the fire from his eyes. "Remember this man . . . for he is the one who truly loves you."

His features blurred. Her tears pooled in her eyes and then ran rampant down her face as he came closer. His lips parted and then centered upon her mouth.

Nokose shook. Covering her mouth with his own, he drank of her sorrow, and breathed in her fear. They would be forever fused in spirit. Then her arms pulled him closer, and her legs parted, letting him in. Everything became a blur but the woman beneath him and the violent surge of emotion that took them over the edge of reason.

Amanda's heart pounded until she thought it might burst as he drove himself into her, again and again. And still it was not enough. His touch was the reverence he could not voice. Their joining was all the more bittersweet because it could be their last.

Sobs raked her throat while she clung to him in desperation. The idea of losing this feeling, and the man who gave it, was impossible to absorb. Every stroke of his body against hers was more beautiful, and at the same time, more painful that anything David had ever done to her.

Tension built within each of them. Body hammered against body, heart against heart. Her sobs echoed his pain. And then it came too suddenly to deny. The soul-shattering, mind-bending flash of white heat that was the omega of love.

"No . . . no . . . no," Amanda sobbed, and wrapped her arms around his neck and held him close against her, unmindful of the weight of his body. "I won't go. I won't."

Her cries shredded his determination, bit by bit, until he had no answer he could give her that didn't cause him shame. He rolled over on his back and took her with him. And then held her till she quieted, and gentled her with a touch. Only when the sobs had ceased, did Nokose dare to look down at her face.

Her eyes were closed, their thick fringe of lashes wet and matted together like reeds after a flood. Flushed cheeks and swollen lips were further proof of her suffering.

His heart swelled within his chest. Inch by inch, breath upon breath, until he feared that it would never beat again. He'd never known that man could feel such pain and still survive.

A maverick sob slipped from between her lips. Even in sleep, her sorrow remained. And yet he could not look away, filling his soul with the sight of her slender form aligned with his. Imprinting forever the memory of soft, silky skin, her laughter, as well as her tears, the feel of her breasts pressing against his chest as she slowly exhaled from spent passion. All that was hers belonged to him.

"And all that I am will go with you," he whispered, clutching her fiercely to his body.

An unexpected gust of air came through the open cabin door. The Dreamcatcher rocked upon its peg, setting the feather to fluttering, the claw to swinging, and the braid of her hair to dangling.

"I hear you, Great Spirit," Nokose said quietly. "It will be done."

David Potter cursed the ground all women walked on, his mother's absent being suffering along with the lot. It gave him great satisfaction to say the words aloud.

"You were a bitch," he shouted, relishing the echo of his voice as it reverberated within the cave. "You made my childhood, and my adult life, a living, breathing hell. But you died, Mother!" The dirt clouded around his knees as he shuffled within the circle his footsteps made. "Do you hear me? You're dead! D. E. A. D."

He stalked to the mouth of the cave and stood at the opening, blinking at the sudden change from dark to light. "And you, Amanda, my beloved wife. You traitorous witch! Come back! You can't escape your fate . . . ate . . . ate."

His shouts rang throughout the valley below, echoing across the hills as his earlier words had done within the confines of the cave. With a curse on his lips and hate in his heart, he spun around and lost himself in the shadows. It was a fitting place for David Potter to be.

Jefferson Dupree's dark, tousled hair whipped across his forehead and into his eyes as it wrestled with the breeze that sprang up at the search site.

The foot of the mountain was before him, the crest far above. His stance was braced. His chin jutted defiantly as he continued to stare at the steep grade and the thick woodlands, contemplating the march he knew lay ahead, while cars and trucks emptied themselves of the officers who'd come to make the search. His eyes glittered, and he looked like what he was: a male animal on the hunt.

Local, state, and federal authorities had converged upon the area in anticipation of finding David Potter. News crews dotted the hillside below, parked on the shoulders of a narrow, two-lane county road, forced to wait behind an imaginary boundary by the county sheriff, who was determined to prevent them from impeding the search, and to keep them out of harm's way when he would rather they not be here at all.

Yet denying them access was impossible. This *was* big news! It wasn't every day that a member of Congress had an arrest warrant issued in his name. Especially for murder. Stories ran rampant concerning Amanda Potter's role in the mess. Most people concluded that she'd become an unwitting victim. Few believed she'd ever be found. A very few still believed she might be found alive.

Jefferson Dupree headed that list. Because he had to. Because losing Amanda was not something he would even consider.

"We're just about ready to start, Dupree."

He spun around, nodding shortly in silent answer to the marshal's warning.

The local authorities had been more than willing to let him join in the search. It was fortunate for them. He would have hated to fight them on the spot when there were much more important issues to face.

"It's going to be dark before we even get halfway up," the marshal grumbled. "Damn, but I hate sleeping outside on the ground."

"If she's there, Amanda Potter has been on the mountain at least four or five days. And I'd be willing to guarantee she doesn't have a sleeping bag."

The marshal flushed. To a man, the searchers were fully aware of Detective Dupree's compulsion to find Potter's wife. They'd seen him pale with fear. They'd heard him rage. What they didn't quite understand was his reason. The woman in question was no relation to him. It was common knowledge that he hardly knew her. But none was willing to question him too closely on the matter.

"Let's get this show on the road!" someone shouted.

Moving in teams, the men began to march up the mountain according to a previously mapped-out plan.

Dupree slung his backpack over his shoulder and started through the brush. He'd traded his shoes for hiking boots, his jacket for a down parka, and added an extra gun and ammunition to his sparse pack. He had little need for extravagant food or clothes. He only wanted Amanda.

And so they moved, slugging up the mountain to get to the point where Dupree had found the keys and ammunition clip. The theory was that if David Potter had planned on coming down, he had done so days ago. No one expected to meet him halfway. And if David Potter was still up there, it was a pretty good guess that he'd gone as far and as high as his legs would take him and had his own reasons for staying. It was a tall peak. They had a long way to go.

Jefferson Dupree walked without stopping, one foot in front of the other, up, up, looking forever forward. Never back. His fate lay in the future, not in the past.

Shadows began to lengthen upon the slope. As the men passed, creatures of the night were startled from their early evening routines. Minutes earlier they had ventured out of their dens, only to scurry back now to the holes from which they'd emerged.

Hawks were seen flying home to roost, while sightings of owls were made by the men who'd taken point. As the day changed from light to dark, so did the life within it. One set slept. Another awoke. The forest was constantly alive.

Dupree felt the air beginning to chill and knew it was partly due to the height they had climbed, as well as the fact that the sun was almost gone. He stopped long enough to pull the parka from his pack. He shrugged into it, fastening it as he resumed his climb. Branches slapped at his face. Twigs snapped beneath his feet. And a hundred men swept up the slopes with careful intent.

About halfway up the slope, Dupree began to move like a man with a purpose. His stride lengthened. His pace increased. He passed the stragglers among the last group, then most of the second wave, on to walk beside the men on point.

There was intensity in his every movement as he made a constant and thorough sweep of the ground ahead. They reached and then passed the area where David Potter had left behind the first clues leading to his whereabouts. Dupree shivered and ignored the feeling that someone was watching their progress. He told himself that he was imagining things.

Trees were taller, the growth thinner and more spread out. The higher they climbed, the sparser the underbrush became. In winter, only the hardiest of plants and animals survived at this level.

His lungs burned, but he didn't notice as he forged ahead. He'd lived with the pain of Amanda's absence for so long that he no longer recognized the signs of a thinner atmosphere.

"Hey, man," an officer called, as Dupree stalked past him. "Where do you think you're going? Or do you know something we don't?"

Dupree caught himself in mid-step and made a mental effort to slow down. No, he didn't know what he was doing. That had been an accepted fact for weeks. Even months. Ever since the day that Amanda Potter had fallen into his arms in the park.

"Sorry," he said. "I just want my hands on that sonofabitch so bad it makes me crazy."

The officer nodded. "You were the one who got the tape, right?"

Bile rose in his throat. Dupree could only nod. Memories of that image were burned so deeply in his brain he sometimes wondered if they'd ever go away.

"Must have been something to see," the officer prodded, perfectly willing to pass the time by talking as well as walking.

Dupree paused. He turned and fixed the man with a cool, amber stare. "Actually, I'd a lot rather have been watching the SuperBowl."

The man got the message immediately. He'd overstepped his bounds, using his authority to cover a morbid curiosity. "Sorry," he said. "I didn't mean it like that."

"It's almost dark."

As far as the officer was concerned, Dupree's remark had nothing to do with the subject. But from the way Dupree pushed through the trees as he moved on ahead, it meant something to him.

Within minutes, darkness surrounded them. Flashlights came out of packs as the men stopped and began to regroup, setting up camps, and laying out sleeping bags in a line that would hopefully prevent whoever might be above them from passing through without detection.

Dupree cursed. Helpless to do anything but follow suit, he unfolded his bag beneath a tree a few feet away from two other searchers. He ate his evening meal to the accompaniment of stories about bossy wives and grouchy bosses. It was no wonder his belly burned as he lay down to sleep. That kind of ambiance would give a billy goat ulcers.

Snores sounded upon the mountain like intermittent animal roars. Dupree lay wide-eyed and sleepless, trying to envision a place where Amanda could be, and still be unharmed. Sudden tears sprang to his eyes. He dug the heels of his hands across burning eyelids and hated the sinking feeling that had entered his gut.

She wasn't dead. He'd know it if she was. And with that thought came another. A reminder that maybe that was why he hurt all over and hadn't slept for days. Maybe his head already knew she was gone. Maybe it was just his heart that hadn't faced the music.

"Amanda . . . baby. If you're out there, tell me where."

.He stared blankly up at the sky above, counting the stars that winked down through the treetops, and while he was watching, an image began to form before his eyes.

It was Amanda. Running toward him. With arms outstretched. Her mouth open wide in a scream he could not hear. In shock, he bolted from his sleeping bag and stared intently through the trees, unable to believe that what he'd seen had only been a dream. It seemed so real.

But she didn't come running. And he couldn't hear a thing but the sounds of night and the snores of the searchers upon the mountain. As his pulse settled into a normal rhythm, he came to realize that this was nothing more than a replay of something he'd seen before. On the day of the picnic. When she'd been running with the children and their kites. He'd suffered the same sensation of déjà vu, and been as frightened and staggered then as he was now. He turned in a circle where he stood, whispering his agony to the night wind, which carried it away.

"Why, lady? Why do I keep seeing you this way? If you're trying to tell me something, I'm not hearing you." And then his voice broke. "Speak louder, love. I'm listening."

He crawled back into the bed and pulled the sleeping bag over his head. If he was going to be able to search tomorrow, he damn well better get some sleep.

"Damned lumpy ground."

It was the first thing Jefferson Dupree heard when he awoke. Remembrance as to where he was and why he was there came to him instantly. He crawled out of his sleeping bag in a leap, and quickly stuffed it into his backpack. Within five minutes, he was once more moving through the trees, even before complete reorganization of the search had taken place.

"Where do you think you're going?" the marshal asked, and grabbed Dupree by the arm.

"I'm going to find Amanda Potter."

"You are one focused sonofabitch," the marshal grunted,

and hefted his own backpack into place. "Move out," he called. The order was repeated down the line.

It was unnecessary for Dupree. He was already more than a hundred yards ahead.

David Potter rose and stretched. He kicked absently at the bag Amanda had left behind. Yesterday he'd eaten the last of the food. It was now going to be a test of his growling belly versus his bullheaded determination in seeing how much longer he would remain.

Sunlight filtered through the narrow opening at the mouth of the cave. It beckoned. Even taunted. David turned toward it and gazed with glassy stare. The thought of warm showers, clean beds, and hearty food made his resolve weaken. Even his mother's voice had been notice-ably absent, ever since the day that he'd told her she was D-E-A-D. He grinned to himself. If he'd known it would be that easy to get rid of her, he'd have done it years ago.

The urge to relieve himself surfaced. Scratching casually at his five-day growth of beard, he headed for the mouth of the cave to do his business. Standing to the side of the opening, he contemplated nature and all her glory. The thought of poached eggs on wheat toast and cinnamon yogurt was so strong he imagined he could taste it, and even smell the cinnamon sprinkled lightly on the top.

Reassembling his clothing gave him time to consider what he would need to buy before he got out of the coun-try. He'd reassured himself yesterday that escape would be simple. All it would take was money in the right hands. At the thought, he decided to count what he had, as well as what he'd found in Amanda's bag.

It was when he began to dig through his pockets that he realized what was gone.

"My keys!"

Money forgotten, he ran back into the cave and grabbed the flashlight. A wild but thorough search of the area he'd been living in revealed nothing but wrappers of the food that he'd eaten.

"Sonofabitch. How will I get away?" In his mind, the motor home was still down on the highway where he'd parked it, not in the police pound where it actually had been taken after Serge had been arrested driving it.

His panic was real. Just when it settled against his empty belly, he heard her whining. Then laughing. Then scolding as always.

I should have known you'd mess up again, she said. *You never could do anything right.*

"Stop! You don't know what you're talking about!" he shouted, kicking wildly about at unseen ghosts until thick clouds of dust boiled within the cave's interior.

Coughing and gasping for air, David staggered back toward the opening, and started outside when something far, far below caught his eye.

The color red . . . and blue. And orange . . . hunter orange. Hunters! No! Not hunters. There were too many and in too orderly a line.

"They've found me," he whined, and ran back into the cave. "What do I do? What do I do?"

The thought of running didn't even occur to him. He'd gone as high and as far as his mind could take him. It was dark here. Dark meant safety. He crawled back into the corner as far as he could go, and sat down. He covered his ears, and closed his eyes. If he couldn't see them, then they couldn't see him.

"There's nothing up here but birds," Dupree's sidekick in search grumbled. "I have a feeling that this is a wasted trip. Are you sure it was Potter's stuff that you found?"

"I'm not sure of anything," Dupree growled. "You know as much as I know. I found an ammunition clip and a set of keys. The damned keys had Potter's address. This area was identified as the place he was last seen by the man who led him up here. What did you want me to do? Get his forwarding address before you crawled out from behind your desk?"

The moment he'd said it, Dupree wished it back. He stopped and wiped his hand across his face. "Dammit, I'm sorry," he said quietly. "This has been a hell of a week. I didn't have to take it out on you."

The man shrugged. "Yeah, no big deal. I *was* whining a little." He grinned. "My therapist says I do that when I'm faced with a situation I don't like."

Dupree grinned. "Don't we all."

The searchers ground to a halt to reassess the situation. A few minutes later, a runner came down the line. And his news sent Dupree's hopes soaring. Something . . . or someone was above them. One of the searchers had distinctly seen sunlight glint off of something shiny. It remained to be seen if it was man-made or man-worn. If it was a beer can they'd seen, someone was due for a ribbing.

Dupree turned around and stared intently upward, trying to discern the place in question. But there was nothing to be seen but the occasional outcropping of rock, as well as trees, trees, and more trees. Nothing glinted. Nothing even moved.

His hopes rose, only to sink. If it was Amanda who'd seen them, then he had to wonder why she hadn't come running. The answer to that made him sick. She didn't come, because she couldn't. If that *was* David Potter hiding above them, what had he done to his wife?

David Potter had more problems than the warrant for his arrest and his missing wife. His mother wouldn't leave him alone.

Get up, you fool! Stand up and fight like a man!

David got to his feet. His pistol was in his hand as he walked to the mouth of the cave. He checked the clip for ammunition. It was nearly full. He'd been saving it for Amanda, but first things first.

He leaned forward, peering intently through the trees.

The men were still there. Only they had stopped searching.

"Maybe they've given up," he muttered.

The only one who's giving up is you, his mother hissed.

"Dammit! I've had just about enough of you," David shouted, and fired.

He didn't even realize that he'd squeezed off the shot until his ears began to ring from the impact.

"Oh damn," he muttered. "Now look what you made me do."

He bolted back inside the cave and began to run in circles, grabbing Amanda's bag, as well as his flashlight. If there was a deeper passageway through here, it was time to investigate.

"Sonofabitch!" a man yelled as Potter's shot went off, and dived headfirst into the bushes.

"That just about sums it up for me, too," Dupree said, as he followed his hiking buddy to cover.

The shot was too far away to put them in danger, but it drove them to their hands and knees beneath some bushes.

"We got us a live one," someone shouted. "Reconnoiter!"

Dupree followed the lawmen, who began to surge toward a thick stand of trees. In minutes, a helicopter that had been on standby was called for. If they were about to storm the wooded castle, they wanted all the backup they could get. The density of the trees was unbelievable. If that was David Potter above them and he decided to run, there were too many places he could hide to elude them.

Jefferson Dupree's adrenaline surged. "I volunteer," he said.

The marshal frowned, and then grinned slightly. "Hell, man, I haven't asked for one, yet."

Dupree dumped his backpack and shoved a clip into his gun.

The marshal frowned again. Obviously the man wasn't listening. "I said . . . I haven't asked for volunteers. Settle down, Dupree. You'll go and get yourself killed and what will that prove? Potter's already going down for Murder

One. If you die, it won't prove a thing, and we can't kill the S.O.B. twice."

Dupree frowned. "You don't get it," he said. "If that bastard claims he's crazy, no one's going to do a thing to him. He'll get a nice padded cell and weekly visits from a state-certified shrink. He'll get away with murder, by reason of insanity."

"Our job is to arrest them and lock them up. It's up to a court of law to do the rest."

Dupree spat. "And we all know what the courts are about, don't we? It's a game of who's got the bucks. David Potter has millions."

The marshal frowned. "The hell you say." He stared long and hard up toward the trees, and then back at the man poised to run. He relented slightly. "Wait for the chopper. And then we'll talk."

Dupree turned toward the mountain slope. "I won't wait long."

"You'll do what I say."

Dupree let the words roll off him like rain from a leaf. He'd come up this mountain for a purpose. To hell with orders.

"If he's as bad as they say, then his wife's either dead or wishes she was."

The shock of the casually uttered statement from the man behind him made Dupree sick. He spun around, his hand curled into a fist. All he could think to do was stop it from being said. Maybe that would keep it from coming true.

"Take that back," Dupree said softly.

The argument died on the other man's lips as his life flashed before his eyes. His acerbic tongue had made more than one enemy in his career on the force, but he'd never had to face one this big.

"Sorry. I didn't know you were standing there."

Dupree shook, from fury as well as despair. He shrugged off the apology and disappeared into the trees, only to surface a few yards away, staring up at the mountain. Waiting for a sign.

SEVENTEEN

Sunlight streamed through the open door of the cabin. A small ground squirrel sat in the doorway, chattering noisily at a blue jay who'd confiscated his nut.

Nokose opened his eyes to witness the dispute between his early-morning visitors and started to smile. It died on his face when he remembered that this morning he had to send away his reason for living.

He rolled over, expecting Amanda to still be asleep. She was sitting cross-legged against the wall with a blanket made of rich, brown beaver pelts lying across her lap. Tears rolled silently down her face as she stared out the door.

"No," he whispered. His voice broke, along with his heart. "Do not do this, Amanda."

She shuddered, then blinked, then turned to look at him. "Don't do what, Seth? Mourn? How can I not? Something inside of me is dying."

"No. It is not," he whispered, and pulled her down into his embrace. "It is just lost. When you return to your world, you will find your way. I promise."

"You can't promise anything. You won't be there."

The palm of his hand centered on her heart. "I am in here. Always."

She clutched fistfuls of his hair and buried her face against his neck, rocking her body to and fro against him in despair.

"I don't want memories. I want the man. I want love at night and a smile in the morning. You gave it all to me . . ." Her voice broke on a fresh sob. "And now you're taking it back."

Nokose's heart felt as if it was shattering, but there were too many things that had to be done to let her continue mourning their losses.

"It is not so, but I don't know how to make you believe. All I ask is that you trust me."

She thumped his chest with her fists. "And all I ask is that you let me stay."

He bolted from the bed and began to dress, desperate to put distance between them before he broke down and relented. It would be disastrous.

"You must dress. We have a distance to go."

Amanda looked up. He held her clothes suspended between them. She yanked them from his hands.

"Damn you," she whispered, as she stared at her jeans, shirt, and shoes. "Where is my tunic? I want to wear what you gave me."

Nokose knelt beside her, smoothing her tangled curls and coaxing the frown from her forehead with the stroke of his hand. "I am sorry, *mon coeur,* but you cannot take back what was never there."

"Is that another damned riddle?" The anger in her voice belied her sorrow.

Nokose smiled gently. He knew the source of her pain and understood her need to strike out at the one who seemed to have hurt her.

"No. It is not a riddle. It is the truth. To go back, you must wear what you wore in." His voice softened. "Don't you understand yet, *ma chérie?* You cannot change what was. Only what is yet to be."

She began pulling on her pants, one leg at a time, in fitful starts and jerks. After the suede-like feel of the deerskin tunic, the fabric of her jeans felt stiff, and the fit too tight and confining. When she had dressed, she turned and looked at him from across the room. Even though the distance between them was small, she felt the gulf widening by the moment.

"Eat." He beckoned for her to sit.

"I wouldn't be able to swallow."

He didn't argue. There was no need. Amanda was arguing enough for the both of them.

"If we've got to do this," she said, "then let's get it over with. No need prolonging the misery. Maybe after I'm gone, your life will return to some kind of order."

She hated herself for the words of anger, but kept saying them in the hopes that he would deny their truth. To her constant dismay, he did not.

"After you have gone, I will have no life, my Amanda. You are taking my heart, remember? A man cannot live without a heart."

"Then why?" Her voice broke as her hands knotted against her sides. She was overwhelmed by the urge to shake him until he reacted with something other than stoicism.

He stood without speaking. There was, after all, nothing left to say.

Tears filled her eyes as she pivoted. The necklace that he'd given her moved beneath her shirt, sliding gently against her skin. She fiddled with the top button, making certain that he did not see. He wouldn't let her take the dress, but she would take her beads. It was all she had to remember him by. A leather string and a handful of beads couldn't possibly matter.

They walked from the clearing, side by side, not touching, not speaking. But the pain they shared was visible upon their faces as they moved through the trees.

The breeze lifted Nokose's long hair, moving it away from his neck and shoulders like black wings taking flight. The early sunlight was kind to their tearstained and burning eyes. It only stung a little bit as they walked east, angling slightly downward toward a destination only he knew.

Several yards from the path they were on, a feeding deer paused to stare at them with wide, nervous eyes.

Amanda recognized the expression. It felt like the one she wore.

How can I let this happen? she asked herself. *Something will surely stop this from taking place. He can't mean it. He loves me. I know it. But if he does, then why . . . why won't he keep me with him?*

While her tumultuous thoughts made hash of her sanity, the pair moved closer and closer to their destination.

Suddenly Nokose stopped, grasping her firmly by the arm as he pointed in front of them. Amanda was completely unprepared for the devastation on his face. When she saw it, she knew that all her last-minute hopes had been for naught. If he was planning to change his mind, he would have already done so.

"We are here," he said.

She started to shake. "This isn't happening!" she cried.

"Yes, my Amanda. It must." And as he pulled her into his arms, he whispered, "Great Spirit give me strength . . . it has to."

Their tears fell, and then mixed, until it was impossible to tell from whose eyes they had fallen. Tortured whispers of love were returned with desperate pleas to relent. She clung to him. And he held her so tightly that when he finally turned her loose, he lost his own balance and stumbled. Without Amanda, he was only half a man.

"We go," he said, and pushed her toward a shadow that wasn't really there.

"Don't make me," she begged, and fell to the dirt at his feet, wrapping her arms around his legs and refusing to turn loose when he pulled.

And then suddenly his anger erupted. "Get up, Amanda. Never yield to another man in the way that you have done in the past. Never let a man raise his hand to you in anger. Never let a man rule your life . . . and your world. You are a strong woman. Fight for what is right. If you must . . . fight for your life."

"I am trying," she sobbed, as she staggered to her feet.

"I'm fighting for my man and his love. He just doesn't want it back."

"No. No! You are wrong! I *do* want it . . . and you. But you aren't looking for me in the right place. Go back, my Amanda, and search. I am already there!"

While trying to absorb this revelation, she let down her guard. It was all that he needed to pull her with him into the shadow. Before she knew it, the same penetrating weight was sinking through the pores of her skin. The breath was being forced from her lungs as the air around them began to hum.

"I love you, Seth," she called, but it was lost in the rush of wind sweeping past them.

Something was wrong. Nokose could feel it. She wasn't moving through as she should. He reached up and pushed her harder, thinking that her mental resistance was keeping them trapped. And then he felt the leather beneath his fingertips and knew. She was wearing the necklace! It belonged in the past with him. She could not take it through.

He grabbed it and pulled. It broke from her neck as he pushed. Suddenly she was gone, and he sensed that she'd passed. A buzzing began in his ears. He only had moments in which to go back, or his own body would be crushed by the weight of the years.

And then he heard her scream.

David Potter was heading for deeper ground. That shot had been the last straw. Thanks to his mother, whoever was below him on the mountain now knew of his presence. He shifted the duffle bag to his other shoulder as he moved farther into the cave. His gun was in one hand, the flashlight with its waning beam in his other.

The last thing he expected to see was Amanda staggering toward him from out of nowhere. In another frame of mind, he might have questioned what he'd just seen. But he was too overwhelmed by his circumstances to consider anything other than that one of his grandest wishes had just been handed to him. Amanda would pay for what she'd done after all.

She stumbled as she fell through, and knew the moment she caught herself from falling that she was back in her own world. Even the air smelled different. But when she looked up only to stare into a single eye of light, all she could hear was an eerie chuckle, and all she could feel was an arm encircling her neck.

"Well, well, well," David growled, and tightened his choke-hold on her neck. "At least one of my prayers has been answered. Welcome back, you bitch!"

"David?"

He swung the flashlight toward the side of her head. It connected with a vicious thump and sent her staggering against the wall. She caught herself and her breath. And then she heard a gun cock and her mind began to whirl as she considered how it would feel to die. *Damn you. I won't give up so easily. Not anymore.*

She struck out at him, and then screamed—never imagining that Nokose, still caught within the passage of time, could hear her.

It echoed. Over and over within the confines of the cavern. When David's curses began to mingle with her shrieks, she knew that she had rattled him.

The last thing she wanted to hear was her name being shouted out from behind her. In shock, she recognized the voice, and knew what was about to happen. Seth was coming to her aid and David was the only one with a gun.

"No!" she screamed. "No, Seth! Go back! Go back!"

David shrieked in fury. "Seth? I knew you couldn't think this up on your own." He swung at her again, but she ducked and then stumbled into another wall. Caught between the beam of the flashlight and her husband, she was as helpless and frightened as a spotlighted deer.

Furious that she'd cuckolded him with another man, David aimed his gun in the direction of the man's voice and fired twice in rapid succession.

Amanda heard the groan of a man in pain, and knew immediately that Seth had been hit.

"No! My God, Seth, no!" she screamed. She would have bolted back into the passageway to him, when suddenly the ceiling and the walls around them began to shake.

Set off by the gunshots inside the mountain, an internal landslide had begun. Rocks rolled and the walls began to crack. The ground shook beneath her feet and dust boiled up into their noses and eyes.

"You've killed him . . . and us!" she shrieked, and rushed toward the beam of light without thought of escape. All she could think to do was stop David from shooting again.

Pain mushroomed inside his chest as Nokose fell out into his world upon his back. Long moments passed while he stared up at the sky and waited to see if he could draw a second breath. Surprised by the fact that it came, and others followed, he tested the blood running down his belly and then traced it to its source. It ran freely from a gaping hole above his heart.

"Amanda," he groaned, and listened to the sound of the avalanche within the mountain. She was on her own.

Realizing that he was losing sensation in his arms and legs, he rolled to his knees, and then waited until the earth stopped spinning. Before it was over, he had one thing left to do.

He pulled himself erect. A long moment passed as he looked around at the world in which he had lived. The sun still shone. Birds still sang. And his blood was running cold. He tilted his head and breathed deeply, for what it was worth, taking a long drink of life. Then he began to move.

One foot after another, his eyes forever forward, he headed toward his father's cabin with the broken necklace dangling from his hand.

With each step that he took, the forest and all within it suddenly silenced. Each living animal slipped quietly into the shadows as death passed by.

The trees began to blur in his vision as sweat beaded upon his forehead. Still he moved as if in a trance. There was a thing yet undone that he must finish. Just when he feared his legs would not make another step, he staggered into a clearing and saw the doorway to the cabin standing open.

His gaze focused on the shape of the door and the shadows within, and he began to move more quickly. His long black hair swung with every motion of his body. His eyes burned brightly with an amber fever of determination that sent a last spurt of adrenaline surging through his system. It was just enough.

He fell through the doorway and onto his knees on the earthen floor. Twice he shook his head to clear his vision, and twice the room tilted and turned upside down. Finally, trusting instinct to get him where he needed to go, Nokose pulled himself up and stumbled to the wall over his bed.

He grabbed the Dreamcatcher and yanked. It came away in his hands and fell with him onto the bed of furs. Weak and spent, breath slipping as quickly from his body as the last of his blood, he tied the bit of leather and beads upon the webbing next to the braid of her hair.

"It is done," he whispered, and fell backward onto nokose's fur.

Full circle. Birthed at the hands of a bear, and imbued with its spirit in life, he now would die upon its fur. His fingers threaded the Dreamcatcher's webbing, his thumb centering on the silken braid of her hair. With his last link to Amanda held close to his heart, he looked up at the rafters above his head and watched them slowly fading out of focus. His final thought was the memory of her face. Then he moved toward the light, this time, forever.

David hadn't expected her to fight. Not with such unrelenting vengeance. Twice he tried to regain the upper hand, but each time Amanda's vicious kick or flailing arms would send him ducking for cover. Only once did he manage to aim the handgun again and fire. The shot missed her, only to ricochet several times against the rock walls of the cave before plowing uselessly into the dirt.

And then her foot connected with his knee and he doubled over in pain while the flashlight fell to the floor and rolled, giving a weak, spotlight effect to everything before it.

Amanda gasped as the light momentarily swept past David. Had she not heard his voice, she would never have recognized him. But the fragmented image she had of him finally fit his inner self. He was now as ugly on the outside as his soul had always been.

And then she saw her bag on the ground at his feet. Her Dreamcatcher had been in there. Knowing that this might be her only chance to get away, she snatched the bag from the dirt and bolted toward the mouth of the cave.

She was doing what Nokose had taught her to do. Yield to no man . . . and fight for the right to her life.

The lawmen were on the move when the faint but certain sounds of gunshots deep inside the mountain were heard. The men moved faster, each of them thinking the same thing. If the man wasn't shooting at them, then he had to have another victim to shoot at. Amanda Potter's welfare came instantly to mind. And then the cave-in began.

To a man, they each felt the ground rumbling beneath their feet, and when dust boiled from a crevice in the rocks several hundred yards above, it pinpointed the cave's opening . . . as well as the possible site of disaster.

Jefferson Dupree was the first to move as he ran uphill as fast as he could. Where some of the lawmen tried to maintain some degree of protection by moving from tree to tree, he opted for the clearings. He was constantly running at an upward angle, and the muscles in his legs began to burn and shake as he pushed himself to the limit and beyond.

The gunshots from within had startled him, and then sickened him beyond belief. He couldn't have come this far only to be too late!

Then the bushes at the cave entrance parted. Just as Dupree thought about aiming his gun, a woman burst out of the cave. He couldn't believe what he was seeing! His heart jerked as hope swelled within him. It was Amanda! He stopped in mid-stride and turned to the men coming behind him.

"Don't shoot! Don't shoot!" he cried. "It's her!"

She ran without looking back. Brush caught the fabric of her jeans, branches tore holes in her shirt and scratched her cheeks as she flew downhill without definite destination. Her only purpose was to get away. Where and how far remained to be seen.

Just as Jefferson Dupree started toward her, another figure bolted from the cave. To the horror of every onlooker below, David Potter chased his wife downhill, firing his gun with every other step.

"You'll pay! You'll pay!" he screamed and squeezed off a round between every shriek of rage.

"Oh Jesus," Dupree groaned, and started to run faster, fear for her life uppermost in his mind. What if he couldn't get to her in time? What if one of Potter's wild shots hit its target before she gained the safety of the searchers?

Amanda heard the shots behind her. Once the bark from a tree directly in her path shattered from a badly aimed bullet, and splattered against her cheek as she passed it on the fly. Another plowed into the dirt inches behind her. Her heart was in her throat. She was so lost in her fear that she was unaware of the help only yards away.

"Get in position!" the marshal yelled, and pointed to the marksmen who were angling for positions that would give them clear shots at Potter without endangering his wife's life. "And when you get a good shot, take it. It may be her only chance," he added. His last remark was under his breath and intended for his ears only.

Sweat ran from her hairline into her eyes. A large tree

root beneath a covering of leaves snagged her toe and sent her sprawling. She hit the earth with such impact that she lost her breath. In that moment, she thought she'd been hit and was in the process of dying.

And then she heard a voice in front of her. Heard the man telling her to run. Her heart jerked, and the air surged from her lungs to her body as adrenaline raced through her system. Someone was coming to her rescue!

She staggered to her knees and then bolted from a half-crouch like a runner out of a starting gate, only seconds ahead of David.

"You stupid, stupid bitch!" he kept screaming. A limb slapped him across the mouth, causing tears to come his eyes. But they were not tears of remorse. Only reflex.

He dodged the next set of limbs and as he did, saw for the first time the lines of men moving toward them from all directions. It was over! The sight of Amanda's retreating figure made it all the more difficult to accept. And she was getting away!

As suddenly as it had begun, he stopped the chase and took slow, careful aim, aligning the gunsight with the center of her back. There was still time for her to pay. Sunlight glimmered in the rich autumn hues of her hair, giving him a colorful target. He held his breath just as he'd been taught, and started to squeeze.

Be careful! Be careful! the voice screeched in his head. *If you don't, you'll miss her again.*

"Goddammit, Mother, don't you ever know when to quit?" he asked, and as he did, his finger jerked on the trigger.

Jefferson Dupree's mind screamed a warning he had no breath left to give voice to as he saw Potter stop and take aim. With his last ounce of strength, he jumped, catching Amanda in mid-flight and taking her to the ground with him as the shot rang in their ears.

Amanda's shock at seeing a man suddenly appear before her was nothing compared to the one that spiraled through her body as the bullet from her husband's gun entered and exited her shoulder as she fell.

Terror subsided as a man's strong arms enfolded her. She heard a thundering heartbeat near her ear, and felt the stroke of his hands as they raked across her body.

Dupree whispered against her ear as they rolled over and over out of the line of fire, only to come to a stop beneath a bush.

"Amanda . . . Amanda! Thank the Lord, I found you at last. You're safe, darling. Safe. And you'll never have to be afraid again."

Amanda would have answered. Joy filled her heart as she heard the familiar voice. But the pain in her shoulder suddenly ballooned. And when his fingers touched the exit wound, she moaned, then sighed, and slipped into unconsciousness.

Dupree's elation faded when he heard her groan. He looked down at the unnatural paleness of her face, the wide, shattered expression in her eyes just before she passed out, and then at the blood that came away on his fingers. Without thought of David Potter's whereabouts, he jumped to his feet and shouted down the mountainside.

"Get me a medic! She's been shot!"

The words brought a smile to Potter's face as he took second aim. But the bullet never left his gun as three different marksmen found their targets. His body bucked from the impact of their shots. His hands went limp as the gun dropped uselessly to the ground. Swaying on his feet, he stared blankly around him at the sunlit clearing in which he stood, and then down at the blood swiftly staining his clothing, unable to believe it was over. He couldn't die. He had a meeting next month in D.C.

No! No! she cried. *I told you it would end like this. You never could do anything right.*

David's lips numbed as his legs began to buckle. "Dammit, Mother, shut the hell up. Why can't you remember? You're already dea . . . "

He hit the ground on his knees and then rolled, coming to a stop against the first tree in his path. His blond hair was stiff and full of bits of grass and leaves. His clear blue eyes stared sightlessly upward toward the sky. Just like his mother, David Potter was D-E-A-D.

A flurry of men descended upon his body as others made their way to Dupree and the wounded victim. Within the space of five minutes, a field dressing had been applied to Amanda Potter's shoulder, and the helicopter that had been en route to assist in the search for the missing felon was now put into use for medical evacuation.

Moments later, Dupree watched it fly out of sight with Amanda inside, and then dropped to the ground as his legs unexpectedly gave way.

"Hell of a run, Dupree," a lawman said, and patted him roughly on the back as he passed. "You probably saved her life."

Dupree folded his arms upon his knees and lowered his head. Black spots danced before his eyes as the man's words rang in his brain.

No, he thought. *I saved my own. If I'd lost her, nothing would have mattered.*

EIGHTEEN

———————— ✦ ————————

Thunder and lightning rattled the windows and rudely jerked Amanda from the drug-induced sleep the doctors had kept her in. The unexpected movement made her wince in the darkness. The pain startled her, and her hands flew to the bulky bandage at her shoulder. For a few seconds, her mind raced in an effort to figure out where she was and how she'd gotten there.

Vague images filtered in and out of her semiconscious mind as she made herself relax while she considered the other twinges of pain she was now feeling. Besides the obvious wound on her shoulder, her legs hurt and her face felt tender. But why?

Lightning flashed again. The shadow of a man moved between her bed and the brief electrical show of light. She gasped.

Jefferson Dupree knew she was awake, but was unaware that she'd spotted him until he heard her swift intake of breath.

"Don't be afraid, Amanda," he whispered, and started toward her bed.

Memories flooded her at the sound of his voice. He'd been with her before in the cave . . . and beyond. Or had it been afterward? She couldn't remember, but she knew that his voice was familiar.

"Who are you?" she whispered.

"Detective Dupree. Morgantown P.D. You remember me, honey," he said softly. "From the park. We even spoke later at the shelter benefit honoring Mrs. Potter."

She sighed, unaware that tears of disappointment had started down her cheeks. The pain of her loss was so fresh that she could not form a word in response. She remembered everything, including the last glimpse she'd had of Seth, and she knew that when David had fired into the passage, he had sealed it between them forever.

"It was you who mailed me the tape, wasn't it, Amanda?"

She shuddered and gulped a sob, then nodded. It didn't occur to her that he could not see her. Lightning flashed again and her eyes squinted as she turned away from the light.

In the brief fluorescent glow of lingering lightning, he saw tears shining on her cheeks and could not prevent a groan of dismay.

"Please . . . Amanda . . . I'll do anything. I'll leave. If you're in pain, I'll call a nurse. Just don't, for God's sake, cry."

Surprised by his vehemence, she choked on a sob and reached behind her for the lamp chain. An artificial glow illuminated the area above and around her bed, bathing her in light.

"It was you who saved me . . . wasn't it?" she asked.

The breath slid out of his body in weak relief. At least she wasn't screaming her head off at the sight of a man in her room. From all he knew of battered women, as well as women who'd been taken hostage, they had lingering or permanent distrust of all men in general. He had to take it slow.

"Yes, it was me, along with about a hundred other lawmen who wouldn't give up on you, lady."

"Then I need to thank them . . . and you. If you hadn't been there, David's aim might have been better the second time."

As soon as she said his name, her gaze slid furtively around the room, as if she expected to see him pop up from the shadows at any moment.

Dupree saw her fear and understood instantly what she was thinking. "You're safe. You don't ever have to be afraid again, Amanda. He's dead."

Her head dropped back onto the pillow and she pulled the sheet up beneath her chin and closed her eyes. Tears slid out from the corners. Unexpectedly, her face crumpled.

"I never thought I'd be glad to say I'm glad another human being is dead . . . but I am," she whispered, and buried her face in her hands.

She looked so small, and sounded so lost. He forgot that he'd meant to maintain his distance. He forgot that she didn't know him in the way that he knew her. Before he thought, Dupree found himself sitting on the side of her bed.

Amanda's sobs came to a halt as Dupree pulled her hands from her face. His voice roughened, the tone deepening as his hand smoothed at the tangles in her hair.

"Never hide from the truth, lady. Never be ashamed that you fought and won. He didn't deserve your love. He damn sure doesn't deserve your tears."

She shuddered. The words were too close to what Seth had said for her to ignore them. How odd.

"I wasn't crying for him," she finally said. "I guess I was crying from the waste of it all."

Slowly, so as not to frighten her, his hand moved from her hair to her cheek. Amanda followed his lead, allowing him to tilt her face until they were eye to eye.

"Nothing is wasted in life that is used."

Amanda's heart jumped. "Is that a riddle?"

Dupree grinned. "Beats the hell out of me. It's just something my father always said. I never got the hang of exactly what it meant, but it sounded good at the time."

The smile on his face made her nervous. Something kept hammering at her memory, making her head throb painfully. And with the thought came Seth's image flooding into her mind. The way he had moved when they made love. The way he had laughed at her insecurities about his world. And then she remembered.

"My bag! I need my bag! Oh, God, I dropped it on the mountain." She started struggling, kicking at the confines of the sheet, when Dupree stayed her panic with a single sentence.

"No. I brought it with me. It's in the drawer."

Thank God! "Please. May I have it?"

He walked around the bed and retrieved it from the drawer opposite her bed. It was dusty, and a bit of leaf was caught in the zipper, but it was more or less still in one piece.

Amanda's fingers shook as she pulled the tab. Crumbs from the snacks that David had eaten mingled with her bits and pieces of clothing. She didn't care. It wasn't clothes she was after. He could have set fire to the lot and it wouldn't have mattered. She dug deeper. All she wanted was . . .

"Oh thank God," she muttered, as her hands felt the taped magazines and the old frame sandwiched between. "It's still here."

Dupree could only stare in puzzlement as she pulled the odd package from inside and laid it in her lap, letting the bag and its meager contents fall to the floor.

Unexpectedly weak, she struggled with the strips of packing tape that she'd used to bind the magazines together, and finally looked up at Dupree with defeat on her face.

"I need help," she said.

She could have asked for the moon and he would have been on his way to NASA in a second to book flight for the next trip.

"What do you want me to do?" he asked gently.

"Cut the tape. But be careful. I don't want what's inside to be damaged."

The blade of his pocket knife made short work of the packing tape. Moments later, he stepped back and let Amanda continue, curious as to what was so important within that she'd risked life and limb to bring it with her as she'd run from the cave.

Amanda held her breath as she moved the first

magazine aside, terrified that in all the turmoil her Dreamcatcher had been broken. But it was just as she'd packed it. The fragile piece had survived this incident, just as it had through the centuries to get to her.

Thunder rumbled low in the distance as lightning moved into the mountains beyond the city. A deep and abiding pain swelled inside her chest until Amanda feared she would die—even wished she could die—as the images upon the webbing jumped out at her from beyond the grave.

"Oh . . . my . . . God."

"What is it, darling?"

Lost in the shock of what she was seeing, Amanda completely missed the term of endearment.

"It can't be," she muttered, as her fingers traced the feather . . . the claw . . . and the beaded medallion. "It stayed behind in the cave when I passed through. So how can this be?"

Her hand shook as she lowered it toward the other two items that had somehow been added to the web. A small bit of something braided and brown hung beside the feather remnant. She touched it carefully, fully aware of its advanced age, and then closed her eyes as she traced the shape, remembering, only three days past, what joy she'd felt as she'd braided it and cut it from her own head before fastening it to the Dreamcatcher.

But that Dreamcatcher had been with Seth. This one had been in the cave all that time. She was unable to grasp the concept of time's puzzle.

She opened her eyes and moved on to the next and last item upon the web. The leather was as hard and stiff as the webbing upon which it hung. The beads were few . . . and small . . . and still azure as a hot summer sky. And they'd been in her possession yesterday, right up until Seth had yanked them from her neck and pushed her through the passage. The last time she'd seen them, they'd been dangling from his hand.

The pain burst, shattering resolve and restraint. Tears

shot to the fore and poured in fresh torrents down her cheeks. She clasped the ancient Dreamcatcher to her breast and rocked in a mindless grief as the last of her odyssey was made known. Whatever connection they'd had was obviously in the past. Even the bits of herself that she'd left behind were as ancient as the Dreamcatcher itself. Seth . . . and their love . . . were just history.

"Oh God," she moaned, whispering to herself as she rocked and rocked against the pillow at her back. "No, Seth, no. You promised you'd be with me always. Why did you lie? Why did you lie?"

Dupree was speechless. Her reaction to what she'd unveiled was obviously traumatic. He feared for her sanity and well-being. And then while he was in the midst of considering calling for a doctor, she'd gone and accused him of lying. None of this made sense. Not a damned bit of sense at all.

"Amanda." He slid onto the side of her bed and tried to pry the frame from her hands. "Honey . . . listen to me," he urged, and succeeded in bringing on nothing but another set of tears, this time accompanied by gut-wrenching sobs that made him want to cry, too.

"Amanda . . . you are my heart. As God is my witness, I *would never*, *could* never, lie to you. What made you think that I did?"

Mon coeur. My heart. The duplication of two different men's endearments shocked her. A sob caught at the back of her throat as she stared at him through a veil of tears. The look in his eyes made her stop and think. And then she looked *into* his eyes and started to shake.

"I've never seen your eyes this close up before," she said, completely ignoring the oddity of the remark.

Dupree grinned. "Yes you have, you've just forgotten. The day you fell in the park? We were eyeball to eyeball, and then some."

She shuddered and swallowed another lingering sob. "They're brown . . . and at the same time gold. Sort of amber, aren't they?"

He shrugged, a little embarrassed. "I guess. I never paid much attention to them unless they were black and blue." He grinned, trying to tease her out of her sorrow. And then a frown slid back into place.

"Amanda, why did you call me a liar? I don't lie. I couldn't lie to you."

She shook her head and swiped at her tears. "I'm sorry," she said. "You misunderstood. I wasn't talking to you. I meant someone else."

Dupree persisted. "I don't think so," he said. "Come on, 'fess up. Whatever it is, you can tell me. After all, you trusted me enough to send me the tape." And as he remembered how remarkable that was, considering what another man had done to her and gotten away with for years, he could only marvel that it had happened at all.

"I did, didn't I? I don't know why. But when it came, you were the only person I could think of who would help." And then she flushed. "Even then, I wasn't sure that you would. I just took the chance and trusted my . . . "

Embarrassed, she looked away, unable to finish her sentence.

"Instincts," Dupree said, and wanted so desperately to hold her that he ached.

She nodded.

"But that still doesn't get past the reason why you called me a liar," he persisted.

She glared at him. It was the first time since she'd awakened that any emotion save sorrow had intervened. Oddly, it felt good to feel something besides pain, even if it was only misplaced frustration.

"For the last damned time," she muttered, staring him in the face, "I did *not* call you a liar. I said *Seth* was the liar."

He shrugged. "I don't know who the hell told, but I'll get even with them somewhere down the line."

She struggled with his odd remark. It made no sense.

"Listen, Dupree," she said slowly, enunciating every word in precise tones.

"Jefferson," he corrected, grinning at the flush of color staining her cheeks.

She rolled her eyes and hugged her Dreamcatcher closer to her breast. "Jefferson, then. No one told me anything. I don't know what you're talking about, either."

"My name is Jefferson," he said. "But my father always calls me Seth. I distinctly heard you . . . "

The room spun. A roar sounded in her ears as Amanda fell backward onto the pillow and stared up at the dark image of the man above her. His hair was short . . . but black as a raven's wing. His skin was considered fair, but it was many shades darker than her own. And those eyes . . . those same rich, warm, amber-colored eyes.

She closed her eyes and heard the words revolving around and around in her head. *I am Nokose, a son of the Muskogee, but my father called me Seth.*

Her eyes flew open. Concern was etched upon his face. She let the Dreamcatcher slide onto the sheet beside her and did something that neither she nor Dupree expected. She held up her arms and made room for him to come in.

"Would you mind very much if I asked you to hold me?" she whispered.

The shock and then unbridled joy on his face was beautiful to see.

"Ah, God, Amanda. It would be my pleasure . . . forever."

He bent down. She closed her eyes and let herself inhale his being, testing her theory as he enfolded her within his arms. The width of his shoulders beneath the jacket, the texture of his hair between her fingers, and the soft whisper of his breath upon her cheek were the same . . . and yet different. But she had to remember. More than two hundred years had come and gone since the man he was before. If this was . . . if he was . . .

She began to shake.

Dupree closed his eyes and said three silent prayers before he could trust himself to speak. And when he did, he chose his words carefully, and gave much thought before they were uttered.

"I don't know why. I don't even know how to explain myself, Amanda. But you need to know that I care for you very, very deeply." He felt her stiffen within his arms. Before she panicked, he hurried on with his explanation. "I never knew you except by name until that day in the park. And then someone yelled, 'Catch her, she's falling,' and seconds later I found myself looking down into the eyes of someone I'd known forever. When you disappeared and I thought you were—" He buried his face in her curls and tried not to think of the blackness that had almost engulfed him. "When I couldn't find you," he corrected, "I nearly went insane. I couldn't sleep. I couldn't eat. I felt like I'd lost the other half of myself, and it made no sense because you were another man's wife. I had . . . have no personal claim on you. Hell . . . I don't even know what your favorite color is."

"Amber . . . I think," she said softly, and sighed as he released her from his embrace. This was almost too much to absorb. But so had the last five days been. If she could accept them, then why was this any less . . . or more?

He grinned, and let his thumb trace the edge of her lower lip.

Amanda caught her breath at the absent affection. It was something Seth had done often. *Oh God, let this be so.*

"Your name is Seth? Truly?"

"Truly. But no one dares call me that but Dad."

"Why?"

He shrugged. "I don't know. It just seemed like a name I always kept to myself."

You were waiting for me to find you, weren't you, Seth? But something happened to us. Somewhere along the way David interfered with our destiny. You had to find a way to heal me . . . and help me find you instead.

"I was wrong," Amanda said. "You didn't lie to me."

He sighed. "Thank God that's settled."

"But I lied to myself. For too many years. If it hadn't been for you . . . if you hadn't found me and saved me . . . if you hadn't interfered, it would have been too late to correct the horrible mistake."

He grinned. His eyes glittered with a deep, rich, amber fire that made her warm to her toes. "It's never too late for things that matter," he said.

"Another damned riddle," Amanda said, and let the love in his gaze come inside where it belonged.

Look for me, Amanda. I am already there.

"I see you, Seth," she whispered.

Dupree's eyebrow cocked. His grin widened, and his arms opened wide.

"Thank God you're beginning to see the light," he said.

Amanda's breath caught on an old sob of regret. "When I see you, I always see light."

EPILOGUE

———————— ✺ ————————

Her head only came to his shoulder. And the hallway leading to the door of his apartment had never seemed this narrow before as he and Amanda drew closer and closer to his front door. Dupree alternated between fits of joy that she was coming home with him, and certain agony that when she walked inside his apartment, she would instantly change her mind.

"Are you sorry you came?" he asked, and then hated himself for asking when she turned those wide green eyes on him and sighed.

"You've asked me that three times since we left the hospital," Amanda said softly. "I would have told you the first time if I had any regrets."

"Chief Morrell says I'm rushing you."

Amanda smiled. It was a small, secretive smile. "Your chief doesn't know all the facts, does he?"

Dupree shook his head and then realized, neither did he. All he knew was that he loved a woman beyond reason and she'd never even let him kiss her.

She'd also given her home and the Potter millions to a homeless shelter without a blink of her eye. It was the talk of the town.

"Your housekeeper, Mabel, wants to take care of you," Dupree reminded her.

"I don't need Mabel." *I already have you.*

Dupree sighed as the key turned in the lock. The door swung wide and she stepped in first. He hit the light switch as she walked inside. The room flooded instantly with a yellow-white illumination, and he remembered the painting and groaned. He supposed it would be a test: If this didn't ruin things, nothing would.

Amanda looked across the room and froze at the sight of it.

"Nokose," she whispered, and then slowly walked first to one side and then the other. No matter where she moved, the bear's shiny black stare seemed to follow her.

"Amanda, I'm sorry. I didn't think about it when . . . "

She turned. The tears on her face startled him. He'd had many reactions to the painting, ranging from shock and horror to disgust. But it had never made anyone cry.

She walked into his arms and buried her face against the buttons on his shirt. The bag he was carrying dropped to the floor as his arms encircled her.

"Oh Seth. I'm sorry. So sorry. I should have known it was you. If I had a last doubt, this put an end to it forever."

She had no rational explanation for what she'd endured, but the acceptance of it all, and of him, was firmly in place.

"I don't know what you're talking about, or what he did," Dupree said, looking over her shoulder to the painting on the opposite wall, "but I'm never taking that damned thing down. Not if this is the kind of response it elicits from you."

She laughed jerky little gulps through her tears. "I love you, Jefferson Seth Dupree. I don't know why it took me so long to find you, but I will thank God every day that it has happened. I've gone from hell to heaven, and I don't ever want to leave it—or you—again."

His heart soared as he realized he'd waited a lifetime to hear those words.

Her lips beckoned, and he took the offer. When his mouth touched hers, the shock of such sweetness made him weak with longing. He tasted tears, and laughter, and the breath of a sob, and knew that he'd willingly die, again and again, just to know this woman's love.

Their lips rocked together in a way that their bodies had not. And when her mouth parted, and he felt the tip of her tongue trace the shape of his lower lip, he nearly went to his knees. His manhood was turgid, his pulse racing. His need for the woman was beyond sanity.

"Ah God, Amanda. Stand still," he whispered, as they broke the kiss.

Amanda moved against the lower part of his body and slid her hands down the middle of his back. "Please, Seth, I have one more request of you."

He groaned. "Anything, lady, as long as you're careful with the goods."

"I am feeling very tired. And I'm not certain that I'm entirely healed. Do you think you might take me to bed?"

He gritted his teeth and closed his eyes against the earlier idea that had popped into his mind. He felt like all kinds of a cad for wanting to make love to her, when she'd just been released from the hospital.

"Sure, sweetheart," he said gently, cursing himself for watching the sway of her hips as she turned away. He missed the long, steady look she gave his bear.

"Before I lie down, there's something I need to do," she said.

He bit the inside of his lip and tried counting to ten as she bent down and pulled something from her bag.

Amanda lifted the Dreamcatcher, and held it in her arms one last time before she turned around and handed it to him.

"Would you mind?" She pointed toward the mantel.

Instantly he understood. Seconds later, it was in position, next to the football . . . inches to the right of the black garter . . . and right below the painting.

Dupree stepped back and squinted his eyes, assessing the arrangement. Oddly enough, it seemed to fit right in.

"Is that okay?" he asked, unaware of the sight he made

beside the Dreamcatcher, which he had created, and the bear, whose spirit had ultimately created him.

Amanda clasped her hands in front of her and resisted the urge to throw herself in his arms. He still did not understand. Maybe he would never understand in the same way that she did. But it didn't matter. What *did* matter was that their hearts had recognized each other long before their minds and bodies had connected.

"Now . . . about that bed," she said, and followed him into the other room. "I need help." She watched his agony with secret delight as he divested her of her outer clothing with shaking hands.

"I only have the one bed," he said, and tried not to look at her long legs and slender body beneath the ivory-colored teddy as he pulled back the covers and helped her get in.

"Just one more thing," she said softly.

"What, baby?" he groaned.

"After everything that's happened, I'm afraid to sleep alone."

"Are you telling me that you want me to get in bed with you?" He could hardly get the words past the knot in his throat.

"Yes."

"And do what?"

Her eyes grew solemn as she contemplated his body beneath his clothing.

"For starters . . . just hold me?"

He shook, and then managed a smile, remembering what hell this woman had endured. It behooved him to suffer a little of it himself just to understand.

"I think I can manage that," he said gently.

"One does what one must," Amanda said softly, watching with growing delight as he pulled off his boots and jacket before sliding into bed beside her.

"Is that a damned riddle?" he growled, and was rewarded with a soft burst of her laughter against his neck. He closed his eyes and resisted the urge to squeeze. There were too many places on her body that had been hurt, he'd be damned if he was responsible for putting another one there.

"Before you go to sleep, there's something I need to ask you," Dupree said.

Amanda sighed and leaned back so that she could see his face. Every day she saw more and more of her Seth in this one. Before long, she knew that they would be forever meshed within her heart.

"Ask and ye shall receive, or something like that," she said.

She was so delightful, he couldn't believe she was actually here, lying in his arms, while he suffered the lust of the damned for his thoughts.

"What is it you wanted to know?" she persisted, as sleep began to beckon.

"Oh! Yeah, right." Now that it came time to say it, he realized how forward and frightening it might seem to her. He took a deep breath and then plunged in. "Amanda, I know you're going to think I'm crazy. In fact, I've been pretty sure of it myself a time or two in the past few weeks. But something is driving me nuts and I have to know."

"What?"

Amber burned within his eyes, giving them a life that she thought she'd lost forever. Amanda held her breath as she waited for him to speak.

"Do you have a small, brown freckle on your right breast?"

Her eyes widened. Her chin trembled, but not from pain, from joy.

"Why yes, I believe I do," she said softly. "Would you like to see?"

He swallowed a lump in his throat while he contemplated the immensity of what she'd said. How had he known? And then he remembered her offer, and smiled as he cradled her face in shaking hands.

"Lord, honey, you have no idea how badly I would. But I don't think my gentlemanly resolve could stand it. Do you understand?"

Amanda smiled and snuggled against his chest as his arms held her close.

"Oh Seth. I understand that . . . and so much more."

Much later, after she'd fallen asleep, Jefferson felt a draft and got out of bed to see if he'd left something open. As he stood in the doorway between living room and bed, he happened to glance up, then watched in absent fascination at the way the sunshine was warming, then framing, the objects upon his mantel.

And as he watched, an odd thing began to happen. He forgot that he was standing, or that Amanda was in the other room asleep.

The sunshine suddenly centered upon the Dream-catcher. He stared, mesmerized by the sight of it as it once must have looked. The feather, a fully formed brown-and-white swath of an eagle's flight, swung freely in a breeze that wasn't there.

The claw was no longer cracked or dulled with age. Instead, its polished surface reflected sunshine. Light moved across and then caught in the warm chestnut color of the braid upon the web, while the string of leather and beads seemed to sway, as if someone had walked by and flipped them as they passed.

Something deep within him ached. Something old . . . and long forgotten. And then he blinked, and the vision vanished.

Thoughtfully, he looked once at the Dreamcatcher, and then back into his room at the woman who'd brought it. An unexpected shudder accompanied by the need to get back to her ended his musing.

When he realized the flow of air had mysteriously ceased as suddenly as it had begun, he started back to bed, then stopped and looked behind him.

Curious, he glanced up at the mantel, but nothing happened. Finally he shrugged. It was, after all, an illusion.